Gone, Baby, Gone

Dennis Lehane

BANTAM BOOKS

LONDON • TORONTO • SYDNEY • AUCKLAND • JOHANNESBURG

GONE, BABY, GONE
A BANTAM BOOK : 9780553818239
0553818236

First publication in Great Britain

PRINTING HISTORY
Bantam edition published 1999
Bantam edition reissued 2006

1 3 5 7 9 10 8 6 4 2

Set in 10/12pt Sabon

Bantam Books are published by Transworld Publishers,
61–63 Uxbridge Road, London W5 5SA,
a division of The Random House Group Ltd,
in Australia by Random House Australia (Pty) Ltd,
20 Alfred Street, Milsons Point, Sydney, NSW 2061, Australia,
in New Zealand by Random House New Zealand Ltd,
18 Poland Road, Glenfield, Auckland 10, New Zealand
and in South Africa by Random House (Pty) Ltd,
Isle of Houghton, Corner of Boundary Road & Carse O'Gowrie,
Houghton 2198, South Africa.

Printed and bound in Germany by
GGP Media GmbH, Pößneck.

Papers used by Transworld Publishers are natural, recyclable
products made from wood grown in sustainable forests. The
manufacturing processes conform to the environmental
regulations of the country of origin.

Acclaim for Dennis Lehane:

'One of the hottest talents to have crossed the Atlantic'
The Times

'Lehane's gritty psychothrillers have carved a distinctive
patch on the map of contemporary crime writing . . .
One of the most electrifying thriller writers'
Guardian

'Discovering Dennis Lehane is a bit like finding a
Mondrian in the attic: surprise followed by ecstasy . . .
Catch up with Lehane soonest'
Independent on Sunday

'He dares the reader to accept his clever misconceptions
and moulds it into a crime story as chillingly compelling
as a car crash. Lehane's world – excellent'
GQ

'His stories are strong, taut with suspense . . .
His characters are vulnerable personalities, with a
plethora of doubts and anxieties, who have known
the downside – just like us'
Irish Times

'The well-oiled plot mechanics, edge-of-the-knife
dialogue and explosive bursts of violence are
polished and primed'
New York Times Book Review

Also by Dennis Lehane

A DRINK BEFORE THE WAR
DARKNESS, TAKE MY HAND
SACRED
GONE, BABY, GONE
PRAYERS FOR RAIN
MYSTIC RIVER

and published by Bantam Books

To my sister, Maureen, and my brothers, Michael,
Thomas, and Gerard:
Thanks for standing by me and
putting up with me.
It couldn't have been easy.

And to

JCP
Who never stood a chance.

Acknowledgments

My editor, Claire Wachtel, and my agent, Ann Rittenberg, once again salvaged a manuscript from a mess and made me look a lot better than I have any right to expect. Mal, Sheila, and Sterling read the crude scribbling and talked me through the difficulties. Thanks also to Sergeant Larry Gillis of the Massachusetts State Police, Department of Public Affairs; Mary Clark of the Thomas Crane Public Library in Quincy; and, for countless gracious intangibles, Jennifer Brawer of William Morrow and Francesca Liversidge of Bantam UK.

Author's Note

Anyone familiar with Boston, Dorchester, South Boston, and Quincy, as well as both the Quincy quarries and the Blue Hills Reservation, will realize that I have taken enormous liberties in describing their geographical and topographical particulars. This was wholly intentional. While these cities, towns, and areas do exist, they have been altered according to the demands of story, as well as my own whims, and therefore should be regarded as entirely fictitious. Further, any similarities between the characters and events in this narrative and real persons, living or dead, is entirely coincidental.

Gone, Baby, Gone

Port Mesa, Texas

October 1998

Long before the sun finds the Gulf, the fishing boats set out into the dark. Shrimpers mostly, an occasional pursuer of marlin or tarpon, the boats are filled almost exclusively with men. The few women who do work the shrimpers keep mostly to themselves. This is the Texas coast, and because so many men have died hard over two centuries of fishing, their offspring and surviving friends feel they've earned their prejudices, their hatred of the Vietnamese competitors, their mistrust of any woman who'd do this ugly work, fumble in the dark with thick cable and hooks that slice through knuckles.

Women, one fisherman says in the black predawn, as the captain cuts the trawler engine to a low rumble and the slate sea roils, should be like Rachel. That's a woman.

That's a woman, all right, another fisherman says. Goddamn, yes, sir.

Rachel is relatively new to Port Mesa. Showed up back in July with her little boy and a battered Dodge pickup, rented a small house on the north side of town, took the HELP WANTED *sign out of the window of Crockett's Last Stand, a wharf bar perched atop ancient pilings that sag toward the sea.*

Took months before anyone even learned her last name: Smith.

Port Mesa attracts a lot of Smiths. A few Does, too. Half the shrimpers are manned by men running from something. Sleeping when most of the world is awake, working while most of it sleeps, drinking the rest of the time in bars few strangers feel comfortable entering, they follow the catch and the seasons, work as far west as Baja, as far south as Key West, and they get paid in cash.

Dalton Voy, owner of Crockett's Last Stand, pays Rachel Smith in cash. Would pay her in gold ingots if she wanted. Ever since she took her place behind the bar, business has jumped twenty percent. Strange as it is, there are fewer fights, too. Usually the men step off the boats with the sun baked straight through their flesh and into their blood, and it makes them irritable, quick to end a discussion with the swing of a bottle, the snap of a pool stick. And when beautiful women are around, in Dalton's experience — well, it just makes the men worse. Quicker to laugh, but quicker to take offense.

Something about Rachel, though, calms the men.

Warns them, too.

It's in her eyes — a quick something that flashes mean and cold when someone steps over the line, touches her wrist too long, makes a sex joke that isn't funny. And it's in her face, the lines etched there, the weathered beauty of it, the sense of a life lived before Port Mesa that knew more dark dawns and hard facts than most of the shrimpers.

Rachel packs a gun in her purse. Dalton Voy saw it once by accident, and the only thing that surprised him about it was that it didn't surprise him at all. Somehow he'd known. Somehow everyone else did, too. No one ever approaches Rachel in the parking lot after work, tries to talk her into his car. No one follows her home.

But when that hard thing isn't in her eyes, and that distance has left her face, man, she lights the place up. She moves up and down that bar like a dancer; every twist and pivot, every tilt of a bottle is smooth and fluid. When she laughs it opens her mouth wide and explodes in her eyes, and everyone in the bar tries to come up with a new joke, a better one, just to feel the thrill of that laugh in their spines again.

And then there's her little boy. Beautiful blond boy. Doesn't look anything like her, but when he smiles, you know he's Rachel's. Maybe a little moody like her, too. You see warning in his eyes sometimes, strange in a child so young. Barely old enough to walk, already showing the world something that says, Don't push.

Old Mrs Hayley watches the boy when Rachel's at work, and she tells Dalton Voy once that you couldn't ask for a better behaved boy, or one who so openly loves his mama. She says that boy is going to be something special. President or something. War hero. You mark my words, Dalton. You mark 'em.

One sunset at Boynton's Cove, Dalton takes his daily walk and comes upon mother and son. Rachel is waist-deep in the warm Gulf, holding the boy under his arms, dipping him up and down in the water. The water is gold, silky in the dying sun, and *it seems to Dalton that Rachel purifies her son in gold, performs some ancient rite that will coat his flesh so it can't be pierced or torn.*

The two of them laugh in the amber sea, and the sun dips red behind them. Rachel kisses her son's neck and props his calves over her hips. He leans back in her hands. And they look into each other's eyes.

Dalton thinks maybe he's never seen anything as beautiful as that look.

Rachel doesn't see him, and Dalton, he doesn't even wave. Feels like an intruder, actually. He keeps his head down, walks back up the way he came.

Something happens to you when you stumble on love that pure. It makes you feel small. Makes you feel ugly and ashamed and unworthy.

Dalton Voy, watching that mother and son playing in the amber water, has realized a cold, simple truth: He's never, not for one second, been loved like that in his life.

Love like that? Hell. It seems so pure, it's damn near criminal.

Part One

Indian Summer, 1997

1

Each day in this country, twenty-three hundred children are reported missing.

Of those, a large portion are abducted by one parent estranged from the other, and over fifty percent of the time the child's whereabouts are never in question. The majority of these children are returned within a week.

Another portion of those twenty-three hundred children are runaways. Again, the majority of them are not gone long, and usually their whereabouts are either known immediately or easily ascertained – a friend's house is the most common destination.

Another category of missing children is the throwaway – those who are cast out of their homes or who run away, and the parents decide not to give chase. These are often the children who fill shelters and bus terminals, street corners in the red-light districts, and, ultimately, prisons.

Of the more than eight hundred thousand children reported missing nationally every year, only thirty-five hundred to four thousand fall into what the Department of Justice categorizes as Non-Family Abductions, or cases in which the police soon rule out family abductions, running away, parental ejection, or the child becoming lost or injured.

Of these cases, three hundred children disappear every year and never return.

No one – not parents, friends, law enforcement, child-care organizations, or centers for missing people – knows where these children go. Into graves, possibly; into cellars or the homes of pedophiles; into voids, perhaps, holes in the fabric of the universe where they will never be heard from again.

Wherever these three hundred go, they stay gone. For a moment or two they haunt strangers who've heard of their cases, haunt their loved ones for far longer.

Without a body to leave behind, proof of their passing, they don't die. They keep us aware of the void.

And they stay gone.

'My sister,' Lionel McCready said, as he paced our belfry office, 'has had a very difficult life.' Lionel was a big man with a slightly houndish sag to his face and wide shoulders that slanted down hard from his collarbone, as if something we couldn't see sat atop them. He had a shaggy, shy smile and a firm grip in a callused hand. He wore a brown UPS deliveryman's uniform and kneaded the brim of the matching brown baseball cap in his beefy hands. 'Our mom was a – well, a boozer, frankly. And our dad left when we were both little kids. When you grow up that way, you – I guess you – maybe you got a lot of anger. It takes some time to get your head straight, figure out your way in life. It's not just Helene. I mean, I had some serious problems, took a hard bust in my twenties. I was no angel.'

'Lionel,' his wife said.

He held up a hand to her, as if he had to spit it out now or he'd never spit it out at all. 'I was lucky. I met Beatrice, straightened my life out. What I'm saying, Mr Kenzie, Miss Gennaro, is that if you're given time, a few breaks, you grow up. You shake that crap. My sister, she's still growing up, what I'm saying. Maybe. Because her life was hard and—'

'Lionel,' his wife said, 'stop making excuses for Helene.' Beatrice McCready ran a hand through her short strawberry hair and said, 'Honey, sit down. Please.'

Lionel said, 'I'm just trying to explain that Helene hasn't had an easy life.'

'Neither have you,' Beatrice said, 'and you're a good father.'

'How many kids do you have?' Angie asked.

Beatrice smiled. 'One. Matt. He's five. He's staying with my brother and his wife until we find Amanda.'

Lionel seemed to perk up a bit at the mention of his son. 'He's a great kid,' he said, and seemed almost embarrassed by his pride.

'And Amanda?' I said.

'She's a terrific kid, too,' Beatrice said. 'And she's way too young to be out there on her own.'

Amanda McCready had disappeared from this neighborhood three days ago. Since then, the entire city of Boston, it seemed, had become obsessed with her whereabouts. The police had put more men on the search than they had on the manhunt for John Salvi after the abortion clinic bombings four years ago. The mayor held a press conference in which he pledged no city business would take precedence over her disappearance until she was found. The press coverage was saturating: front page of both papers each morning, lead story in all three major telecasts at night, hourly updates inserted between the soaps and talk shows.

And in three days – nothing. Not a hint of her.

Amanda McCready had been on this earth four years and seven months when she vanished. Her mother had put her to bed on Sunday night, checked in on her once around eight-thirty, and the next morning, shortly after nine, had looked in at Amanda's bed and seen nothing but sheets dented with the wrinkled impression of her daughter's body.

The clothes Helene McCready had laid out for her daughter – a pink T-shirt, denim shorts, pink socks, and white sneakers – were gone, as was Amanda's favorite doll, a blond-haired replica of a three-year-old that bore an eerie resemblance to its owner, and whom Amanda had named Pea. The room showed no signs of struggle.

Helene and Amanda lived on the second floor of a three-decker, and while it was possible Amanda had been abducted by someone who'd placed a ladder under her bedroom window and pushed the screen open to gain entry, it was also unlikely. The screen and windowsills had shown no signs of disturbance, and the ground at the foundation of the house bore no ladder marks.

What was far more likely, if one assumed a four-year-old didn't suddenly decide to leave home on her own in the middle of the night, was that the abductor entered the apartment through the front door, without picking the lock or prying the hinges loose from the jamb, because such actions were unnecessary on a door that had been left unlocked.

Helene McCready had taken a hell of a beating in the press when that information came out. Twenty-four hours after her daughter's disappearance, the *News*, Boston's tabloid answer to the *New York Post*, ran as its front-page headline:

COME ON IN:
LITTLE AMANDA'S MOM LEFT DOOR UNLOCKED

Beneath the headline were two photographs, one of Amanda, the other of the front door to the apartment. The door was propped wide open, which, police stated, was not how it was discovered the morning of Amanda McCready's disappearance. Unlocked, yes; wide open, no.

Most of the city didn't care much about the distinction, though. Helene McCready had left her four-year-old daughter alone in an unlocked apartment while she went next door to her friend Dottie Mahew's house. There she and Dottie watched TV – two sitcoms and a movie of the week entitled *Her Father's Sins* starring Suzanne Somers and Tony Curtis. After the news, they watched half of *Entertainment Tonight Weekend Edition* and then Helene returned home.

For roughly three hours and forty-five minutes, Amanda McCready had been left alone in an unlocked apartment. At some point during that time, the assumption went, she had either slipped out on her own or been abducted.

Angie and I had followed the case as closely as the rest of the city, and it baffled us as much as it seemed to baffle everyone else. Helene McCready, we knew, had submitted to a polygraph regarding her daughter's disappearance and passed. Police were unable to find a single lead to follow; rumor had it they were consulting psychics. Neighbors on the street that night, a warm Indian summer night when most windows were open and pedestrians strolled at random, reported seeing nothing suspicious, hearing nothing that sounded like a child's screams. No one remembered seeing a four-year-old wandering around alone or a suspicious person or persons carrying either a child or an odd-looking bundle.

Amanda McCready, as far as anyone could tell, had vanished so completely it was as if she'd never been born.

Beatrice McCready, her aunt, had called us this afternoon. I told her I didn't think there was much we could do that a hundred cops, half the Boston press corps, and thousands of everyday people weren't already doing on her niece's behalf.

'Mrs McCready,' I said, 'save your money.'

'I'd rather save my niece,' she said.

Now, as the Wednesday evening rush-hour traffic dwindled to some distant beeps and engine revs on the avenue below, Angie and I sat in our office in the belfry of St Bartholomew's Church in Dorchester and listened to Amanda's aunt and uncle plead her case.

'Who's Amanda's father?' Angie said.

The weight seemed to resettle onto Lionel's shoulders. 'We don't know. We think it's a guy named Todd Morgan. He left the city right after

24

Helene got pregnant. Nobody's heard from him since.'

'The list of possible fathers is long, though,' Beatrice said.

Lionel looked down at the floor.

'Mr McCready,' I said.

He looked at me. 'Lionel.'

'Please, Lionel,' I said. 'Have a seat.'

He fitted himself into the small chair on the other side of the desk after a bit of a struggle.

'This Todd Morgan,' Angie said, as she finished writing the name on a pad of paper. 'Do police know his whereabouts?'

'Mannheim, Germany,' Beatrice said. 'He's stationed in the army over there. And he was on the base when Amanda disappeared.'

'Have they discounted him as a suspect?' I said. 'There's no way he would have hired a friend to do it?'

Lionel cleared his throat, looked at the floor again. 'The police said he's embarrassed by my sister and doesn't think Amanda is his child anyway.' He looked up at me with those lost, gentle eyes of his. 'They said his response was: "If I want a rug rat to shit and cry all the time, I can have a German one."'

I could feel the wave of hurt that had washed through him when he'd had to call his niece a 'rug rat,' and I nodded. 'Tell me about Helene,' I said.

There wasn't much to tell. Helene McCready was Lionel's younger sister by four years, which put her at twenty-eight. She'd dropped out of Monsignor Ryan Memorial High School in her junior year, never got the GED she kept saying she would. At seventeen, she ran off with a guy fifteen years older, and they'd lived in a trailer park in New Hampshire for six months before Helene returned home with a face bruised purple and the first of three abortions behind her. Since then she'd worked a variety of jobs – Stop & Shop cashier, Chess King clerk, dry cleaner's assistant, UPS receptionist – and never managed to hold on to any for more than eighteen months. Since the disappearance of her daughter, she'd taken leave from her part-time job running the lottery machine at Li'l Peach, and there weren't any indications she'd be going back.

'She loved that little girl, though,' Lionel said.

Beatrice looked as if she were of a different opinion, but she kept silent.

'Where is Helene now?' Angie said.

'At our house,' Lionel said. 'The lawyer we contacted said we should keep her under wraps as long as we can.'

'Why?' I said.

'Why?' Lionel said.

'Yeah. I mean, her child's missing. Shouldn't she be making appeals to the public? Canvassing the neighborhood at least?'

Lionel opened his mouth, then closed it. He looked down at his shoes.

'Helene is not up to that,' Beatrice said.

'Why not?' Angie said.

'Because – well, because she's Helene,' Beatrice said.

'Are the police monitoring the phones at her place in case there's a ransom demand?'

'Yes,' Lionel said.

'And she's not there,' Angie said.

'It got to be too much for her,' Lionel said. 'She

26

needed her privacy.' He held out his hands, looked at us.

'Oh,' I said. 'Her privacy.'

'Of course,' Angie said.

'Look' – Lionel kneaded his cap again – 'I know how it seems. I do. But people show their worry in different ways. Right?'

I gave him a halfhearted nod. 'If she'd had three abortions,' I said, and Lionel winced, 'what made her decide to give birth to Amanda?'

'I think she decided it was time.' He leaned forward and his face brightened. 'If you could have seen how excited she was during that pregnancy. I mean, her life had purpose, you know? She was sure that child would make everything better.'

'For her,' Angie said. 'What about the child?'

'My point at the time,' Beatrice said.

Lionel turned to both women, his eyes wide and desperate again. 'They were good for each other,' he said. 'I believe that.'

Beatrice looked at her shoes. Angie looked out the window.

Lionel looked back at me. 'They were.'

I nodded, and his hound dog's face sagged with relief.

'Lionel,' Angie said, still looking out the window, 'I've read all the newspaper reports. Nobody seems to know who would have taken Amanda. The police are stymied, and according to reports, Helene says she has no ideas on the subject either.'

'I know.' Lionel nodded.

'So, okay.' Angie turned from the window and looked at Lionel. 'What do you think happened?'

'I don't know,' he said, and gripped his hat so

hard, I thought it might come apart in those big hands. 'It's like she was sucked up into the sky.'

'Has Helene been dating anybody?'

Beatrice snorted.

'Anybody regular?' I said.

'No,' Lionel said.

'The press is suggesting she hung around with some unsavory characters,' Angie said.

Lionel shrugged, as if that was a matter of course.

'She hangs out at the Filmore Tap,' Beatrice said.

'That's the biggest dive in Dorchester,' Angie said.

'And think how many bars contend for that honor,' Beatrice said.

'It's not that bad,' Lionel said, and looked to me for support.

I held out my hands. 'I carry a gun on a regular basis, Lionel. And I get nervous going into the Filmore.'

'The Filmore's known as a druggies' bar,' Angie said. 'Supposedly they move coke and heroin in and out of there like buffalo wings. Does your sister have a drug problem?'

'You mean, like heroin?'

'They mean like anything,' Beatrice said.

'She smokes a little weed,' Lionel said.

'A little?' I asked. 'Or a lot?'

'What's a lot?' he said.

'Does she keep a water bong and a roach clip on her nightstand?' Angie said.

Lionel squinted at her.

'She's not addicted to any particular drug,' Beatrice said. 'She dabbles.'

'Coke?' I said.

She nodded and Lionel looked at her, stunned.

28

'Pills?'

Beatrice shrugged.

'Needles?' I said.

'Oh, no,' Lionel said.

Beatrice said, 'Not as far as I know.' She thought about it. 'No. We've seen her in shorts and tank tops all summer. We'd have seen tracks.'

'Wait.' Lionel held up a hand. 'Just wait. We're supposed to be looking for Amanda, not talking about my sister's bad habits.'

'We have to know everything about Helene and her habits and her friends,' Angie said. 'A child goes missing, usually the reason is close to home.'

Lionel stood up and his shadow filled the top of the desk. 'What's that mean?'

'Sit down,' Beatrice said.

'No. I need to know what that means. Are you suggesting my sister could have had something to do with Amanda's disappearance?'

Angie watched him steadily. 'You tell me.'

'No,' he said loudly. 'Okay? No.' He looked down at his wife. 'She's not a criminal, okay? She's a woman who's lost her child. You know?'

Beatrice looked up at him, her face inscrutable.

'Lionel,' I said.

He stared down at his wife, then looked at Angie again.

'Lionel,' I said again, and he turned to me. 'You said yourself it's like Amanda disappeared into thin air. Okay. Fifty cops are looking for her. Maybe more. You two have been working on it. People in the neighborhood . . .'

'Yeah,' he said. 'Lots of them. They've been great.'

'Okay. So where is she?'

He stared at me as if I might suddenly pull her out of my desk drawer.

'I don't know.' He closed his eyes.

'No one does,' I said. 'And if we're going to look into this – and I'm not saying we will . . .'

Beatrice sat up in her chair and looked hard at me.

'But *if*, we have to work under the assumption that if she has been abducted, it was by someone close to her.'

Lionel sat back down. 'You think she was taken.'

'Don't you?' Angie said. 'A four-year-old who ran off on her own wouldn't still be out there after almost three full days without having been seen.'

'Yeah,' he said, as if facing something he'd known was true but had been holding at bay until now. 'Yeah. You're probably right.'

'So what do we do now?' Beatrice said.

'You want my honest opinion?' I said.

She cocked her head slightly, her eyes holding steadily with my own. 'I'm not sure.'

'You have a son who's about to enter school. Right?'

Beatrice nodded.

'Save the money you would have spent on us and put it toward his education.'

Beatrice's head didn't move; it stayed cocked slightly to the right, but for a moment she looked as if she'd been slapped. 'You won't take this case, Mr Kenzie?'

'I'm not sure there's any point to it.'

Beatrice's voice rose in the small office. 'A child is—'

'Missing,' Angie said. 'Yes. But a lot of people are

looking for her. The news coverage has been extensive. Everyone in this city and probably most of the state knows what she looks like. And, trust me, most of them have their eyes peeled for her.'

Beatrice looked at Lionel. Lionel gave her a small shrug. She turned from him and locked eyes with me again. She was a small woman, no more than five foot three. Her pale face, sparkled with freckles the same color as her hair, was heart-shaped, and there was a child's roundness to her button nose and chin, the cheekbones that resembled acorns. But there was also a furious aura of strength about her, as if she equated yielding with dying.

'I came to you both,' she said, 'because you find people. That's what you do. You found that man who killed all those people a few years ago, you saved that baby and his mother in the playground, you—'

'Mrs McCready,' Angie said, holding up a hand.

'Nobody wanted me to come here,' she said. 'Not Helene, not my husband, not the police. "You'd be wasting your money," everyone said. "She's not even your child," they said.'

'Honey.' Lionel put his hand on hers.

She shook it off, leaned forward until her arms were propped on the desk and her sapphire eyes were holding mine.

'Mr Kenzie, you can find her.'

'No,' I said softly. 'Not if she's hidden well enough. Not if a lot of people who are just as good at this as we are haven't been able to find her either. We're just two more people, Mrs McCready. Nothing more.'

'Your point?' Her voice was low, again, and icy.

'Our point,' Angie said, 'is what help could two more sets of eyes be?'

'What harm, though?' Beatrice said. 'Can you tell me that? What harm?'

2

From a detective's perspective once you rule out running away or abduction by a parent, a child's disappearance is similar to a murder case: If it's not solved within seventy-two hours, it's unlikely it ever will be. That doesn't necessarily mean the child is dead, though the probability is high. But if the child is alive, she's definitely worse off than when she went missing. Because there's very little gray area in the motivations of adults who encounter children who aren't their own; you either *A*, help that child or, *B*, exploit her. And while the methods of exploitation vary – ransoming children for money, using them for labor, abusing them sexually for personal and/or profit concerns, murdering them – none of them stem from benevolence. And if the child doesn't die and is eventually found, the scars run so deep that the poison can never be removed from her blood.

In the last four years, I'd killed two men. I'd watched my oldest friend and a woman I barely knew die in front of me. I'd seen children desecrated in the worst possible ways, met men and women who killed as if it were a reflex action, watched relationships burn in the violence with which I'd actively surrounded myself.

And I was tired of it.

Amanda McCready had been missing for at least sixty hours by this point, maybe as long as seventy, and I didn't want to find her stuffed in a Dumpster somewhere, her hair matted with blood. I didn't want to find her six months down the road, vacant-eyed and used up by some freak with a video camera and a mailing list of pedophiles. I didn't want to look in a four-year-old's eyes and see the death of everything that had been pure in her.

I didn't want to find Amanda McCready. I wanted someone else to.

But maybe because I'd become as caught up in this case over the last few days as the rest of the city, or maybe because it had happened here in my neighborhood, or maybe just because 'four-year-old' and 'missing' aren't words that should go together in the same sentence, we agreed to meet Lionel and Beatrice McCready at Helene's apartment in half an hour.

'You'll take the case, then?' Beatrice said, as she and Lionel stood.

'That's what we need to discuss between ourselves,' I said.

'But—'

'Mrs McCready,' Angie said, 'things are done a certain way in this business. We have to consult privately before we agree to anything.'

Beatrice didn't like it, but she also realized there was very little she could do about it.

'We'll drop by Helene's in half an hour,' I said.

34

'Thank you,' Lionel said, and tugged his wife's sleeve.

'Yes. Thanks,' Beatrice said, though she didn't sound real sincere. I had a feeling that nothing less than a presidential deployment of the National Guard to search for her niece would satisfy her.

We listened to their footfalls descend the belfry stairs and then I watched from the window as they left the schoolyard beside the church and walked to a weather-beaten Dodge Aries. The sun had drifted west past my line of sight, and the early October sky was still a pale summer white, but wisps of rust had floated into the white. A child's voice called, 'Vinny, wait up! Vinny!' and from four stories above the ground there was something lonely about the sound, something unfinished. Beatrice and Lionel's car U-turned on the avenue, and I watched the puff of its exhaust until it had pulled out of sight.

'I don't know,' Angie said, and leaned back in her chair. She propped her sneakers up on the desk and pushed her long thick hair off her temples. 'I just don't know about this one.'

She wore black Lycra biking shorts and a loose black tank top over a tight white one. The black tank top bore the white letters NIN on the front and the words PRETTY HATE MACHINE on the back. She'd owned it for about eight years and it still looked like she was wearing it for the first time. I'd lived with Angie for almost two years. As far as I could see, she didn't take any better care of her apparel than I did mine, but I owned shirts that looked like they'd been run through a car engine half an hour after I removed the price tags, and she had socks from high school that were still as white as palace linen. Women and their clothes often astounded me this way, but I figured it was one of those mysteries I'd never solve – like what really happened to Amelia Earhart or the bell that used to occupy our office.

'Don't know about this case?' I said. 'In what way?'

'A missing child, a mother who apparently isn't looking too hard, a pushy aunt—'

'You thought Beatrice was pushy?'

'Not any more so than a Jehovah with one foot in the door.'

'She's worried about that kid. Tear-her-hair-out worried.'

'And I feel for that.' She shrugged. 'Still don't enjoy being pushed, though.'

'It's not one of your stronger qualities, true.'

She flipped a pencil at my head, caught my chin. I rubbed at the spot and looked for the pencil so I could throw it back.

'It's all fun and games until someone loses an eye,' I mumbled, as I felt under my chair for the pencil.

'We're doing real well,' she said.

'We are.' The pencil wasn't below my chair or the desk, as far as I could see.

'Made more this year than last.'

'And it's only October.' No pencil by the floorboard or under the mini-fridge. Maybe it was with Amelia Earhart and Amanda McCready and the bell.

'Only October,' she agreed.

'You're saying we don't need this case.'

'Pretty much the size of it.'

I gave up on the pencil and looked out the window

for a bit. The wisps of rust had deepened to blood red, and the white sky was gradually darkening into blue. The first yellow lightbulb of the evening clicked on in a third-story apartment across the street. The smell of the air coming through the screen made me think of early adolescence and stickball, long, easy days leaking into long, easy nights.

'You don't agree?' Angie said after a few moments.

I shrugged.

'Speak now or forever hold your peace,' she said lightly.

I turned and looked at her. The gathering dusk was gold against her window, and it swam in her dark hair. Her honeycomb skin was darker than usual from the long dry summer that had somehow continued to extend well into autumn, and the muscles in her calves and biceps were pronounced after months of daily basketball games at the Ryan playground.

In my previous experience with women, once you've been intimate with someone for a while, her beauty is often the first thing you overlook. Intellectually, you know it's there, but your emotional capacity to be overwhelmed or surprised by it, to the point where it can get you drunk, diminishes. But there are still moments every day when I glance at Angie and feel a gust cleave through my chest cavity from the sweet pain of looking at her.

'What?' Her wide mouth broke into a grin.

'Nothing,' I said softly.

She held my gaze. 'I love you, too.'

'Yeah?'

'Oh, yeah.'

'Scary, ain't it?'

'Sometimes, yeah.' She shrugged. 'Sometimes, not at all.'

We sat there for a bit, saying nothing, and then Angie's eyes drifted to her window.

'I'm just not sure we need this . . . mess right now.'

'This mess being?'

'A missing child. Worse, a completely vanished child.' She closed her eyes and inhaled the warm breeze through her nose. 'I like being happy.' She opened her eyes but kept them fixed on the window. Her chin quivered slightly. 'You know?'

It had been a year and a half since Angie and I had consummated what friends claimed was a love affair that had been going on for decades. And those eighteen months had also been the most profitable our detective agency had ever experienced.

A little less than two years ago, we'd closed – or maybe just merely survived – the Gerry Glynn case. Boston's first known serial killer in thirty years had garnered a lot of attention, as had those of us credited with catching him. The spate of publicity – national news coverage, never-ending rehashes in the tabloids, two true-crime paperbacks with a rumored third on the way – had made Angie and me two of the better-known private investigators in the city.

For five months after Gerry Glynn's death, we'd refused to take cases, and this seemed only to whet the appetites of prospective clients. After we completed an investigation into the disappearance of a woman named Desiree Stone, we returned to publicly accepting cases again, and for the first few weeks the staircase leading up to the belfry was jammed with people.

Without ever acknowledging it to each other, we refused out-of-hand any cases that smelled of violence or glimpses into the darker caverns of human nature. Both of us, I think, felt we'd earned a break, so we stuck to insurance fraud, corporate malfeasance, simple divorces.

In February, we'd even accepted an elderly woman's plea that we locate her missing iguana. The hideous beast's name was Puffy, and he was a seventeen-inch-long iridescent green monstrosity with, as his owner put it, 'a negative disposition toward humanity.' We found Puffy in the wilds of suburban Boston as he made a dash across the soggy plains of the fourteenth green at Belmont Hills Country Club, his spiky tail wagging like mad as he lunged for the hint of sunlight he spied on the fairway of the fifteenth. He was cold. He didn't put up a fight. He did almost get turned into a belt, though, when he relieved himself in the backseat of our company car, but his owner paid for the cleaning and gave us a generous reward for her beloved Puffy's return.

It had been that kind of year. Not the best for war stories down at the local bar but exceptional for the bank account. And as potentially embarrassing as it was to chase a pampered lizard around a frozen golf course, it beat getting shot at. Beat the hell out of it, actually.

'You think we've lost our nerve?' Angie asked me recently.

'Absolutely,' I'd said. And smiled.

*   *   *

'What if she's dead?' Angie said, as we descended the belfry steps.

'That would be bad,' I said.

'It would be worse than bad, depending on how deep we got into it.'

'You want to tell them no, then.' I opened the door that led out to the rear schoolyard.

She looked at me, her mouth half open, as if afraid to put it into words, hear them hit the air, and know that it made her someone who refused to help a child in need.

'I don't want to tell them yes quite yet,' she managed, as we reached our car.

I nodded. I knew the feeling.

'Everything about this disappearance smells bad,' Angie said, as we drove down Dorchester Avenue toward Helene and Amanda's apartment.

'I know.'

'Four-year-olds don't vanish without help.'

'Definitely not.'

Along the avenue, people were beginning to come out of their homes now that dinner was over. Some placed lawn chairs on their small front porches; others walked up the avenue toward bars or twilight ball games. I could smell sulfur in the air from a recently discharged bottle rocket, and the moist evening hung like an untaken breath in that bruised hue between deep blue and sudden black.

Angie pulled her legs up to her chest and rested her chin on her knees. 'Maybe I've become a coward, but I don't mind chasing iguanas across golf courses.'

I looked through the windshield as we turned

off Dorchester Avenue onto Savin Hill Avenue.

'Neither do I,' I said.

When a child disappears, the space she'd occupied is immediately filled with dozens of people. And these people – relatives, friends, police officers, reporters from both TV and print – create a lot of energy and noise, a sense of communal intensity, of fierce and shared dedication to a task.

But amid all that noise, nothing is louder than the silence of the missing child. It's a silence that's two and a half to three feet tall, and you feel it at your hip and hear it rising up from the floorboards, shouting to you from corners and crevices and the emotionless face of a doll left on the floor by the bed. It's a silence that's different from the one left at funerals and wakes. The silence of the dead carries with it a sense of finality; it's a silence you know you must get used to. But the silence of a missing child is not something you want to get used to; you refuse to accept it, and so it screams at you.

The silence of the dead says, Goodbye.

The silence of the missing says, Find me.

It seemed like half the neighborhood and a quarter of the Boston Police Department were inside Helene McCready's two-bedroom apartment. The living room stretched through an open portico into the dining room, and these two rooms were the center of most of the activity. The police had set up banks of phones on the floor of the dining room, and all were in use; several people used their personal cell phones as well. A burly man in a PROUD TO BE A DOT RAT T-shirt looked up from a stack of flyers on the coffee table in front of him and said, 'Beatrice, Channel Four wants Helene at six tomorrow night.'

A woman put her hand over the receiver of her cell phone. 'The producers of *Annie in the AM* called. They want Helene to go on the show in the morning.'

'Mrs McCready,' a cop called from the dining room, 'we need you in here a sec.'

Beatrice nodded at the burly man and the woman with the cell phone and said to us, 'Amanda's bedroom is the first on the right.'

I nodded, and she cut off into the crowd and headed for the dining room.

Amanda's bedroom door was open, and the room itself was still and dark, as if the sounds from the street below couldn't penetrate up here. A toilet flushed, and a patrolman came out of the bathroom and looked at us as his right hand finished zipping up his fly.

'Friends of the family?' he asked.

'Yes.'

He nodded. 'Don't touch anything, please.'

'We won't,' Angie said.

He nodded and went up the hall into the kitchen.

I used my car key to turn on the light switch in Amanda's room. I knew that every item in the room had been dusted and analyzed for fingerprints by now, but I also knew how perturbed cops get when you touch anything with bare hands at a crime scene.

A bare lightbulb hung from a cord above Amanda's bed, the copper housing plate gone and the exposed wires dusty. The ceiling was badly in need of a paint job, and the summer heat had done its work on the posters that had hung from the walls. There were three that I could see, and they lay curled and rumpled by the baseboards. Squares of tape were spaced in uneven rectangle formations on the wall where the posters had been. I had no idea how long they'd lain there, wrinkling, growing hairline creases like veins.

The apartment was identical in layout to my own, and to that of apartments in most three-deckers in the neighborhood, and Amanda's bedroom was the smaller of the two by about half. Helene's bedroom, I assumed, was the master and would be past the bathroom on the right, directly across from the kitchen and looking out on the rear porch and small yard below. Amanda's bedroom looked out on the three-decker next door and was probably as deprived of light at noon as it was now, at eight o'clock in the evening.

The room was musty, the furniture sparse. The dresser across from the bed looked as if it had been picked up at a yard sale, and the bed itself had no frame. It was a single mattress and box spring placed on the floor, covered in a top sheet that didn't match the bottom and a Lion King comforter that had been pushed aside in the heat.

A doll lay at the foot of the bed, looking up at the ceiling with flat doll's eyes; a stuffed bunny turned on its side against the foot of the dresser. An old black-and-white TV sat up on the dresser, and there was a small radio on the bedside table, but I couldn't see any books in the room, not even coloring books.

I tried to picture the girl who'd slept in this room. I'd seen enough photos of Amanda in the last few days to know what she looked like, but a physical likeness couldn't tell me what set her face had taken when she walked into this room at the end of a day or woke to it first thing in the morning.

Had she tried to put those posters back up on the wall? Had she asked for the bright blue and yellow pop-up books she'd seen in malls? In the dark and quiet of this room late at night, when she was awake and alone, did she fixate on the lone nail sticking out from the wall across from the bed or the sallow brown water mark that puddled down from the ceiling at the east corner?

I looked at the doll's shiny, ugly eyes, and I wanted to close them with my foot.

'Mr Kenzie, Miss Gennaro.' It was Beatrice's voice, calling from the kitchen.

Angie and I took one last look at the bedroom, and then I used my key to switch the light off and we walked down the hall into the kitchen.

There was a man leaning against the oven, hands stuffed in his pockets. By the way he watched us as we approached, I knew he was waiting for us. He was a few inches shorter than I am, wide and round as an oil drum with a boyish, jolly face, slightly ruddy, as if he spent a lot of time outdoors. His throat had that paradoxically pinched and flabby look of someone nearing retirement age, and there was a hardness to him, an implacability that seemed a hundred years old, seemed to have judged you and your entire life in a glance.

'Lieutenant Jack Doyle,' he said, as he fired his hand into my own.

I shook the hand. 'Patrick Kenzie.'

Angie introduced herself and shook his hand, too, and we stood before him in the small kitchen as he

44

peered intently into our faces. His own face was unreadable, but the intensity of his gaze had a magnet's pull, something in there you wanted to look into even when you knew you should look away.

I'd seen him on TV a few times over the last few days. He ran the BPD's Crimes Against Children squad, and when he stared into the camera and spoke of how he'd find Amanda McCready no matter what it took, you felt a momentary pity for whoever had abducted her.

'Lieutenant Doyle was interested in meeting you,' Beatrice said.

'Now we've met,' I said.

Doyle smiled. 'You got a minute?'

Without waiting for an answer, he crossed to the door leading out to the porch, opened it, and looked back over his shoulder at us.

'Apparently we do,' Angie said.

The porch railing needed a paint job even more than the ceiling in Amanda's bedroom. Every time one of us leaned on it, the chipped, sun-baked paint crackled under our forearms like logs in a fire.

On the porch I could smell the odor of barbecue a few houses away, and from somewhere on the next block came the sounds of a backyard gathering – a woman's loud voice complaining about a sunburn, a radio playing the Mighty Mighty Bosstones, laughter as sharp and sudden as ice cubes shifting in a glass. Hard to believe it was October. Hard to believe winter was near.

Hard to believe Amanda McCready floated farther and farther away out there, and the world continued turning.

'So,' Doyle said, as he leaned over the railing. 'You solve the case yet?'

Angie looked at me and rolled her eyes.

'No,' I said, 'but we're close.'

Doyle chuckled softly, his eyes on the patch of concrete and dead grass below the porch.

Angie said, 'We assume you advised the McCreadys not to contact us.'

'Why would I do that?'

'Same reason I would if I were in your position,' Angie said, as he turned his head to look at her. 'Too many cooks.'

Doyle nodded. 'That's part of it.'

'What's the other part?' I said.

He laced his fingers together, then pushed the hands out until the knuckles cracked. 'These people look like they're rolling in dough? Like they got cigarette boats, diamond-studded candelabras I don't know about?'

'No.'

'And ever since the Gerry Glynn thing, I hear you two charge pretty steep rates.'

Angie nodded. 'Pretty steep retainers, too.'

Doyle gave her a small smile and turned back to the railing. He gripped it lightly with both hands and leaned back on his heels. 'Time this little girl is found, Lionel and Beatrice could be a hundred grand in the hole. At least. They're only the aunt and uncle, but they'll buy spots on TV to find her, take out full-page ads in every national paper, plaster her picture on highway billboards, hire psychics, shamans, and PIs.' He looked back at us. 'They'll go broke. You know?'

'Which is one of the reasons we've been trying not to take this case,' I said.

'Really?' He raised an eyebrow. 'Then why are you here?'

'Beatrice is persistent,' Angie said.

He looked back at the kitchen window. 'She is that, isn't she?'

'We're a little confused why Amanda's mother isn't as well.'

Doyle shrugged. 'Last time I saw her, she was doped up on tranquilizers, Prozac, whatever they give the parents of missing kids these days.' He turned back from the railing, his hands out by his side. 'Whatever. Lookit, I don't want to get off on the wrong foot with two people who might help me find this kid. No shit. I just want to make sure that, A, you don't get in my way; B, you don't tell the press how you were brought on board because the police are such boneheads they couldn't find water from a boat; or, C, you don't exploit the worry of those people in there for money. Because I happen to like Lionel and Beatrice. They're good people.'

'What was B again?' I smiled.

Angie said, 'Lieutenant, as we said, we're trying hard not to take this case. It's doubtful we'll be around long enough to get in your way.'

He looked at her a long time with that hard, open gaze of his. 'Then why are you standing on this porch talking to me?'

'So far Beatrice refuses to take no for an answer.'

'And you think that's somehow going to change?' He smiled softly and shook his head.

'We can hope,' I said.

He nodded, then turned back to the railing. 'Long time.'

'What?' Angie said.

His eyes remained on the backyard and the one just beyond it. 'For a four-year-old to be missing.' He sighed. 'Long time,' he repeated.

'And you have no leads?' Angie asked.

He shrugged. 'Nothing I'd bet the house on.'

'Anything you'd bet a second-rate condo on?' she said.

He smiled again and shrugged.

'I take that as a "not really,"' Angie said.

He nodded. 'Not really.' The dry paint sounded like brittle leaves under his clenched hands. 'Tell you how I got into the kid-finding racket. 'Bout twenty years ago, my daughter, Shannon? She disappears. For one day.' He turned to us, held up his index finger. 'Not even one day, really. Actually, it was from like four o'clock one afternoon till about eight the next morning, but she was six. And I'll tell you, you have no clue how long a night can be until your child goes missing in one. The last time Shannon's friends had seen her she was heading home on her bicycle, and a couple of them said they saw a car following her real slow.' He rubbed his eyes with the heels of his hand and blew a rush of air out of his mouth at the memory. 'We found her the next morning in a drainage ditch near a park. She'd cracked up the bike and broken both ankles, passed out from the pain.'

He noticed the looks on our faces and held up his hand.

'She was fine,' he said. 'Two broken ankles hurt like hell and she was one scared kid for a while, but

48

that was the worst trauma her or my wife and me suffered through her whole childhood. That's good luck. Hell, that's amazing luck.' He blessed himself quickly. 'My point, though? When Shannon was missing and the whole neighborhood and all my cop buddies are looking for her, and me and Tricia are driving or walking everywhere and tearing our hair out, we stopped for a cup of coffee. To go, believe me. But for two minutes, while we're standing in this Dunkin' Donuts waiting for our coffee, I look at Tricia and she looks at me and both of us, without saying a word, know that if Shannon is dead, we're dead too. Our marriage – over. Our happiness – over. Our lives would be one long road of pain. Nothing else, really. Everything good and hopeful, everything we lived for, really, would die with our daughter.'

'And that's why you joined Crimes Against Children?' I said.

'That's why I *built* Crimes Against Children,' he said. 'It's my baby. I created it. Took me fifteen years, but I did it. CAC exists because I looked at my wife in that doughnut shop and I knew, right then and beyond any doubt, that no one can survive the loss of a child. No one. Not you, not me, not even a loser like Helene McCready.'

'Helene's a loser?' Angie said.

He cocked an eyebrow. 'Know why she went to her friend Dottie's instead of vice versa?'

We shook our heads.

'The picture tube was going on her TV. The color went in and out, and Helene didn't like that. So she left her kid behind and went next door.'

'For TV.'

49

He nodded. 'For TV.'

'Wow,' Angie said.

He looked at us steadily for a full minute, then hitched his pants and said, 'Two of my best guys, Poole and Broussard, will contact you. They'll be your liaisons. If you can help, I'm not going to stand in your way.' He rubbed his face with his hands again, shook his head. 'Shit, I'm tired.'

'When's the last time you slept?' Angie said.

'Beyond a catnap?' He chuckled softly. 'Few days at least.'

'You must have someone who relieves you,' Angie said.

'Don't want relief,' he said. 'I want this child. And I want her in one piece. And I want her yesterday.'

3

Helene McCready was watching herself on TV when we entered Lionel's house with Lionel and Beatrice.

The on-screen Helene wore a light blue dress and matching jacket with the bulb of a white rose pinned to the lapel. Her hair flowed down to her shoulders. Her face carried just a hint of excessive makeup, hastily applied around the eyes perhaps.

The real Helene McCready wore a pink T-shirt with the words BORN TO SHOP on the front and a pair of white sweatpants that had been shorn just above the knees. Her hair, tied in a loose ponytail, looked like it had been through so many dye jobs it had forgotten its original color and was stuck somewhere between platinum and greasy wheat.

Another woman sat on the couch beside the real Helene McCready, about the same age but thicker and paler, dimples of cellulite pocking the white flesh under her upper arms as she raised a cigarette to her lips and leaned forward to concentrate on the TV.

'Look, Dottie, look,' Helene said. 'There's Gregor and Head Sparks.'

'Oh, yeah!' Dottie pointed at the screen as two

men walked behind the reporter interviewing Helene. The men waved at the camera.

'Look at 'em waving.' Helene smiled. 'The punks.'

'Smart-asses,' Dottie said.

Helene raised a can of Miller to her lips with the same hand that held her cigarette, and the long ash curled down toward her chin as she drank.

'Helene,' Lionel said.

'One sec, one sec.' Helene waved her beer can at him, her eyes fixed on the screen. 'This is the best part.'

Beatrice caught our eyes and rolled her own.

On TV, the reporter asked Helene who she thought could be responsible for the abduction of her child.

'How do you answer a question like that?' the TV Helene said. 'I mean, like, who would take my little girl? What's the point? She never did nothing to nobody. She was just a little girl with a beautiful smile. That's what she did all the time, she smiled.'

'She did have a beautiful smile,' Dottie said.

'Does,' Beatrice said.

The women on the couch seemed not to have heard her.

'Oh, it was,' Helene said. 'It was perfect. Just perfect. Break your heart.' Helene's voice cracked, and she put down her beer long enough to grab a Kleenex from a box on the coffee table.

Dottie patted her knee and clucked. 'There, there,' Dottie said. 'There, there.'

'Helene,' Lionel said.

TV coverage of Helene had given way to footage of O.J. playing golf somewhere in Florida.

'I still can't believe he got away with it,' Helene said.

Dottie turned to her. 'I *know*,' she said, as if she'd been unburdened of a great secret.

'If he wasn't black,' Helene said, 'he'd be in jail now.'

'If he wasn't black,' Dottie said, 'he'd have gotten the chair.'

'If he wasn't black,' Angie said, 'you two wouldn't care.'

They turned their heads and looked back at us. They seemed mildly surprised by the four people standing behind them, as if we'd suddenly appeared there like Magi.

'What?' Dottie said, her brown eyes darting across our chests.

'Helene,' Lionel said.

Helene looked up into his face, her mascara smudged under puffy eyes. 'Yeah?'

'This is Patrick and Angie, the two detectives we talked about.'

Helene gave us a limp wave with her sodden Kleenex. 'Hi-ya.'

'Hi,' Angie said.

'Hi-ya,' I said.

'I 'member you,' Dottie said to Angie. 'You 'member me?'

Angie smiled kindly and shook her head.

'MRM High,' Dottie said. 'I was, like, a freshman. You were a senior.'

Angie gave it some thought, shook her head again.

'Oh, yeah,' Dottie said. 'I 'member you. Prom Queen. That's what we called you.' She swigged some beer. 'You still like that?'

'Like what?' Angie said.

'Like you think you're better than everyone else.'

53

She peered at Angie with eyes so tiny it was hard to tell if they were bleary or not. 'That was you all over. Miss Perfect. Miss—'

'Helene.' Angie turned her head to concentrate on Helene McCready. 'We need to speak to you about Amanda.'

But Helene had her eyes on me, her cigarette frozen a quarter inch from her lips. 'You look like someone. Dottie, doesn't he?'

'What?' Dottie said.

'Look like someone.' Helene took two quick hits from her cigarette.

'Who?' Dottie stared at me now.

'You know,' Helene said. 'That guy. That guy on that show, you know the one.'

'No,' Dottie said, and gave me a hesitant smile. 'What show?'

'That show,' Helene said. 'You gotta know the one I'm talking about.'

'No, I don't.'

'You gotta.'

'What show?' Dottie turned her head to look at Helene. 'What show?'

Helene blinked at her and frowned. Then she looked back at me. 'You look just like him,' she assured me.

'Okay,' I said.

Beatrice leaned against the hallway doorjamb and closed her eyes.

'Helene,' Lionel said, 'Patrick and Angie have to talk to you about Amanda. Alone.'

'What,' Dottie said, 'I'm some kind of freak?'

'No, Dottie,' Lionel said carefully. 'I didn't say that.'

54

'I'm some kind of fucking loser, Lionel? Not good enough to be with my best friend when she needs me most?'

'He's not saying that,' Beatrice said in a tired voice, her eyes still closed.

'Then again . . .' I said.

Dottie screwed up her blotchy face, looked at me.

'Helene,' Angie said hurriedly, 'it would go a lot faster if we could just ask you some questions alone and be out of your hair.'

Helene looked at Angie. Then at Lionel. Then at the TV. Finally she focused on the back of Dottie's head.

Dottie was still looking at me, confused, trying to decide if the confusion should mutate into anger or not.

'Dottie,' Helene said, with the air of someone about to deliver a state address, 'is my best friend. My *best* friend. That means something. You want to talk to me, you talk to her.'

Dottie's eyes left mine and she turned to look at her *best* friend, and Helene nudged her knee with her elbow.

I glanced at Angie. We've been working together so long, I could sum up the look on Angie's face in two words:

Screw this.

I met her eyes and nodded. Life was too short to spend another quarter second with either Helene or Dottie.

I looked at Lionel and he shrugged, his body puddled with resignation.

We would have walked out right then – in fact, we were starting to – but Beatrice opened her eyes and blocked our path and said, 'Please.'

'No,' Angie said quietly.

'An hour,' Beatrice said. 'Just give us an hour. We'll pay.'

'It's not the money,' Angie said.

'Please,' Beatrice said. She looked past Angie, locked eyes with me. She shifted her weight from her left foot to her right and her shoulders sagged.

'One more hour,' I said. 'That's it.'

She smiled and nodded.

'Patrick, right?' Helene looked up at me. 'That's your name?'

'Yes,' I said.

'Think you could move a little to your left, Patrick?' Helene said. 'You're blocking the TV.'

Half an hour later, we'd learned nothing new.

Lionel, after a lot of wheedling, had convinced his sister to turn off the TV while we talked, but a lack of TV seemed only to further diminish Helene's attention span. Several times during our conversation, her eyes darted past me to the blank screen as if hoping it would turn back on through divine intervention.

Dottie, after all her bitching about sticking by her best friend, left the room as soon as we turned off the TV. We heard her knocking around the kitchen, opening the refrigerator for another beer, rattling through the cupboards for an ashtray.

Lionel sat beside his sister on the couch, and Angie and I sat on the floor against the entertainment center. Beatrice took the end of the couch as far away from Helene as possible, stretched one leg out in front of her, held the other by the ankle between both hands.

We asked Helene to tell us everything regarding the day of her daughter's disappearance, asked if there'd been any sort of argument between the two of them, if Helene had angered anyone who'd have a reason to abduct her daughter as an act of vengeance.

Helene's voice bore what seemed a constant tone of exasperation as she explained that she never argued with her daughter. How could you argue with someone who smiled all the time? In between the smiling, it seemed, Amanda had only loved her mother and been loved by her, and they'd spent their time loving and smiling and smiling some more. Helene could think of no one she'd angered, and as she'd told the police, even if she had, who would abduct her child to get back at her? Children took work, Helene said. You had to feed them, she assured us. You had to tuck them in. You had to play with them sometimes.

Hence, all that smiling.

In the end, she told us nothing we hadn't learned already from either news reports or Lionel and Beatrice.

As for Helene herself – the more time I spent with her, the less I wanted to be in the same room. As we discussed her child's disappearance, she let us in on the fact that she hated her life. She was lonely; there were no good men left; they needed to put a fence up around Mexico to keep out all those Mexicans who were apparently stealing jobs up here in Boston. She was sure there was a liberal agenda to corrupt every decent American but she couldn't articulate what that agenda was, only that it affected her ability to be happy and it was determined to keep blacks on welfare. Sure, she was on welfare herself, but she'd been trying hard these last seven years to get off.

She spoke of Amanda as one would speak of a stolen car or an errant pet – she seemed more annoyed than anything else. Her child had disappeared and, boy, had that fucked up her life.

God, it appeared, had anointed Helene McCready Life's Great Victim. The rest of us could step out of line now. The competition was over.

'Helene,' I said, near the end of our conversation, 'is there anything you could tell us that you might have forgotten to tell the police?'

Helene looked at the remote control on the coffee table. 'What?' she said.

I repeated my question.

'It's hard,' she said. 'You know?'

'What?' I said.

'Raising a kid.' She looked up at me and her dull eyes widened, as if she were about to impart great wisdom. 'It's hard. It's not like in the commercials.'

When we left the living room, Helene turned on the TV and Dottie swept past us, two beers in hand, as if she'd been given her cue.

'She's got some emotional problems,' Lionel told us, once we'd settled in the kitchen.

'Yeah,' Beatrice said. 'She's a cunt.' She poured coffee into her mug.

'Don't say that word,' Lionel said. 'For God's sake.'

Beatrice poured some coffee into Angie's cup, looked at me.

I held up my can of Coke.

'Lionel,' Angie said, 'your sister doesn't seem too concerned that Amanda's missing.'

'Oh, she's concerned,' Lionel said. 'Last night? She cried all night. I think she's just cried out at the moment. Trying to get a handle on her . . . grief. You know.'

'Lionel,' I said, 'with all due respect, I see self-pity. I don't see grief.'

'It's there,' Lionel blinked, looked at his wife. 'It's there. Really.'

Angie said, 'I know I've said this before, but I really don't see what we can do that the police aren't already doing.'

'I know.' Lionel sighed. 'I know.'

'Maybe later,' I said.

'Sure,' he agreed.

'If the police get completely stumped and pull off the case,' Angie said. 'Maybe then.'

'Yeah.' Lionel came off the wall and held out his hand. 'Look, thanks for dropping by. Thanks for . . . everything.'

'Any time.' I went to shake his hand.

Beatrice's voice, jagged but clear, stopped me. 'She's four.'

I looked at her.

'Four years old,' she said, her eyes on the ceiling. 'And she's out there somewhere. Maybe lost. Maybe worse.'

'Honey,' Lionel said.

Beatrice gave a small shake of her head. She looked at her drink, then tilted her head and slugged it back, her eyes closed. When it was empty, she tossed her mug on the table and bent over, her hands clasped together.

'Mrs McCready,' I said, but she cut me off with a wave of her hand.

'Every second people aren't trying to find her is a second she feels.' She raised her head and opened her eyes.

'Honey,' Lionel said.

'Don't "honey" me.' She looked at Angie. 'Amanda is afraid. She is missing. And Lionel's bitch sister sits out in my living room with her fat friend sucking down beers and watching herself on TV. And who speaks for Amanda? Huh?' She looked at her husband. She looked at Angie and me, her eyes red. She looked at the floor. 'Who shows that little girl that someone gives a shit whether she lives or dies?'

For a full minute, the only sound in that kitchen came from the hum of the refrigerator motor.

Then, very softly, Angie said, 'I guess we do.'

I looked at her and raised my eyebrows. She shrugged.

An odd hybrid of laugh and sob escaped Beatrice's mouth, and she placed a fist to her lips and stared at Angie as tears filled her eyes but refused to fall.

4

The section of Dorchester Avenue that runs through my neighborhood used to have more Irish bars on it than any other street outside Dublin. When I was younger, my father used to participate in a marathon pub crawl to raise money for local charities. Two beers and one shot per bar, and the men would move onto the next one. They'd begin in Fields Corner, the next neighborhood over, and move north up the avenue. The idea was to see which man could remain standing long enough to cross the border into South Boston, less than two miles north.

My father was a hell of a drinker, as were most of the men who signed up for the pub crawl, but in all the years of its existence, not one man ever made it to Southie.

Most of those bars are gone now, replaced by Vietnamese restaurants and corner stores. Now known as the Ho Chi Minh Trail, this four-block section of the avenue is actually a lot more charming than many of my white neighbors seem to find it. You drive it early in the morning, and you often find old men leading fellow senior citizens in tai chi exercises along the sidewalks, see people wearing their native dress of dark silk pajamas and wide straw hats. I've heard about the alleged gangs, or tongs, working down here, but I've never encountered them; mostly I've seen young Vietnamese kids with spiked, gel-saturated hair and Gargoyle sunglasses, standing around trying to look cool, trying to look hard, and I find them no different than I was at their age.

Of the old bars that have survived the latest flux of immigration into our neighborhood, the three that front the avenue itself are very good bars. The owners and their clientele have a laissez-faire attitude toward the Vietnamese, and the Vietnamese treat them in kind. Neither culture seems particularly curious about the other, and that suits both just fine.

The only other bar near the Ho Chi Minh Trail was off the avenue, at the end of a dirt road that was stunted when the town ran out of funds to complete it in the mid-forties. The alley that remained never saw the sunlight. A trucking company's hangar-sized depot loomed over it from the south. A dense thicket of three-deckers blocked it from the north. At the end of this alley sat the Filmore Tap, as dusty and seemingly forgotten as the aborted road it sat on.

Back in the days of the Dot Ave pub crawl, even men of my father's ilk – brawlers and boozers all – didn't go in the Filmore. It was stricken from the pub crawl map as if it didn't exist, and in my entire life I never knew anyone who frequented the place on a regular basis.

There's a difference between a tough working-class bar and a sleazy white-trash bar, and the

Filmore epitomized the latter. Fights in working-class bars break out frequently enough but usually involve fists, maybe a beer bottle over someone's head at worst. Fights broke out in the Filmore about every second beer and usually involved switch-blades. Something about the place attracted men who'd lost anything worth caring about a long, long time ago. They came in here to nurse their drug habits and their alcoholism and their hate. And while you wouldn't think there were a lot of people clamoring to get in their club, they didn't look kindly upon potential applicants.

The bartender glanced at us as we came in from the sunlight on Thursday afternoon and adjusted our eyes to the sallow dark green ambience of the place. Four guys huddled around the corner of the bar closest to the door, and they turned slowly, one by one, and looked at us.

'Where's Lee Marvin when you need him?' I said to Angie.

'Or Eastwood,' Angie said. 'I'd take Clint about now.'

Two guys shot pool in the back. Well, they *were* shooting pool. And then we came in and somehow messed up their game, and one of them looked up from the table and frowned.

The bartender turned his back to us. He stared at the TV above him, intently focused on an episode of *Gilligan's Island*. The Skipper was hitting Gilligan on the head with his cap. The Professor was trying to break it up. The Howells laughed. Maryann and Ginger were nowhere to be found. Maybe that had something to do with the plot.

Angie and I took stools at the far corner of the

bar, near the bartender, and waited for him to acknowledge us.

The Skipper kept hitting Gilligan. He was apparently mad about something involving a monkey.

'This is a great one,' I said to Angie. 'They almost get off the island.'

'Really?' Angie lit a cigarette. 'Pray tell, what stops them?'

'Skipper professes his love for his little buddy and they get all caught up in the wedding arrangements and the monkey steals the boat and all their coconuts.'

'Right,' Angie said. 'I remember this one now.'

The bartender turned and looked down at us. 'What?' he said.

'A pint of your finest ale,' I said.

'Two,' Angie said.

'Fine,' the bartender said. 'But then you shut up until the show's over. Some of us haven't seen this one.'

After *Gilligan*, the bar TV was tuned to an episode of *Public Enemies*, a fact-based crime show in which the exploits of wanted felons were reenacted by actors so inept they made Van Damme and Seagal look like Olivier and Gielgud. This particular episode concerned a man who'd sexually molested and then carved up his children in Montana, shot a state trooper in North Dakota, and seemed to have spent his entire life making sure everyone he encountered had one bad fucking day.

'You ask me,' Big Dave Strand said to Angie and me, as they flashed the felon's face onscreen, 'that's the guy you should be talking to. Not bothering my people.'

Big Dave Strand was the owner and chief bartender of the Filmore Tap. He was, true to his name, big – at least six four, with a wide body that seemed as if the thick flesh had wrapped itself in layers over the bone as opposed to expanding organically as the body grew. Big Dave had a bushel of beard and mustache around his lips and dark green jailhouse tattoos on both biceps. The one on the left arm depicted a revolver and bore the word FUCK below it. The one on the right seemed to be of a bullet impacting with a skull and said YOU below it.

Oddly, I'd never run into Big Dave in church.

'Knew guys like him in the joint,' Big Dave said. He drew himself another pint of Piel's from the tap. 'Freaks. They'd keep 'em out of general population 'cause they knew what we'd do to them. They knew.' He downed half his pint, looked up at the TV again, and belched.

The bar smelled of sour milk for some reason. And sweat. And beer. And buttered popcorn from the baskets spaced out along the bar at every fourth stool. The floor was rubber tile, and Big Dave kept a hose behind the bar. By the looks of the floor, it had been a few days since he'd used it. Cigarette butts and popcorn were ground into the rubber, and I was pretty sure the small movements I saw coming from the shadows under one of the tables were those of mice nibbling on something along the baseboard.

We'd questioned all four men at the bar about Helene McCready, and none of them had been much help. They were older men, the youngest in his mid-thirties but looking a decade older. They all looked Angie up and down as if she were hanging naked in a butcher's window. They weren't particularly hostile, but they weren't helpful either. They all knew Helene but didn't seem to feel one way or another about her. They all knew her daughter was missing and didn't seem to feel one way or another about that either. One of them, a busted heap of red veins and yellowing skin named Lenny, said, 'The kid's missing. So? She'll turn up. They always do.'

'You've misplaced children before?' Angie said.

Lenny nodded. 'They showed back up.'

'Where are they now?' I said.

'One's in prison, one's in Alaska or someplace.' He whacked the shoulder of the man nodding off beside him. 'This here's the youngest.'

Lenny's son, a pale skinny guy with two brightly blackened eyes, said, 'You're fucking *A*,' and dropped his head into his arms on the bar.

'We already been through this with the cops,' Big Dave told us. 'We told 'em, Yeah, Helene comes in here; no, she don't bring the kid with her; yeah, she likes her beer; no, she didn't sell the kid to pay off a drug debt.' He narrowed his eyes at us. 'Least not to anyone in here.'

One of the pool players came to the bar. He was a skinny guy with a shaved head, cheap jailhouse tats on his arms, but none done with the attention to detail and fine aesthetic sense of Big Dave's. He leaned in between Angie and me, even though there were a few car lengths of space to our right. He ordered two more beers from Dave and stared at Angie's breasts.

'You got a problem?' Angie said.

'No problem,' the guy said. 'I don't have a problem.'

'He's problem-free,' I said.

The guy continued staring at Angie's breasts with eyes that looked as if they'd been zapped with a lightning bolt and seared of life.

Dave brought his beers, and the guy picked them up.

'These two are asking about Helene,' Dave said.

'Yeah?' The guy's voice was so flat it was hard to tell if he had a pulse. He pulled his two beers in between our heads and tilted the mug in his left hand so that some beer spilled on my shoe.

I looked down at my shoe, then back up into his eyes. His breath smelled like an athlete's sock. He waited for me to respond. When I didn't, he looked at the mugs in his hands and his fingers tightened around the handles. He looked back up at me, and those stunted eyes were black holes.

'I don't have a problem,' he said. 'Maybe you do.'

I shifted my weight slightly in my chair so that my elbow had more leverage on the bar in case I had to bob or weave suddenly and waited for the guy to make whatever move was floating through his head like a cancer cell.

He looked down at his hands again. 'Maybe you do,' he repeated loudly, and then stepped out from in between us.

We watched him walk back to his friend by the pool table. His friend took his beer, and the guy with the shaved head gestured in our direction.

'Did Helene have a big drug problem?' Angie asked Big Dave.

'The fuck would I know?' Big Dave said. 'You implying something?'

'Dave,' I said.

'Big Dave,' he corrected me.

'Big Dave,' I said. 'I don't care if you keep kilos under the bar. And I don't care if you sell them to Helene McCready on a daily basis. We just want to know if she had enough of a drug problem that she was in deep to somebody.'

He held my gaze for about thirty seconds, long enough for me to see how much of a badass he was. Then he watched some more TV.

'Big Dave,' Angie said.

He turned his bison's head.

'Is Helene an addict?'

'You know,' Big Dave said, 'you're pretty hot. You ever want to go a few rounds with a real man, give a call.'

Angie said, 'You know some?'

Big Dave looked back up at the TV.

Angie and I glanced at each other. She shrugged. I shrugged. The attention-deficit afflicting Helene and her friends was apparently widespread enough to fill a psych ward.

'She didn't have no big debts,' Big Dave said. 'She's into me for maybe sixty bucks. If she was into anybody else for . . . party favors, I'd have heard about it.'

'Hey, Big Dave,' one of the men down the end of the bar called, 'you ask her yet if she blows?'

Big Dave held out his arms to them and shrugged. 'Ask her yourself.'

'Hey, honey,' the man called. 'Hey, honey.'

'What about guys?' Angie kept her eyes on Dave, her voice clear, as if whatever these assholes were talking about had nothing to do with her. 'Was she seeing anybody who might be pissed off at her?'

'Hey, honey,' the man called. 'Look at me. Look over here. Hey, honey.'

Big Dave chuckled and turned away from the four guys long enough to put a fresh head on his beer. 'There's chicks who can make you crazy, and chicks you'd fight over.' He smiled over his pint glass at Angie. 'You, for instance.'

'And Helene?' I said.

Big Dave smiled at me as if he thought his come-ons to Angie had me worried. He glanced down the bar at the four men. He winked.

'And Helene?' I repeated.

'You saw her. She's all-right looking. She'd *do*, I guess. But one look at her, you know she ain't worth much in the sack.' He leaned on the bar in front of Angie. 'Now, you, I bet you've fucked guys in half. Right, honey?'

She shook her head and chuckled softly.

All four guys at the bar were fully awake now. They watched us with high beams in their pupils.

Lenny's son came off his stool and walked over to the door.

Angie looked down at the bar top, fingered her grimy coaster.

'Don't look away when I'm talking to you,' Big Dave said. His voice was thicker now, as if his throat were clogged with phlegm.

Angie raised her head, looked at him.

'That's better.' Big Dave leaned in closer. His left arm slid off the bar and reached for something below.

There was a loud snap in the still bar as Lenny's son turned the bolt on the front door.

So this is how it happens. A woman with intelligence,

pride, and beauty enters a place like this and the men get a glimpse of all they've been missing, all they can never have. They're forced to confront the deficiencies of character that drove them to a dump like this in the first place. Hate, envy, and regret all smash through their stunted brains at once. And they decide to make the woman regret, too – regret her intelligence, her beauty, and, especially, her pride. They decide to smash back, pin the woman to the bar, spew and gorge.

I looked at the glass front of the cigarette machine, saw my reflection and the reflection of the two men behind me. They approached from the pool table, sticks in hand, the bald one in the lead.

'Helene McCready,' Big Dave said, his eyes still locked on Angie, 'is a nothing. A loser. Means her kid woulda been a loser. So whatever happened to the kid, she's better off. What I don't like is people coming in my bar, implying I'm a dealer, running their mouths like they're better than me.'

Lenny's son leaned against the door and crossed his arms over his chest.

'Dave,' I said.

'Big Dave,' he said through gritted teeth, his eyes never leaving Angie.

'Dave,' I said, 'don't be a fuckup here.'

'Did you hear him, Big Dave?' Angie said, a hint of tremor in her voice. 'Don't be stupid.'

I said, 'Look at me, Dave.'

Dave glanced in my direction, more to check on the progress of the two pool players coming up behind me than because of what I'd said, and his head froze as he spotted the .45 Colt Commander in my waistband.

I'd moved it there from the holster at the small of my back the moment Lenny's son had walked over to block the door, and Dave raised his eyes from my waist to my face and quickly recognized the difference between someone who exposes a gun for show and someone who does so to use it.

'Either of those guys behind me takes another step,' I told Big Dave, 'and this situation's going nuclear.'

Dave glanced over my shoulder and shook his head quickly.

'Tell that asshole to move away from the door,' Angie said.

'Ray,' Big Dave called, 'sit back down.'

'Why?' Ray said. 'The fuck for, Big Dave? Free country and shit.'

I tapped the butt of the .45 with my index finger.

'Ray,' Big Dave said, his eyes locked on me now, 'get away from the door or I'll fucking put your head through it.'

'Okay,' Ray said. 'Okay, okay. Jeez, Big Dave. I mean, jeez and shit.' Ray shook his head, but instead of returning to his seat, he unlocked the door and walked out of the bar.

'Quite the orator, our Ray,' I said.

'Let's go,' Angie said.

'Sure.' I pushed my bar stool away with my leg.

The two pool players stood just off to my right as I turned toward the door. I glanced at the one who'd spilled beer on my shoe. He held his pool stick upside down in both hands, the hilt resting on his shoulder. He was stupid enough to still be standing there, but not so stupid he was going to move any closer.

'*Now*,' I told him, 'you have a problem.'

He glanced at the stick in his hands, at the sweat darkening the wood below his hands.

I said, 'Drop the stick.'

He considered the distance between us. He considered the butt of the .45 and my right hand resting a half inch away from it. He looked into my face. Then he bent and placed the stick by his feet. He stepped back from it as his friend's stick clattered loudly to the floor.

I turned away and took five steps down the bar and then stopped. I looked back at Big Dave. 'What?' I said.

'Excuse me?' Dave watched my hands.

'I thought you said something.'

'I didn't say anything.'

'I thought you said that maybe you hadn't told us everything you could have about Helene McCready.'

'I didn't,' Big Dave said, and held up his hands. 'I didn't say anything.'

'Angie,' I said, 'you think Big Dave told us everything?'

She had stopped by the door, her .38 held loosely in her left hand as she leaned against the doorjamb. 'Nope.'

'We think you're holding out, Dave.' I shrugged. 'Just an opinion.'

'I told you everything. Now I think you both should just—'

'Come back when you're closing up tonight?' I said. 'That's a great idea, Big Dave. You got it. We'll come back then.'

Big Dave shook his head several times. 'No, no.'

'Say about two, two-fifteen?' I nodded. 'See you then, Dave.'

I turned and walked down the rest of the bar. Nobody would meet my eyes. Everyone looked at their beers.

'She wasn't over at her friend Dottie's house,' Big Dave said.

We turned and looked back at him. He leaned over the bar sink and fired a spurt of water into his face from the dispenser hose.

'Hands up on the bar, Dave,' Angie said.

He raised his head and blinked against the liquid. He placed his palms flat on the bar top. 'Helene,' he said. 'She wasn't over at Dottie's. She was here.'

'With who?' I said.

'With Dottie,' he said. 'And Lenny's kid, Ray.'

Lenny raised his head from his beer and said, 'Shut the fuck up, Dave.'

'The skeevy guy who manned the door?' Angie said. 'That's Ray?'

Big Dave nodded.

'What were they doing in here?' I said.

'Don't you say another word,' Lenny said.

Big Dave glanced at him desperately, then back at Angie and me. 'Just drinking. Helene knew it looked bad enough she left her kid alone in the first place. If the press or the cops knew she was actually ten blocks away at a bar and not next door, it would look even worse.'

'What's her relationship with Ray?'

'They do each other sometimes, I think.' He shrugged.

'What's Ray's last name?'

'David!' Lenny said. 'David, you shut the—'

73

'Likanski,' Big Dave said. 'He lives on Harvest.' He took a gulp of air.

'You are shit,' Lenny told him. 'That's what you are, and it's all you'll ever be, and all your retarded fucking offspring will be and everything you touch. Shit.'

'Lenny,' I said.

Lenny kept his back to me. 'You think I'm going to say a word to you, boy, you are on fucking angel dust. I might be watching my beer, but I know you got a gun, and I know that girl has one too. And so fucking what? Shoot me or leave.'

Outside, I could hear the sound of a siren approaching.

Lenny turned his head, and a smile broke across his face. 'Sounds like they're coming for you, don't it?' His smile broke into a hard, bitter laugh that exposed a red sore of a mouth with almost no teeth.

He waved at me as the siren grew so close I knew they were in the alley. 'Bye-bye now. Smoke 'em if you got 'em.'

His bitter laugh came out even harder this time and sounded more like the coughing of ravaged lungs. After a few seconds, his cronies joined in, nervously at first but then openly, as we heard the doors of the cop car opening outside.

By the time we walked out the door, it sounded like a party in there.

5

When we stepped out of the bar into the alley, we met the grille of a black Ford Taurus parked a matter of inches from the front door. The younger of the two detectives, a big guy beaming a little boy's smile, leaned in through the open driver's window and turned off the siren.

His partner sat cross-legged on the hood, a colder smile on his round face, and said, '*Woo, woo, woo.*' He held an index finger aloft and rotated his wrist and made the sound again. '*Woo, woo, woo.*'

'Frighteningly realistic,' I said.

'Ain't it?' He clapped his hands together and slid down the car hood until his feet rested on the grille and his knees were almost touching my legs.

'You'd be Pat Kenzie.' His hand shot out toward my chest. 'Glad to make your acquaintance.'

'Patrick,' I said, and shook the hand.

He gave it two vigorous pumps. 'Detective Sergeant Nick Raftopoulos. Call me Poole. Everyone does.' His sharp elfin face tilted toward Angie. 'You'd be Angela.'

She shook his hand. 'Angie.'

'Pleasure to meet you, Angie. Anyone ever tell you that you have your father's eyes?'

Angie placed a hand over her eyebrows, took a step toward Nick Raftopoulos. 'You knew my father?'

Poole held his palms up on his knees. 'In passing. In a member-of-opposing-teams capacity. I liked the man, miss. He had genuine class. To tell you the truth, I mourned his . . . passing, if that's the word. He was a rarity.'

Angie gave him a soft smile. 'That's nice of you to say.'

The bar door opened behind us and I could smell stale whiskey again.

The younger cop looked up at whoever stood behind us. 'Back inside, mutt. I know someone holding paper on your ass.'

The stale whiskey stench dissipated and the door closed behind us.

Poole jerked his thumb over his shoulder. 'That young man there with the sweet disposition is my partner, Detective Remy Broussard.'

We nodded at Broussard, and he nodded back. At closer glance, he was older than he'd first appeared. I put him at forty-three or forty-four. When I'd first come outside I'd pegged him for my age because of the Tom Sawyer innocence in that grin of his, but the crow's-feet around his eyes, the lines etched in the hollows of his cheeks, and the deep pewter-gray streaked through his curly dirty-blond hair added a decade upon a second look. He had the build of a man who worked out at least four times a week, a physique of solid bulked-up muscle mass that was softened by the double-breasted olive Italian suit he wore over a loosened blue-and-gold Bill Blass tie and subtly pinstriped shirt unbuttoned at the collar.

A clotheshorse, I decided, as he brushed some dust from the edge of his left Florsheim, the kind of man who probably never passed a mirror without casting a lingering glance into it. But as he leaned over the open driver's door and stared at us, I sensed a piercing calculation in him, a prodigious intelligence. He might pause at mirrors, but I doubted he ever missed anything going on behind him when he did.

'Our dear Lieutenant Jack-the-impassioned Doyle said we should look you up,' Poole said. 'So here we are.'

'Here you are,' I said.

'We're driving up the avenue toward your office,' Poole said, 'and we see Skinny Ray Likanski come running out of this alley. Ray's father, you see, a snitch of snitches in the old days, goes way back with me. Detective Broussard wouldn't know Skinny Ray from Sugar Ray, but I say, "Stop the chariot, Remy. That plebeian is none other than Skinny Ray Likanski and he looks a might distressed."' Poole smiled and drummed his fingers on his kneecaps. 'Ray is screaming about someone waving a gun inside this fine establishment.' He cocked his eyebrow at me. '"A gun?" I say to Detective Broussard. "In a gentleman's club like the Filmore Tap? Why, I never."'

I looked at Broussard. He leaned against the driver's door, arms folded across his chest. He shrugged as if to say, My partner, what a character.

Poole did a fast drumbeat on the hood of the Taurus to get my attention. I looked back at him, and he smiled up at me with his weathered elf's face. He was in his late fifties probably, squat, and the hair cropped tight to his head was the color of cigarette ash. He rubbed the bristles and squinted into the midafternoon sunlight. 'Would said alleged gun be that Colt Commander I see by your alleged right hip, Mr Kenzie?'

'Allegedly,' I said.

Poole smiled, looked up at the Filmore Tap. 'Our Mr Big Dave Strand – is he still in one piece in there?'

'Last I checked,' I said.

'Should we be arresting you two for assault?' Broussard pulled a stick of gum from a pack of Wrigley's, popped it in his mouth.

'He'd have to press charges.'

'And you don't think he will?' Poole said.

'We're pretty sure he won't,' Angie said.

Poole looked at us, his eyebrows raised. He turned his head, looked back at his partner. Broussard shrugged and then both of them broke out in wide grins.

'Well, ain't that terrific,' Poole said.

'Big Dave tried his brand of charm on you, I assume?' Broussard asked Angie.

'"Tried" being the operative word,' Angie said.

Broussard chewed his gum, smiling around it, and then straightened to his full height, his eyes locked on Angie as if reconsidering her.

'In all seriousness,' Poole said, though his voice was still light, 'did either of you discharge your firearms in there?'

'No,' I said.

Poole held out his hand and snapped his fingers.

I removed my gun from my waistband and handed it to him.

He dropped the clip from the gun butt into his

hand. He racked the slide, then peered into the chamber to make sure it was clear before he sniffed the barrel. He nodded to himself. He passed the clip to my left hand, placed the gun in my right.

I placed the gun back in the holster at the small of my back, slid the clip into the pocket of my jacket.

'And your permits?' Broussard said.

'Up-to-date and in our wallets,' Angie said.

Poole and Broussard grinned at each other again. Then they stared at us until we figured out what they were waiting for.

We each produced our permits and handed them over the car hood to Poole. Poole gave them a cursory glance and handed them back.

'Should we interview the patrons, Poole?'

Poole looked back at Broussard. 'I'm hungry.'

'I could eat, too,' Broussard said.

Poole raised his eyebrows at us again. 'How about you two? You hungry?'

'Not particularly,' I said.

'That's okay. The place I'm thinking of,' Poole said, and placed his hand gently under my elbow, 'the food's awful anyway. But they got water you wouldn't believe. Best around. Straight out of the tap.'

The Victoria Diner was in Roxbury, just over the dividing line from my neighborhood, and actually served great food. Nick Raftopoulos had pork chops. Remy Broussard had a turkey club.

Angie and I drank coffee. 'So you're getting nowhere,' Angie said.

Poole dipped a chunk of pork in applesauce. 'In truth, no.'

Broussard wiped his mouth with his napkin. 'Neither of us has ever worked a case with this much publicity that went on for so long and didn't turn out bad.'

'You don't think Helene's involved?' I said.

'We did at first,' Poole said. 'My operating theory was that she sold the kid or else some dealer she owed kidnapped the little girl.'

'What changed your mind?' Angie said.

Poole chewed some food, nudged Broussard to answer.

'Polygraph. She passed with flying colors. Also, this guy wolfing pork chops and me? It's pretty hard to lie to us when we're working on you together. Helene lies, don't get me wrong, but not about her daughter's disappearance. She honestly doesn't know what happened to her.'

'What about Helene's whereabouts the night Amanda disappeared?'

Broussard's sandwich stalled halfway to his mouth. 'What about them?'

'You believe the story she told the press?' Angie said.

'Is there a reason we shouldn't?' Poole dipped his fork in the applesauce.

'Big Dave told us a different story.'

Poole leaned back in his chair, slapped the crumbs from his hands. 'And what was that?'

'Did you or did you not believe Helene's story?' Angie asked.

'Not entirely,' Broussard said. 'According to the polygraph, she was with Dottie, but maybe not in Dottie's apartment. She's sticking to the lie, though.'

'Where was she?' Poole said.

'According to Big Dave, she was in the Filmore.'

Poole and Broussard looked at each other, then back at us.

'So,' Broussard said slowly, 'she did bullshit us.'

'Didn't want to spoil her fifteen seconds,' Poole said.

'Her fifteen seconds?' I asked.

'In the spotlight,' Poole said. 'Used to be minutes; these days it's seconds.' He sighed. 'On the TV, playing her role as the grieving mother in the pretty blue dress. You remember that Brazilian woman in Allston, her little boy went missing about eight months back?'

'And was never found.' Angie nodded.

'Right. The point is, though, that mother – she was dark-skinned, she didn't dress well, she always looked sorta stoned on camera? After a while, the general public really didn't give a shit about her missing boy because they disliked the mother so much.'

'But Helene McCready,' Broussard said, 'she's white. And she fixes herself up, she looks good on camera. Maybe she doesn't come across as the brightest bulb in the box, but she's likable.'

'No, she's not,' Angie said.

'Oh, in person?' Broussard shook his head. 'In person, she's about as likable as a case of crabs. But on camera? When she's speaking for all of fifteen seconds? The lens loves her, the public loves her. She leaves her kid alone for almost four hours, there's some outrage, but mostly people are saying, "Cut her some slack. We all make mistakes."'

'And she's probably never been loved in her life like that,' Poole said. 'And as soon as Amanda is found, or let's say something happens to knock the case off the front page – and that something always happens – then Helene goes back to being who she was. But for now, what I'm saying, she's grabbing her fifteen seconds.'

'And that's all you think her lying about her whereabouts amounts to?' I said.

'Probably,' Broussard said. He wiped the corners of his mouth with his napkin, pushed his plate away. 'Don't get us wrong. We're going over to her brother's place in a few minutes, and we're going to tear her a new asshole for lying to us. And if there is more to it, we'll find out.' He tipped his hand towards us. 'Thanks to you two.'

'How long have you been on this case?' Poole asked.

Angie looked at her watch. 'Since late last night.'

'And you already uncovered something we missed?' Poole chuckled. 'You two might be as capable as we've heard.'

Angie batted her eyelashes. 'Gee, gosh.'

Broussard smiled. 'I hang out with Oscar Lee sometimes. We both came up through the Housing Police about a million years ago. After Gerry Glynn got put down in that playground a couple years back, I asked Oscar about you two. Want to know what he said?'

I shrugged. 'Knowing Oscar, it was probably profane.'

Broussard nodded. 'He said you two were major fuckups in most aspects of your lives.'

'Sounds like Oscar,' Angie said.

'But he also said once you both got it into your

heads that you were going to close a case, not even God himself could call you off.'

'That Oscar,' I said, 'he's a peach.'

'So now you're on the same case we are.' Poole folded his napkin delicately and placed it on top of his plate.

'That bother you?' Angie said.

Poole looked at Broussard. Broussard shrugged.

'It doesn't bother us in principle,' Poole said.

'But,' Broussard said, 'there should be some ground rules.'

'Such as?'

'Such as . . .' Poole removed a pack of cigarettes. He pulled off the cellophane slowly, then removed the tinfoil and pulled out an unfiltered Camel. He sniffed it, inhaling the tobacco scent deep into his nostrils as he leaned his head back and closed his eyes. Then he leaned forward and ground the unlit cigarette into the ashtray until it snapped in half. He placed the pack back in his pocket.

Broussard smiled at us, his left eyebrow cocked.

Poole noticed us staring at him. 'I beg your pardon. I quit.'

'When?' Angie said.

'Two years ago. But I still need the rituals.' He smiled. 'Rituals are important.'

Angie reached into her purse. 'Do you mind if I smoke?'

'Oh, God, would you?' Poole said.

He watched Angie light her cigarette; then his head shifted slightly and his eyes cleared and found mine, seemed capable of gaining entrance to the core of my brain or my soul with a blink.

'Ground rules,' he said. 'We can't have any press leaks. You're friends with Richie Colgan of the *Trib*.'

I nodded.

'Colgan's no friend of the police,' Broussard said.

Angie said, 'It's not his job to be a friend. It's his job to be a reporter.'

'And I have no argument with that,' Poole said. 'But I can't have anyone in the press knowing anything we don't want him to regarding this investigation. Agreed?'

I looked at Angie. She studied Poole through her cigarette smoke. Eventually, she nodded. I said, 'Agreed.'

'Magic!' Poole said with a Scottish accent.

'Where did you get this guy?' Angie asked Broussard.

'They pay me an extra hundred a week to work with him. Hazardous duty pay.'

Poole leaned into the current of Angie's cigarette smoke, sniffed it. 'Second,' he said. 'You two are unorthodox. That's fine. But we can't have you associated with this case and find out you're exposing firearms and threatening information out of people, à la Mr Big Dave Strand.'

Angie said, 'Big Dave Strand was about to rape me, Sergeant Raftopoulos.'

'I understand,' Poole said.

'No, you don't,' Angie said. 'You have no idea.'

Poole nodded. 'I apologize. However, you assure us that what happened to Big Dave this afternoon was an aberration? One that won't be repeated?'

'We do,' Angie said.

'Well, I'll take you at your word. How do you feel about our terms so far?'

'If we're going to agree not to leak to the press, which, believe me, will strain our relationship with Richie Colgan, then you have to keep us in the loop. If we think you're treating us like you treat the press, Colgan gets a phone call.'

Broussard nodded. 'I don't see a problem with that. Poole?'

Poole shrugged, his eyes on me.

Angie said, 'I find it hard to believe a four-year-old could vanish so completely on a warm night without anyone seeing her.'

Broussard turned his wedding ring in half revolutions around his finger. 'So do I.'

'So what have you got?' Angie said. 'Three days, you must have something we didn't read about in the papers.'

'We have twelve confessions,' Broussard said, 'ranging from "I took the girl and ate her" to "I took the girl and sold her to the Moonies," who apparently pay top dollar.' He gave us a rueful smile. 'None of the twelve confessions check out. We got psychics who say she's in Connecticut; she's in California; no, she's still in the state but in a wooded region. We've interrogated Lionel and Beatrice McCready, and their alibis are airtight. We've checked the sewers. We've interviewed every neighbor on that street inside their houses, not just to see what they might have heard or saw that night but to check their homes casually for any evidence of the girl. We now know which neighbor does coke, which has a drinking problem, which beats his wife, and which beats her husband, but we haven't found anything to tie any of them to Amanda McCready's disappearance.'

'Zero,' I said. 'You really have nothing.'

Broussard turned his head slowly, looked at Poole.

After about a minute of staring across the table at us, his tongue rolling around and pushing against his lower lip, Poole reached into the battered attaché case on the seat beside him and removed a few glossy photographs. He handed the first one across the table to us.

It was a black-and-white close-up of a man in his late fifties with a face that looked as if the skin had been pulled back hard against the bone, bunched up, and clipped by a metal clamp at the back of his skull. His pale eyes bulged from their sockets, and his tiny mouth all but disappeared under the shadow of his curved talon of a nose. His sunken cheeks were so puckered, he could have been sucking on a lemon. Ten or twelve strands of silver hair were finger-combed across the exposed flesh at the top of his pointy head.

'Ever seen him?' Broussard asked.

We shook our heads.

'Name's Leon Trett. Convicted child molester. He's taken three falls. The first got him sentenced to a psych ward, the last two to the pen. He finished his last bit about two and a half years ago, walked out of Bridgewater, and disappeared.'

Poole handed us a second photo, this one a full-length color shot of a gigantic woman with the shoulders of a bank vault and the wide girth and shaggy brown mane of a Saint Bernard standing upright.

'Good God,' Angie said.

'Roberta Trett,' Poole said. 'The lovely missus of

the aforementioned Leon. That picture was taken ten years ago, so she could have changed some, but I doubt she's shrunk. Roberta has a renowned green thumb. She usually supports herself and her dear heart, Leon, as a florist. Two and a half years ago, she quit her job and moved out of her apartment in Roslindale, and no one has seen either of them since.'

'But . . .' Angie said.

Poole handed the third and final photograph across the table. It was a mug shot of a small toffee-skinned man with a lazy right eye and scrunched, confused features. He peered into the lens as if he were looking for it in a dark room, his face a knot of helpless anger and agitated bewilderment.

'Corwin Earle,' Poole said. 'Also a convicted pedophile. Released one week ago from Bridgewater. Whereabouts unknown.'

'But he's connected to the Tretts,' I said.

Broussard nodded. 'Bunked with Leon in Bridgewater. After Leon rotated back to the world, Corwin Earle's roommate was a Dorchester mugger named Bobby Minton, who in between stomping the shit out of Corwin for being a baby-raper was privy to the retard's musings. Corwin, according to Bobby Minton, had a favorite fantasy: When he was released from prison, he was going to look up his old bunkmate Leon and his wonderful wife, Roberta, and they were going to live together as one big happy family. But Corwin wasn't going to show up on the door without a gift. Bad form, I guess. And, according to Bobby Minton, the gift wasn't going to be a bottle of Cutty for Leon and a dozen roses for Roberta. It was going to be a kid. Young, Bobby told us. Corwin and Leon like 'em young. No older than nine.'

'This Bobby Minton call you?' Angie said.

Poole nodded. 'As soon as he heard about Amanda McCready's disappearance. Mr Minton, it seems, had consistently taunted Corwin Earle with vivid stories about what the good people of Dorchester do to baby-rapers. How Corwin wouldn't be able to walk ten yards down Dorchester Avenue without getting his penis chopped off and stuffed in his mouth. Mr Minton thinks Corwin Earle specifically chose Dorchester in which to pick up his homecoming present for the Tretts because he wanted to spit in Mr Minton's face.'

'And where's Corwin Earle now?' I asked.

'Gone. Vanished. We've staked out his parents' home in Marshfield, but so far, nothing. He left the pen in a taxi, took it to a strip club in Stoughton, and that's the last anyone's seen of him.'

'And this Bobby Minton's phone call or whatever – that's all you have to tie Earle and the Tretts to Amanda?'

'Pretty thin, huh?' Broussard said. 'I told you we don't have much. Chances are, Earle doesn't have the balls for a straight kidnapping in an unknown neighborhood. Nothing in his sheet points toward it. The kids he molested were kids at a summer camp where he worked seven years ago. No violence, no forced captivity. He was probably just talking big for his cell mate.'

'What about the Tretts?' Angie said.

'Well, Roberta's clean. The only felony she's ever been convicted of was as an accessory-after-the-fact in a liquor store stickup in Lynn back in the late seventies. She did a year, completed her probation, and hasn't spent so much as a night in county jail since.'

'But Leon?'

'Leon.' Broussard raised his eyebrows at Poole and whistled. 'Leon's bad, bad, bad. Convicted three times, accused twenty. Most cases were dropped when the victims refused to testify. And I don't know if you know the logic regarding baby-rapers, but it's the same for rats and roaches: You see one, there's another hundred nearby. You catch a freak molesting a kid, you can bet there's another thirty he's never been bagged for if he's halfway intelligent. So Leon, by our conservative estimates, has probably raped a good fifty kids. And he was living in Randolph and later in Holbrook when kids disappeared for good, so the feds and local cops have him at the head of their lists of suspects for those kids' murders. Let you in on another aspect of Leon's character – last time he was busted, Kingston P.D. found a shitload of automatic weapons buried near his house.'

'Did he take a fall for them?' Angie asked.

Broussard shook his head. 'He was smart enough to bury them on his next-door neighbor's property. Kingston P.D. knew the shit was his – his house was filled with NRA newsletters, gun manuals, *The Turner Diaries*, all the usual well-armed paranoid's paraphernalia – but they couldn't prove it. Very little sticks to Leon. He's very careful, and he knows how to drop out of sight.'

'Apparently,' Angie said, with a bitter edge.

Poole put a hand lightly on hers. 'Keep the photos. Study them. And have your eyes open for any of the three. I doubt they're involved – nothing points to it besides a convict's theory – but they are the most prominent child-rapers in the area these days.'

Angie smiled at Poole's hand. 'Okay.'

Broussard lifted his silk tie and picked at some lint. 'Who was Helene McCready with at the Filmore Sunday night?'

'Dottie Mahew,' Angie said.

'That all?'

Neither Angie nor I spoke for a moment.

'Remember,' Broussard said, 'full disclosure.'

'Skinny Ray Likanski,' I said.

Broussard turned to Poole. 'Tell me more about this guy, partner.'

'The rascal,' Poole said. 'And to think we had His Skinniness in our hands not an hour ago.' He shook his head. 'Well, that's a miss.'

'How so?' I said.

'Skinny Ray's a professional lowlife. Learned from his daddy. He probably knows we're looking for him, so he's gone. Least for a while. Probably the only reason he told us you two were waving weapons around in the Filmore was so we'd leave him be, give him time to get out of Dodge. The Likanskis got relatives in Allegheny, Rem. Maybe you could—'

'I'll call the P.D. down there,' Broussard said. 'Can we trace him?'

Poole shook his head. 'He hasn't taken a fall in five years. No outstandings. No parole officer. He's clean.' Poole tapped the table with his index. 'He'll surface eventually. Disease always does.'

'We done?' Broussard asked, as the waitress approached.

Poole paid the check, and the four of us walked out into the darkening afternoon.

'If you were betting men,' Angie said, 'what would you bet happened to Amanda McCready?'

Broussard took out another stick of gum, popped it in his mouth, and chewed slowly. Poole straightened his tie and studied his reflection in the passenger window of his car.

'I'd say,' Poole said, 'that nothing good can come when a four-year-old has been missing for eighty-plus hours.'

'Detective Broussard?' Angie said.

'I'd say she's dead, Ms Gennaro.' He walked around the car to the driver's door and opened it. 'It's a nasty world out there, and it's never been nice to children.'

6

The Astros were playing the Orioles in a sunset game at Savin Hill Park, and both teams seemed to be having some problems with their mechanics. When a slugger for the Astros hit one down the third-base line, the Orioles' third baseman failed to field it because he was more interested in tugging at a weed by his feet. So the Astros' base runner picked up the ball and ran toward home with it. Just before he reached the plate, he threw the ball in the general direction of the pitcher, who picked it up and threw it toward first. The first baseman caught the ball, but instead of tagging a runner, he turned and threw it into the outfield. The centerfielder and the right fielder met at the ball and tackled each other. The left fielder waved to his mom.

The North Dorchester T-ball league for ages four through six met once a week down at Savin Hill Park and played on the smaller of two fields, which was separated from the Southeast Expressway by about fifty yards and a chain-link fence. Savin Hill overlooks the expressway and a small bay known as Malibu Beach, and it's here that the Dorchester Yacht Club moors its boats. I've lived in this neighborhood my entire life and have never seen an actual yacht drop anchor anywhere near here, but maybe I'm always looking on the wrong days.

When I was between four and six, we played baseball because they didn't have T-ball back then. We had coaches, and parents who screamed and demanded concentration, kids who'd already been taught how to lay down bunts and dive under the second baseman's tag, fathers who tested us from the mound with fast balls and curves. We had seven-inning games and bitter rivalries with other parishes, and by the time we entered Little League at seven or eight, the teams from St Bart's, St William's, and St Anthony's in North Dorchester were justifiably feared.

As I stood by the bleachers with Angie and watched about thirty small boys and girls run around like spastics and miss balls because they'd pulled their hats over their eyes or were busy staring up at the setting sun, I was pretty certain that the method used when I was their age better prepared a child for the rigors of the actual sport of baseball, but the T-ball kids seemed to be having a lot more fun.

In the first place, there were no outs that I could see. The entire lineup of each team hit through a rotation. Once all fifteen or so kids had hit (and they all hit; there was no such thing as a strikeout), they switched bats for gloves with the other team. Nobody kept score. If one child was actually alert enough to both catch the ball and tag out the runner, both kids were congratulated profusely by the base coach and then the runner stayed on base. A few parents yelled, 'Pick up the ball for God's sake, Andrea,' or 'Run, Eddie, run! No, no – that way.

That way!' But for the most part, the parents and coaches clapped for every hit that dribbled more than four feet, for every ball fielded and thrown back somewhere in the same zip code as the park, for every successful run from first base to third, even if the kid ran over the pitcher's mound to get there.

Amanda McCready had played in this league. Signed up and brought to the games by Lionel and Beatrice, she'd been an Oriole, and her coach told us she usually played second base and could catch the ball pretty well when she wasn't transfixed by the bird on her shirt.

'She missed a few that way.' Sonya Garabedian smiled and shook her head. 'She'd be right out there where Aaron is now, and she'd be tugging at her shirt, staring at the bird, talking to it every now and then. And if a ball came her way – well, it would just have to wait until she was done looking at the pretty bird.'

The boy standing at the tee, a round and rather large kid for his age, smashed the ball into deep left, and all the outfielders and most of the infielders ran after it. As he rounded second base, the big boy decided, What the heck, he was going to try and field it too, and he ran into the outfield to join the party as the kids tackled and rolled and bounced off one another like bumper cars.

'That's something you'd never see Amanda do,' Sonya Garabedian said.

'Hit a home run?' Angie said.

Sonya shook her head. 'Well, that too. But, no, you see that pig pile out there? If we don't get somebody to stop it, they'll start playing King of the Mountain and forget why they came in the first place.'

94

As two parents walked out on the field toward the melee and kids somersaulted off the pile like circus performers, Sonya pointed to a small girl with red hair who was playing third base. She was probably five and smaller than almost anyone on either team. Her team shirt hung to her shins. She looked at the party going onto the outfield as more kids ran toward it, and then she bent to her knees and began digging in the dirt with a rock.

'That's Kerry,' Sonya said. 'No matter what happens – if an elephant walks out onto the field and starts letting all the kids play with its trunk – Kerry won't join in. It simply wouldn't occur to her.'

'She's that shy?' I said.

'That's part of it.' She nodded. 'But more than that, she simply doesn't respond to what other children predictably respond to. She's never really sad, but she's never really happy either. You understand?'

Kerry looked up from the dirt for a moment, her freckled face squinting as the dying sun bounced off the pitcher's stop, and then she went back to digging.

'Amanda is like Kerry in that way,' Sonya said. 'She doesn't respond much to immediate stimulation.'

'She's introverted,' Angie said.

'Partially, but not in a way that makes you think there's all that much going on behind her eyes. It's not that she's locked in her own little world, it's that she doesn't see much that interests her in this world either.' She turned her face and looked up at me, and there was something sad and hard in the set of her jaw, the flatness of her gaze. 'You've met Helene?'

'Yes.'

'What'd you think?'

I shrugged.

She smiled. 'She makes people shrug, doesn't she?'

'Did she come to games?' Angie asked.

'Once,' Sonya said. 'Once, and she was drunk. She was with Dottie Mahew and they were both half in the bag, and they were very loud. I think Amanda was embarrassed. She kept asking me when the game would be over.' She shook her head. 'Kids this age, they don't grasp time the way we do. They just notice if it seems long or short. That day, the game must have seemed real long to Amanda.'

More parents and coaches had gone out to the field now, as had most of the Astros. Several kids were still bouncing in the original pile, but just as many had broken up into separate groups, playing tag, throwing their gloves at one another, or just rolling around on the grass like seals.

'Miss Garabedian, did you ever notice strangers lurking around the games?' Angie showed her the pictures of Corwin Earle, Leon, and Roberta Trett.

She looked at them, blinked at the size of Roberta, but eventually shook her head.

'See that big guy out there by the pile?' She pointed at a tall thick guy in his early forties with a bristly crew cut. 'That's Matthew Hoagland. He's a professional bodybuilder, former Mr Massachusetts a couple years in a row. A very sweet guy. And he loves his kids. Last year, we had a mangy-looking guy come by the field and watch the game for a few minutes, and none of us liked his eyes. So Matt made him leave. I have no idea what he said to the guy, but the guy turned white and left in a hurry. No one's come back since. Maybe that type of . . . person has a network and spreads the word or whatever. I wouldn't know. But no strangers come to these games.' She looked at us. 'Until you two, that is.'

I touched my hair. 'How's my mange?'

She chuckled. 'A few of us recognized you, Mr Kenzie. We remember how you saved that child in the playground. You can baby-sit for any of us any time you want.'

Angie nudged me. 'Our hero.'

'Shut up,' I said.

It took another ten minutes for order to be restored in the outfield and play, such as it was, to resume.

During that time, Sonya Garabedian introduced us to some of the parents who'd remained in the bleachers. A few of them knew Helene and Amanda, and we spent the rest of the game talking with them. What emerged from our conversations – other than further reinforcement of our perception of Helene McCready as a creature committed to self-interest – was a fuller portrait of Amanda.

Contrary to Helene's depiction of some mythic sitcom moppet who lived only to smile and smile, the people we spoke to usually mentioned how little Amanda smiled, how she was generally listless and far too quiet for a four-year-old.

'My Jessica?' Frances Neagly said. 'From the time she was two until she was five, she bounced off walls. And the questions! Everything was, "Mommy, why don't animals talk like we do? How come I have toes? How come some water's cold and some water's hot?"' Frances gave us a tired smile. 'I mean, it was constant. Every mother I know talks

97

about how exasperating a four-year-old can be. They're four, right? The world surprises them every ten seconds.'

'But Amanda?' Angie said.

Frances Neagly leaned back and looked around the park as the shadows deepened and crept across the children in the field, seemed to shrink them. 'I baby-sat her a few times. Never by arrangement. Helene would drop by, say, "Could you just watch her a sec?" And six or seven hours later she'd come pick her up. I mean, whatta you gonna do, say no?' She lit a cigarette. 'Amanda was so quiet. Never a problem. Not once. But, really, who expects that from a four-year-old? She'd just sit wherever you left her and stare at the walls or the TV or whatever. She didn't investigate my kids' toys or pull the cat's tail or anything. She'd just sit there, like a lump, and she never asked when her mother was coming back to get her.'

'Is she mentally handicapped?' I said. 'Autistic, maybe?'

She shook her head. 'No. If you talked to her, she responded fine. She always seemed a little surprised, but she'd be sweet, speak very well for her age. No, she's a smart kid. She just isn't a very excitable one.'

'And that seemed unnatural,' Angie said.

She shrugged. 'Yeah, I guess. You know what it is? I think she was used to being ignored.' A pigeon swooped in low over the pitcher's mound, and some kid threw his glove at it and missed. Frances smiled weakly at us. 'And I think that sucks.'

She turned away from us as her daughter came up to the plate, a bat held awkwardly in her hands as she considered the ball and tee in front of her.

'Hit it out of the park, honey,' Frances called. 'You can do it.'

Her daughter turned and looked at her. She smiled. Then she shook her head several times and threw the bat onto the field.

7

After the game, we stopped in the Ashmont Grille for a meal and a beer, and Angie had what I can only describe as a delayed-stress reaction to what had happened in the Filmore Tap.

The Ashmont Grille served the sort of food my mom used to make – meat loaf and potato and lots of gravy – and the waitresses all acted like moms, too. If you didn't clean your plate, they asked you if the starving children in China would waste food. I always half expected to be told I couldn't leave the table until I'd eaten every last bite.

If that were the case, Angie would have been there until next week, the way she picked at her chicken Marsala. For someone so petite and slim, Angie can out-eat truck drivers fresh off the road. But tonight, she swirled the linguine on her fork, then seemed to forget about it. She'd drop the fork on the plate, sip some beer, and stare off into space as if she were Helene McCready looking for a television set.

By the time she'd reached her fourth bite, my meal was gone. Angie took this as an indication that dinner was over and pushed her plate into the center of the table.

'You can never know people,' she said, her eyes

on the table. 'Can you? Understand them. It's not possible. You can't . . . fathom what makes them do the things they do, think the way they do. If it's not the way you think, it never makes sense. Does it?' She looked up at me and her eyes were red and wet.

'You talking about Helene?'

'Helene' – she cleared her throat – 'Helene, and Big Dave, and those guys in the bar, and whoever took Amanda. They don't make sense. They don't . . .' A tear fell to her cheek and she wiped at it with the back of her hand. 'Shit.'

I took her hand and she chewed the inside of her mouth, and looked up at the ceiling fan above her.

'Ange,' I said, 'those guys in the Filmore were human waste. They're not worth a single moment's thought.'

'Uh-huh.' She took a deep breath through her mouth, and I could hear it rattle its way through the liquid clogging her throat. 'Yeah.'

'Hey,' I said. I stroked her forearm with my palm. 'I'm serious. They're nothing. They're—'

'They would have raped me, Patrick. I'm sure of it.' She looked at me, and her mouth jerked erratically until it froze for a moment in a smile, one of the strangest smiles I've ever seen. She patted my hand and the flesh around her mouth crumbled, and then her whole face crumbled with it. The tears poured from her eyes, and she kept trying to hold that smile and pat my hand.

I've known this woman all my life, and I can count on one hand how many times she's wept in my presence. I didn't understand completely at the moment what had brought this on – I'd seen Angie face far more dire situations than the one we faced in the bar today and shrug them off – but whatever the cause, the pain was real, and seeing it in her face and body killed me.

I came out from my side of the booth, and she waved me away, but I slid in beside her, and she caved into me. She gripped my shirt and wept silently into my shoulder. I smoothed her hair, kissed her head, and held her. I could feel the blood coursing through her body as she shook in my arms.

'I feel like such a goof,' Angie said.

'Don't be ridiculous,' I said.

We'd left the Ashmont Grille and Angie asked me to stop at Columbia Park in South Boston. A horseshoe of bleachers set in granite surrounded the dusty track at the tip of the park, and we bought a sixpack and took it down there with us, dusted some splinters off a bleacher plank before sitting down.

Columbia Park is Angie's sacred place. Her father, Jimmy, disappeared in a mob hit over two decades ago, and the park is where her mother chose to tell Angie and her sister that their father was dead, corpse or no corpse. Angie returns to the park sometimes during her dark nights, when she can't sleep, when the ghosts crawl around in her head.

The ocean was fifty yards to our right, and the breeze coming off it was cool enough for us to wrap up in each other to keep from shivering.

She leaned forward, staring out at the track and the wide swath of green park beyond. 'You know what it is?'

'Tell me.'

'I don't understand people who choose to hurt

other people.' She turned on the bleacher until she was facing me. 'I'm not talking about people who *respond* to violence with violence. I mean, we're as guilty of that as anyone. I'm talking about people who hurt other people without provocation. Who enjoy ugliness. Who get off on dragging everyone down into the muck with them.'

'The guys in the bar.'

'Yeah. They would have raped me. Raped. Me.' Her mouth remained open for a moment, as if the full implication of that were truly hitting her for the first time. 'And then they would have gone home and celebrated. No, no, wait.' She raised her arm in front of her face. 'No, that's not it. They wouldn't have celebrated. That's not the worst thing. The worst thing is, they wouldn't have given it much thought at all. They would have opened up my body, violated me in every sick way they could think of, and then after they were done, they'd remember it the way you'd remember a cup of coffee. Not as something to celebrate, just as one more thing that got you through your day.'

I didn't say anything. There wasn't anything to say. I held her eyes and waited for her to go on.

'And Helene,' she said. 'She's almost as bad as those guys, Patrick.'

'With all due respect, that's pushing it, Ange.'

She shook her head, her eyes wide. 'No, it's not. Rape is instant violation. It burns your insides out and reduces you to nothing in the time it takes some asshole to shove his dick in you. But what Helene does to her child . . .' She glanced at the dusty track below, took a slug from her beer. 'You heard the stories from those mothers. You saw how she's dealing with her little girl's disappearance. I bet she violates Amanda every day, not with rape or violence but with apathy. She was burning that child's insides out in tiny doses, like arsenic. That's Helene. She's arsenic.' She nodded to herself and repeated in a whisper, 'She's arsenic.'

I took her hands in mine. 'I can make a phone call from the car and drop this case. Now.'

'No.' She shook her head. 'No way. These people, these selfish, fucking people – these Big Daves and Helenes – they pollute the world. And I know they'll reap what they sow. And good. But I'm not going anywhere until we find that child. Beatrice was right. She's alone. And nobody speaks for her.'

'Except us.'

'Except us.' She nodded. 'I'm going to find that girl, Patrick.'

There was an obsessive light in her eyes I'd never seen shine so brightly before.

'Okay, Ange,' I said. 'Okay.'

'Okay.' She tapped my beer can with her own.

'What if she's dead already?' I said.

'She isn't,' Angie said. 'I can feel it.'

'But if she is?'

'She isn't.' She drained her beer, tossed the can into the bag at my feet. 'She just isn't.' She looked at me. 'Understand?'

'Sure,' I said.

Back at the apartment, all Angie's energy and fire drained out of her at once, and she passed out on top of the bedcovers. I slid them out from under her, then pulled them over her and turned out the light.

I sat at the kitchen table, wrote *Amanda*

McCready on a file folder, and scribbled a few pages of notes regarding the last twenty-four hours: our interviews with the McCreadys and the men at the Filmore and the parents at the ball game. When I was through, I got up, took a beer from the fridge, and stood in the middle of the kitchen floor as I drank some of it. I hadn't pulled the shades on the kitchen windows, and every time I looked at one of the dark squares, Gerry Glynn's face leered back at me, his hair soaked with gasoline, his face spotted with the blood of his last victim, Phil Dimassi.

I pulled the shades.

Patrick, Gerry whispered from the center of my chest, *I'm waiting for you.*

When Angie, Oscar, Devin, Phil Dimassi, and I had gone head-to-head with Gerry Glynn, his partner, Evandro Arujo, and an imprisoned psychotic named Alec Hardiman, I doubt any of us had realized the toll it would take. Gerry and Evandro had been eviscerating people, decapitating and disemboweling and crucifying them, out of a sense of fun or spite, or because Gerry was mad at God, or just because. I never fully understood the reasons behind it. I'm not sure anyone could. Sooner or later motives pale in light of the actions they give birth to.

I had nightmares about Gerry often. Always Gerry. Never Evandro, never Alec Hardiman. Just Gerry. Probably because I'd known him my entire life. Back when he'd been a cop, walking the local beat, always with a smile and a friendly ruffle of the hair for us kids. Then, after he'd retired, as owner and chief bartender of the Black Emerald. I drank with Gerry, had conversations long into the night with Gerry, felt at ease with him, trusted him. And all that time, over the course of three decades, he'd been killing runaway kids. A whole forgotten populace that nobody was looking for and nobody missed.

My nightmares varied, but usually Gerry killed Phil in them. In front of me. In reality, I hadn't seen him slice Phil's throat, even though I'd been only eight feet away. I'd been on the floor of Gerry's bar, trying to keep his German shepherd from plunging its teeth into my eye, but I'd heard Phil scream; I'd heard him say, 'No, Gerry. No.' And I'd held him while he died.

Phil Dimassi had been Angie's husband for twelve years. Until their wedding, he'd also been my best friend. After Angie filed for divorce, Phil quit drinking, became gainfully employed again, was on the road to a kind of redemption, I think. But Gerry blew all that away.

Gerry fired a bullet into Angie's abdomen. Gerry cut fissures into my jaw with a straight razor. Gerry helped end the relationship I had with a woman named Grace Cole and her daughter, Mae.

Gerry, the left side of his body on fire, had a shotgun pointed at my face when Oscar fired three bullets into him from behind.

Gerry damn near destroyed all of us.

And I wait for you down here, Patrick. I wait.

I had no logical reason to think that searching for Amanda McCready was going to lead to the sort of carnage my encounter with Gerry Glynn and his pals had created, no logical reason at all. It was this night, I reasoned, the first cool night in a few weeks, the dark-slate feel of it all. If it were last night, moist and balmy, I wouldn't be feeling this way.

But then again . . .

What we'd learned, unequivocally, during our pursuit of Gerry Glynn was exactly what Angie had spoken of tonight – that people could rarely be understood. We were slippery creatures, our impulses ruled by a variety of forces, many of them incomprehensible even to ourselves.

Why would someone abduct Amanda McCready? I had no idea.

Why would someone – several someones, actually – want to rape a woman?

Once again, I had no idea.

I sat for a while with my eyes closed, trying to see Amanda McCready, to conjure up a concrete inner sense of whether she was alive or not. But behind my eyelids, I saw only the dark.

I finished my beer and looked in on Angie.

She slept on her stomach in the middle of the bed, one arm splayed across the pillow on my side, the other clenched in a fist against her throat. I wanted to go to her and hold her until what happened in the Filmore stopped happening in her head, until her fear went away, until Gerry Glynn went away, until the world and everything ugly in it passed over our bodies and rode the night wind out of our lives.

I stood in the doorway a long time, watching her sleep, hoping my silly hopes.

8

After her estrangement from Phil and before she and I became lovers, Angie dated a producer with New England Cable News Network. I'd met the guy once and hadn't been particularly impressed, though I do recall he had great taste in ties. Wore too much after-shave, though. And mousse. And dated Angie. So the chances of us getting together for late-night Nintendo games and Saturday softball were pretty slim from the get-go.

The guy proved useful after the fact, however, because Angie kept in touch and occasionally, when we needed them, scored us tapes of local news broadcasts. It's always amazed me how she can do that – stay in touch, remain friends, get a guy she dumped two years ago to do her favors. I'd be lucky to call an ex-girlfriend and get my own toaster back. Maybe I need to work on my breakup technique.

The next morning, while Angie showered, I went downstairs and signed off with the FedEx guy for a box from Joel Calzada of NECN. This city has eight news channels: the major network affiliates, Four, Five, and Seven; the UPN, WB, and Fox channels; NECN; and finally a mom-and-pop independent at the top of the dial. Among these eight stations, all have noon and six P.M. broadcasts, three have five o'clocks, two have five-thirtys, four have ten in the evenings, and four wrap up at eleven. They broadcast at various times throughout the morning, beginning at five, and each has one-minute updates at several different times, during the day.

Joel had, at Angie's request, gotten his hands on every broadcast by every station concerning Amanda's disappearance since the night she'd vanished. Don't ask me how he pulled this off. Maybe producers trade tapes all the time. Maybe Angie can sweet-talk with the best of them. Maybe it was Joel's ties.

I'd spent a few hours last night rereading all the newspaper articles about Amanda, and I'd come up with nothing new except for hands stained so deeply with black ink I'd made a fingerprint collage on a sheet of legal paper before going to bed. When a case seems as dense and protective of its secrets as marble, sometimes the only thing to do is attempt a fresh approach, or at least an approach that feels fresh. That was the idea here – watch the tapes, see what jumped out at us.

I removed eight VHS tapes from the FedEx box, stacked them on the floor of the living room by the TV, and Angie and I ate breakfast at the coffee table and compared case notes and tried to come up with a plan of attack for the day. Short of trying to track down Skinny Ray Likanski and reinterviewing Helene, Beatrice and Lionel McCready – in the desperate hope they'd remember something crucial they'd heretofore forgotten regarding the night Amanda disappeared – very little occurred to us.

Angie leaned back against the couch as I picked up her empty breakfast plate. 'And then,' she said, 'there are times you think, A job with the electric company – now why didn't I take that?' She looked up at me as I placed her plate on top of my own. 'Great benefits.'

'Excellent retirement plan.' I took the plates into the kitchen, placed them in the dishwasher.

'Regular hours.' Angie called from the living room, and I heard the snap of her Bic as she lit the morning's first cigarette. 'Stellar dental.'

I made us each a cup of coffee and returned to the living room. Angie's thick hair was still damp from the shower, and the man's sweatpants and T-shirt combination she usually wore in the morning made her seem smaller and less substantial than she really was.

'Thanks.' She took her coffee cup from my hand without looking up, turned a page of her notes.

'Those things'll kill you,' I said.

She took her cigarette from the ashtray, eyes still on her notes. 'I've been smoking since I was sixteen.'

'Long time.'

She turned another page. 'And in all that time, you never gave me shit.'

'Your body, your mind,' I said.

She nodded. 'But now that we're sleeping together, it's somehow partly your body, too. That it?'

Over the last six months, I'd become accustomed to her morning moods. Often she was insanely energetic – back from aerobics and a walk along Castle Island before I woke up – but even in the best of times, she was far from a Chatty Cathy in the morning. And if she felt she'd exposed some part of herself the night before, been vulnerable or weak (which in her mind was usually the same thing), a thin, cold mist would surround her like ground fog at dawn. You could see her, know she was there, but then you'd take your eyes off her for a second and she'd be gone, had drifted back behind wisps of white fog, wasn't coming out for a while.

'Am I nagging?' I said.

She looked up at me, smiled coldly. 'Just a bit.' She sipped her coffee and looked down at her notes again. 'There's nothing here.'

'Patience.' I turned on the TV, popped the first tape into the VCR.

The leader counted down from seven, the numbers black and slightly fuzzy against a blue backdrop, a header flashed the date of Amanda's disappearance, and suddenly we were in the studio with Gordon Taylor and Tanya Biloskirka, anchors extraordinaire for Channel Five. Gordon always seemed to have trouble keeping his dark hair from falling to his forehead, unusual in this age of freeze-dried anchor heads, but he had piercing, righteous eyes and a constant quaver of outrage in his voice that made up for the hair thing, even when he was reporting on Christmas tree lightings and Barney sightings. Tanya, of the unpronounceable last name, wore glasses to give her an air of intellectualism, but every guy I knew still thought she was a babe, which I guess was the point.

Gordon straightened his cuffs and Tanya did this cool squirming/settling thing in her chair as she shuffled some papers in her hand and prepared to read from the TelePrompTer. The words MISSING CHILD appeared in the pop-up box image between their heads.

'A child disappears in Dorchester,' Gordon said gravely. 'Tanya?'

'Thanks, Gordon.' The camera moved in for a close-up. 'A four-year-old Dorchester girl's disappearance has police baffled and neighbors worried. It happened just a few hours ago. Little Amanda McCready vanished from her Sagamore Street home, without, police say' – she leaned forward a hair and her voice dropped an octave – 'a trace.'

They cut back to Gordon, who hadn't been expecting it. His hand froze halfway up his forehead, a lock of his annoying hair spilling over his fingers. 'For more on this breaking story, we go live to Gert Broderick. Gert?'

The street was crowded with neighbors and the curious as Gert Broderick stood with microphone in hand and reported the information Gordon and Tanya had just told us. About twenty feet behind Gert, on the other side of a stream of yellow caution tape and uniformed cops, an hysterical Helene was being held by Lionel on her front porch. She was shouting something that was hard to decipher amid the crowd noise, the hum of light generators from the news crews, the gaspy words of Gert's reportage.

'. . . and that's what police seem to know now – precious little.' Gert stared into the camera, trying not to blink.

Gordon Taylor's voice cut into the live feed. 'Gert.'

Gert touched a hand to her left ear. 'Yes, Gordon. Gordon?'

'Gert.'

'Yes, Gordon. I'm here.'

'Is that the little girl's mother on the porch behind you?'

The camera lens zoomed toward the porch, racked focus, and closed tight on Helene and Lionel. Helene's mouth was open and tears poured down her cheeks and her head made an odd up-and-down, up-and-down motion, as if, like a newborn's, it had lost the support of the neck muscles.

Gert said, 'We *believe* that's Amanda's mother, though it has not been officially confirmed at this time.'

Helene's fists hit Lionel's chest and her eyes snapped open. She wailed and her left hand surged over Lionel's shoulder, the index finger pointing at something off-camera. It was a live crumbling we were being made witness to on that porch, a deep invasion of the privacy of grief.

'She seems upset,' Gordon said. That Gordon, nothing slipped past him.

'Yes,' Tanya agreed.

'Since time is of the essence,' Gert said, 'police are asking for any information, anyone who may have seen little Amanda—'

'*Little* Amanda?' Angie said, and shook her head. 'What is she supposed to be at four, humongous Amanda? Mature Amanda?'

'—anyone who has *any* information on this little girl—'

Amanda's photograph filled the screen.

'—please call the number listed below.'

The number for the Crimes Against Children squad flashed below Amanda's photo for a few moments, and then they cut back to the studio. In place of MISSING CHILD in the pop-up box, they'd inserted the live feed, and a smaller Gert Broderick fondled her microphone and looked into the camera with a blank, vaguely confused look on her blank, vaguely confused face as Helene continued to go ballistic on the porch and Beatrice joined Lionel and tried to hold her in place.

'Gert,' Tanya said, 'have you been able to talk to the mother at all?'

Gert's sudden tight smile covered an annoyed spark that crossed her blank eyes like smoke. 'No, Tanya. As of yet, the police have not allowed us past that caution tape you see behind me, so, again, we have yet to confirm if Helene McCready is in fact the hysterical woman you see on the porch behind me.'

'Tragic,' Gordon said, as Helene lunged into Lionel again and wailed so sharply that Gert's shoulders tensed.

'Tragic,' Tanya agreed, as Amanda's face and the phone number for Crimes Against Children filled the screen for another half second.

'In another breaking story,' Gordon said as they cut back to him, 'a home invasion in Lowell has left at least two people dead and a third wounded by gunfire. For that story we go to Martha Torsney in Lowell. Martha?'

They cut to Martha, and a slash of snow burst across the screen for a split second before being replaced momentarily by a black screen and we settled in to watch the rest of the tape, confident Gordon and Tanya would be there to tell us how to feel about the events transpiring before us, fill in the emotional blanks.

*   *   *

Eight tapes and ninety minutes later, we'd come up with nothing except stiff bodies and an even more depressingly jaded view of broadcast journalism than we'd had before. Except for the camera angles, nothing distinguished one report from another. As the search for Amanda dragged on, the newscasts showed numbingly similar footage of Helene's house, Helene herself being interviewed, Broussard or Poole giving statements, neighbors pounding the pavements with flyers, cops leaning over car hoods shining flashlights over maps of the neighborhood or reining in their search dogs. And all the reports were followed by the same pithy, rankly maudlin commentary, the same studied sadness and head-shaking morality in the eyes and jaws and foreheads of the newscasters. *And now, back to our regularly scheduled program . . .*

'Well,' Angie said, and stretched so hard I heard the vertebrae in her back crack like walnuts hit with a cleaver, 'outside of seeing a bunch of people we know from the neighborhood on TV, what have we accomplished this morning?'

I sat forward, cracking my own neck. Pretty soon we'd have a band. 'Not much. I did see Lauren Smythe. Always thought she'd moved.' I shrugged. 'Guess she was just avoiding me.'

'Is that the one who attacked you with a knife?'

'Scissors,' I said. 'And I prefer to think it was fore-play. She just wasn't very good at it.'

She whacked my shoulder with the back of her hand. 'Let's see. I saw April Norton and Susan Siersma, who I haven't seen since high school and Billy Boran and Mike O'Connor, who's lost a lotta hair, don't you think?'

I nodded. 'Lost a lotta weight, too.'

'Who notices? He's bald.'

'Sometimes I think you're more shallow than I am.'

She shrugged and lit a cigarette. 'Who else did we see?'

'Danielle Genter,' I said. 'Babs Kerins. Friggin' Chris Mullen was everywhere.'

'I noticed that too. In the early stuff.'

I sipped some cold coffee. 'Huh?'

'In the early stuff. He was always hanging around the periphery in the early parts of every tape, never the later stuff.'

I yawned. 'He's a periphery guy, ol' Chris.' I picked up her empty coffee cup, hung it off my finger beside my own. 'More?'

She shook her head.

I went into the kitchen, put her cup in the sink, poured myself a fresh cup. Angie came in as I opened the refrigerator and removed the cream.

'When's the last time you saw Chris Mullen in the neighborhood?'

I closed the door, looked at her. 'When's the last time you saw half the people we saw watching those tapes?'

She shook her head. 'Forget about everyone else. I mean, they've been here. Chris? He moved uptown. Got himself a place in Devonshire Towers around, like, 'eighty-seven.'

I shrugged. 'Again – so?'

'So what's Chris Mullen do for work?'

I put the cream carton down on the counter beside my cup. 'He works for Cheese Olamon.'

'Who happens to be in prison.'

'Big surprise.'

'For?'

'What?'

'What is Cheese in prison for?'

I picked up the cream carton again. 'What else?' I turned in the kitchen as I heard my words, let the carton dangle by my thigh. 'Drug dealing,' I said slowly.

'You are so goddamned right.'

9

Amanda McCready wasn't smiling. She stared at me with still, empty eyes, her ash-blond hair falling limply around her face, as if it had been plastered to the sides of her head with a wet palm. She had her mother's tremulous chin, too square and too small for her oval face, and the sallow crevices under her cheeks hinted of questionable nutrition.

She wasn't frowning, nor did she appear to be angry or sad. She was just *there*, as if she had no hierarchy of responses to stimuli. Getting her photograph taken had been no different from eating or dressing or watching TV or taking a walk with her mother. Every experience in her young life, it seemed, had existed along a flat line, no ups, no downs, no anythings.

Her photograph lay slightly off-center on a white sheet of legal-sized paper. Below the photograph were her vital statistics. Directly below those were the words – IF YOU SEE AMANDA, PLEASE CALL – and below that were Lionel and Beatrice's names and their phone number. Following that was the number of the CAC squad, with Lieutenant Jack Doyle listed as the contact person. Under that number was 911.

And at the bottom of the list was Helene's name and number.

The stack of flyers sat on the kitchen counter in Lionel's house, where he'd left them after he'd come home this morning. Lionel had been out all night plastering them to streetlight poles and subway station support beams, across temporary walls at construction sites and boarded-up buildings. He had covered downtown Boston and Cambridge, while Beatrice and three dozen neighbors had divided up the rest of the greater metro area. By dawn, they'd put Amanda's face in every legal and illegal spot they could find in a twenty-mile radius of Boston.

Beatrice was in the living room when we entered, going through her morning routine of contacting all police and press assigned to the case and asking for progress reports. After that, she'd call the hospitals again. Next she'd call any businesses that had refused to put up a flyer of Amanda in their break rooms or cafeterias and ask them to explain why.

I had no idea when, or if, she'd sleep.

Helene was in the kitchen with us. She sat at the table and ate a bowl of Apple Jacks and nursed a hangover. Lionel and Beatrice, possibly sensing something in the simultaneous arrival of Angie and myself with Poole and Broussard, followed us into the kitchen, Lionel's hair still wet from the shower, dots of moisture speckling his UPS uniform, Beatrice's small face carrying a war refugee's weariness.

'Cheese Olamon,' Helene said slowly.

'Cheese Olamon,' Angie said. 'Yes.'

Helene scratched her neck where a small vein

pulsed like a beetle trapped under the flesh. 'I don't know.'

'Don't know what?' Broussard said.

'I mean, the name sounds sorta familiar.' Helene looked up at me and fingered a tear in the plastic tabletop.

'Sorta familiar?' Poole said. 'Sorta familiar, Miss McCready? Can I quote you on that?'

'What?' Helene ran a hand through her thin hair. 'What? I said it sounded familiar.'

'A name like Cheese Olamon,' Angie said, 'doesn't *sound* any kind of way. You're either acquainted with it or you're not.'

'I'm thinking.' Helene touched her nose lightly, then pulled back the hand and stared at the fingers.

A chair scraped as Poole dragged it across the floor, set it down in front of Helene, sat in it.

'Yes or no, Miss McCready. Yes or no.'

'Yes or no what?'

Broussard sighed loudly and fingered his wedding band, tapped his foot on the floor.

'Do you know Mr Cheese Olamon?' Poole's whisper sounded drenched in gravel and glass.

'I don't—'

'Helene!' Angie's voice was so sharp even I started.

Helene looked up at her, and the beetle in her throat lapsed into a seizure under her skin. She tried to hold Angie's gaze for about a tenth of a second, and then she dropped her head. Her hair fell over her face, and a tiny rasping noise came from behind it as she crossed one bare foot on top of the other and clenched the muscles in her calves.

'I knew Cheese,' she said. 'A bit.'

'A little bit or a lot of bit?' Broussard pulled out a stick of gum, and the sound of the foil wrapper as he removed it was like teeth on my spine.

Helene shrugged. 'I knew him.'

For the first time since we'd come into their kitchen, Beatrice and Lionel moved from their places against the wall, Beatrice over to the oven between Broussard and me, Lionel to a seat in the corner on the other side of the table from his sister. Beatrice lifted a cast-iron kettle off the burner and placed it under the faucet.

'Who's Cheese Olamon?' Lionel reached out and took his sister's right hand from her face. 'Helene? Who's Cheese Olamon?'

Beatrice turned her head to me. 'He's a drug dealer or something, isn't he?'

She'd spoken so softly that over the running water no one but Broussard and I had heard her.

I held out my hands and shrugged.

Beatrice turned back to the faucet.

'Helene?' Lionel said again, and there was a high, uneven pitch to his voice.

'He's just a guy, Lionel.' Helene's voice was tired and flat and seemed to come from a million years away.

Lionel looked at the rest of us.

Both Angie and I looked away.

'Cheese Olamon,' Remy Broussard said, and cleared his throat, 'is, among other things, a drug dealer, Mr McCready.'

'What else is he?' Lionel had a child's broken curiosity in his face.

'What?'

'You said "among other things." What other things?'

Beatrice turned from the faucet, placed the kettle on the burner, and ignited the flame underneath. 'Helene, why don't you answer your brother's question?'

Helene's hair remained in her face and her voice a million years away. 'Why don't you go suck a nigger's dick, Bea?'

Lionel's fist hit the table so hard, a fissure rippled through the cheap covering like a stream through a canyon.

Helene's head snapped back and the hair flew off her face.

'You listen to me.' Lionel pointed a quaking finger an inch from his sister's nose. 'You don't insult my wife, and you don't make racist remarks in my kitchen.'

'Lionel—'

'In my kitchen!' He hit the table again. 'Helene!'

It wasn't a voice I'd heard before. Lionel had raised his voice that first time in our office, and that voice I was familiar with. But this was something else. Thunder. A thing that loosened cement and launched tremors through oak.

'Who,' Lionel said, and his free hand gripped the corner of the table, 'is Cheese Olamon?'

'He is a drug dealer, Mr McCready.' Poole searched his pockets, came up with a pack of cigarettes. 'And a pornographer. And a pimp.' He removed a cigarette from the pack, placed it upright on the table, leaned in to sniff from the top. 'Also a tax evader, if you can believe that.'

Lionel, who'd apparently never seen Poole's tobacco ritual before, seemed momentarily transfixed by it. Then he blinked and turned his attention back to Helene.

'You associate with a pimp?'

'I—'

'A pornographer, Helene?'

Helene turned away from him, rested her right arm on the table, and looked out at the kitchen without meeting the eyes of any of its occupants.

'What'd you do for him?' Broussard said.

'Muling occasionally.' Helene lit a cigarette, cupped the match in her hand, and shook it out with the same motion she'd use to chalk a pool cue.

'Muling,' Poole said.

She nodded.

'From where to where?' Angie asked.

'Here to Providence. Here to Philly. It depended on the supply.' She shrugged. 'Depended on the demand.'

'And for that you got what?' Broussard said.

'Some cash. Some stash.' Another shrug.

'Heroin?' Lionel said.

She turned her head, looked at him, her cigarette dangling from between her fingers, her body loose and puddling. 'Yeah, Lionel. Sometimes. Sometimes coke, sometimes Ex, and sometimes' – she shook her head, turned it back toward the rest of the room – 'whatever the fuck.'

'Track marks,' Beatrice said. 'We would have seen track marks.'

Poole patted Helene's knee. 'She snorted it.' He flared his nostrils, slid them over his cigarette. 'Didn't you?'

Helene nodded. 'Less addictive that way.'

Poole smiled. 'Of course it is.'

Helene removed his hand from her knee and stood up, crossed to the refrigerator, and pulled out a can of Miller. She opened it with a hard snap and the beer foamed to the top and she slurped it up into her mouth.

I looked at the clock: ten-thirty in the morning.

Broussard called two CAC detectives and told them to locate and begin immediate surveillance of Chris Mullen. In addition to the original detectives searching for Amanda, and the two who'd been assigned to locate Ray Likanski, the entire CAC division was now clocking overtime on one case.

'This is strictly need-to-know,' he said into the phone. 'That means only I need to know what you're doing for the time being. Clear?'

When he hung up, we followed Helene and her morning beer onto Lionel and Beatrice's back porch. Flat cobalt clouds drifted overhead and the morning turned sluggish and gray, gave the air a moist thickness, a promise of afternoon rain.

The beer seemed to give Helene a concentration she usually lacked. She leaned against the porch rail and met our eyes without fear or self-pity and answered our questions about Cheese Olamon and his right-hand man, Chris Mullen.

'How long have you known Mr Olamon?' Poole asked.

She shrugged. 'Ten, maybe twelve years. From around the neighborhood.'

'Chris Mullen?'

''Bout the same.'

'Where did your association begin?'

Helene lowered her beer. 'What?'

'Where did you meet this Cheese guy?' Beatrice said.

'The Filmore.' She took a slug off the beer can.

'When did you start working for him?' Angie asked.

Another shrug. 'I did some small stuff over the years. 'Bout four years ago I needed more money to take care of Amanda—'

'Jesus Christ,' Lionel said.

She glanced at him, then back at Poole and Broussard. '—so he sent me on a few buys. Hardly ever big stuff.'

'Hardly ever,' Poole said.

She blinked, then nodded quickly.

Poole turned his head, his tongue pushing against the inside of his lower lip. Broussard met his eyes and pulled another stick of gum from his pocket.

Poole chuckled softly. 'Miss McCready, do you know what squad Detective Broussard and I worked for before we were asked to join Crimes Against Children?'

Helene grimaced. 'I care?'

Broussard popped the gum in his mouth. 'No reason you should, really. But just for the record—'

'Narcotics,' Poole said.

'CAC is pretty small, not much in the way of camaraderie,' Broussard said, 'so we still hang out mostly with narcs.'

'Keep abreast of things,' Poole said.

Helene squinted at Poole, tried to figure out where this was going.

'You said you ran dope through the Philadelphia corridor,' Broussard said.

'Uh-huh.'

'Who to?'

She shook her head.

'Miss McCready,' Poole said, 'we're not here on a narco bust. Give us a name so we can confirm whether you really muled for Cheese Ol—'

'Rick Lembo.'

'Ricky the Dick,' Broussard said, and smiled.

'Where did the deals go down?'

'The Ramada by the airport.'

Poole nodded at Broussard.

'You do any New Hampshire runs?'

Helene took a hit off the beer and shook her head.

'No?' Broussard raised his eyebrows. 'Nothing up Nashua way, no quick sales to the biker gangs?'

Again Helene shook her head. 'No. Not me.'

'How much you hit Cheese for, Miss McCready?'

'Excuse me?' Helene said.

'The Cheese violates his parole three months ago. He takes a ten-to-twelve fall.' Broussard spit his gum over the railing. 'How much you take off him when you heard he got dropped?'

'Nothing.' Helene's eyes stayed on her bare feet.

'Bullshit.'

Poole stepped over to Helene and gently took the beer can from her hand. He leaned over the railing and tipped the can, poured the contents into the driveway behind the house.

'Miss McCready,' he said, 'word I've heard on the proverbial street the past few months is that Cheese Olamon sent a goody bag up to some bikers in a Nashua motel just before his arrest. The goody bag was recovered in a raid, but not the money. Since the bikers – hale fellows all – had yet to partake of

126

the contents of the bag, speculation among our northern law enforcement friends was that the deal had gone down only moments before the raid. Further speculation led many to believe that the mule walked off with the money. Which, according to current urban lore, was news to the members of Cheese Olamon's camp.'

'Where's the money?' Broussard said.

'I don't know what you're talking about.'

'Care to take a polygraph?'

'I already took one.'

'Different questions this time.'

Helene turned to the railing, looked out on the small tar parking lot, the withered trees just beyond.

'How much, Miss McCready?' Poole's voice was soft, without a hint of pressure or urgency.

'Two hundred thousand.'

The porch was silent for a full minute.

'Who rode shotgun?' Broussard said eventually.

'Ray Likanski.'

'Where's the money?'

The muscles in Helene's scrawny back clenched. 'I don't know.'

'Liar, liar,' Poole said. 'Pants on fire.'

She turned from the railing. 'I don't know. I swear to God.'

'She swears to God.' Poole winked at me.

'Oh, well then,' Broussard said, 'I guess we have to believe her.'

'Miss McCready?' Poole pulled his shirt cuffs from underneath his suit coat, smoothed them against his wrists. His voice was light and almost musical.

'Look, I—'

'Where's the money?' The lighter and more melodious the singsong got, the more threatening Poole seemed.

'I don't . . .' Helene ran a hand over her face, and her body sagged against the railing. 'I was stoned, okay? We left the motel; two seconds later every cop in New Hampshire is running through the parking lot. Ray snuggled up to me, and we just walked right through them. Amanda was crying, so they must have thought we were just a family who'd been on the road.'

'Amanda was there with you?' Beatrice said. 'Helene!'

'What,' Helene said, 'I was going to leave her in the car?'

'So you drove away,' Poole said. 'You got stoned. And then what?'

'Ray stopped at a friend's place. We were in there, like, an hour.'

'Where was Amanda?' Beatrice said.

Helene scowled. 'The fuck I know, Bea? In the car or in the house with us. One of the two. I told you, I was fucked up.'

'Was the money with you when you left the house?' Poole asked.

'I don't think so.'

Broussard flipped open his steno pad. 'Where was this house?'

'In an alley.'

Broussard closed his eyes for a moment. 'Where was it located? The address, Miss McCready.'

'I told you, I was stoned. I—'

'The fucking *town* then.' Broussard's teeth were clenched.

'Charlestown,' she said. She cocked her head, thought about it. 'Yeah. I'm almost sure. Or Everett.'

'Or Everett,' Angie said. 'That narrows it down.'

I said, 'Charlestown's the one with the big monument, Helene.' I smiled my encouragement. 'You know the one. Looks like the Washington Monument, except it's on Bunker Hill.'

'Is he making fun of me?' Helene asked Poole.

'I wouldn't hazard a guess,' Poole said. 'But Mr Kenzie has a point. If you were in Charlestown, you'd remember the monument, wouldn't you?'

Another long pause as Helene searched what remained of her brain. I wondered if I should go grab another beer for her, see if it would speed things up.

'Yeah,' she said, very slowly. 'We drove over the big hill by the monument on our way out.'

'So the house,' Broussard said, 'was on the east side of town.'

'East?' Helene said.

'You were closer to Bunker Hill project, Medford Street or Bunker Hill Avenue, than you were to Main or Warren streets.'

'If you say so.'

Broussard tilted his head, ran the back of his hand slowly across the stubble on his cheek, took a few shallow breaths.

'Miss McCready,' Poole said, 'besides the fact that the house was at the end of an alley, do you remember anything else about it? Was it a one-family or two?'

'It was really small.'

'We'll call it a one-family.' Poole jotted in his notepad. 'Color?'

'They were white.'

'Who?'

'Ray's friends. A woman and a guy. Both white.'

'Excellent,' Poole said. 'But the house. What color was that?'

She shrugged. 'I don't remember.'

'Let's go look for Likanski,' Broussard said. 'We can go to Pennsylvania. Hell, I'll drive.'

Poole held up a hand. 'Give us another minute here, Detective. Miss McCready, please search your memory. Remember that night. The smells. The music Ray Likanski played on his stereo. Anything that will help put you back in that car. You drove from Nashua to Charlestown. That's about an hour's drive, maybe a little less. You got stoned. You pulled over into this alley, and you—'

'We didn't.'

'What?'

'Pull into the alley. We parked on the street because there was an old broken-down car in the alley. We had to drive around for like twenty minutes till we found a parking space, too. That place sucks for parking.'

Poole nodded. 'This broken-down car in the alley, was there anything memorable about it?'

She shook her head. 'It was just a rust heap, up on blocks. No wheels or nothing.'

'Hence the blocks,' Poole said. 'Nothing else?'

Helene was midway through another shake of her head when she stopped and giggled.

'Care to share your joke with the class?' Poole said.

She looked over at him, still smiling. 'What?'

'Why are you laughing, Miss McCready?'

'Garfield.'

'James A.? Our twentieth president?'

'Huh?' Helene's eyes bulged. 'No. The cat.'

We all stared at her.

'The cat!' She held out her hands. 'In the comic strip.'

'Uh-huh,' I said.

''Member when everyone used to have those Garfields stuck to the back of their windows? Well, this car had one, too. That's how I knew it had been there, like, forever. I mean, who puts Garfields on their windows anymore?'

'Indeed,' Poole said. 'Indeed.'

10

When Winthrop and the original settlers arrived in the New World, they chose to settle on a square mile's worth of land, most of it hill, that they named Boston, after the town in England they'd left behind. During the one harsh winter Winthrop's pilgrims spent there, they found the water inexplicably brackish, so they moved across the channel, taking the name Boston with them and leaving what would become Charlestown without a name or purpose for a while.

Since then, Charlestown has held tight to an outpost's identity. Historically Irish, home to deca-generations of fishermen, merchant marines, and dockworkers, Charlestown is infamous for its code of silence, a resistance to speaking to the police, which has left it with a murder rate that, while low, boasts the highest percentage of unsolved cases in the nation. This adherence to keeping one's mouth shut even extends to simple directions. Ask a townie how to get to such-and-such street and his eyes will narrow. 'The fuck you doing here if you don't know where you're going?' might be the polite response, followed by an extended middle finger if he really likes you.

So Charlestown is an easy place to get confused. Signs bearing street names disappear all the time, and the houses are often stacked so close together they conceal small alleys that lead to other homes behind. The streets that climb the hill are apt to dead-end or else force the driver to turn in the opposite direction from where he was headed.

The sections of Charlestown change character with bewildering speed as well. Depending on which direction one is heading, the Mishawum Housing Project can give way to the gentrified brownstones surrounding Edwards Park in a horseshoe; the roads passing through the grandeur of the red-brick and white-trim colonial town houses fronting Monument Square drop without warning or respect for gravity into the dark gray of Bunker Hill Project, one of the most poverty-stricken white housing developments this side of West Virginia.

But speckled throughout it all, one finds a sense of history – of brick and mortar, colonial clapboard and cobblestone, pre-Revolutionary taverns and post-Treaty of Versailles sailors quarters – that's hard to duplicate in most of America.

Still sucks to drive through, though.

Which is what we'd been doing for the last hour, following Poole and Broussard, accompanied by Helene in the backseat of their Taurus, up and over and around and across Charlestown. We'd criss-crossed the hill, loped around the back of both housing projects, jerked bumper-to-bumper through the yuppie enclaves up by the Bunker Hill Monument and down at the base of Warren Street. We'd driven along the docks, rolled past Old Ironsides and the naval quarters and once-dingy warehouses and tanker-repair hangars converted into pricey condos, rumbled along the cracked roads that skirted the burned-out shells of long-forgotten fisheries at the edge of the land mass, where more than one wise guy had gazed at his final vista of moonlight bathing the Mystic River as a bullet cracked through a breech and into his head.

We'd tailed the Taurus along Main Street and Rutherford Avenue, followed the hill up to High Street and down to Bunker Hill Avenue and beyond to Medford Street, and we'd cased every tiny street in between, idling at the alleys that appeared suddenly out of the corners of our eyes. Looking for a car on blocks. Looking for two hundred grand. Looking for Garfield.

'Sooner or later,' Angie said, 'we're going to run out of gas.'

'Or patience,' I said, as Helene pointed at something through the Taurus window.

I applied the brakes, and once again the Taurus stopped ahead of us, and Broussard got out with Helene and they walked over to an alley and stared in. Broussard asked her something and Helene shook her head and they walked back to the car and I took my foot off the brake.

'Why are we looking for the money again?' Angie asked a few minutes later as we dropped over the other side of the hill and the hood of our Crown Victoria pointed straight down and the brakes clacked and the pedal jumped against my foot.

I shrugged. 'Maybe because, A, this is the closest lead there's been in a while to anything and, B, maybe Broussard and Poole figure it's a drug-related kidnapping now.'

'So where's the ransom demand? How come Chris Mullen or Cheese Olamon or one of their boys hasn't contacted Helene yet?'

'Maybe they're waiting for her to figure it out.'

'That's expecting a lot from someone like Helene.'

'Chris and Cheese ain't rocket scientists.'

'True, but—'

We'd stopped again, and this time Helene was out of the car before Broussard, gesturing maniacally at a construction Dumpster on the sidewalk. The construction crew working on the house across the street was nowhere to be seen; I knew they were somewhere nearby, though, if only for the scaffolding erected against the building facade.

I pressed down the emergency brake and stepped out of the car, and pretty soon I saw why Helene was so excited. The Dumpster, five feet tall and four feet wide, had obscured the alley behind it. There in the alley sat a late-seventies Grand Torino, up on blocks, one fat orange cat attached by suction cups to the rear window, paws spread wide, smiling like an idiot through the dirty glass.

It was impossible to double-park on the street without blocking it entirely, so we spent another five minutes finding parking spaces back up the hill on Bartlett Street. Then the five of us walked back toward the alley. The construction crew had returned in the interim and milled around the scaffolding with their coolers and liters of Mountain Dew. They whistled at Helene and Angie as we walked down the hill.

Poole saluted one of them as we neared the alley, and the man quickly looked away.

'Mr Fred Griffin,' Poole said. 'Still have a taste for the amphetamines?'

Fred Griffin shook his head.

'Apologize,' Poole said in that threatening singsong of his, as he turned into the alley.

Fred cleared his throat. 'Sorry, ladies.'

Helene flipped him the bird and the rest of the construction crew hooted.

Angie nudged me as we lagged behind the other three. 'You get the feeling Poole's a bit tightly wound behind that big smile?'

'Personally,' I said, 'I wouldn't fuck with him. But I'm a wuss.'

'That's our secret, babe.' She patted my ass as we turned into the alley, which drew another round of hoots from across the street.

The Gran Torino hadn't been used in a while. Helene was right about that. Chips of rust and sallow beige spots stained the cinder blocks under the wheels. The windows had accumulated so much dust it was a wonder we'd been able to discern Garfield in the first place. A newspaper that bore a headline detailing Princess Diana's peace mission to Bosnia lay on the dashboard.

The alley was cobblestone, cracked in places, shattered in others, to reveal a pink-gray earth beneath. Two plastic trash cans spilled garbage beneath a cobwebbed gas meter. The alley cut so narrowly between two three-deckers, I was surprised they'd been able to fit the car in.

At the end of the alley, about ten yards off the street, sat a single-story box of a house, dating back to the forties or fifties, from the unimaginative look of the construction. It could have been the foreman's shack on a construction site or a small radio station, and probably wouldn't have stood out quite so much if it were in a less architecturally rich neighborhood, but even so it was an eyesore. There were no steps, just a crooked door raised about an inch off the foundation, and the wood shingles were covered in black tarpaper, as if someone had once considered aluminum siding but then quit before the delivery was made.

'You remember the names of the occupants?' Poole asked Helene, as he unsnapped his holster strap with a flick of his thumb.

'No.'

''Course not,' Broussard said, his eyes scanning the four windows fronting the alley, the grimy plastic shades pulled down to their sills. 'You said there were two?'

'Yeah. A guy and his girlfriend.' Helene looked up and around at the three-deckers casting their shadows over us.

A window behind us shot open, and we spun toward the sound.

'Jesus Christ,' Helene said.

A woman in her late fifties stuck her head out a second-story window and peered down at us. She held a wooden spoon in one hand, and a strand of linguine fell off the edge and dropped to the alley.

'You the animal people?'

'Ma'am?' Poole squinted up at her.

'The SPCA,' she said and waggled the wooden spoon. 'You with them?'

'All five of us?' Angie said.

'I been calling,' the woman said. 'I been calling.'

'Pertaining to what?' I asked.

'Pertaining to those friggin' cats, smart-ass, that's what. I gotta listen to my grandson Jeffrey whining in one ear and my husband bitching in the other. I look like I got a third ear at the back of my head to listen to those friggin' cats?'

'No, ma'am,' Poole said. 'No third ear I can see.'

Broussard cleared his throat. 'Of course, we can only see your front from here, ma'am.'

Angie coughed into her fist and Poole dropped his head, looked at his shoes.

The woman said, 'You're cops. I can tell.'

'What gave it away?' Broussard asked.

'The lack of respect for working people.' The woman slammed the window back down so hard the panes shook.

'We can only see your front.' Poole chuckled.

'You like that?' Broussard turned to the door of the small house and knocked.

I looked in the overstuffed trash cans by the gas meter, saw at least ten small tins of cat food.

Broussard knocked again. 'I respect working people,' he said, to no one in particular.

'Most times,' Poole agreed.

I looked over at Helene. Why hadn't Poole and Broussard left her in the car?

Broussard knocked a third time, and a cat yowled from inside.

Broussard stepped back from the door. 'Miss McCready?'

'Yeah.'

He pointed at the door. 'Would you be so kind as to turn the doorknob?'

Helene gave him a look but did so, and the door opened inward.

Broussard smiled at her. 'And would you take one step inside?'

Again, Helene did so.

'Excellent,' Poole said. 'See anything?'

She looked back at us. 'It's dark. Smells funny, though.'

Broussard said as he jotted in his notebook, 'Citizen stated premises smelled abnormal.' He capped his pen. 'Okay. You can come out, Miss McCready.'

Angie and I looked at each other, shook our heads. You had to hand it to Poole and Broussard. By getting Helene to open the door and step in first, they'd avoided the need for a warrant. 'Abnormal smell' was good enough for probable cause, and once Helene had opened the door, just about anyone could legally enter.

Helene stepped out onto the cobblestones and looked back up at the window where the woman had complained about the cats.

One of them – an emaciated orange tabby, with sharply defined ribs – shot past Broussard and then around me, leaped into the air, landed atop one of the trash cans, and dove its head into the collection of tins I'd seen.

'Guys,' I said.

Poole and Broussard turned from the doorway.

'The cat's paws. There's dried blood on them.'

'Oh, gross,' Helene said.

Broussard pointed at her. 'You stay here. Don't move until we call for you.'

She fished in her pockets for her cigarettes. 'You don't have to tell me twice.'

Poole stuck his head in the doorway and sniffed.

He turned back to Broussard, frowned, and nodded at the same time.

Angie and I came up beside them.

'Bloaters,' Broussard said. 'Anyone got cologne or perfume?'

Angie and I shook our heads. Poole produced a small vial of Aramis from his pocket. Until then, I hadn't known they still manufactured it.

'Aramis?' I said. 'What, they were out of Brut?'

Poole raised his eyebrows up and down several times. 'Old Spice, too, unfortunately.'

He passed the bottle around, and we each applied it liberally to our upper lips. Angie doused a handkerchief with it as well. Nasty as it smelled as it scorched the insides of my nostrils, it was still preferable to smelling a bloater without anything at all.

Bloaters are what some cops, paramedics, and doctors call bodies that have been dead for a while. Once the body's gases and acids have been allowed to run rampant after rigor mortis, the body will bloat and balloon and do all sorts of other really appetizing things.

A porch the width of my car greeted us. Winter boots caked with dried salt sat stuck to last February's newspapers beside a spade with gashes in the wood handle, a rusted hibachi, and a bag of empty beer cans. The thin green rug was ripped apart in several places, and the bloody footprints of several cats had dried into the fabric.

The next room we entered was a living room, and light from the windows was joined by the silver shaft from a TV with the volume turned down. The inside of the house was dark, but gray light came in from the side windows, filling the rooms with a pewter haze that didn't do much to improve the squalid surroundings. The rugs on the floors were a mismatched shag, patched together with a drug addict's sense of aesthetics. In several places, you could see the tufts rising in ridges where the sections had been cut and placed side by side. The walls were paneled in blond plywood, and the ceilings flaked white paint. A shredded futon couch sat against the wall, and as we stood in the center of the room, our eyes adjusting to the gray light, I noticed several sets of sparkling eyes brighten from the torn fabric.

A soft electric hum, like cicadas buzzing around a generator, rolled out from the futon, and the several sets of eyes moved in a jagged line.

And then they attacked.

Or at least it seemed that way at first. A dozen high-pitched meows preceded a scratch-and-scramble exodus as the cats – Siamese and calicoes and tabbies and one Hemingway – shot off the couch and over the coffee table, hit the shag carpet sections, burst through our legs, and banged off the baseboards on their way toward the door.

Poole said, 'Mother of God,' and hopped up on one leg.

I flattened against the cheap wall, and Angie joined me, and a hunk of thick fur slithered over my foot.

Broussard jerked to his right and then left, whacked at the hem of his suit jacket.

The cats weren't after us, though. They were after sunlight.

Outside, Helene shrieked as they poured through the open doorway. 'Holy shit! Help!'

'What I tell ya?' A voice I recognized as the middle-aged lady's yelled. 'A blight. A goddamned blight on the city a' Charlestown!'

Inside the house, it was suddenly so quiet I could hear the tick of a clock coming from the kitchen.

'Cats,' Poole said with thick disdain, and wiped his brow with a handkerchief.

Broussard bent to check his pant cuffs, dusted a wisp of cat hair off his shoes.

'Cats are smart.' Angie came off the wall. 'Better than dogs.'

'Dogs get the paper for you, though,' I said.

'Dogs don't scratch the shit out of couches, either,' Broussard said.

'Dogs don't eat their owners' corpses when they're hungry,' Poole said. 'Cats do.'

'Ugh,' Angie managed. 'That's not true. Is it?'

We moved slowly into the kitchen.

As soon as we entered, I had to stop for a moment, catch my breath, and suck in the cologne on my upper lip with flared nostrils.

Angie said, 'Shit,' and buried her face in her handkerchief.

A naked man was tied to a chair. A woman knelt on the floor a few feet away from him, her chin to her chest, the straps of her bloody white negligee hanging down to her elbows, her wrists and ankles hog-tied together behind her back. Both bodies had thickened with gas and turned the white of volcanic ash after blood stopped pumping through their veins.

The man had taken a large blast to his chest that had demolished his sternum and upper rib cage. By the size of the hole, I had to assume the blast had been unleashed from a shotgun at close range. And unfortunately, Poole had been right about the feeding habits and questionable loyalty of felines. More than just buckshot had chewed into the man's flesh. Between the damage wrought by the blast, time, and the cats, his upper chest looked as if it had been pushed open by surgical shears from the inside.

'Those aren't what I think they are,' Angie said, her eyes on the gaping hole.

'Sorry to inform you,' Poole said, 'but those are the man's lungs.'

'It's official,' Angie said. 'I'm nauseous.'

Poole tilted the man's chin up with a ballpoint pen. He took a step back. 'Well, hello, David!'

'Martin?' Broussard said, and took a step closer to the body.

'The same.' Poole dropped the chin and touched the man's dark hair. 'You're looking peaked, David.'

Broussard turned to us. 'David Martin. Also known as Wee David.'

Angie coughed into her handkerchief. 'He looks pretty tall to me.'

'It has nothing to do with his height.'

Angie glanced at the man's groin. 'Oh.'

'This must be Kimmie,' Poole said, and stepped over a puddle of dried blood to the woman in the negligee.

He lifted her head with the pen, and I said, 'Christ almighty.'

A black wound cut a small canyon across Kimmie's throat. Her chin and cheekbones were splattered with black blood and her eyes looked upward, as if asking for deliverance or help or proof that something, anything, waited for her beyond this kitchen.

Her arms bore several deep cuts, thick and caked black with blood, and holes I recognized as cigarette burns dotted her shoulders and collarbone.

'She was tortured.'

Broussard nodded. 'In front of the boyfriend. "Tell me where it is or I cut her again." That sort of thing.' He shook his head. 'This kinda sucks. Kimmie was all right for a cokehead.'

Poole stepped back from Kimmie's corpse. 'The cats didn't touch her.'

'What?' Angie said.

He pointed at Wee David. 'As you can see, they feasted on Mr Martin. Not Kimmie, though.'

'What's your point?' I said.

He shrugged. 'They liked Kimmie. Didn't like Wee David. Too bad the killers didn't feel the same way.'

Broussard stepped up beside his partner. 'You think Wee David gave up the goods?'

Poole lowered Kimmie's head gently back to her chest, made a *tsk* noise. 'He was a greedy bastard.' He looked over his shoulder at us. 'Not to speak ill of the dead, but—' He shrugged.

'Wee David and a previous girlfriend broke into a drugstore a couple of years ago, raided the place for Demerol, Darvon, Valium, whatever. Anyway, the cops are coming and Wee Dave and his girl go out a back door, have to jump down to an alley from a second-story fire escape. The girls sprains her ankle. Wee Dave loves her so much he unburdens her of her supply and leaves her there in the alley.'

First Big Dave Strand. Now Wee Dave Martin. Time to stop naming our children David.

I looked around the kitchen. The floor tiles had been torn up, the pantry shelves swept clear of food; piles of canned goods and empty potato-chip bags littered the floor. The ceiling slats had been removed and lay in a pile of white dust by the kitchen table. The oven and refrigerator had been pulled away from the wall. The cupboard doors lay open.

Whoever had killed Wee David and Kimmie seemed to have been thorough.

'You want to call it in?' Broussard said.

Poole shrugged. 'Why don't we poke around a bit first?'

Poole produced several pairs of thin plastic gloves from his pocket. He separated them and passed a pair each to Broussard, Angie, and me.

'This is a crime scene,' Broussard said to Angie and me. 'Don't queer it.'

The bedroom and bathroom were in the same state of distress as the kitchen and living room. Everything had been overturned, cut open, emptied onto the floor. Given the houses of other drug addicts I've seen, it wasn't noticeably worse than most.

'The TV,' Angie said.

I stuck my head out of the bedroom as Poole came out of the kitchen and Broussard exited the bathroom. We joined Angie around the TV.

'No one thought to touch it.'

'Probably because it's on,' Poole said.

'So?'

'Kind of hard to hide two hundred grand in there and keep all the parts working,' Broussard said. 'Don't you think?'

Angie shrugged, looked at the screen, watched one

145

of Jerry Springer's guests being restrained. She turned up the volume.

One of Jerry Springer's guests called another guest a *ho*', called an amused man a *dirty dog*.

Broussard sighed. 'I'll get a screwdriver.'

Jerry Springer looked at the audience knowingly. The audience hooted. Many words were bleeped out.

Behind us, Helene said, 'Oh, cool. Springer Time.'

Broussard came out of the bathroom with a tiny screwdriver with a red rubber handle. 'Miss McCready,' he said, 'I need you to wait outside.'

Helene sat on the edge of the torn-up futon, eyes on the TV. 'That lady's yelling 'cause of the cats. She said she's calling the police.'

'You tell her we *are* the police?'

Helene smiled distantly as one of Jerry's female guests threw a lopping punch at another one. 'I told her. She said she was going to call 'em anyway.'

Broussard brandished the screwdriver and nodded at Angie. She shut off the TV in mid-bleep.

Helene said, 'Damn.' She sniffed the air. 'Smells in here.'

'Want some cologne?'

She shook her head. 'My old boyfriend's trailer smelled worse. He used to, like, leave dirty socks soaking in the sink. Now that's a smell, lemme tell you.'

Poole tilted his head as if about to say something, but then he glanced at her and changed his mind, exhaled a loud, hopeless sigh.

Broussard unscrewed the back of the TV, and I helped slide it off. We peered in.

'Anything?' Poole said.

'Cables, wires, internal speakers, a motor, picture tube,' Broussard said.

We slid the casing back on.

'Shoot me,' Angie said. 'It wasn't the worst idea of the day.'

'Oh, no.' Poole held up his hands.

'Wasn't the best, either,' Broussard said out of the side of his mouth.

'What?' Angie said.

Broussard flashed his million-dollar smile at her. 'Hmm?'

'Could you turn it back on?' Helene said.

Poole narrowed his eyes in her direction, shook his head. 'Patrick?'

'Yeah?'

'There's a backyard behind here. Could you take Miss McCready out there while we finish up in here?'

'What about the show?' Helene said.

'I'll fill in the blanks,' I said. 'Ho', I said. 'You dirty dog,' I said. 'Bleep,' I said.

Helene looked up at me as I offered her my hand. 'You don't make sense a lot.'

'*Whoo-whoo*,' I said.

As we approached the kitchen, Poole said, 'Close your eyes, Miss McCready.'

'What?' Helene reared back from him a bit.

'You don't want to see what's in here.'

Before either of us could stop her, Helene leaned forward and craned her head over his shoulder.

Poole's face sagged and he stepped aside.

Helene entered the kitchen and stopped. I stood behind her, waited for her to scream or faint or fall to her knees or run back into the living room.

'They dead?' she said.

'Yeah,' I said. 'Very.'

She moved into the kitchen, headed for the back door. I looked at Poole. He raised an eyebrow.

As Helene passed Wee Dave, she paused to look at his chest.

'It's like in that movie,' she said.

'Which?'

'The one with all the aliens who pop out of people's chests, bleed acid. What was it called?'

'*Alien*,' I said.

'Right. They came out of your chest. But what was the movie called?'

Angie made a run to the local Dunkin' Donuts and joined Helene and me out in the backyard a few minutes later, while Poole and Broussard went through the house with notebooks and cameras.

The yard was barely a yard. The closet in my bedroom was bigger. Wee Dave and Kimmie had placed a rusted metal table and chairs out there, and we sat and listened to the sounds of the neighborhood as the day bled into midafternoon and the air chilled – mothers calling for children, the construction crew using mortar drills on the other side of the house, a whiffle-ball game in progress a couple of blocks over.

Helene sipped her Coke through a straw. 'Too bad. They seemed like nice people.'

I took a sip of coffee. 'How many times did you meet them?'

'Just that one time.'

Angie asked. 'You remember anything special about that night?'

Helene sucked some more Coke through the straw as she thought about it. 'All those cats. They were, like, everywhere. One of them scratched Amanda's hand, the little bitch.' She smiled at us. 'The cat, I mean.'

'So Amanda was in the house with you.'

'I guess.' She shrugged. 'Sure.'

'Because earlier you weren't sure if you'd left her behind in the car.'

She shrugged again, and I resisted an urge to reach out with both hands and slap her shoulders back down. 'Did I? Well, till I remembered the cat scratching her, I wasn't sure. No, she was in the house.'

'Anything else you remember?' Angie's fingers drummed the tabletop.

'She was nice.'

'Who, Kimmie?'

She pointed a finger at me, smiled. 'Yeah. That was her name: Kimmie. She was cool. She took me and Amanda in her bedroom, showed us pictures of her trip to Disney World. Amanda was, like, psyched. Everything on the ride home was, "Mommy, can we go see Mickey and Minnie? Can we go to Disney World?"' She snorted. 'Kids. Like I had the money.'

'You had two hundred thousand dollars when you entered that house.'

'But that was Ray's deal. I mean, I wouldn't rip off a nut job like Cheese Olamon on my own. Ray said he'd cut me in at some point. He'd never lied to me before, so I figured it's his deal, his problem if Cheese finds out.' Another shrug.

'Me and Cheese go way back,' I said.

'That right?'

I nodded. 'Chris Mullen, too. We all played Babe Ruth together, hung on the corner, et cetera.'

She raised her eyebrows. 'No shit?'

I held up a hand. 'Swear to God. And Cheese. Helene, you know what he'd do if he thought someone had ripped him off?'

She picked up her soda cup, placed it back down again. 'Look, I told you, it was Ray. I didn't do nothing but walk into that motel room with—'

'Cheese – and this was when we were kids, fifteen maybe – he saw his girlfriend glance at another guy one night? Cheese shattered a beer bottle against a streetlight and slashed her face with it. Tore her nose off, Helene. That was Cheese at fifteen. What do you think he's like now?'

She sucked on her straw until the air rattled the ice at the bottom. 'It was Ray's—'

'You think he'll lose any sleep killing your daughter?' Angie said. 'Helene.' She reached across the table and grasped Helene's bony wrist. 'Do you?'

'Cheese?' Helene said, and her voice cracked. 'You think he had something to do with Amanda's disappearance?'

Angie stared at her for a full thirty seconds before she shook her head and dropped Helene's wrist. 'Helene, let me ask you something.'

Helene rubbed her wrist and looked at her soda cup again. 'Yeah?'

'What fucking planet are you from exactly?'

Helene didn't say anything for a while after that.

Autumn died in technicolor all around us. Bright yellows and reds afire, burnished oranges and rusty greens painted the leaves that floated from the branches, collected in the grass. That vibrant odor of dying things, so particular to fall, creased the blades of air that cut through our clothing and made us tense our muscles and widen our eyes. Nowhere does death occur so spectacularly, so proudly, as it does in New England in October. The sun, broken free of the storm clouds that had threatened this morning, turned windowpanes into hard squares of white light and washed the brick row houses that surrounded the tiny yard in a smoked tint that matched the darker leaves.

Death, I thought, is not this. Death is directly behind us. Death is the grungy kitchen of Wee David and Kimmie. Death is black blood and disloyal cats who feed on anything.

'Helene,' I said.

'Yeah?'

'While you were in the room with Kimmie looking at pictures of Disney World, where were Wee David and Ray?'

Her mouth opened slightly.

'Quick,' I said. 'Off the top of your head. Don't think.'

'The backyard,' she said.

'The backyard.' Angie pointed at the ground. 'Here.'

She nodded.

'Could you see the backyard from Kimmie's bedroom?' I asked.

'No. The shades were drawn.'

'Then how'd you know they were out here?' I asked.

'Ray's shoes were filthy when we left,' she said slowly. 'Ray is a slob in a lot of ways.' She reached out and touched my arm as if she were about to share a deeply personal secret with me. 'But, man, he takes care of his shoes.'

11

GTwo Hundred + Composure = Child

'Gee two hundred?' Angie said.

'Two hundred grand,' Broussard said quietly.

'Where'd you find that note?' I said.

He looked over his shoulder at the house. 'Curled up tight and stuck in the waistband of Kimmie's lacy Underalls. An attention grabber, I think.'

We stood in the backyard.

'It's here,' Angie said, and pointed at a small mound by a dry and withered elm tree. The dirt was freshly turned there, the mound the only ridge in the plot of land that was otherwise as flat as a nickel.

'I believe you, Miss Gennaro,' Broussard said. 'So now what do we do?'

'Dig it up,' I said.

'And impound it and make it public knowledge,' Poole said. 'Tie it, through the press, to Amanda McCready's disappearance.'

I looked around at the dead grass, the burgundy leaves curled atop the blades. 'No one's touched this place in a while.'

Poole nodded. 'Your conclusion?'

'If it *is* buried there' – I pointed at the mound – 'then Wee David kept it to himself even though they tortured Kimmie to death in front of him.'

'No one ever accused Wee Dave of being a candidate for the Peace Corps,' Broussard said.

Poole walked over to the tree, placed a foot on either side of the mound, stared down at it.

Inside the house, Helene sat in the living room, fifteen feet from two bloating corpses, and watched TV. Springer had given way to Geraldo or Sally or some other ringmaster sounding the cowbell for the latest cavalcade of carnival freaks. The public 'therapy' of confession, the continued watering down of the meaning of the word 'trauma,' a steady stream of morons shouting at the void from a raised dais.

Helene didn't seem to mind. She only complained about the smell, asked if we could open a window. Nobody had a good enough reason why we couldn't, and once we did, we left her there, her face bathed in flickers of silver light.

'So we're out of this,' Angie said, a note of quiet, sad surprise in her voice, a sudden confronting of the anticlimax that comes when a case ends abruptly.

I thought about it. It was a kidnapping now, complete with a ransom note and logical suspects with a motive. The FBI would take over, and we could follow the case through the news like every other couch potato in the state, wait for Helene to show up on Springer Time with other parents who'd misplaced their kids.

I held out my hand to Broussard. 'Angie's right. It was nice working with you.'

Broussard shook the hand and nodded but didn't

say anything. He looked over at Poole.

Poole toed the small ridge of dirt with his shoe, his eyes on Angie.

'We *are* out of this,' Angie said to him, 'aren't we?'

Poole held her gaze for a bit, then looked back at the tiny mound.

No one spoke for a couple of minutes. I knew we should go. Angie knew we should go. Yet we stayed, planted, it seemed, in that tiny yard with the dead elm.

I turned my head toward the ugly house behind us, could see Wee David's head from here, the top of the chair he'd been bound to. Had he been aware of the feel of his bare shoulder blades against the cheap wicker backing of the chair? Had that been the last sensation he'd acknowledged before the buckshot opened up his chest cavity as if the bone and flesh were made of tissue paper? Or was it the sensation of the blood draining to his bound wrists, the fingers turning blue and numb?

The people who'd entered this house that last day or night of his life had known they'd kill Kimmie and Wee David. That was a professional execution back in that kitchen. Kimmie's throat had been sliced as a last-ditch effort to get Wee David to talk, but she'd also been killed with a knife, out of prudence.

Neighbors will almost always attribute one gunshot to something else – a car backfiring, maybe, or, in the case of a shotgun blast, an engine blowing or a china cabinet falling to the floor. Particularly when the sound may have come from the home of drug dealers or users, people who are known by their neighbors to make odd sounds at all times of night.

No one wants to think they actually heard a gunshot, were actually witness – if only aurally – to a murder.

So the killers had killed Kimmie quickly and silently, probably without warning. But Wee David – they'd been pointing that shotgun at him for a while. They'd wanted him to see the curl of the finger against the trigger, hear the hammer hit the shell, the explosive click of ignition.

And these were the people who held Amanda McCready.

'You want to trade the two hundred thousand for Amanda,' Angie said.

There it was. What I'd known for the last five minutes. What Poole and Broussard were unwilling to put into words. A cataclysmic breach of police protocol.

Poole studied the trunk of the dead tree. Broussard lifted a red leaf off the green grass with the toe of his shoe.

'Right?' Angie said.

Poole sighed. 'I'd prefer that the kidnappers not open a suitcase full of newspaper or marked money and kill the child before we get to them.'

'That's happened to you before?' Angie said.

'It's happened to cases I've turned over to the FBI,' Poole said. 'That's what we're dealing with here, Miss Gennaro. Kidnapping is federal.'

'We go federal,' Broussard said, 'the money goes into an evidence locker, and the Feds do the negotiating, get a chance to show how clever they are.'

Angie looked out at the tiny yard, the dying violet petals growing through the chain-link fence from the other side. 'You two want to negotiate with the kidnappers without the Feds.'

Poole dug his hands into his pockets. 'I've found too many dead children in closets, Miss Gennaro.'

She looked at Broussard. 'You?'

He smiled. 'I hate Feds.'

I said, 'This goes bad, you'll lose your pensions, guys. Maybe worse.'

On the other side of the yard, a man hung a throw rug out his third-story window and started beating it with a hockey stick that was missing the blade. The dust rose in angry, ephemeral clouds, and the man kept whacking without seeming to notice us.

Poole lowered himself to his haunches, picked at a blade of grass by the mound. 'You remember the Jeannie Minelli case? Couple years back?'

Angie and I shrugged. It was sad how many horrible things you forgot.

'Nine-year-old girl,' Broussard said. 'Disappeared riding her bike in Somerville.'

I nodded. It was coming back.

'We found her, Mr Kenzie, Miss Gennaro.' Poole snapped the blade of grass between his fingers at both ends. 'In a barrel. Soaked in cement. The cement hadn't hardened yet because the geniuses who killed her had used the wrong ratio of water to cement in the mix.' He slapped his hands together, to clear them of dust or pollen or just because. 'We found a nine-year-old's corpse floating in a barrel of watery cement.' He stood. 'Sound pleasant?'

I looked over at Broussard. The memory had blanched his face, and several tremors spilled down his arms until he put his hands in his pockets, tightened his elbows against the sides of his torso.

'No,' I said, 'but if this goes wrong, you'll—'

'What?' Poole said. 'Lose my benefits? I'm retiring soon, Mr Kenzie. You ever see what the policemen's union can do to someone trying to take away the retirement money of a decorated officer with thirty years in?' Poole pointed a finger at us, wagged it. 'It's like watching starving dogs go after meat hung on a man's balls. Not pretty.'

Angie chuckled. 'You're something else, Poole.'

He touched her shoulder. 'I'm a broken-down old man with three ex-wives, Miss Gennaro. I'm nothing. But I'd like to go out my last case a winner. With luck, take down Chris Mullen and bury Cheese Olamon deeper in jail while I'm at it.'

Angie glanced at his hand, then up into his face. 'And if you blow it?'

'Then I drink myself to death.' Poole removed the hand and ran it through the hard stubble on his head. 'Cheap vodka. The best I can do on a cop's pension. Sound okay to you?'

Angie smiled. 'Sounds fine, Poole. Sounds fine.'

Poole glanced over his shoulder at the guy whacking his throw rug, then back at us. 'Mr Kenzie, did you notice that gardening spade on the porch?'

I nodded.

Poole smiled.

'Oh,' I said. 'Right.'

I went back through the house and got the spade. As I came back through the living room, Helene said, 'We outa here soon?'

'Pretty soon.'

She looked at the spade and the plastic gloves on my hands. 'You find the money?'

I shrugged. 'Maybe.'

She nodded, looked back at the TV.

I started walking again, and her voice stopped me at the doorway to the kitchen.

'Mr Kenzie?'

'Yeah.'

Her eyes sparkled in the glow from the TV screen in such a way they reminded me of the cats'. 'They wouldn't hurt her. Would they?'

'You mean Chris Mullen and the rest of Cheese Olamon's crew?'

She nodded.

On the TV a woman told another woman to stay away from my daughter, you dyke. The audience hooted.

'Would they?' Helene's eyes remained fixed on the TV.

'Yes,' I said.

She turned her head sharply in my direction. 'No.' She shook her head, as if doing so would make her wish come true.

I should have told her I was kidding. That Amanda would be fine. That she'd be returned and things would go back to normal and Helene could drug herself with TV and booze and heroin and whatever else she used to cocoon herself from just how nasty the world could be.

But her daughter was out there, alone and terrified, handcuffed to a radiator or a bedpost, electrical tape tied around the lower half of her face so she couldn't make any noise. Or she was dead. And part of the reason for that was Helene's self-indulgence, her determination to act as if she could do whatever she chose and there'd be no consequence, no opposite and equal reaction.

'Helene,' I said.

She lit a cigarette, and the match head jumped around the target several times before the tobacco ignited. 'What?'

'Are you getting all this finally?'

She looked to the TV, then back at me, and her eyes were moist and pink. 'What?'

'Your daughter was abducted. Because of what you stole. The men who have her don't give a shit about her. And they might not give her back.'

Two tears rolled down Helene's cheeks, and she wiped at them with the back of her wrist.

'I know that,' she said, her attention back on the TV. 'I'm not stupid.'

'Yes you are,' I said, and walked out to the back-yard.

Standing in a circle around the mound, we blocked it from the view of any neighboring row houses. Broussard pushed the spade into the dirt and over-turned it several times before we saw the wrinkled top of a green plastic bag appear.

Broussard dug a little more, and then Poole looked around and bent over, pulled at the bag, and wrenched it free from the hole.

They hadn't even tied the top of the bag, just twisted it several times, and Poole allowed it to revolve in his hand, the green plastic crinkling as the tight lines spread apart at the neck and the bag grew wider. Poole dropped it to the ground and the top of the bag opened up.

A pile of loose bills greeted us, mostly hundreds and fifties, old and soft.

'That's a lot of money,' Angie said.

Poole shook his head. 'That, Miss Gennaro, is Amanda McCready.'

Before Poole and Broussard called in the forensics team and medical examiner, we shut off the TV in the living room and ran it down for Helene.

'You'll trade the money for Amanda,' she said.

Poole nodded.

'And she'll be alive.'

'That's the hope.'

'And I have to do what again?'

Broussard lowered himself to his haunches in front of her. 'You don't have to *do* anything, Miss McCready. You just have to make a choice right now. Us four here' – he waved his hand at the rest of us – 'happen to think this might be the right approach. But if my bosses find out I plan to do it this way, I'll get suspended or fired. You understand?'

She half nodded. 'If you tell people, they'll want to arrest Chris Mullen.'

Broussard nodded. 'Possibly. Or, we think, the FBI might put the capture of the kidnapper before your daughter's safety.'

Another half nod, as if her chin kept meeting an invisible barrier on its way down.

Poole said, 'Miss McCready, the bottom line is, it's your decision. If you want us to, we'll call this in right now, hand over the money, and let the pros handle it.'

'Other people?' She looked at Broussard.

He touched her hand. 'Yes.'

'I don't want other people. I don't . . .' She stood up a bit unsteadily. 'What do I have to do if we do it your way?'

'Keep quiet.' Broussard came off his haunches. 'Don't talk to the press or the police. Don't even tell Lionel and Beatrice what's going on.'

'Are you going to talk to Cheese?'

I said, 'That's probably our next move, yeah.'

'Mr Olamon seems to be holding the cards at the moment,' Broussard said.

'What if you just, like, followed Chris Mullen? Maybe he'd take you to Amanda without knowing it?'

'We'll be doing that as well,' Poole said. 'But I have a feeling they'll be expecting it. I'm sure they have Amanda well hidden.'

'Tell him I'm sorry.'

'Who?'

'Cheese. Tell him I didn't mean nothing bad. I just want my kid back. Tell him not to hurt her. Could you do that?' She looked at Broussard.

'Sure.'

'I'm hungry,' Helene said.

'We'll get you some—'

She shook her head at Poole. 'Not me. Not me. That's what Amanda said.'

'What? When?'

'When I put her to bed that night. That's the last thing she said to me: "Mommy, I'm hungry."' Helene smiled, but her eyes filled. 'I said, "Don't worry, honey. You'll eat in the morning."'

No one said anything. We waited to see if she'd crumble.

'I mean, they'd have fed her, right?' She held the smile as tears rolled down her face. 'She's not still hungry, is she?' She looked at me. 'Is she?'

'I don't know,' I said.

12

Cheese Olamon was a six-foot-two four-hundred-and-thirty-pound yellow-haired Scandinavian who'd somehow arrived at the misconception that he was black.

Though his flesh jiggled when he walked and his fashion sense ran toward the fleece or thick cotton sweats favored by overweight men everywhere, it would have been a large error to mistake Cheese for a jolly fat guy or confuse his bulk with a lack of speed.

Cheese smiled a lot, and there was a very real joy that seemed to overtake him in the presence of some people. And for all the wincing that his dated, pseudo Shaft-speak could induce in people, there was something strangely endearing and infectious about it. You'd find yourself listening to him talk and you'd wonder if his adoption of a slang very few people – black or white – had ever truly spoken this side of a Fred Williamson/Antonio Fargas opus was misplaced affection for black ghetto culture, deranged racism, or both. In any case, it could be damn catchy.

But I was also familiar with the Cheese who'd

glanced at a guy in a bar one night with such self-possessed malevolence you knew the guy's life expectancy had just dropped to about a minute and a half. I knew the Cheese who employed girls so thin and skagged out they could disappear by ducking behind a baseball bat, took rolls of bills from them as they leaned into his car, patted their bony asses, and sent them back to work.

And all the rounds he bought at the bar, all the fins and sawbucks he pressed into the flesh of broken rummies and then drove them to get Chinese with it, all the turkeys he handed out to the neighborhood poor at Christmas couldn't erase the junkies who'd died in hallways with spikes still sticking out of their arms; the young women who turned into craven hags seemingly overnight, gums bleeding, begging in the subways for money to spend on AZT treatments; the names he'd personally edited from next year's phone books.

A freak of both nature and nurture, Cheese had been small and sickly through most of grade school; his rib cage had shone through his cheap white shirt like an old man's fingers; he sometimes had coughing fits so violent he'd vomit. He rarely spoke. He had no friends that I remember, and while most of us ate lunch from *Adam-12* and Barbie lunch boxes, Cheese carried his in a brown paper bag that he carefully folded after he was done and took home to use again.

Both parents walked him up to the schoolyard gate every morning for the first few years. They'd speak to him in a foreign tongue, and their brusque voices carried into the schoolyard as they fussed with their son's hair or scarf, fiddled with the buttons on his heavy peasant's coat, before setting him free. They'd walk back down the avenue – giants, both of them – Mr Olamon wearing a satin fedora at least fifteen years out of fashion with a weathered orange feather in the band, his head cocked slightly, as if he expected taunts or trash to be hurled down on him and his wife from second-story porches. Cheese would watch them until they were out of sight, wincing if his mother paused to pull a sagging sock back up over her thick ankle.

For whatever reason, the memories I have of Cheese and his parents seem trapped in the saber-blade sunlight of early winter: snapshots of an ugly little boy at the edge of a schoolyard pocked with half-frozen puddles watching his gigantic parents stoop their shoulders and walk under shivering black trees.

Cheese took multiple shit and multiple beatings for his light accent, his parents' far thicker ones, his country-village clothes, and his skin, which had a soapy, yellowish luster that reminded kids of bad cheese. Hence the name.

During Cheese's seventh year at St Bart's, his father, a janitor at an exclusive grade school in Brookline, was indicted for physically assaulting a ten-year-old student who'd spit on the floor. The child, the son of a Mass General neurosurgeon and visiting professor at Harvard, had received a broken arm and nose in the few seconds of Mr Olamon's sudden attack, and the penalty promised to be stiff. The same year, Cheese grew ten inches in five months.

The next year – the year of his father's conviction and sentence to three-to-six – Cheese bulked up.

Fourteen years of being pissed on went into the muscle mass, fourteen years of being taunted and having his slight accent aped, fourteen years of humiliation and swallowed rage turned into a hot, calcified cannonball of bile in his stomach.

That summer between eighth grade and high school became Cheese Olamon's Summer of Payback. Kids got sucker-punched rounding corners, looked up from the sidewalk to see one of Cheese's size twelves descending into their ribs. There were broken noses and broken arms, and Carl Cox – one of Cheese's oldest and most merciless tormentors – got a rock dropped on his head from a three-decker roof that, among other things, tore off half his ear and left him talking funny for the rest of his life.

It wasn't just the boys from our graduating class at St Bart's who got it, either; several fourteen-year-old girls spent that summer with bandages over their noses or making trips to the dentist to repair broken teeth.

Even then, though, Cheese knew how to pick his targets. The ones whom he correctly guessed were too timid or powerless to come back against him saw his face when he hurt them. The ones he hurt worst – and therefore those most likely to speak to the police or their parents – never saw anything at all.

Among the ones who escaped Cheese's revenge were Phil, Angie, and myself, who'd never tormented him, if only because we each had at least one unfashionably immigrant parent ourselves. And Cheese left Bubba Rogowski alone, as well. I don't remember if Bubba had ever messed with Cheese or not, but even if he had, Cheese was smart enough to know that, when it came to warfare, Cheese would be the German army and Bubba the Russian winter. So Cheese stuck to the fronts and battles he knew he could win.

No matter how much bigger, craftier, and more dangerously psychotic Cheese became over the years, he maintained an almost sycophantic persona in Bubba's presence, even going so far as to personally feed and groom Bubba's dogs when Bubba was overseas on various weapons buys.

That's Bubba for you. The people who terrify you and me feed his dogs.

'"Mother institutionalized when subject was seventeen,"' Broussard read from Cheese Olamon's file, as Poole drove past Walden Pond Nature Preserve toward Concord Prison. '"Father released from Norfolk a year later, disappeared."'

'Rumor has it Cheese killed him,' I said. I lounged in the backseat, head against the window, Concord's glorious trees floating past.

After Broussard and Poole had called in the double homicide at Wee David's, Angie and I took the bag of money and drove Helene back to Lionel's house. We dropped her off and drove to Bubba's warehouse.

Two o'clock in the afternoon is prime sleeping time for Bubba, and we were greeted at the door by the sight of him in a flaming red Japanese kimono and a somewhat irritated look on that deranged cherub's face of his.

'Why am I awake?' he said.

'We need your safe,' Angie said.

'You own a safe.' He glowered at me.

167

I looked up into his glare. 'Ours doesn't have a minefield protecting it.'

He held out his hand, and Angie placed the bag in it.

'Contents?' Bubba said.

'Two hundred grand.'

Bubba nodded as if we'd just said Grandmother's heirlooms. We could have told him Proof of extraterrestrials, and the reaction would have been the same. Unless you could hook him up on a date with Jane Seymour, Bubba's pretty hard to impress.

Angie pulled the pictures of Corwin Earle and Leon and Roberta Trett from her bag, fanned them up in front of Bubba's sleepy face. 'Know any of them?'

'Hot goddamn!' he said.

'You do?' Angie said.

'Huh?' He shook his head. 'No. That's one big hairy bitch, though. She walk upright and everything?'

Angie sighed and put the photos back in her bag.

'The other two were cons,' Bubba said. 'Never met 'em, but you can always tell.'

He yawned, nodded, and shut the door in our faces.

'It wasn't his presence I missed when he was in jail,' Angie said.

'It was the engaging verbal discourse,' I said.

Angie dropped me back at my apartment, where I waited for Poole and Broussard, while she drove over to Chris Mullen's condo building to begin surveillance. She opted for the duty because she's never been real keen on entering men's prisons. Besides, Cheese gets kind of funny around her, takes to blushing and asking her who she's dating these days. I took the ride with Poole and Broussard because I was an allegedly friendly face, and Cheese has never been known for cooperating with the men in blue.

'Suspect in the death of one Jo Jo McDaniel, 1986,' Broussard said, as we wound our way up Route 2.

'Cheese's mentor in the drug trade,' I said.

Broussard nodded. 'Suspect in the disappearance and suspected death of Daniel Caleb, 1991.'

'Didn't hear about that one.'

'Accountant.' Broussard flipped a page. 'Supposedly cooked books for a few unsavory characters.'

'Cheese caught him with his hand in the till.'

'Apparently.'

Poole caught my eyes in the rearview mirror. 'Quite the association you have with the criminal element, Patrick.'

I sat up in the seat. 'Gee, Poole, whatever could you mean?'

'Friends with Cheese Olamon and Chris Mullen,' Broussard said.

'They're not friends. Just guys I grew up with.'

'Didn't you also grow up with the late Kevin Hurlihy?' Poole brought the car to a stop in the left lane, waiting for a break in traffic on the other side of the road so he could cross Route 2 and enter the prison driveway.

'Last I heard, Kevin was just missing,' I said.

Broussard smiled over the seat at me. 'And let's not forget the infamous Mr Rogowski.'

I shrugged. I was used to my association with

Bubba raising eyebrows. Especially cops' eyebrows.

'Bubba's a friend,' I said.

'Hell of a friend,' Broussard said. 'Is it true he's got a floor of his warehouse mined with explosives?'

I shrugged. 'Drop in on him sometime, see for yourself.'

Poole chuckled. 'Talk about your early retirement plans.' He turned into the gravel driveway of the prison. 'Some neighborhood you come from, Patrick, that's all. Some neighborhood.'

'We're just misunderstood down there,' I said. 'Hearts of gold, every one of us.'

When we stepped out of the car, Broussard stretched and said, 'Oscar Lee tells me you're not comfortable with judgment.'

'With what?' I said, and looked up at the prison walls. Typical of Concord. Even the prison looked inviting.

'Judgment,' Broussard said. 'Oscar says you hate judging people.'

I followed the cyclone wire at the top of the wall. A little less inviting, suddenly.

'Says that's why you hang with a psycho like Rogowski, maintain relations with the likes of Cheese Olamon.'

I squinted into the bright sun. 'No,' I said. 'I'm not very good at judging people. Every now and then I've had to.'

'And?' Poole said.

I shrugged. 'Left a bad taste in my mouth.'

'So you judged poorly?' Poole said lightly.

I thought of my calling Helene 'stupid' just a couple of hours ago; the way the word seemed to shrink her and stab her at the same time. I shook my head. 'No. My judgment was correct. Just left a bad taste in my mouth. Simple as that.'

I stuck my hands in my pockets and walked toward the front door of the prison before Poole and Broussard could think of any more questions regarding my character or lack thereof.

The warden posted a guard at each of the two gates that led in and out of the small visitors' yard at Concord Prison, and the guards in the towers shifted their attention to us. Cheese was already there when we arrived. He was the only convict in the yard, Broussard and Poole having requested as much privacy as possible.

'Yo, Patrick, how's it hanging?' Cheese called, as we crossed the yard. He stood by a water fountain. In comparison to the Orca with yellow hair that was Cheese, the fountain looked like a golf tee.

'Not bad, Cheese. It's a nice day.'

'I am fucking down with that, brother.' He brought his fist down on top of my own. 'Day like this is like righteous pussy, Jack Daniel's, and a pack of Kools all rolled into one. Know what I'm saying?'

I didn't, but I smiled. That's how it worked with Cheese. You nodded, you smiled, you wondered when he'd start making some sense.

'Damn!' Cheese reared back on his heels. 'You brought yourself the law with you. The Man is in the house!' he shouted. 'In da house. Poole and . . .' – he snapped his fingers - 'Broussard. Right? Thought you boys left Narco.'

Poole smiled into the sun. 'We did, Mr Cheese, sir. We certainly did.' He pointed to a long dark scab on Cheese's chin. It looked like a slice left by a jagged blade. 'You've been making enemies here?'

'This? Shit.' Cheese rolled his eyes at me. 'Motherfucker ain't been born yet can put the Cheese down.'

Broussard chuckled and toed the dirt with his left foot. 'Yeah, Cheese, sure. You been talking your black rap and pissed off some brother don't like white boys with a confused sense of identity. That it?'

'Yo, Poole,' Cheese said, 'what's a cool-as-ice-cream cat like yourself doing with this deadweight-nappy-headed-couldn't-find-his-own-ass-with-a-map motherfucker?'

'Slumming,' Poole said, and a small smile twitched the corners of Broussard's mouth.

'Heard you lost a bag of cash,' Broussard said.

'You did?' Cheese rubbed his chin. 'Hmm. Can't rightly recall that, officer, but you got a bag of cash you're looking to unload – well, I'll be happy to take it off your hands. Give it to my man Patrick, he'll hold it for me till I get out.'

'Aww, Cheese,' I said, 'that's touching.'

'We down, brother, 'cause I *know* your shit's straight. How's Brother Rogowski?'

'Fine.'

'Motherfucker did a year in Plymouth? Cons still shaking in that place. 'Fraid he might come *back*, he seemed to like it so much.'

'He ain't going back,' I said. 'He missed a year of TV he's still catching up on.'

'How're the dogs?' Cheese whispered, as if they were a secret.

'Belker died about a month ago.'

The information rocked Cheese in place for a

moment. He looked up at the sky as a soft breeze found his eyelids. 'How'd he die?' He looked at me. 'Poison?'

I shook my head. 'Hit by a car.'

'Intentional?'

I shook my head again. 'Little old lady was driving. Belker just beelined into the avenue.'

'How's Bubba taking it?'

'He'd had Belker neutered the month before.' I shrugged. 'He's pretty sure it was suicide.'

'Makes sense.' Cheese nodded. 'Sure.'

'The money, Cheese.' Broussard waved a hand in front of Cheese's face. 'The money.'

'Ain't missing none, officer. What I tol' you.' Cheese shrugged and turned away from Broussard, walked over to a picnic bench, and took a seat on top, waited for us to join him.

'Cheese,' I said, as I sat down beside him, 'we got a missing girl in the neighborhood. Maybe you heard about it?'

Cheese lifted a blade of grass off his shoelaces, twirled it between his chubby fingers. 'Heard a bit. Amanda something, wasn't it?'

'McCready,' Poole said.

Cheese pursed his lips, seemed to give it about a millisecond's worth of thought, then shrugged. 'Don't ring a bell. What's this about a bag of cash?'

Broussard chuckled softly and shook his head.

'Let's try a hypothetical,' Poole said.

Cheese clasped his hands together between his legs and looked at Poole with an eager small-boy's expression on his buttery face. 'Okeydokey.'

Poole placed a foot up on the bench by Cheese's. 'Let us say, just for argument—'

'Just for argument,' Cheese said happily.

'—that someone stole some money from a gentleman on the same day he was incarcerated by the state for a parole violation.'

'This story got any tit in it?' Cheese asked. 'The Cheese likes him some story with tit.'

'I'm getting to it,' Poole said. 'I promise.'

Cheese nudged me with his elbow, gave me a huge grin, then turned back to Poole. Broussard leaned back on his heels, looked out at the guard towers.

'So this person – who does in fact have breasts – steals from a man she shouldn't. And a few months later, her child disappears.'

'Pity,' Cheese said. 'A god*damn* shame, you ask the Cheese.'

'Yes,' Poole said. 'A shame. Now a known associate of the man this woman angered—'

'Stole from,' Cheese said.

'Excuse me.' Poole tipped an imaginary hat. 'A known associate of the man this woman stole from was seen in the crowd gathered outside the woman's house the night her daughter disappeared.'

Cheese rubbed his chin. 'Interesting.'

'And that man works for you, Mr Olamon.'

Cheese raised his eyebrows. 'Straight up and shit?'

'Mmm.'

'You said there was a crowd outside this house?'

'I did.'

'So, lookee here, I bets a whole boatload of folks were standing there who *don't* work for me.'

'This is true.'

'You gonna question them, too?'

'The mother didn't rip them off,' I said.

Cheese turned his head. 'How do you know? A

174

bitch crazy enough to take from the Cheese, she may be ripping off the whole motherfucking *neighborhood*. Am I right, brother?'

'So you admit she stole from you?' Broussard said.

Cheese looked at me, jerked his thumb in Broussard's direction. 'I thought this was a hypothetical.'

'Of course.' Broussard held up a hand. 'Excuse me, Your Cheeseness.'

'Here's the deal,' Poole said.

'Ooooh,' Cheese said. 'A deal.'

'Mr Olamon, we'll keep this quiet. Between just us.'

'Just us,' Cheese said, and rolled his eyes at me.

'But we want that child returned safely.'

Cheese looked at him for a long time, a smile steadily growing on his face. 'Let me get this straight. You saying that you – the Man – are going to let my hypothetical boy pick up this hypothetical money in return for one hypothetical kid, and then we all's just walk away friends? That the shit you trying to sell me, officer?'

'Detective sergeant,' Poole said.

'Whatever.' Cheese snorted, threw his hands out in front of him.

'You're familiar with the law, Mr Olamon. Just by offering you this deal, we are entrapping you. Legally, you can do whatever you want with this offer and not suffer any charges.'

'Bullshit.'

'No shit,' Poole said.

'Cheese,' I said, 'who gets hurt with this deal?'

'Huh?'

'Seriously. Someone gets his money back.

Someone else gets her kid back. Everyone walks away happy.'

He wagged a finger at me. 'Patrick, my brother, do not attempt a career in sales. Who gets hurt? That what you're asking? Who gets motherfucking hurt?'

'Yeah. Tell me.'

'The motherfucker who got ripped off, that's who!' He threw his hands up in the air, slapped them down on his enormous thighs, leaned his head in toward mine until we were almost touching. 'That motherfucker gets hurt. That motherfucker gets motherfucking buttfucked. What, he supposed to trust the Man? The Man and his deal?' He put a hand on the back of my neck, squeezed. 'Fuck, nigger, you been smoking motherfucking *crack*?'

'Mr Olamon,' Poole said, 'how do we convince you that we're on the level?'

Cheese let go of my neck. 'You don't. Y'all step back, maybe let things cool down a bit, let folks work shit out amongst themselves.' He wagged his thick finger at Poole. 'Maybe then, everybody get happy.'

Poole extended his arms, palms up. 'We can't do that, Mr Olamon. You must know that.'

'Okay, okay.' Cheese nodded hurriedly. 'Maybe someone needs to offer a certain righteous motherfucker some kind of reduction of sentence for his help in facilitating a certain transaction. What you think about that?'

'That would mean bringing in the District Attorney,' Poole said.

'So?'

'Maybe you missed the part where we said we want to keep this quiet,' Broussard said. 'Get the girl back, go on our merry way.'

'Well, then, your hypothetical man, he take that sort of deal, he's a chump. Motherfucking hypothetical dumb-ass, and that's for damn sure.'

'We just want Amanda McCready,' Broussard said. He placed his palm on the back of his neck, kneaded the flesh. 'Alive.'

Cheese leaned back on the table, tilted his head to the sun, sucked in the air through nostrils so wide they could vacuum rolls of quarters off a rug.

Poole stepped back from the table, crossed his arms over his chest, and waited.

'Used to keep a bitch in my stable name of McCready,' Cheese said eventually. 'Occasional trade, not regular. Didn't look like much, but you gave her the right party favor, that girl could *go*. Know what I'm saying?'

'Stable?' Broussard stepped over to the table. 'Are you telling us you exploited Helene McCready for the purposes of prostitution, Cheese Whiz?'

Cheese leaned forward and laughed. 'P-p-p-purposes of p-p-p-prostitution. Dang, that's got a nice ring to it, don't it now? Form myself a band, call it Purposes of Prostitution, pack the clubs like a motherfucker.'

Broussard flicked his wrist and hit Cheese Olamon in the center of the nose with the back of his hand. It wasn't a love tap, either. Cheese got his hands up to his nose and blood immediately seeped through the fingers, and Broussard stepped between the big man's open legs and grabbed his right ear in his hand, squeezed until I heard cartilage rattle.

'Listen to me, mutt. You listening?'

Cheese made a noise that sounded like an affirmative.

'I don't give a fuck about Helene McCready and whether you turned her out on Easter Sunday to a roomful of priests. I don't care about your bullshit scag deals and the street you're still running from behind these walls. I care about Amanda McCready.' He leaned into the ear, twisted his vise-grip hold. 'You hear that name? Amanda McCready. And if you don't tell me where she is, you Richard Roundtree – wannabe piece of shit, I'm going to get the names of the four biggest black-buck cons who hate your dumb ass and make sure they spend a night with you in solitary with nothing but their dicks and a Zippo. You following this or should I hit you again?'

He let go of Cheese's ear and stepped back.

Sweat had darkened Cheese's hair, and the thick rattle he made behind his cupped hands was the same one he'd made as a kid between coughing attacks, often just before he vomited.

Broussard flourished a hand in Cheese's direction and looked over at me. 'Judgment,' he said, and wiped the hand on his pants.

Cheese dropped his hands from his nose and leaned back on the picnic bench as blood trickled over his upper lip and into his mouth. He took several deep breaths, his eyes never leaving Broussard.

The guards in the towers looked off into the sky. The two guards manning the gates studied their shoes as if they'd each received a new pair that morning.

I could hear a distant clank of steel as someone worked out with weights inside the prison walls. A tiny bird swooped across the visitors' yard. It was so small and moved so fast, I couldn't even tell what color it was before it shot up the wall and over the cyclone wire, disappeared from view.

Broussard stood back from the bench, his feet spread, staring at Cheese, his gaze so devoid of emotion or life he could have been studying tree bark. This was another Broussard, one I hadn't met before.

As fellow investigators, Angie and I had been treated by Broussard with professional respect and even a bit of charm. I'm sure that's the Broussard most people knew – the handsome, articulate detective with flawless grooming and a movie star's smile. But in Concord Prison, I was seeing the street cop, the alley brawler, the interrogation-by-nightstick Broussard. As he leveled his dark gaze at Cheese, I saw the righteous, win-at-all-costs menace of a guerrilla fighter, a jungle warrior.

Cheese spit a thick mix of phlegm and blood onto the grass.

'Yo, Mark Fuhrman,' he said, 'kiss my black ass.'

Broussard lunged for him, and Poole caught the back of his partner's jacket as Cheese scrambled backward and swung his huge body off the picnic table.

'These are some sorry-ass crackers you hanging with, Patrick.'

'Hey, mutt!' Broussard shouted. 'You remember me that night in solitary! You got it?'

'Got a picture of your wife doing it with a pile of dwarfs in my cell,' Cheese said. 'That's what I got. Want to come look?'

Broussard made another lunge, and Poole wrapped his arms around his partner's chest, lifted the bigger man off his feet, and pivoted away from the bench.

Cheese headed for the prisoners' gate and I trotted to catch up.

'Cheese.'

He looked back over his shoulder, kept walking.

'Cheese, for Christ's sake, she's four years old.'

Cheese kept walking. 'I'm real sorry about that. Tell the man he need to work on his social skills.'

The guard stopped me at the gate as Cheese passed through. The guard had mirrored sunglasses, and I could see my funhouse reflection in each eye as he pushed me back. Two little shimmering versions of me, the same goofy, dismayed look in each face.

'Come on, Cheese. Come on, man.'

Cheese turned back to the fence, put his fingers through the rungs, stared at me for a long time.

'I can't help you, Patrick. Okay?'

I gestured over my shoulder at Poole and Broussard. 'Their deal was real.'

Cheese shook his head slowly. 'Shit, Patrick. Cops are like cons, man. Motherfuckers always got an angle.'

'They'll come back with an army, Cheese. You know how this works. They're working a red ball and they're pissed.'

'And I don't know shit.'

'Yes, you do.'

He smiled broadly, the blood beginning to clot

and thicken on his upper lip. 'Prove it,' he said, and turned away, walked along the pebbled path that led across a short lawn and back into the prison.

I walked back past Broussard and Poole on my way to the visitors' gate.

'Nice judgment,' I said. 'Picture-fucking-perfect.'

13

Broussard caught up with me as we made our way down the corridor toward the sign-in desk. His hand gripped my elbow from behind and turned me toward him.

'Problem with my method, Mr Kenzie?'

'Fucking *method*?' I pulled my arm out of his grasp. 'That what you call what you did back there?'

Poole and the guard reached us, and Poole said, 'Not here, gentlemen. There are appearances to maintain.'

Poole steered us both down the corridor and through the metal detectors and the last remaining gate. Our weapons were returned to us by a sergeant with hair plugs springing from the top of his head in tiny, tightly wrapped bundles, and then we walked out into the parking lot.

Broussard started in as soon as our shoes hit gravel. 'How much bullshit were you willing to swallow from that slug, Mr Kenzie? Huh?'

'Whatever it took to—'

'Maybe you'd like to go back in, talk about dog suicides and—'

'—get a fucking deal, Detective Broussard! That's what I—'

'—how much you're *down* with your man Cheese.'

'Gentlemen.' Poole stepped in between us.

The echo of our voices was raw in that parking lot, and our faces were red from shouting. The tendons in Broussard's neck bulged like lines of rope stretched taut, and I could feel adrenaline shake my blood.

'My methods were sound,' Broussard said.

'Your methods,' I said, 'sucked.'

Poole put a hand on Broussards's chest. Broussard looked down at it and kept his eyes there for a bit, his jaw muscles rolling up under the flesh.

I walked across the parking lot, felt the adrenaline turning to jelly in my calves, the gravel crunching underfoot, heard the sharp cry of a bird slicing through the air from the direction of Walden Pond, saw the sun soften and spread against the tree trunks as it died. I leaned against the back of the Taurus, placed a foot up on the bumper. Poole still had a hand on Broussard's chest, was talking to him, his lips close to the younger man's ear.

All the shouting aside, my temper hadn't really shown itself yet. If I'm truly angry, if that switch in my head has been tripped, my voice rides a flat line, becomes dead and monotonous, and a red marble of light drills through my skull and blots out all fear, all reason, all empathy. And the hotter the red marble glows, the colder my blood chills, until it's the blue of fine metal, and the monotone becomes a whisper.

That whisper – rarely with any warning to myself or anyone else – is then broken by the lash of my hand, the kick of my foot, the fury of muscle extending in an instant from that pool of red marble and ice-metal blood.

It is my father's temper.

So even before I was aware I had it, I knew its character. I'd felt its hand.

The crucial difference between my father and me – I hope – has always been a matter of action. He acted on his anger, whenever and wherever it beset him. His temper ruled him the way alcohol or pride or vanity rules other men.

At a very early age, just as the child of an alcoholic swears he'll never drink, I swore to guard against the advance of the red marble, the cold blood, the tendency toward monotone. Choice, I've always believed, is all that separates us from animals. A monkey can't choose to control his appetite. A man can. My father, at certain hideous moments, was an animal. I refuse to be.

So while I understood Broussard's rage, his desperation to find Amanda, his lashing out at Cheese Olamon's refusal to take us seriously, I refused to condone it. Because it got us nowhere. It got Amanda nowhere – except, maybe, deeper down the hole in which she already lay and that much farther away from us.

Broussard's shoes appeared on the gravel below the bumper. I felt his shadow cool the sun on my face.

'I can't do this anymore.' His voice was so soft it almost disappeared on the breeze.

'What's that?' I said.

'Let scumbags hurt kids and walk away, feel like they're clever. I can't.'

'Then quit your job,' I said.

'We have his money. He has to go through us and trade the girl to get it.'

I looked up into his face, saw the fear there, the rabid hope he'd never see another dead or hopelessly fucked-up kid again.

'What if he doesn't care about the money?' I said.

Broussard looked away.

'Oh, he cares.' Poole came over to the car, rested his hand on the trunk, but he didn't sound so sure.

'Cheese has a shitload of money,' I said.

'You know these guys,' Poole said, as Broussard stood very still, a frozen curiosity in his face. 'There's never enough money. They always want more.'

'Two hundred grand isn't pocket change to Cheese,' I said, 'but it ain't house money either. It's bribe and property-tax petty cash. For one year. What if he wants to make a moral point?'

Broussard shook his head. 'Cheese Olamon has no morals.'

'Yes, he does.' I kicked the bumper with my heel, as surprised as anyone, I think, by the vehemence in my voice. More quietly, I repeated, 'Yes, he does. And the number one moral law in his universe is: Don't fuck with Cheese.'

Poole nodded. 'And Helene did.'

'Goddamn right.'

'And if Cheese is pissed off enough, you think he'll kill the girl and say "fuck it" to the money just to send that message.'

I nodded. 'And sleep right through the night.'

Poole's face took on a gray cast as he stepped into the shadow between Broussard and me. He suddenly looked very old, no longer vaguely threatening so much as vaguely threatened, and the sense of elfin mischief had left him.

'What if,' he said, so quietly I had to lean in to hear, 'Cheese wishes to make both his moral point *and* a profit?'

'Run a bait-and-switch?' Broussard said.

Poole dug his hands into his pockets, steeled his back and shoulders against the sudden late-afternoon bite in the breeze.

'We may have tipped our hand in there, Rem.'

'How so?'

'Cheese now knows we're so desperate to get the child back that we're willing to break the rules, leave the badge at home, and step into a money-for-child scenario with no official authority.'

'And if Cheese wants to walk away a winner . . .'

'Then no one else walks away at all,' Poole said.

'We've got to get to Chris Mullen,' I said. 'See who he leads us to. Before the trade goes down.'

Poole and Broussard nodded.

'Mr Kenzie.' Broussard offered his hand. 'I was out of line in there. I let that mug get the better of me, and I could have fucked us on this.'

I took the hand. 'We'll bring her home.'

He tightened his grip on my hand. 'Alive.'

'Alive,' I said.

'You think Broussard's cracking under the strain?' Angie said.

We sat parked at the edge of the financial district on Devonshire Street, covering the rear of Devonshire Place, Chris Mullen's condo tower. The CAC detectives who'd tailed Mullen back here had gone home for the night. Several other two-man teams covered all the other key players in Cheese's crew, while we watched Mullen. Broussard and Poole covered the front of the building from the Washington Street side. It was just past midnight. Mullen had been inside for three hours.

I shrugged. 'Did you see Broussard's face when Poole talked about finding Jeannie Minelli's body in the barrel of cement?'

Angie shook her head.

'It was worse than Poole's. He looked like he was going to have a nervous breakdown just hearing about it. Hands started to shake, face got all white and shiny. The man looked bad.' I looked up at the three yellow squares on the fifteenth floor that we'd identified as Mullen's windows as one of them went black. 'Maybe he *is* losing it. He overreacted with Cheese, that's for sure.'

Angie lit a cigarette and cracked her window. The street was still. Brooked by canyons of white limestone facades and shimmering blue-glass skyscrapers, it looked like a film set at night, a giant model of a world no real people occupied. In the daytime, Devonshire would be packed with the vaguely joyous, vaguely violent hustle of pedestrians and stockbrokers, lawyers and secretaries and bicycle messengers, trucks and cabs honking their horns, briefcases, power ties, and cell phones. But after nine or so it shut down, and sitting in a car packed between all that vast and empty architecture felt like we were just one more prop in a giant museum piece, after the lights have been dimmed and the security guards have left the room.

''Member the night Glynn shot me?' Angie said.

'Yeah.'

'Just before it happened, I remember struggling with you and Evandro in the dark, all the candles in my bedroom flickering like eyes, and I thought: I can't do this anymore. I can't *invest* any more of myself – not one more piece – in all this violence and . . . shit.' She turned on the seat. 'Maybe that's what Broussard feels. I mean, how many kids can you find in pools of cement?'

I thought about the pure nothing that had come into Broussard's eyes after he'd slapped Cheese. A nothing so complete it had overwhelmed even his fury.

Angie was right: How many dead kids could you find?

'He'll burn down the city if he thinks it'll lead to Amanda,' I said.

Angie nodded. 'Both of them will.'

'And she may already be dead.'

Angie flicked her cigarette ash over the top of her window. 'Don't say that.'

'Can't help it. It's a distinct possibility. You know it. So do I.'

The towering quiet of the empty street slipped into the car for a bit.

'Cheese hates witnesses,' Angie said eventually.

'Hates 'em,' I agreed.

'If that child is dead,' Angie said, and cleared her throat, 'then Broussard definitely – and Poole most probably – will snap.'

I nodded. 'And God help whoever they think was involved.'

'You think God'll help?'

'Huh?'

'God,' she said, and crushed her cigarette in the

ashtray. 'You think He'll help Amanda's kidnappers any more than He helped her?'

'Probably not.'

'Then again . . .' She looked out the windshield.

'What?'

'If Amanda is dead and Broussard flips out, kills her kidnappers, maybe God *is* helping.'

'Heck of a strange God.'

Angie shrugged. 'You take what you can get,' she said.

14

I'd heard about Chris Mullen's banker's hours, his determination to run a nighttime business during daylight hours, and the next morning, at exactly 8:55, he walked out of Devonshire Towers and turned right on Washington.

I was parked on Washington a half block up from the condo towers, and when I picked up Mullen walking toward State in my rearview mirror, I depressed the transmit button on the walkie-talkie lying on the seat and said, 'He just left through the front.'

From her post on Devonshire Street, where no cars were allowed to park or even idle in the morning, Angie said, 'Gotcha.'

Broussard, wearing a gray T-shirt, black sweats, and a dark blue and white warm-up jacket, stood across from my car in front of Pi Alley. He sipped coffee from a Styrofoam cup and read the sports page like a jogger just finished his run. He'd rigged a headset to a receiver strapped to his waistband and painted both the earphones and receiver yellow and black to look like a Discman. He'd even sprayed water down the front of his shirt five minutes ago to make it look like sweat. These ex-vice and narcotics guys – masters of the small details of disguise.

As Mullen took a right at the flower stand in front of the Old State House, Broussard crossed Washington and followed. I saw him raise his coffee to his mouth and his lips move as he spoke into the transmitter strapped under his watchband.

'Moving east on State. I got him. Showtime, kids.'

I turned the walkie-talkie off and slipped it into my coat pocket until my part had been played. In keeping with the disguise motif of the day, I was dressed in the rattiest gray trench coat this side of a subway bum, and I'd stained it freshly this morning with egg yolk and Pepsi. My soiled T-shirt was torn across the chest and my jeans and the tops of my shoes were speckled with paint and dirt. The tips of my shoe soles were separated from the top and clapped softly as I walked, and my bare toes peeked out. I'd brushed my hair straight off my forehead and blown it dry to give it that Don King look, and what remained of the egg I'd used on the trench coat I'd rubbed into my beard.

Styling.

I unzipped my fly as I stumbled across Washington Street and poured the rest of my morning coffee down my chest. People saw me coming and sidestepped my lumbering steps and swinging arms, and I mumbled a whole stream of words I'd never learned from my mom and pushed through the gilt-edged front doors of Devonshire Place.

Boy, did the security guard look psyched to see me.

So did the three people who exited the elevator and cut a wide swath around me on the marble floor.

I leered at the two women in the trio, smiled at the cut of their legs dropping from the hems of their Anne Klein suits.

'Join me for a pizza?' I asked.

The businessman steered the women even farther away as the security guard said, 'Hey! Hey, you!'

I turned toward him as he came out from behind his gleaming black horseshoe desk. He was young and lean, and he had a finger rudely pointed in my direction.

The businessman pushed the women out of the building and pulled a cell phone from his inside pocket, extended the antenna by gripping it between his teeth, but kept walking up Washington.

'Come on,' the security guard said. 'Turn around and go out the way you came in. Right now. Come on.'

I swayed in front of him and licked my beard, came back with eggshell. I left my mouth open as I chewed on it and it crackled.

The security guard set his feet on the marble and placed a hand on his nightstick. 'You,' he said, like he was talking to a dog. 'Go.'

'Uh-ah,' I mumbled, and swayed some more.

The elevator bank dinged as another car reached the lobby.

The security guard reached for my elbow, but I pivoted and his fingers snapped at air.

I reached into my pocket. 'Got something to show you.'

The security guard pulled his nightstick from its holster. 'Hey! Keep your hands where I can see—'

'Oh, my God,' someone said as the crowd exited

the elevator and I pulled a banana from my trench coat, pointed it at the rent-a-cop.

'Jesus Christ, he's got a banana!' The voice came from behind me. Angie.

Always the improviser. Couldn't stick to the script.

The crowd from the elevator was trying to cross the lobby, avoid eye contact with me, and still see enough of the incident to have the day's best story at the watercooler.

'Sir,' the security guard said, trying to sound authoritative and yet polite, now that several tenants bore witness, 'put the banana down.'

I pointed the banana at him. 'Got this from my cousin. He's an orangutan.'

'Shouldn't someone call the police?' a woman asked.

'Ma'am,' the security guard said, a bit desperately, 'I have this under control.'

I tossed the banana at him. He dropped his nightstick and jumped back as if he'd been shot.

Someone in the crowd yelped, and several people jogged for the doors.

At the elevator bank, Angie caught my eye and pointed at my hair. 'Very hot,' she mouthed, and then she slipped into the elevator and the doors closed.

The security guard picked up his nightstick and dropped the banana. He looked ready to rush me. I didn't know how many people remained behind me – maybe three – but at least one of them could be thinking about heroically rushing the vagrant as well.

I turned so that my back was to the horseshoe desk

and elevators. Only two men, one woman, and the security guard remained. And both men were inching toward the doors. The woman seemed fascinated, however. Her mouth was open, and one hand was pressed against the base of her throat.

'Whatever happened to Men at Work?' I asked her.

'What?' The security guard took another step toward me.

'The Australian band.' I turned my head, locked the security guard in a kind, curious stare. 'Very big in the early eighties. Huge. Do you know what happened to them?'

'What? No.'

I cocked my head as I stared at him, scratched my temple. For a long moment, no one in the lobby moved or even breathed it seemed.

'Oh,' I said eventually. I shrugged. 'My mistake. Keep the banana.'

I stepped over it on my way out, and the two men flattened against the wall.

I winked at one of them. 'First-rate security guard you got. Without him, I'da busted up the place.' I pushed open the doors onto Washington Street.

I was about to give a covert thumbs-up to Poole, who sat in the Taurus on the corner of School and Washington, when the heels of two palms hit my shoulder and chucked me into the side of the building.

'Out of my way, you fucking derelict.'

I turned my head in time to see Chris Mullen walk back through the revolving doors, gesture toward the frozen security guard in my direction, and keep walking toward the elevator bank.

I broke into the stream of pedestrians filling the street, cleared the walkie-talkie from my pocket, and turned it on.

'Poole, Mullen's back.'

'Affirmative, Mr Kenzie. Broussard's contacting Ms Gennaro as we speak. Turn around, go to your car. Do not blow our covers.' I could see his lips move behind his windshield, and then he dropped his walkie-talkie back onto his seat and glared at me.

I turned in the crowd.

A woman with coke-bottle glasses and hair tied back so tightly off her forehead her face looked like a bug's stared up at me.

'Are you some kind of cop?'

I raised a finger to my lips. 'Sssh.' I put the walkie-talkie back in my trench coat, left her standing there, mouth open, and walked back to my car.

As I opened the trunk, I saw Broussard leaning against the window of Eddie Bauer. He held his hand up by his ear and spoke into his wrist.

I tuned to his channel as I leaned under the open trunk.

'. . . . say again, Miss Gennaro, subject en route. Abort immediately.'

I brushed all the eggshell from my beard and put a baseball cap over my head.

'Say again,' Broussard whispered. 'Abort. Out.'

I tossed the trench coat in the trunk, removed my black leather jacket, placed the walkie-talkie in the pocket, and closed the jacket over my soiled T-shirt. I closed the trunk and cut back through the crowds to Eddie Bauer, stared through the window at the mannequins.

'She respond?'

'No,' Broussard said.

'Was her walkie-talkie working?'

'Couldn't tell. We have to assume she heard me and clicked off before Mullen could hear it.'

'We go up,' I said.

'You take a move toward that building, I'll blow your leg off at the knee.'

'She's exposed up there. If her walkie-talkie was on the fritz and she didn't hear your—'

'I won't allow you to queer this surveillance just because you're sleeping with her.' He came off the window and passed me in a loose, loping, post-jog stride. 'She's a professional. Why don't you start acting like one?'

He walked up the street and I looked at my watch: 9:15 A.M.

Mullen had been inside four minutes. Why'd he turn around in the first place? Had Broussard blown the tail?

No. Broussard was too good. I'd only seen him because I knew to look for him, and even then he blended into crowds so well my eyes had skipped over him once before I'd identified him.

I looked at my watch again: 9:16.

If Angie had gotten Broussard's message as soon as he'd realized Mullen was headed back to Devonshire Place, she would have been in the elevators, or possibly have gotten as far as the outside of Mullen's door. She would have turned and headed right for the stairwell. And she'd be down by now.

9:17.

I watched the entrance to Devonshire Place. A pair of young stockbrokers stepped out in shiny Hugo

196

Boss suits, Gucci shoes, and Geoffrey Beene ties, hair so thick with gel it would take a woodchipper to muss it. They stepped aside for a slim woman in a dark-blue power suit and a matching pair of wafer-thin Revos over her eyes, checked out her ass as she stepped into a taxi.

9:18.

The only way Angie would still be up there was if she'd been forced to hide in Mullen's apartment or if he'd caught her, either inside or at his door.

9:19.

She'd never have been dumb enough to hop back in the elevators if she had, in fact, gotten Broussard's message. Stand there and see the car door open to Chris Mullen on the other side . . .

Hey, Ange, long time no see.

You too, Chris.

What brings you by my building?

Visiting a friend.

Yeah? Aren't you working that missing girl case?

Why do you have a gun pointed at me, Chris?

9:20.

I glanced across Washington to the corner of School Street.

Poole met my eyes, shook his head very deliberately.

Maybe she had reached the lobby but was being harassed by the security guard.

Miss, hold on. I don't remember seeing you in here before.

I'm new.

I don't think so. His hand goes to the phone, dials 911 . . .

But she'd be out the door by then.

197

9:22.

I took a step toward the building. Took another one. Then stopped.

If nothing had gone wrong, if Angie had simply turned off her walkie-talkie so the squawk wouldn't alert anyone to her presence and was, as I stood there, standing on the other side of a fifteenth-floor exit door, watching Mullen's apartment door through a small square of glass, and I stepped in front of the entrance just as Mullen walked out, recognized me . . .

I leaned back against the wall.

9:24.

Fourteen minutes since Mullen had shoved me into the wall and entered the building.

The walkie-talkie in my jacket purred against my chest. I pulled it out and there was a quick low bleat, followed by: 'He's coming back down.'

Angie's voice.

'Where are you?'

'Thank God for fifty-inch TVs, is all I can say.'

'You're *inside?*' Broussard said.

''Course. Nice place, but easy locks, man, I swear.'

'What brought him back?'

'His suit. It's a long story. Tell you later. He should be reaching the street any second.'

Mullen exited the building wearing a blue suit instead of the black one he'd worn on the way in. His tie was different, too. I was staring at the knot when the head above it swung my way and I glanced down at my shoes without moving my head. Quick movements are the first thing your paranoid drug dealer types notice in a crowd, so I wasn't about to turn away.

I counted down from ten very slowly, thumbed down the volume on the walkie-talkie in my pocket, and barely heard Broussard's voice. 'He's moving again. I got him.'

I looked up as Mullen's shoulders moved in front of a young girl in a bright yellow jacket, and I turned my head slightly and picked up Broussard sliding through the crowd where Court became State Street as Mullen turned right before the Old State House and cut through the alley again.

I turned back to the window of Eddie Bauer, met my reflection.

'Whew,' I said.

15

An hour later, Angie opened the passenger door of the Crown Victoria and said, 'Wired for sound, man. Wired for sound.'

I'd moved the car to the fourth story of the Pi Alley garage and pointed it toward Devonshire Place.

'You bugged every room?'

She lit a cigarette. 'The phones, too.'

I looked at my watch. She'd been in there an hour flat. 'What're you, CIA?'

She smiled around her cigarette. 'I tell you, I might have to kill you later, babe.'

'So what was up with the suit?'

She had a far-off look in her eyes as she stared through the windshield at the facade of Devonshire Place. Then she shook her head slightly.

'The suits. Right. He talks to himself.'

'Mullen?'

She nodded. 'In the third person.'

'Must have picked it up from Cheese.'

'He comes in the door going, "Great fucking choice, Mullen. A black suit on a Friday. You out of your fucking mind?" Like that.'

'I'd like Inane Superstitions for three hundred, Alex.'

She chuckled. 'Exactly. So then he goes in his bedroom and he's thrashing around in there, ripping his suit off, slamming hangers together in the closet, ya ya ya. Anyway, it takes him a few minutes, and then he selects a new suit and he puts it on, and I'm thinking, Good, he's outa here, because I'm getting real cramped behind that TV, piles of cables back there like snakes . . .'

'And?'

Angie can get lost in moments like these, so sometimes a gentle prodding helps.

She scowled at me. 'Mister Cut-to-the-Chase, over here. *So* . . . then suddenly I hear him talking again. He's going. "Fuckhead. Hey, fuckhead! Yeah, you!"'

'What?' I leaned forward.

'Interested again, are we?' She winked. 'Yeah, so I think he's spotted me. I think I'm bagged. Cooked. Right?' Her large brown eyes had grown huge.

'Right.'

She took a drag off her cigarette. 'Nah. Talking to himself again.'

'He calls himself "fuckhead"?'

'When the mood strikes him, apparently. "Hey, fuckhead, you're going to wear a yellow tie with *this* suit? That's good. Real good, fuck face."'

'Fuck face.'

'I swear to God. A bit limited on the vocabulary, I'd say. So then there's more thrashing around as he gets another tie, puts it on, mumbles under his breath the whole way. And I'm thinking, He'll get the tie right, be halfway out the door, and decide the shirt's wrong. I'll be so cramped, I'll need traction to get out from behind his TV.'

'And?'

'He left. I called you guys.' She flicked her cigarette out the window. 'End of story.'

'Were you in the apartment when Broussard walkie-talkied he was on his way back?'

She shook her head. 'At Mullen's door with picks in hand.'

'You kidding me?'

'What?'

'You broke in *after* you knew he was coming back?'

She shrugged. 'Something came over me.'

'You're nuts.'

She gave me a throaty chuckle. 'Nuts enough to keep you interested, Slick. That's all I need.'

I couldn't decide whether I wanted to kiss her or kill her.

The walkie-talkie squawked on the seat between us, and Broussard's voice popped through the speaker. 'Poole, you got him?'

'Affirm. Taxi moving south on Purchase, heading for the expressway.'

'Kenzie.'

'Yeah?'

'Miss Gennaro with you?'

'Affirm,' I said in my deepest voice. Angie punched my arm.

'Stand by. Let's see where he's going. I'm going to start walking back.'

We listened to a minute or so of dead air before Poole came back on. 'He's on the expressway and heading south. Ms Gennaro?'

'Yeah, Poole.'

'Are all our friends in place?'

'Every last one.'

'Turn on your receivers and leave your position. Pick up Broussard and head south.'

'You got it. Detective Broussard?'

'I'm heading west on Broad Street.'

I put the car in reverse.

'We'll meet you at the corner of Broad and Batterymarch.'

'Copy that.'

As I left the garage, Angie turned on the boxy portable receiver in the backseat and adjusted the volume until we heard the soft hiss of Mullen's empty apartment. I cut through the parking ramp under Devonshire Place, took a left on Water, rolled through Post Office and Liberty squares, and found Broussard leaning against a street lamp in front of a deli.

He hopped in the car as Poole's voice came over the walkie-talkie. 'Getting off the expressway in Dorchester by the South Bay Shopping Center.'

'Back to the old neighborhood,' Broussard said. 'You Dorchester boys just can't stay away.'

'It's like a magnet,' I assured him.

'Scratch that,' Poole said. 'He's taking a left on Boston Street, heading toward Southie.'

I said, 'Not a very strong magnet, however.'

Ten minutes later we passed Poole's empty Taurus on Gavin Street in the heart of Old Colony Project in South Boston and parked half a block up. Poole's last transmission had told us he was following Mullen into Old Colony on foot. Until he contacted us again, there wasn't much to do but sit and wait and look at the project.

Not a bad-looking sight, actually. The streets are clean and tree-lined and curve gracefully through red-brick buildings with freshly painted white trim. Small hedges and squares of grass lie under most first-floor windows. The fence encircling the garden is upright, rooted, and free of rust. As far as projects go, Old Colony is one of the most aesthetically pleasing you're apt to find in this country.

It has a bit of a heroin problem, though. And a teen suicide problem, which probably stems from the heroin. And the heroin probably stems from the fact that even if you do grow up in the prettiest project in the world, it's still a project, and you're still growing up there, and heroin ain't much but it beats staring at the same walls and the same bricks and the same fences your whole life.

'I grew up here,' Broussard said, from the back-seat. He peered out the window, as if expecting it to shrink or grow in front of him.

'With your name?' Angie said. 'You can't be serious.'

He smiled and gave her a small shrug. 'Father was a merchant marine from New Orleans. Or "Nawlins," as he called it. He got in some trouble down there, ended up working the docks, in Charlestown and then Southie.' He cocked his head toward the brick buildings. 'We settled here. Every third kid was named Frankie O'Brien and the rest were Sullivans and Sheas and Carrolls and Connellys. And if their first name wasn't Frank, it was Mike or Sean or Pat.' He raised his eyebrows at me.

I held up my hands. 'Oops.'

'So having a name like Remy Broussard . . . yeah,

I'd say it toughened me up.' He smiled broadly and looked out at the projects, whistled softly. 'Man, talk about going home again.'

'You don't live in Southie anymore?' Angie asked.

He shook his head. 'Haven't since my dad died.'

'You miss it?'

He pursed his lips and glanced at some kids running past on the sidewalk, shouting, throwing what appeared to be bottle caps at each other for no apparent reason.

'Not really, no. Always felt like a misplaced country boy in the city. Even in New Orleans.' He shrugged. 'I like trees.'

He turned the frequency dial on his walkie-talkie, raised it to his lips. 'Detective Pasquale, this is Broussard. Over.'

Pasquale was one of the CAC detectives assigned to watch Concord Prison for any visitors who'd come to see Cheese. 'This is Pasquale.'

'Anything?'

'Nothing. No visitors since you guys yesterday.'

'Phone calls?'

'Negative. Olamon lost phone privileges when he got in a beef on the yard last month.'

'Okay. Broussard out.' He dropped the walkie-talkie on the seat. He raised his head suddenly and watched a car come up the street toward us. 'What have we here?'

A smoke-gray Lexus RX 300 with a vanity plate that read PHARO pulled past us and drove another twenty or thirty yards before banging a U-turn and pulling into a space along the curb and blocking an alley. It was a fifty-thousand-dollar sport utility vehicle built for off-road travel and those occasional jungle safaris that come through these parts, and every inch of it gleamed as if it had been polished with silk pillows. It fit right in with all the Escorts, Golfs, and Geos parked along the street, the early eighties Buick with green trash bags taped over the shattered rear window.

'The RX 300,' Broussard said, in the deep bass of a commercial announcer. 'Pristine comfort for the drug dealer who can't be hindered by snowstorms and bad roads.' He leaned forward and rested his arms on the seat back between us, his eyes on the rearview mirror. 'Ladies and gentlemen, meet Pharaoh Gutierrez, Lord High of the city of Lowell.'

A slim Hispanic man stepped out of the Lexus. He wore black linen trousers and a lime-green shirt, clasped at the neck with a black stud, underneath a black silk dinner jacket with tails that fell to the bend in his knees.

'Quite the fashion plate,' Angie said.

'Ain't he just?' Broussard said. 'And he's dressing conservative today. You should see the man when he goes out clubbing.'

Pharaoh Gutierrez straightened his tails and smoothed the thighs of his trousers.

'What the fuck is he doing here?' Broussard said softly.

'Who is he?'

'He handles Cheese's action in Lowell and Lawrence, all the real sexy old mill towns. Rumor has it he's the only one can deal with all the psycho fishermen up in New Bedford to boot.'

'So then it makes sense,' Angie said.

Broussard's eyes remained fixed on the mirror. 'What's that?'

'Him meeting with Chris Mullen.'

Broussard shook his head. 'No, no, no. Mullen and the Pharaoh despise each other. Something to do with a woman, I heard; goes back a decade. That's why Gutierrez was banished to the 495 Beltway dumps, and Mullen gets to stay cosmopolitan. This makes *no* sense.'

Gutierrez looked up and down the street, using both hands to grasp the lapels of his dinner jacket like a judge, his chin tilted up slightly. His long thin nose sniffed the air. There was something recalcitrant and illogical in his stiff bearing; it didn't go with his slim build. He cut the figure of a man who brooked no offense, yet always seemed to be expecting one. So insecure he'd kill to prove he wasn't.

He reminded me of a few guys I've known – shorter guys, usually, or slight of build, but so ferociously determined to prove they could be just as dangerous as the big guys that they never stopped fighting, never paused for breath, ate too quickly. The men I'd known like this either became cops or criminals. There didn't seem to be much room in between. And they often died quickly and young, an angry question frozen in their faces.

'He looks like a pain in the ass,' I said.

Broussard placed his hands on the seat back, rested his chin on them. 'Yeah, that about sums the Pharaoh up. Too much to prove, not enough time to prove it. I always figured him for snapping, maybe walking up to Chris Mullen and busting a cap in his forehead some day, Cheese Olamon be damned.'

'Maybe this is that day,' Angie said.

'Maybe,' Broussard said.

Gutierrez walked around the Lexus and leaned back against the front quarter panel. He looked down the alley he blocked, then at his watch.

'Mullen's coming your way.' Poole's voice was a whisper over the walkie-talkie.

'Unfriendly third party out front,' Broussard said. 'Hang back, man.'

'Copy.'

Angie reached up and tilted the rearview mirror a bit to the right so we had a clear view of Gutierrez, the Lexus, and the edge of the alley.

Mullen appeared at the end of the alley. He ran a palm down his tie, looked at Gutierrez and the Lexus blocking his path for a still moment.

Broussard leaned back from the front seat, removed his Glock from his waistband, and racked the slide.

'This goes bad, don't move from this car, just call 911.'

Mullen held up a slim black valise and smiled.

Gutierrez nodded.

Broussard ducked down on the seat and hooked his fingers over the passenger door handle.

Mullen reached out his free hand, and after a moment Gutierrez took it. Then the two men hugged, clapped each other's backs with their fists.

Broussard let go of the door handle. 'Oh, this is interesting.'

When they broke their clinch, Gutierrez held the valise. He turned to the Lexus and opened the door with a flourish and small bow, and Mullen climbed into the passenger seat. Then Gutierrez walked around to the driver's door, climbed in, and started the engine.

'Poole,' Broussard said into his walkie-talkie, 'we got Pharaoh Gutierrez and Chris Mullen out here acting like long-lost brothers.'

'Hush your mouth.'

'Swear to God, man.'

Pharaoh Gutierrez's Lexus pulled away from the curb and rolled past us.

As it continued up the street, Broussard raised the walkie-talkie to his lips. 'Clear, Poole. We're tailing a dark-gray Lexus SUV driven by Gutierrez with Mullen riding shotgun. They're heading out of the project.'

As we passed the second alley, Poole came jogging out. He wore a vagrant's disguise similar to my own except he'd added the dash of a dark-blue bandanna. He removed it as he crossed behind our car and trotted to the Taurus, and we followed the Lexus back onto Boston Street. Gutierrez took a right, and we followed into Andrew Square and then over to the annex road that ran parallel to the expressway.

'If Mullen and Gutierrez are friends now,' Angie said, 'what does that mean?'

'Shitload of bad news for Cheese Olamon.'

'Cheese is in prison, his two lieutenants – supposedly mortal enemies – join up against him?'

Broussard nodded. 'Take over the empire.'

'Where's that leave Amanda?' I said.

Broussard shrugged. 'In the middle somewhere.'

'The middle of what?' I said. 'Crosshairs?'

16

One of the things that happens when you follow scumbags around for a while is that you grow a little envious of their lifestyles.

Oh, it's not the big things – the sixty-thousand-dollar cars, the million-dollar condos, the fifty-yard-line seats at Patriots' games – that really get to you, though they can be annoying. It's the small, everyday carte blanche a good drug dealer enjoys that seems truly alien to the rest of us working folk.

For example, in all the time we watched them, I rarely saw Chris Mullen, or Pharaoh Gutierrez obey traffic signals. Red lights, apparently, were for the wee people, stop signs for suckers. The fifty-five-miles-per-hour speed limit on the expressway? Please. Why go fifty-five when ninety gets you there all that much faster? Why use the passing lane when the breakdown lane is free and clear?

And then there was the parking situation. A parking space in Boston is about as common as a ski slope in the Sahara. Little old ladies in mink stoles have fought gun battles over a contested spot. In the mid-eighties some moron actually paid a quarter million dollars for a deeded parking slip in a Beacon

Hill garage, and that didn't include monthly maintenance fees.

Boston: We're small, we're cold, but we'll kill for a good parking space. Come on up. Bring the family.

Gutierrez and Mullen and several of their minions we followed over the next few days didn't have that problem. They simply double-parked: wherever and whenever the mood struck them, for as long as they desired.

Once, on Columbus Avenue in the South End, Chris Mullen finished his lunch and walked out of Hammersleys to find a very pissed-off artiste complete with signature goatee and three studs in one ear waiting for him. Chris had blocked in the artiste's dumpy Civic with his sleek black Benz. The artiste's girlfriend was with him, so he had to make a stink. From where we sat, idling a half block up on the other side of the street, we couldn't hear what was said, but we got the gist. The artiste and his girlfriend shouted and pointed. As Chris approached he tucked his cashmere scarf under his dark Armani raincoat, smoothed his tie, and kicked the artiste in the kneecap so deftly the guy was on the ground before his girlfriend ran out of things to say. Chris stood so close to the woman they could have been mistaken for lovers. He placed his index finger against her forehead and cocked his thumb, held it there for what probably seemed like hours to her. Then he dropped the hammer. He took his finger back from the woman's head and blew on it. He smiled at her. He leaned in and gave her a quick peck on the cheek.

Then Chris walked around to his car, got in, and drove off, left the girl staring after him, stunned, still unaware, I think, that her boyfriend was howling in pain, writhing on the sidewalk like a cat with a broken back.

Besides ourselves and Broussard and Poole, several cops from the CAC unit worked the surveillance, and in addition to Gutierrez and Mullen we observed a rogues' gallery of Cheese Olamon's men. There was Carlos 'the Shiv' Orlando, who oversaw the day-to-day operations in the housing projects and kept a stack of comic books with him wherever he went. There was JJ MacNally, who'd worked his way up to head pimp of all non-Vietnamese hookers in North Dorchester but dated and doted upon a Vietnamese girl who looked to be all of fifteen. Joel Green and Hicky Vister oversaw loansharking and bookmaking from a booth in Elsinore's, a bar Cheese owned in Lower Mills, and Buddy Perry and Brian Box – two guys so dumb they'd need maps to find their own bathrooms – ran the muscle.

It was not, from even a cursory glance, a think tank. Cheese had risen through the ranks by paying his dues, showing respect, paying homage to anyone who could hurt him, and stepping up whenever there was a power vacuum. The biggest of these happened a few years back when Jack Rouse, godfather of the Irish mob in Dorchester and Southie, vanished along with his chief henchman, Kevin Hurlihy, a guy who had a hornet's nest in his brain and industrial corrosive for blood. When they disappeared, Cheese put in a bid for upper Dorchester and got the action. Cheese was smart, Chris Mullen was halfway there, and Pharaoh Gutierrez seemed to have a bit on the ball. The rest of Cheese's guys, though, conformed to his policy of never hiring anyone who, besides being greedy (which Cheese regarded as a given in this business), was smart enough to do anything about it.

So he hired chuckleheads and adrenaline freaks and guys who liked to wad their money in rubber bands and talk like James Caan and swagger, but who had very little ambition beyond that.

Every time Mullen or Gutierrez went anywhere indoors – an apartment, a warehouse, an office building – the place was immediately tagged for CAC surveillance and over the next three days was watched around the clock and infiltrated if possible.

The bugs we'd placed in Mullen's place revealed that he called his mother every night at seven and had the same conversation about why he wasn't married, why he was too selfish to give his mother grandkids, why he didn't date nice girls, and how come he always looked so pale when he had such a good job working for the Forest Service. At seven-thirty every night, he watched *Jeopardy!*, and answered the questions aloud, batting about .300. He had a real gift for geography questions but flat-out sucked when it came to seventeenth-century French artists.

We heard him talk to several girlfriends, bullshit with Gutierrez about cars and movies and the Bruins, but like a lot of criminals, he seemed to have a healthy distrust of talking business over the phone.

The search for Amanda McCready had failed on all other fronts, and police manpower was gradually being shifted away from CAC and into other areas.

On the fourth day of surveillance, Broussard and Poole got a call from Lieutenant Doyle telling them to be down at the precinct in half an hour and to make sure they had us with them.

'This could be ugly,' Poole said, as we drove downtown.

'Why us?' Angie said.

'That's what we meant about ugly,' Poole said, and smiled as Angie stuck her tongue out at him.

Doyle didn't seem to be having a great day. His skin was gray and the flesh under his eyes was dark and his entire body smelled of cold coffee.

'Close the door,' he said to Poole, as we entered.

We took seats across the desk from him as Poole shut the door behind us.

Doyle said, 'When I set up CAC and was looking for good detectives, I looked everywhere but Vice and Narcotics. Now why would I do that, Detective Broussard?'

Broussard played with his tie. 'Because everyone's afraid to work with Vice and Narco, sir.'

'And why is that, Sergeant Raftopoulos?'

Poole smiled. 'Because we're so pretty, sir.'

Doyle made a keep-it-coming gesture with his hand and nodded several times to himself.

'Because,' he said eventually, 'Narco and Vice detectives are cowboys. Crazy cops. They like the juice, like the jack, like the rush. Like to do things their own way.'

Poole nodded. 'Often an unfortunate side effect of the assignments, yes, sir.'

'But I was assured by your lieutenant at the Oh-Six that you two were stand-up guys, very effective, very by-the-book. Yes?'

'That's the rumor, sir,' Broussard said.

Doyle gave him a tight smile. 'You made Detective First last year. Correct, Broussard?'

'Yes, sir.'

'Care to be busted back to Second or Third? Patrolman, possibly?'

'Uh, no, sir. That I would not enjoy much, sir.'

'Then stop breaking my balls with the wise-ass shit, Detective.'

Broussard coughed into his fist. 'Yes, sir.'

Doyle picked a sheet of paper off his desk, read it for a bit, placed it back down. 'You've got half the detectives in the CAC working the surveillance of Olamon's men. When I asked why, you said you'd received an anonymous tip that Olamon was involved in the disappearance of Amanda McCready.' He nodded to himself again, then looked up and locked eyes with Poole. 'Care to revise that statement?'

'Sir?'

Doyle looked at his watch and stood up. 'I'll count down from ten. Tell me the truth before I get to one, and maybe you'll keep your jobs. Ten,' he said.

'Sir.'

'Nine.'

'Sir, we don't know—'

'Oooh. Eight. Seven.'

'We believe Amanda McCready was kidnapped by Cheese Olamon in order to ensure the return of money her mother stole from Olamon's organization.' Poole sat back, shrugged at Broussard.

'So, it's kidnapping,' Doyle said, and sat down.

'Possibly,' Broussard said.

'Which is federal.'

'Only if we're sure,' Poole said.

Doyle opened a desk drawer and removed a tape recorder, which he tossed on top of the desk. He looked at Angie and me for the first time since we'd entered the office and pressed PLAY.

There was a bit of scratchy static, then the sound of a phone ringing, then a voice I recognized as Lionel's said, 'Hello.'

A woman's voice on the other end of the line said, 'Tell your sister to send the old cop, the good-looking cop, and the two private detectives to the Granite Rail Quarry tomorrow night at eight o'clock. Tell them to approach from the Quincy side, up the old railway slope.'

'Excuse me. Who is this?'

'Tell them to bring what they found in Charlestown.'

'Ma'am I'm not sure what—'

'Tell them what they found in Charlestown will be traded for what we found in Dorchester.' The woman's voice, low and flat, lightened. 'You got that, honey?'

'I'm not sure. Can I get a piece of paper?'

A throaty chuckle. 'You're a caution, honey. Really. It's all on tape. For anyone who's listening? If we see anyone but the four I mentioned at Granite Rail tomorrow night, that package from Dorchester goes over a cliff.'

'No one's—'

'Bye-bye, honey. You stay sweet now. You hear?'

'No, wait—'

There was a click, followed by the harsh sound of Lionel's breathing, followed by a dial tone.

Doyle turned the tape recorder off. He leaned

back in his chair and made a steeple of his fingers, tapped it against his lower lip.

After a few minutes' silence, he said, 'What did you find in Charlestown, guys?'

No one said anything.

He swiveled his chair, looked at Poole and Broussard. 'You want me to do the countdown thing again?'

Poole looked at Broussard. Broussard held out a hand, palm up, and swung it back in Poole's direction.

'Thanks, sweetie.' Poole turned to Doyle. 'We found two hundred thousand dollars in the backyard of David Martin and Kimmie Niehaus.'

'The bloaters in C-Town,' Doyle said.

'Yes, sir.'

'And this two hundred thousand – it's been tagged as evidence, of course.'

Poole swung his hand in Broussard's direction.

Broussard looked at his shoes. 'Not exactly, sir.'

'Really.' Doyle picked up a pencil, jotted something in the notepad by his elbow. 'And after I call Internal Affairs and you're both summarily fired by this department, which security firm do you think you'll work for?'

'Well, you see—'

'Or will it be a bar?' Doyle smiled broadly. 'Civilians love that – knowing their bartender's a former cop. Get to hear all those war stories.'

'Lieutenant,' Poole said, 'with all due respect, we'd love to keep our jobs.'

'I'm sure you would.' Doyle wrote some more on the notepad. 'Should have thought of that before you misappropriated evidence in a murder

217

investigation. That's a felony, gentlemen.' He picked up the phone, punched two numbers, waited. 'Michael, get me the names of the investigating officers on the David Martin/Kimmie Niehaus homicides. I'll hold.' He tucked the phone against his shoulder, tapped the pencil eraser against the desktop, and whistled lightly through his teeth. A small, tinny voice emanated from the receiver, and he leaned into the phone again. 'Yeah. Got it.' He scribbled on the notepad and hung up. 'Detectives Daniel Guden and Mark Leonard. Know 'em?'

'Vaguely,' Broussard said.

'I can assume then that you failed to let them know what you found in the backyard of their victims.'

'Yes, sir.'

'Yes, sir, you let them know? Or yes, sir, you failed to let them know?'

'The latter,' Poole said.

Doyle placed his hands behind his head and leaned back in his chair again. 'Run it down for me now, gentlemen. If it doesn't smell as bad as it does at the moment, maybe – and I mean only *maybe* – you'll have jobs next week. But I promise you this: They won't be with CAC. I want fucking cowboys, I'll watch *Rio Bravo*.'

Poole told him everything, from the time Angie and I had spotted Chris Mullen on the newscast videos until now. The only thing he left out was the ransom note they'd found in Kimmie's underwear, and once I replayed the tape of Lionel's conversation with the woman in my head, I realized that without the note there was no hard evidence that Lionel's caller was

218

demanding money for a child. No evidence of kidnapping: no Feds.

'Where's the money?' Doyle asked, when Poole finished.

'I have it,' I said.

'You do, do you?' he said, without glancing in my direction. 'This is very good, Sergeant Poole. Two hundred thousand dollars in stolen money – and stolen evidence, I might add – in the hands of a private citizen whose name has been brought up over the years in connection with three unsolved homicides and – some say – the disappearance of Jack Rouse and Kevin Hurlihy.'

'Not me,' I said. 'Must be confusing me with that other Patrick Kenzie guy.'

Angie kicked my ankle.

'Pat,' Doyle said, and leaned forward in his chair, looked at me.

'Patrick,' I said.

''Scuse me,' Doyle said, 'Patrick, I have you dead to rights on receiving stolen property, obstruction of justice, interfering in a capitol felony investigation, and tampering with evidence in the same. Care to fuck with me some more and see what I can dig up if I really don't like you?'

I shifted in my chair.

'What's that?' Doyle said. 'I didn't hear you.'

'No,' I said.

He put his hand behind his ear. 'Again?'

'No,' I said. 'Sir.'

He smiled, slapped the desk with his fingers. 'Very good, son. Speak when spoken to. Otherwise, keep it zipped.' He nodded at Angie. 'Like your partner there. Always heard you were the brains of the operation, ma'am. Seems to be holding true here.' He swiveled back toward Poole and Broussard. 'So you two geniuses decided to play at Cheese Olamon's level and swap the money for the kid.'

'Pretty much, sir.'

'And the reason I shouldn't turn this over to the Feds is?' He held out his hands.

'Because there's been no official ransom demand,' Broussard said.

Doyle glanced down at the tape recorder. 'What did we just listen to, then?'

'Well, sir.' Poole leaned across the desk, pointed at the tape recorder. 'If you listen to it again you'll hear a woman suggesting a trade of "something" found in Charlestown for "something" found in Dorchester. That woman could be discussing the trade of stamps for baseball cards.'

'The fact that she called the mother of a missing child, that wouldn't intrigue our federal law enforcement brothers?'

'Well, technically,' Broussard said, 'she called the brother of the missing child's mother.'

'And said, "Tell your sister,"' Doyle said.

'Yes, true, but still, sir, no hard evidence that we're talking about a kidnapping. And you know the Feds, they fucked up Ruby Ridge, Waco, cut insane deals with the Boston mob, they—'

Doyle held up a hand. 'We're all aware of recent Bureau transgressions, Detective Broussard.' He looked down at the tape recorder, then at the notes he'd jotted by his elbow. 'The Granite Rail Quarry is not our jurisdiction. It's shared between the State

Police and the Quincy P.D. So . . .' He clapped his hands together. 'Okay.'

'Okay?' Broussard said.

'Okay means no explicit mention of the McCready kid means we propose a joint effort with the Staties and the Quincy blues. Leave the Feds at home. The caller said no cops besides you two on the Granite Rail Quarry trail. Fine. But we're going to lock down those hills, gentlemen. We're going to tie a rope around the Quincy quarries, and as soon as that kid's out of harm's way, we're going to throw a lead blanket over Mullen, Gutierrez, and whoever else thinks he's going to have a two-hundred-grand payday.' He slapped his fingers on the desktop again. 'Sound good?'

'Yes, sir.'

'Yes, sir.'

He gave them that broad, icy smile of his. 'And once that's done, I'm transferring you humps out of my division and out of my precinct. Anything goes wrong at that quarry tomorrow night? I'm transferring you to the Bomb Squad. You get to mark time till your retirements climbing under cars and hoping they don't go boom. Any questions?'

'No, sir.'

'No, sir.'

A swivel back our way. 'Mr Kenzie and Miss Gennaro, you are civilians. I don't like your being in this office, never mind going up that hill tomorrow night, but I don't have much choice. So here's the deal: You will not engage the suspects in any exchange of gunfire. You will not speak with the suspects. Should there be a confrontation, you will drop to your knees and cover your heads. When this is over, you will not discuss any aspects of the operation with the press. And you will not write books about the affair. Clear?'

I nodded.

Angie nodded.

'If you fail me on any of these points, I'll have your licenses and gun permits revoked, and I'll put the Cold Case squad on the Marion Socia homicide, call my friends in the press, and have them do a retrospective on the strange disappearance of Jack Rouse and Kevin Hurlihy. Understood?'

We nodded.

'Give me a "Yes, Lieutenant Doyle."'

'Yes, Lieutenant Doyle,' Angie murmured.

'Yes, Lieutenant Doyle,' I said.

'Excellent.' Doyle leaned back in his chair and held his arms out wide to the four of us. 'Now get the fuck out of my sight.'

'Swell guy,' Angie said, when we reached the street.

'He's just an old softie,' Poole said.

'Really?'

Poole looked at me like I was sniffing glue and shook his head very slowly.

'Oh,' I said.

'The money is safe, isn't it, Mr Kenzie?'

I nodded. 'You want it now?'

Poole and Broussard looked at each other, then shrugged.

'No point,' Broussard said. 'There'll be a war room meeting sometime tomorrow between us and the Staties and the Quincy boys. Bring it then.'

'Who knows?' Poole said. 'Maybe, with all the

manpower we have staking out Olamon's people, we'll catch one of them leaving the house for the quarries tomorrow with the child in tow. We'll drop 'em then and this whole thing'll be over.'

'Sure, Poole,' Angie said. 'Sure. It'll be that easy.'

Poole sighed and rocked back on his heels.

'Man,' Broussard said, 'I don't want to work for no Bomb Squad.'

Poole chuckled. 'This,' he said, 'is the Bomb Squad, boy.'

We sat on the steps of Beatrice and Lionel's front porch and gave them as much of an update and recent case history as we could, fudging any details that could possibly put them under federal indictment if this blew up in our faces at a later date.

'So,' Beatrice said when we finished, 'this all happened because Helene pulled one of her fucked-up schemes and ripped off the wrong guy.'

I nodded.

Lionel picked at a large callus on the side of his thumb, blew air out of his mouth in a steady rush. 'She's my sister,' he said eventually, 'but this – this is . . .'

'Unforgivable,' Beatrice said.

He looked back at her, then turned back to me as if he'd had tonic water splashed in his face. 'Yeah. Unforgivable.'

Angie came over to the railing and I stood up, felt her warm hand slide into mine.

'If it's any consolation,' she said, 'I doubt anyone could have seen this coming.'

Beatrice crossed the porch and sat on the steps beside her husband. She took both his large hands in hers and they looked far off down the street for a minute or so, their faces drawn and empty and angry and resigned all at the same time.

'I just don't understand,' Beatrice said. 'I just don't understand,' she whispered.

'Will they kill her?' Lionel looked over his shoulder at us.

'No,' I said. 'There's no sense in that.'

Angie squeezed my hand to hold me up against the weight of the lie.

Back at the apartment, I took the first shower to wash off four days of sitting in cars and following scumbags around town, and Angie took the second.

When she came out, she stood in the living room doorway, the white towel wrapped tightly around her honey skin, and ran a brush back through her hair, watching me as I sat in the armchair and jotted notes of our meeting with Lieutenant Doyle.

I looked up, met her eyes.

They are amazing eyes, the color of caramel and very large. I sometimes think they could drink me if they wanted to. Which would be fine, believe me. Perfectly fine.

'I've missed you,' she said.

'We've been locked in a car for three and a half days. What was to miss?'

She tilted her head slightly, held my gaze until I got it.

'Oh,' I said. 'You mean you've *missed* me.'

'Yeah.'

I nodded. 'How much?'

She dropped the towel.

'That much,' I said and something caught in my throat. 'My, my.'

After making love, I live for a time in a world of echoes and snapshot memories. I lie in the damp dark with Angie's heart beating atop my own, her spine pressed against my fingertips or her hip warming my palm, and I can hear the echo of her soft groans, a sudden gasp, the low, throaty chuckle she emits after we're spent and she tosses her head back for a moment and her dark hair falls from her face and down her back. With my eyes closed, I see in close-up the bite of her upper teeth on her lower lip, the cut of her calf on the white mattress, the press of a shoulder blade against her flesh, the wisps of dream and appetite that suddenly cloud and moisten her eyes, the points of her dark pink nails sinking into the skin above my abdomen.

After making love with Angie, I'm no good for anything for half an hour or so. Most times, I need someone to draw me a diagram just to dial a phone. All but the most basic motor skills are largely beyond me. Intelligent conversation is out of the question. I just float in echoes and snapshots.

'Hey.' She drummed her fingers on my chest, tightened her thigh against the inside of my own.

'Yeah?'

'You ever think—'

'Not at the moment.'

She laughed, hooked a foot around my ankle, and rose up my chest a bit, ran a tongue along my throat. 'Seriously, just for a sec.'

'Shoot,' I managed.

'You ever think, I mean, when you're inside me, that what we're doing could, if we let it, produce life?'

I tilted my head and opened my eyes, looked into hers. She stared back calmly. A smudge of mascara under her left eye looked like a bruise in the soft dark of our bedroom.

And it was *our* bedroom now, wasn't it? She still owned the house she'd grown up in on Howes Street, still kept most of her furniture there, but she hadn't spent a night there in almost two years.

Our bedroom. Our bed. Our sheets tangled around these two bodies lying together, heartbeats drumming, flesh pressed together so tightly it would be hard for an observer to decide where one of us ended and the other began. Hard for me sometimes, too.

'A child,' I said.

She nodded.

'Bring a child,' I said slowly, 'into this world. With our jobs.'

Another nod, and this time her eyes glistened.

'You want that?'

'I didn't say that,' she whispered, and leaned in and kissed the tip of my nose. 'I said, "Did you ever think about it?" Did you ever think about the power we have when we're making love in this bed and the springs are making noise and we're making noise and everything feels . . . well, wonderful, and not just because of the physical sensation, but because we're joined – me and you – right here?' She pressed a palm against my groin. 'We're capable of creating life, baby. Me and you. One pill I forget to take – one chance in, what is it, a hundred thousand? – and

I could have life growing in me right now. Your life. Mine.' She kissed me. 'Ours.'

Lying like this, so close, so warm with the other's heat, so deeply, deeply *enthralled* with each other, it was easy to wish life was beginning at this moment in her womb. All that was sacred and mysterious about a woman's body in general and Angie's in particular seemed locked in this cocoon of sheets, this soft mattress and rickety bed. It all seemed so clear suddenly.

But the world was not this bed. The world was cement-cold and jaggedly sharp. The world was filled with monsters who'd once been babies, who'd started as zygotes in the womb, who'd emerged from woman in the only miracle the twentieth century has left, yet emerged angry or twisted or destined to be so. How many other lovers had lain in similar cocoons, similar beds, and felt what we felt now? How many monsters had they produced? And how many victims?

'Speak,' Angie said, and pushed the damp hair off my forehead.

'I've thought about it,' I said.

'And?'

'And it awes me.'

'Me too.'

'Scares me.'

'Me too.'

'A lot.'

Her eyes grew small. 'How come?'

'Little kids found in cement barrels, the Amanda McCreadys who vanish like they'd never lived, pedophiles out there roaming the streets with electrical tape and nylon cord. This world is a shit hole, honey.'

She nodded. 'And?'

'And what?'

'And it's a shit hole. Okay. But then what? I mean, our parents probably knew it was a shit hole, but they had us.'

'Great childhoods we had, too.'

'Would you prefer never to have been born?'

I placed both hands on her lower back and she leaned back into them. Her body rose off mine and the sheet fell from her back and she settled on my lap and looked down at me, her hair falling from behind her ears, naked and beautiful and as close to sheer perfection as any thing or any person or any fantasy I'd ever known.

'Would I prefer never to have been born?'

'That's the question,' she said softly.

'Of course not,' I said. 'But would Amanda McCready?'

'Our child wouldn't be Amanda McCready.'

'How do we know?'

'Because we wouldn't rip off drug dealers who'd take our child to get the money back.'

'Kids disappear every day for a lot less reason than that, and you know it. Kids disappear because they were walking to school, on the wrong corner at the wrong time, got separated from their parents at a mall. And they die, Ange. They die.'

A single tear fell to her breast, and after a moment it slid over the nipple and fell to my chest, already cold by the time it hit my skin.

'I know that,' she said. 'But be that as it may, I want your child. Not today, maybe not even next year. But I want it. I want to produce something beautiful from my body that is us and yet a person completely unlike us.'

'You want a baby.'

She shook her head. 'I want your baby.'

At some point we dozed.

Or I did. I woke a few minutes later to find her gone from the bed, and I got up and walked through the dark apartment into the kitchen, found her sitting at the table by the window, her bare flesh paled by the fractured moonlight cutting through rips in the shade.

There was a notepad by her elbow, the case file in front of her, and she looked up as I came through the doorway and said, 'They can't let her live.'

'Cheese and Mullen?'

She nodded. 'It's a dumb tactical move. They have to kill her.'

'They've kept her alive so far.'

'How do we know? And even if they have, they'll only do so, maybe, until they get the money. Just to be sure. But then they'll have to kill her. She's too much of a loose end.'

I nodded.

'You've already faced this,' she said.

'Yes.'

'So tomorrow night?'

'I expect to find a corpse.'

She lit a cigarette, and her skin was momentarily flushed by the lighter flame. 'Can you live with that?'

'No.' I came over to the table by her, put my hand on her shoulder, was aware of our nakedness in the kitchen, and I found myself thinking again of the power we held in our bed and our bodies, that potential third life floating like a spirit between our bare skin.

'Bubba?' she said.

'Most certainly.'

'Poole and Broussard won't like it.'

'Which is why we won't tell them he's there.'

'If Amanda is still alive when we reach the quarries, and we can locate her, or at least pinpoint her location—'

'Then Bubba will drop anyone holding her. Drop 'em like a sack of shit and disappear back into the night.'

She smiled. 'You want to call him?'

I slid the phone across the table. 'Be my guest.'

She crossed her legs as she dialed, tilted her head into the receiver. 'Hey, big boy,' she said, when he answered, 'want to come out and play tomorrow night?'

She listened for a moment, and her smile widened.

'If you're particularly blessed, Bubba, sure, you'll get to shoot someone.'

17

Major John Dempsey of the Massachusetts State Police had a wide Irish face as flat as a pancake and the wary, bulging eyes of an owl. He even blinked like an owl; a sudden snap of the ocular muscles would clamp his thick lids down over his eyes, where they'd remain a tenth of a second longer than normal before they'd snap back up like window shades and disappear under the brows.

Like most state troopers I've encountered, his spine seemed forged of lead pipe and his lips were pale and too thin; in the flat whiteness of his face they appeared to have been etched into the flesh by a weak pencil. His hands were a creamy white, the fingers long and feminine, the nails manicured as smooth as the edge of a nickel. But those hands were the only softness in him. The rest of him was constructed of shale, his slim frame so hard and stripped of body fat that if he fell from the podium I was sure he'd break apart in chips.

The uniforms of our state troopers have always unsettled me, and none more so than that of the upper ranks. There's something aggressively Teutonic in all that spit-polished black leather, those pronounced epaulets and shiny silver brass, the hard strap of the Sam Browne as it clamps across the chest from right shoulder to left hip, the extra quarter inch of height in the cap brim so that it settles over the forehead and shrouds the eyes.

City cops always remind me of the grunts in old war movies. No matter how nicely dressed, they seem one step away from crawling on their bellies up the beach at Normandy, wet cigar clenched between their teeth, dirt raining on their backs. But when I look at the average Statie – the clenched jaw and arrogant turn of chin, the sun glinting off all those uniform parts built to glint – I instantly picture them goose-stepping down the autumn streets of Poland circa 1939.

Major Dempsey had removed his large hat shortly after we were all assembled, to reveal an alarmingly orange tuft of hair underneath. It was shorn to bright stubbled pikes that rose from the scalp like Astroturf, and he seemed aware of the disconcerting effect it had on strangers. He smoothed the sides with his palms, lifted the pointer off his desk, and tapped it against his open palm as his own eyes surveyed the room with a bemused contempt. To his left, in a small row of chairs under the seal of the Commonwealth, Lieutenant Doyle sat with the police chief of Quincy, both dressed in their funereal best, all three watching the room with imposing stares.

We'd convened in the briefing room of the State Police barracks in Milton, and the entire left side of the room was commandeered by the Staties themselves, all hawk-eyed and smooth-skinned, hats tucked crisply under their arms, not so much as a hairline wrinkle in their trousers or shirts.

The left side of the room was made up of Quincy cops in the front rows and Boston in the rear. The Quincy cops seemed to be emulating the Staties, though I spotted a few wrinkles, a few hats cast to the floor by their feet. They were mostly young men and women, cheeks as smooth and shiny as striped bass, and I'd have bet hard cash none of them had ever fired their guns in the line of duty.

The rear of the room, by comparison, looked like the waiting area at a soup kitchen. The uniformed cops looked okay, but the CAC guys and women, as well as the host of other detectives brought in from other squads on temporary assignment, were a color-clashing, coffee-stained collection of five o'clock shadow, cigarette-stink breath, rumpled hair, and clothes so wrinkled you could lose small appliances in their folds. Most of the detectives had been working the Amanda McCready case since the outset, and they had that 'fuck-you-if-you-don't-like-it' demeanor of all cops who've been clocking too much overtime and banging on too many doors. Unlike the Staties and the Quincy cops, the members of the Boston contingent sprawled in their seats, kicked at each other, and coughed a lot.

Angie and I, arriving just before the meeting began, took our seats in the rear. In her freshly laundered black jeans and untucked black cotton shirt under a brown leather jacket, Angie looked good enough to sit up with the Quincy cops, but I was strictly post-Seattle grunge in a torn flannel shirt over a white Ren & Stimpy T-shirt and jeans speckled with flecks of white paint. My hi-tops were brand-spanking-new, though.

'Those the kind you pump?' Broussard asked, as

we slid into the seats beside him and Poole.

I brushed a piece of lint off my new kicks. 'Nope.'

'Too bad. I like the pump.'

'According to the commercial,' I said, 'they'll help me jump as high as Penny Hardaway and get two chicks at once.'

'Oh, well, then. Worth the cash.'

Behind Major Dempsey, two troopers hung a large topographical map of the Quincy quarries and the Blue Hills Reservation on the wall. As soon as it was fastened, Dempsey lifted his pointer and tapped a spot midway up the map.

'Granite Rail Quarry,' he said crisply. 'Recent developments in the Amanda McCready disappearance lead us to believe that an exchange will be made tonight at twenty hundred hours. The kidnappers wish to trade the child for a satchel of stolen money which is currently in the care of the Boston Police Department.' He drew a large circle around the map with his pointer. 'As you can see, the quarries were probably chosen because of the myriad potential escape routes.'

'Myriad,' Poole said under his breath. 'Good word.'

'Even with helicopters at our disposal and a full-scale task force waiting at strategic points around both the quarries and the Blue Hills Reservation, this will not be an easy area to contain. To make things even more difficult, the kidnappers have demanded that only four people approach the area tonight. Until the exchange occurs, we have to maintain a completely invisible presence.'

A trooper raised his hand and cleared his throat. 'Major, how are we to establish a perimeter around the area and still keep from being seen?'

'There's the rub.' Dempsey ran a hand over his chin.

'He didn't just say that,' Poole whispered.

'He did.'

'Wow.'

'Command Post One,' Dempsey said, 'will be set up in this valley, at the base of the bunny slope in the Blue Hills. From there, the top of Granite Rail Quarry is less than one minute by helicopter. The majority of our forces will be on standby there. As soon as we have word that the exchange has been completed, we will sweep out and around the reservation, block Quarry Street at both ends, Chickatawbut and Saw Cut Notch roads at both ends, seal off both the south and north exits and entrance ramps to the southeast expressway, and throw a blanket over the whole kit and kaboodle.'

'Kit,' Poole said.

'Kaboodle,' Broussard said.

'Command Post Two will be here at the entrance to Quincy Cemetery, and Command Post Three . . .'

We listened for the next hour as Dempsey outlined the plan of containment and carved up duties between state and local police departments. Over one hundred and fifty cops would be deployed and camping out around the Quincy quarries and at the edge of the Blue Hills. They had three helicopters at their disposal. The elite BPD Hostage Negotiation Team would be on-site. Lieutenant Doyle and the Quincy police chief would act as 'rovers' – each in his own car, headlamps off, circling the quarries in the dark.

'Pray they don't crash into each other,' Poole said.

The quarries comprised a large land mass. At the height of the New England granite boom, more than sixty were in operation. Granite Rail remained one of twenty-two that hadn't been filled in, and the sites of the rest spread wide across the torn hills between the expressway and the Blue Hills. We'd be entering at night with very little light. Even the rangers Dempsey brought in to speak about the area admitted that there were so many trails in those hills that some were known only to the few people who used them.

But the trails weren't really the issue. Trails eventually led somewhere and that somewhere was a small number of roads, a public park or two. Even if the kidnappers could slip through the dragnet on the hills, they'd be nabbed somewhere below. If it were a case of just the four of us and a few cops monitoring the hills, I'd give the edge to Cheese's people. But with one hundred and fifty cops, I was hard-pressed to see how anyone planned to move in and out of there unnoticed.

And no matter how dumb most of the people in Cheese's organization were, even they had to know that, no matter what their demands, in a hostage situation there would be a lot of cops.

So how were they planning to get out?

I raised my hand the next time Dempsey paused, and when he saw me, he looked like he was considering ignoring me, so I said, 'Major.'

He looked down at his pointer. 'Yes.'

'I don't see how the kidnappers can escape.'

Several cops chuckled and Dempsey smiled.

'Well, that's the point, Mr Kenzie, isn't it?'

I smiled back. 'I understand that, but don't you think the kidnappers do too?'

'How do you mean?'

'They picked this location. They would have realized that you'd surround it. Right?'

Dempsey shrugged. 'Crime makes you stupid.'

Another round of polite laughter from the boys in blue.

I waited for it to die down. 'Major, if they had planned for such a contingency, though, what then?'

His smile widened, but his owl eyes didn't follow suit. They narrowed at me, slightly confused, slightly angry. 'There's no way out, Mr Kenzie. No matter what they think. It's a billion to one.'

'But they think they're the one.'

'Then they're wrong.' Dempsey looked at his pointer and scowled. 'Any more dumb questions?'

At six, we met with Detective Maria Dykema of Hostage Negotiation in a van they'd parked under a water tower about thirty yards off Ricciuti Drive, the road that was carved through the heart of the Quincy quarries. She was a slim, petite woman in her early forties with short hair the color of milk and almond eyes. She wore a dark business suit and tugged idly at the pearl earring on her left ear throughout most of our conversation.

'If any of you come face-to-face with the kidnapper and the child, what do you do?' Her glance swept across the four of us and settled on the wall of the van, where someone had taped a copy of the *National Lampoon* picture in which a hand held a pistol to the head of a dog and the caption read:

BUY THIS MAGAZINE OR WE'LL KILL THIS DOG. 'I'm waiting,' she said.

Broussard said, 'We tell the suspect to release—'

'You *ask* the suspect,' she corrected.

'We ask the suspect to release the child.'

'And if he replies "Fuck off" and cocks his pistol, what then?'

'We—'

'You back off,' she said. 'You keep him in sight, but you give him room. He panics, the kid dies. He feels threatened, same thing. The first thing you do is give him the illusion of space, of breathing room. You don't want him to feel in command, but you don't want him to feel helpless either. You want him to feel he has options.' She turned her head away from the photo, tugged her earring, and met our eyes. 'Clear?'

I nodded.

'Don't draw a bead on the suspect, whatever you do. Don't make sudden moves. When you are going to do something, tell him. As in: "I'm going to back up now. I'm lowering my gun now." Et cetera.'

'Baby him,' Broussard said. 'That's your recommendation.'

She smiled slightly, her eyes on the hem of her skirt. 'Detective Broussard, I've got six years in with Hostage Negotiation, and I've only lost one. You want to puff out your chest and start screaming, "Down, motherfucker!" should you run into this sort of situation, be my guest. But do me a favor and spare me the talk-show circuit after the perp blows Amanda McCready's heart all over your shirt.' She raised her eyebrows at him. ''Kay?'

'Detective,' Broussard said. 'I wasn't questioning

how you do your job. I was just making an observation.'

Poole nodded. 'If we have to baby someone to save this girl, I'll put the fella in a carriage and sing lullabies to him. You have my word.'

She sighed and leaned back, ran both hands through her hair. 'The chances of anyone running into the perp with Amanda McCready are slim to none. But if you do, remember – that girl is all they got. People who take hostages and then get into a standoff, they're like rats backed into a corner. They're usually very afraid and very lethal. And they won't blame themselves and they won't blame you for the situation. They'll blame her. And unless you're very careful, they'll cut her throat.'

She let that sink in. Then she removed four business cards from her suit pocket and handed one to each of us. 'You all have cell phones?'

We nodded.

'My number is on the back of that card. If you do get into a standoff with this perp and you run out of things to say, call me and hand the phone to the kidnapper. Okay?'

She looked out the back window at the black craggy mass of the hills and quarry outcroppings, the jutting silhouettes of jagged granite peaks.

'The quarries,' she said. 'Who would pick a place like that?'

'It doesn't seem the easiest place to escape from,' Angie said. 'Under the circumstances.'

Detective Dykema nodded. 'And yet they picked it. What do they know that we don't?'

* * *

At seven, we assembled in the BPD's Mobile Command Post, where Lieutenant Doyle gave us his version of a pep talk.

'If you fuck up, there are plenty of cliffs up there to jump from. So' – he patted Poole's knee – 'don't fuck up.'

'Inspiring speech, sir.'

Doyle reached under the console table and removed a light blue gym bag, tossed it onto Broussard's lap. 'The money Mr Kenzie turned in this morning. It's all been counted, all serial numbers recorded. There is exactly two hundred thousand dollars in that bag. Not a penny less. See that it's returned that way.'

The radio that took up a good third of the console table squawked: 'Command, this is Unit Five-niner. Over.'

Doyle lifted the receiver off its cradle and flicked the SEND switch. 'This is Command. Go ahead, Fifty-nine.'

'Mullen has left Devonshire Place in a Yellow taxi heading west on Storrow. We are attached. Over.'

'West?' Broussard said. 'Why's he going west? Why's he on Storrow?'

'Fifty-nine,' Doyle said, 'did you establish positive ID on Mullen?'

'Ah . . .' There was a long pause amid crackles of static.

'Say again, Fifty-nine. Over.'

'Command, we intercepted Mullen's transmission with the cab company and watched him step into it on Devonshire at the rear entrance. Over.'

'Fifty-nine, you don't sound so sure.'

'Uh, Command, we saw a man matching Mullen's

physical description wearing a Celtics hat and sunglasses . . . Uh . . . Over.'

Doyle closed his eyes for a moment, placed the receiver in the center of his forehead. 'Fifty-nine, did you or did you not make a positive ID on the suspect? Over.'

Another long pause filled with static.

'Uh, Command, come to think of it, that's a negative. But we're pretty sure—'

'Fifty-nine, who was covering Devonshire Place with you? Over.'

'Six-seven, Command. Sir, should we—'

Doyle cut them off with a flick of a switch, punched a button on the radio, and spoke into the receiver.

'Sixty-seven, this is Command. Respond. Over.'

'Command, this is Sixty-seven. Over.'

'What is your location?'

'South on Tremont, Command. Partner on foot. Over.'

'Sixty-seven, why are you on Tremont? Over.'

'Following suspect, Command. Suspect is on foot, walking south along the Common. Over.'

'Sixty-seven, are you saying you're following Mullen south on Tremont?'

'Affirmative, Command.'

'Sixty-seven, instruct your partner to detain Mr Mullen. Over.'

'Ah, Command, we don't—'

'Instruct your partner to detain the suspect, Sixty-seven. Over.'

'Affirmative, sir.'

Doyle placed the receiver on the console table for a moment, pinched the bridge of his nose, and sighed.

Angie and I looked at Poole and Broussard. Broussard shrugged. Poole shook his head in disgust.

'Uh, Command, this is Sixty-seven. Over.'

Doyle picked up the receiver. 'Go ahead.'

'Yeah, Command, well, um—'

'The man you're following is not Mullen. Affirmative?'

'Affirmative, Command. Individual was dressed like suspect, but—'

'Out, Sixty-seven.'

Doyle tossed the receiver into the radio, shook his head. He leaned back in his chair, looked at Poole.

'Where's Gutierrez?'

Poole folded his hands on his lap. 'Last I checked, he was in a room at the Prudential Hilton. Arrived last night from Lowell.'

'Who's on him?'

'A four-man team. Dean, Gallagher, Gleason, and Halpern.'

Doyle cross-checked the names with the list by his elbow which gave their unit numbers. He flicked a switch on the radio.

'Unit Forty-nine, this is command. Come in. Over.'

'Command, this is Forty-nine. Over.'

'What is your location? Over.'

'Dalton Street, Command, by the Hilton. Over.'

'Forty-nine, where is' – Doyle consulted the list by his elbow – 'unit Seventy-three? Over.'

'Detective Gleason is in the lobby, Command. Detective Halpern is covering the rear exit. Over.'

'And where is the suspect? Over.'

'Suspect is in his room, Command. Over.'

242

'Confirm that, Forty-nine. Over.'

'Affirmative. Will get back to you. Over and out.'

While we waited for an answer no one spoke. We didn't even look at each other. The same way you can watch a football game, and know that even though your team has a six-point lead with four minutes to go that they're somehow going to blow it, so the five of us in the rear of the command post seemed to feel any edge we may have had slipping out under the door into the gathering dark. If Mullen had so easily given four experienced detectives the slip, then how many other times had he done it over the last few days? How many times had the police been sure they were watching Mullen, when in fact they were tailing someone else? Mullen, for all we knew, could have been making visits to Amanda McCready. He could have been establishing his escape route out of these hills tonight. He could have been buying off cops to look the other way or picking which ones he'd have removed from the equation sometime after eight in the pitch black of the hills at night.

Mullen, if he'd known we were on him from the get-go, could have been showing us everything he wanted us to see, and, while we were looking at that, the things he didn't want us to see were going on behind our backs.

'Command, this is Forty-nine. We've got a problem. Gutierrez is gone. I repeat: Gutierrez is gone. Over.'

'How long, Forty-nine? Over.'

'Hard to say, Command. His rental car is still parked in the garage. Last physical observation occurred at oh-seven-hundred hours. Over.'

'Command out.'

Doyle seemed to consider crushing the receiver in his hand for a moment, but then he laid it gently and precisely on the corner of the console table.

Broussard said, 'He probably had another car placed in the garage a day or two before he checked in.'

Doyle nodded. 'When I check with the other teams, how many of Olamon's men, do you think, will be unaccounted for?'

No one had an answer, but I don't think he'd expected one.

18

If you head south out of my neighborhood and cross the Neponset River, you end up in Quincy, long thought of by my father's generation as a way station for the Irish prosperous enough to escape Dorchester but not quite wealthy enough to reach Milton, the tony two-toilet-Irish suburb a few miles northwest. As you drive south along Interstate 93, just before you reach Braintree, you'll see a cluster of sandy brown hills rising to the west that always seem on the verge of sudden crumbling.

It was in these hills that the grand old men of Quincy's past discovered granite so rich with black silicates and smoky quartz that it must have shimmered at their feet like a diamond stream. The first commercial railway in the country was constructed in 1827, with the first rail clamped to the land with swinging spikes and metal bolts in Quincy, up in the hills, so that granite could be transported down to the banks of the Neponset River, where it was loaded onto schooners and transported to Boston or down to Manhattan, New Orleans, Mobile, and Savannah.

This hundred-year granite boom created buildings erected to withstand both time and fashion –

imposing libraries and seats of government, towering churches, prisons that smothered noise, light, and hopes of escape, the fluted monolithic columns in custom houses across the country, and the Bunker Hill Monument. And what was left in the wake of all this rock lifted from the earth were holes. Deep holes. Wide holes. Holes that have never been filled by anything but water.

Over the years since the granite industry died, the quarries have become the favored dumping ground for just about everything: stolen cars, old refrigerators and ovens, bodies. Every few years when a kid vanishes after diving into them or a Walpole lifer tells police he dumped a missing hooker over one of the cliffs, the quarries are searched and newspapers run photos of topographical maps and underwater photography that reveal a submerged landscape of mountain ranges, rock violently disrupted and disgorged, sudden jagged needles rising from the depths, jutting crags of cliff face appearing like ghosts of Atlantis under a hundred feet of rain.

Sometimes, those bodies are found. And sometimes, they're not. The quarries, given to underwater storms of black silt and sudden illogical shifts in their landscape, rife with undocumented shelves and crevices, yield their secrets with all the frequency of the Vatican.

As we trudged up the old railway incline, snapping branches out of our faces, trampling weeds and stumbling over rocks in the dark, slipping on sudden smooth stones and cursing under our breath, I found myself thinking that if we were pioneers trying to pass through these hills to reach the reservoir on the other side in the Blue Hills, we'd be dead by now.

Some bear or pissed-off moose or Indian war party would have killed us just for disturbing the peace.

'Try and be a little louder,' I said, as Broussard slipped in the dark, banged his shin on a boulder, and straightened up long enough to kick it.

'Hey,' he said, 'I look like Jeremiah Johnson to you? Last time I was in the woods, I was drunk, I was having sex, and I could see the highway from where I was.'

'You were having sex?' Angie said. 'My God.'

'You have something against sex?'

'I have something against bugs,' Angie said. 'Ick.'

'Is it true that if you have sex in the woods, the smell attracts bears?' Poole said. He supported himself on a tree trunk for a moment, sucked in the night air.

'There aren't any bears left around here.'

'You never know,' Poole said, and looked off into the dark trees. He placed the gym bag of money by his feet for a moment, removed a handkerchief from his pocket, dabbed at the sweat on his neck, wiped his reddening face. He blew air out of his cheeks and swallowed a few times.

'You okay, Poole?'

He nodded. 'Fine. Just out of shape. And, oh, yeah, old.'

'Want one of us to carry the bag?' Angie asked.

Poole grimaced at her and picked up the bag. He pointed up the slope. '"Once more unto the breach."'

'That's not a breach,' Broussard said. 'That's a hill.'

'I was quoting Shakespeare, you vulgarian.' Poole came off the tree and began trudging up the hill.

'Then you should have said, "My kingdom for a horse,"' Broussard said. 'Would have been more appropriate.'

Angie took a few deep breaths, caught Broussard's eyes as he did the same. 'We're old.'

'We're old,' he agreed.

'Think it's time we hung 'em up?'

'Love to.' He smiled, leaned over, and took another breath. 'My wife? Got in a car accident just before we were married, fractured some bones. No health insurance. You know what a fracture cost to fix? Man, I'll be able to retire about the same time I'm chasing perps with a walker.'

'Somebody say a walker?' Poole said. He looked up at the steep slope. 'That'd be sweet.'

As a kid I'd taken this path several times to reach the watering holes of Granite Rail or Swingle's Quarry. It was supposedly off-limits, of course, surrounded by fences and patrolled by rangers for the MDC, but there were always jagged doors cut through the chain link if you knew where to look, and if you didn't, you brought the equipment to make your own. The rangers were in short supply, and even with a small army they'd have been hard-pressed to patrol the dozens of quarries and the hundreds of kids who made their way up to them on a blistering summer day.

So I'd climbed this ridge before. Fifteen years ago. In the daylight.

It was a little different now. For one, I wasn't in the shape I'd been in when I was a teenager. Too many bruises and too many bars and far too many on-the-job collisions with people and pool tables – and, once, both a windshield and the road waiting on the other side – had given my body the creaks and aches and constant dull throbs of either a man twice my age or a professional football player.

Second, like Broussard, I wasn't exactly Grizzly Adams. My exposure to a world without asphalt and a good deli was limited. Once a year, I took a hiking trip with my sister and her family up Washington's Mount Rainier; four years ago I'd been coerced into a camping trip in Maine by a woman who'd fancied herself a naturalist because she shopped at army-navy stores. The trip had been scheduled for three days, but we'd lasted one night and a can of insect repellent before we drove to Camden for white sheets and room service.

I considered my companions as we climbed the slope toward Granite Rail Quarry. My guess was none of them would have made it through the first night of that camping trip. Maybe with sunlight, proper hiking boots, a sturdy staff, and a first-rate ski lift, we'd have made respectable progress, but it was only after twenty minutes of thumping and banging up the hill, our flashlights trained on the imprints and the occasional embedded railroad tie of a railway that had stopped running almost a century ago, that we finally got a whiff of the water.

Nothing smells so clean and cold and promising as quarry water. I'm not sure why this is, because it's merely decades of rain piled up between walls of granite and fed and freshened by underground springs, but the moment the scent found my nostrils, I was sixteen again and I could feel the plunge in my chest as I jumped over the edge of Heaven's Peak, a seventy-foot cliff in Swingle's Quarry, saw the light-green water yawn open below me like a waiting hand, felt weightless and bodiless and pure spirit hanging in the empty, awesome air around me. Then I dropped, and the air turned into a tornado shooting straight up from the advancing pool of green, and the graffiti exploded from the shelves and walls and cliffs all around me, burst forth in reds and blacks and golds and blues, and I could smell that clean, cold, and suddenly frightening odor of a century's raindrops just before I hit the water, toes pointed down, wrists tucked tight against my hips, dropped deep below the surface where the cars and the refrigerators and the bodies lay.

Over the years, as the quarries have claimed one young life every four years or so, not to mention all the corpses dumped over the cliffs in the dead of night and discovered, if at all, years later, I've read the newspapers as editorialists, community activists, and grieving parents ask, 'Why? Why?'

Why do kids – quarry rats, we called ourselves in my generation – feel the need to jump from cliffs as high as one hundred feet into water two hundred feet deep and mined with sudden outcroppings, car antennas, logs, and who knows what else?

I have no idea. I jumped because I was a kid. Because my father was an asshole and my home was a constant police action, and most of the time finding a place to hide was how my sister and I spent our lives, and that didn't seem much like living. Because often, as I stood on those cliffs and looked over the edge at an overturned bowl of green that turned and revealed itself the more I craned my neck, I felt a cold sizzle in my stomach and an awareness of every limb, every bone, and every blood vessel in my body. Because I felt pure in the air and clean in the water. I jumped to prove things to my friends and, once those things had been proven, because I was addicted to it, needed to find higher cliffs, longer drops. I jumped for the same reason I became a private detective – because I hate knowing exactly what's next.

'I need to catch a breath,' Poole said. He grabbed a thick vine growing out of the ground in front of us and twisted with it toward the ground. The gym bag fell from his hand, and his foot slipped in the dirt, and he fell on top of the bag, clenching the vine tightly in his hand.

We were about fifteen yards from the top. I could see the faintest green shimmer of water, like a wisp of cloud, reflecting off the dark cliffs and hovering in the cobalt pitch of sky just beyond the last ridge.

'Sure, buddy, sure.' Broussard stopped and stood by his partner as the older man placed his flashlight on his lap and gasped for breath.

In the dark, Poole was as white as I'd ever seen him. He shone. His raspy breath clawed its way into the night, and his eyes swam in their sockets, seemed to float in search of something they couldn't locate.

Angie knelt by him and put a hand under his jaw, felt his pulse. 'Take a deep breath.'

Poole nodded, his eyes bulging, and sucked air.

Broussard lowered himself to his haunches. 'You okay, buddy?'

'Fine,' Poole managed. 'Aces.'

The shine on his face found his throat and dampened his collar.

'Too fucking old to be humping my ass up some' – he coughed – 'hill.'

Angie looked at Broussard. Broussard looked back at me.

Poole coughed some more. I tilted my flashlight, saw tiny dots of blood speckle his chin.

'Just a minute,' he said.

I shook my head and Broussard nodded, pulled his walkie-talkie from his jacket.

Poole reached up and grasped his wrist. 'What are you doing?'

'Calling it in,' Broussard said. 'We got to get you off this hill, my man.'

Poole tightened his grip on Broussard's wrist, coughed so hard I thought he'd lurch into a convulsion for a minute.

'You don't call anything in,' he said. 'We're supposed to be alone.'

'Poole,' Angie said, 'you're in some trouble here.'

He looked up at her and smiled. 'I'm fine.'

'Bullshit,' Broussard said, and looked away from the blood on Poole's chin.

'Really.' Poole shifted on the ground, wrapped the inside of his forearm around the vine. 'Go over the hill, children. Go over the hill.' He smiled, but the corners of his mouth twitched against his shiny cheeks.

We looked down at him. He looked like he was one arch of the back or roll of the eyes from a headstone. His flesh was the color of raw scallop and his eyes wouldn't stay focused. His breathing sounded like rain through a window screen.

His grip on Broussard's wrist was still as tight as a jailer's, though. He glanced at the three of us and seemed to guess what we were thinking.

'I'm old and in debt,' he said. 'And I'll be fine. You don't find that girl, she won't be.'

Broussard said, 'I don't *know* her, Poole. Get it?'

Poole nodded and tightened his grip on Broussard's wrist until the flesh in his hand turned red. "Preciate that, son. Really do. What's the first thing I taught you?'

Broussard looked away, and his eyes glistened in the light bouncing from Angie's flashlight, off his partner's chest and into his pupils.

'What's the first thing I taught you?' Poole said.

Broussard cleared his throat, spit into the woods. 'Huh?'

'Close the case,' Broussard said, and his voice sounded as if Poole's hand had left his wrist and found his throat.

'Always,' Poole said. He rolled his eyes in the direction of the ridge behind him. 'So, go close it.'

'I—'

'Don't you dare pity me, kid. Don't you dare. Take the bag.'

Broussard lowered his chin to his chest. He reached under Poole and pulled the bag out, slapped the dirt off the bottom.

'Go,' Poole said. 'Now.'

Broussard pulled his wrist from Poole's fingers and stood up. He looked off into the dark woods like a kid who's just been told what alone means.

Poole glanced at me and Angie and smiled. 'I'll survive. Save the girl, call for evac.'

I looked away. Poole, to the best of my knowledge, had just suffered either a small heart attack or a stroke. And the blood that had shot from his lungs didn't exactly give cause for optimism. I was looking down at a man who, unless he got immediate help, would die.

Angie said, 'I'll stay.'

We looked at her. She'd remained on her knees by Poole since he'd sat down, and she ran a palm over his white forehead, ran it back through the bristles of his hair.

'The hell you will,' Poole said, and swatted at her hand. He tilted his head, looked up into her face. 'That child is going to die tonight, Miss Gennaro.'

'Angie.'

'That child is going to die tonight, Angie.' He gritted his teeth for a moment and grimaced at something shooting up his sternum, swallowed hard to force it back down. 'Unless we do something. We need every person we have to get her out of here in one piece. Now' – he struggled with the vine, pulled himself up a bit – 'you're going up to those quarries. And so are you, Patrick.' He turned his head to Broussard. 'And you most definitely fucking are. So go. Go now.'

None of us wanted to. That was obvious. But then Poole held out his arm and tilted the wrist up toward us until we could all read the illuminated hands of his watch: 8.03.

We were late.

'Go!' he hissed.

I looked at the top of the hill, then off into the dark woods behind Poole, then down at the man himself. Splayed there, legs spread and one foot lolling off to the side, he looked like a scarecrow tossed from his perch.

'Go!'

We left him there.

We scrambled up the hill, Broussard taking the lead as the path was narrowed by thickets of weeds and brambles. Except for the sounds of our progress, the night was so still it would have been easy to believe we were the only creatures out in it.

Ten feet from the top, we met a chain-link fence twelve feet high, but it didn't prove much of an obstacle. A section of it as wide and tall as a garage door had been cut out, and we walked through the hole without pausing.

At the top of the hill, Broussard stopped long enough to engage his walkie-talkie and whisper into it. 'Have reached the quarry. Sergeant Raftopoulos is ill. On my signal – repeat, on my signal – send evac to the railroad slope fifteen yards from the top. Wait for my signal. Copy.'

'Affirmative.'

'Out.' Broussard placed the walkie-talkie back in his raincoat.

'What now?' Angie said.

We stood on a cliff about forty feet above the water. In the dark, I could see the silhouettes of other cliffs and crags, bent trees, and jutting rock shelves. A line of cut, strewn, and disrupted granite rose off to our immediate left, a few jagged peaks another ten to fifteen feet higher than the one on which we stood. To our right, the land rolled flat for about sixty yards, then curved and became jagged and erratic again, erupting into the dark. Below, the water waited, a wide circle of light gray against the black cliff walls.

'The woman who called Lionel said wait for instructions,' Broussard said. 'You see any instructions?'

Angie shone her flashlight at our feet, bounced it off the granite walls, arced it off the trees and bushes. The dancing light was like a lazy eye that gave us fractured glimpses into a dense, alien world that could alter itself dramatically within inches – go from stone to moss to battered white bark to mint-green vegetation. And flowing through the tree line like reams of dental floss were silver stripes of chain link.

'I don't see any instructions,' Angie said.

Bubba, I knew, was out there somewhere. He could probably see us right now. Maybe he could see Mullen and Gutierrez and whoever was working with them. Maybe he could see Amanda McCready. He'd approached from the Milton side and cut through Cunningham Park and up along a path he'd found years before, when he'd gone there to dump hot weapons, or a car, or a body – whatever it was guys like Bubba dumped in the quarries.

He'd have a target scope on his rifle equipped with a light amplification device, and through the scope we'd all look like we stood in a misty seaweed world, moved within a photograph that was still developing before his eyes.

The walkie-talkie on Broussard's hip went off, and the squawk was like a scream in the midst of all that quiet. He fumbled with it and brought it up to his mouth.

'Broussard.'

'This is Doyle. Sixteenth Precinct just received a call from a woman with a message for you. We think it's the same woman who called Lionel McCready.'

'Copy. What's the message?'

'You're to walk to your right, Detective Broussard, up onto the southern cliffs. Kenzie and Gennaro are to walk to their left.'

'That's it?'

'That's it. Doyle out.'

Broussard clipped the walkie-talkie back on his hip, looked off at the line of cliffs on the far side of the water. 'Divide and conquer.'

He looked at us, and his eyes were small and empty. He looked much younger than usual, nerves and fear stripping ten years from his face.

'Be careful,' Angie said.

'You too,' he said.

We stood there for another few seconds, as if by not moving we could stave off the inevitable, the moment when we'd discover whether Amanda McCready was alive or dead, the moment when all this hoping and planning would be out of our hands and whoever was hurt or lost or killed wouldn't be up to us any longer.

'Well,' Broussard said. 'Shit.' He shrugged and then walked off along the flat path, the flashlight beam bouncing in front of him through the dust.

Angie and I moved back from the edge about ten feet and followed the stone until a gap appeared and another granite slab rose six inches on the other side. I gripped her hand and we stepped over the gap and up onto the next slab, followed that stone another thirty feet until we met a wall.

It rose a good ten feet above us, and its creamy beige color was mixed with swirls of chocolate. It reminded me of a marble cake. A six-ton marble cake, but still.

We shone our flashlights to the left of it and found nothing but sheer mass back about thirty feet and into the trees. I brought the light back to the section in front of me, found cuts in the rock, as if layers had been chipped away in places like shale. A small lip about a foot wide opened like a smile two and a half feet up the face, and four feet above that I saw another, wider smile.

'Done much rock climbing lately?' I asked Angie.

'You're not thinking . . . ?' Her light beam danced across the rock face.

'Don't see any alternative.' I handed her my flashlight and raised the toe of my shoe until it found the first small lip. I looked back over my shoulder at Angie. 'I wouldn't stand directly behind me, if I were you. I might be coming back down real quick.'

She shook her head and stepped to my left, kept both flashlights shining on the rock as I flexed the toe of my shoe against the lip and pushed up and down a couple of times to see if the smile crumbled. When it didn't, I took a deep breath and pushed up off it, grabbed for the higher shelf. I got my fingers in there, and they slid on dust and rock salt and then popped back out again, and I bounced back off the rock face and fell on my ass.

'That was good,' Angie said. 'You definitely have a genetic predisposition toward all things athletic.'

I stood and wiped the dust off my fingers, smeared it on my jeans. I scowled at Angie and tried again, and again I fell back on my ass.

'It's getting nervous, though,' Angie said.

The third try, I actually held my fingers in the shelf for a good fifteen seconds before I lost my grip.

Angie's lights shone down in my face as I looked up at the beast slab of stubborn granite.

'May I?' she said.

I took the flashlights from her, shone them on the rock. 'Be my guest.'

She walked backward several feet and peered at the rock. She squatted and rose up and down on her haunches several times, stretched her torso from the small of her back, and flexed her fingers. Before I even knew what her plan was, she rose, took off, and ran full speed at the rock face. A few inches before she would have smacked into it like Wile E. Coyote into a painted-on door, her foot dug into the lower shelf, her right hand grabbed the upper one, and her small body vaulted up another two feet as her left arm slapped over the top.

She hung there for a good thirty seconds like that, pressed flat into the rock as if she'd been hurled there.

'Now what are you going to do?' I said.

'I thought I'd just lie here awhile.'

'That sounds like sarcasm.'

'Oh, you recognize it?'

'One of my talents.'

'Patrick,' she said, in a tone that reminded me of my mother and several nuns I've known, 'get under me and push.'

I shoved one flashlight into my belt buckle, so that the light shone up into my face, and the other in my back pocket, stood under Angie, got both hands under her heels, and pushed up. Both flashlights together were probably heavier than she was. She shot up the rock face and I extended my arms until they were straight above my head and her heels left the palms. She turned around on top of the rock, looked down at me from her hands and knees, and extended her hand.

'Ready, my Olympian?'

I coughed into my hand. 'Bitch.'

She withdrew the hand and smiled. 'What was that?'

'I said I have to *switch* the other flashlight to my back pocket.'

'Oh.' She lowered the hand again. 'Of course.'

After she'd pulled me up, we shone the lights across the top of the rock. It ran unbroken for at least twenty yards and was as smooth as a bowling ball. I lay on my stomach and stuck my head and flashlight over the edge, watching the cliff face drop straight and smooth another sixty-five feet to the water.

We were about midway up the north side of the quarry. Directly across the water was a row of cliffs and shelves, littered with graffiti and even a stray climber's piton. The water, when under my beam, shimmered against the rock like heat waves off a summer road. It was the pale green I remembered, slightly milkier, but I knew the color was deceptive. Divers looking for a body in this water last summer had been forced to abandon their search when a high concentration of silt deposits combined with the natural lack of visibility in depths of more than one hundred and fifty feet made it impossible to see more than two to three feet in front of their faces. I brought my beam back across the water toward our side, skipped over a crumpled license plate floating in the green, a chunk of log that had been gnawed open in the center by animals until it resembled a canoe, and then the edge of something round and the color of flesh.

'Patrick,' Angie said.

'Wait a sec. Shine your light down here.' I darted my beam back to my right, back to where I'd seen the curve of flesh, found only more green water.

'Ange,' I said. 'Now, for Christ's sake.'

She lay on the rock beside me and flashed her light beside my own. Having to travel sixty-five feet down weakened the light, and the soft green of the water didn't help much either. Our circles of light ran parallel like a pair of eyes and swayed back and forth across the water, then up and down, in tight squares.

'What did you see?'

'I don't know. Could have been a rock . . .'

The coffee-brown bark of the log floated under my beam, then the license plate again, crumpled as if by thick angry hands.

Maybe it *had* been a rock. The white light, green water, and surrounding black could be playing tricks with my eyes. If it had been a body, we'd have found it by now. Besides, bodies don't float. Not in the quarries.

'I got something.'

I tilted my wrist, followed Angie's shaft of light, and the twin beams bathed the curved head and dead eyes of Amanda McCready's doll, Pea. It floated on its back in the green water, its flower-print dress soiled and wet.

Oh, Jesus, I thought. No.

'Patrick,' Angie said, 'she could be down there.'

'Wait—'

'She could be down there,' she repeated, and I heard a kicking sound as she rolled onto her back and pushed one shoe off her left heel.

'Angie. Wait. We're supposed to—'

On the other side of the quarry, the tree line behind the cliffs exploded. Gunfire ripped through the branches, and light popped and erupted in sudden blasts of yellow and white.

'I'm pinned down! I'm pinned down!' Broussard's voice screamed over the walkie-talkie. 'Need immediate support! Repeat: Need immediate support!'

A chip of marble jumped off the cliff and into my cheek, and then suddenly the trees behind us buzzed and sheared their branches, and sparks and metallic pings popped off the rock face.

Angie and I rolled back from the edge and I grabbed my walkie-talkie. 'This is Kenzie. We're taking fire. Repeat: We are taking fire from the south side of the quarry.'

I rolled back farther into the darkness, saw my flashlight where I'd left it on the edge, still pointing its shaft of light out over the quarry. Whoever was shooting from the other side of the water was probably using the flashlight as a homing beacon.

'You hit?'

Angie shook her head. 'No.'

'Be right back.'

'What?'

Another barrage of bullets hammered the rocks and trees behind us, and I held my breath, waited for a pause. When it came in a roar of silence, I scrambled through the dark and swung the back of my hand into the flashlight, sent it over the edge and dropping toward the water.

'Christ,' Angie said, as I scrambled back to her. 'What do we do?'

'I don't know. If they got LAD scopes on their rifles, we're dead.'

The shooter opened up again. Leaves in the trees behind Angie leaped into the night and bullets spit into the trunks, snapped thin branches. The gunfire paused for a half second as the shooter realigned his aim, and then metal slapped the cliff face below us, just on the other side of the lip, hammering the rock like a hailstorm. One shift of the gun an inch or two up in the shooter's arms, and the bullets would streak over the cliff top and into our faces.

'Need evac!' Broussard screamed over the walkie-talkie. 'Immediately! Drawing fire from both sides!'

'Evac en route,' a calm, cold voice replied.

I depressed the transmit button as the gunfire stopped again. 'Broussard.'

'Yeah. You two okay?'

'Pinned.'

'Me too.' From his end, I heard a sudden stream of bullets and when I looked across the quarry I could see the steady white flash of muzzle fire in the trees.

'Son of a bitch!' Broussard shouted.

Then the sky opened up and poured white light as two helicopters streaked over the center of the quarry, lights powerful enough to bathe a football stadium strapped to their noses. For a moment, I was blinded by the sheer mass of the sudden white glow. Everything lost its color and turned white with the light: white tree line, white cliff face, white water.

The fury of white was disrupted by a long, dark object as it arced from the tree line on the other side, somersaulted in the air, end over end, and then dropped over the cliff and toward the water. I followed its descent enough to identify it as a rifle before it disappeared from view, but still more gunfire burst from the tree line across the water from us.

And then it stopped. I searched the white light and just glimpsed the butt end of another rifle as it dropped through the night toward the water.

One helicopter banked above the tree line on Broussard's side and I heard the chatter of automatic fire, heard Broussard scream over the walkie-talkie, 'Hold your fire! Hold your fire, you fucking lunatic!'

The green treetops were shredding themselves in the white light, popping and snapping into the air, and then the chatter of the weapon fired from the helicopter stopped as the second helicopter banked and pointed its light directly in my face. The wind from its rotor blades found my body and knocked me off my feet, and Angie grabbed the walkie-talkie and said, 'Back off. We're fine. You are in the line of fire.'

The white light disappeared for a moment, and when my vision cleared and the wind lessened, I saw that the helicopter had drifted up about forty feet, hovered over the quarry, and dipped its light toward the water.

All gunfire had stopped. The fury of mechanical noise, though, had been replaced by the whine of copter turbines and the chop of rotors.

I looked into the pool of white and saw the green water churn, the chunk of log and license plate bounce off Amanda's doll. I turned back toward Angie in time to see her kick her right shoe off her foot and pull her sweatshirt over her head at the same time. She wore only a black bra and blue jeans as she shivered in the crisp air and blew color into her cheeks.

'You're not going down there,' I said.

'You're right.' She nodded and bent toward her

sweatshirt, and then she burst past me and by the time I spun toward her, she was airborne, kicking her legs and throwing her chest out in front of her. The helicopter canted to its right and Angie's body twisted in the light and then straightened.

She dropped like a missile.

In the white light, her body was dark. With her hands clamped tight to her thighs, she looked like a slim statue as she plummeted.

She hit the water like a butcher knife, sliced in clean, and disappeared.

'We've got one in the water,' someone said over the walkie-talkie. 'We've got one in the water.'

As if certain I'd follow her lead, the helicopter swung back in toward the cliff, turned to its right, and hovered there, jerking slightly from side to side but forming an immediate wall in front of me.

The trick to jumping off quarry cliffs has always been one of speed and lunging. You have to jump out as far as possible so that the air and gravity's whims don't push you back into the walls and outcroppings as you fall. With the helicopter in front of me, even if I could manage to dive below its legs, the downdraft would swat me into the cliff, leave me plastered there like a stain.

I lay on my stomach and watched for Angie. The way she'd hit the water, even if she'd begun kicking as soon as her head went under, she'd still dropped deep. And with these quarries, anything could have been lying in wait as soon as she hit the water: logs, an old refrigerator perched on a submerged shelf.

She surfaced fifteen yards from the doll, looked around wildly, and dove under again.

On the south side of the quarry, Broussard

appeared on the top of a ragged outcropping of rocks. He waved his arms and the helicopter on that side swung in toward him. Broussard reached up and a scream of turbine – like the wail of a dentist's drill – pierced the night as the helicopter lowered its legs toward Broussard. He reached out for the leg but a breeze pushed the entire carriage away from him in a lurch.

The same gust of wind buffeted the helicopter in front of me, and it almost drifted into the side of the cliff. It pulled back and banked to its right, turned in the center of the quarry, and started coming back as I kicked off my shoes and removed my jacket.

Below, Angie surfaced again and swam over to the doll. She turned her head, looked up at the helicopters, and went under.

Across the quarry, the other helicopter swung in toward Broussard. He stepped back on the craggy outcropping, seemed to lose his footing, but then he got his arms up and wrapped around the leg as the helicopter swayed back from the cliff and turned its nose out over the water. Broussard's legs kicked at the air, and his body dipped and rose, dipped and rose, and then he was pulled up into the cabin.

The helicopter on my side came straight at me, and I realized almost too late that it was trying to land. I scooped up shoes and jacket and stumbled back from the ledge and then to my left as the front of the legs dipped toward rock, then jerked back and swung its tail rotor to the left.

When it came back at a slightly higher elevation, the blast from the rotors was strong enough to knock me down, and the whine of the turbine dug against my eardrums like a metal pick.

As I scrambled to my feet, the helicopter bounced once, then twice off the smooth stone. I could see the pilot's face tighten in the cockpit as he fought for purchase, and the nose dipped and the tail rose and for a second I thought the rotors would scrape the crop of rocks that separated the cliff top from the tree line.

A cop in a dark blue jumpsuit and black helmet jumped from the cabin and kept his head low and his knees bent as he ran across the rock toward me.

'Kenzie?' he shouted.

I nodded.

'Come on.' He grabbed my arm and pushed my head down as the other helicopter shot away from the water and off toward the slope where we'd left Poole. There was no way they'd land over there, I knew. It was too tight, no clearing to speak of. Their only hope of getting him out of there was to drop a man and a basket over the side and pull Poole up and out.

The cop shoved me into the cabin as the rotors continued to whip overhead, and as soon as I was inside, the machine lurched off the rock and dropped over the side.

I could see Angie below us as we swooped down toward her. She held Amanda's doll in one hand and dropped below the surface. As the helicopter slid over the surface, the water began to churn and swirl.

'Go back up!' I screamed.

The co-pilot looked back at me.

I jerked my thumb toward the ceiling. 'You'll drown her! Go back up!'

The co-pilot nudged the pilot and the pilot pulled back on the throttle and my stomach slid into my intestines as the helicopter banked to the right and a graffiti-strewn cliff loomed through the cockpit window and then broke away from us as we rose and turned in a full circle and hovered from a height of about thirty feet over the last place we'd seen Angie.

She came up and flailed at the eddies engulfing her, spit water from her mouth, and turned onto her back.

'What's she doing?' the cop beside me said.

'Going to shore,' I said, as Angie backstroked toward the rocks, the doll arcing with the windmill motion of her left arm.

The cop nodded, his rifle aimed at the tree line.

Angie's high school had no swim team, so she competed for the Girls Clubs of America, won a silver medal when she was sixteen in a regional competition. Even with the years of smoking, she still had the stroke. Her body cut cleanly through the water, barely disturbing it, leaving so little in her wake that she could have been an eel as she slid toward shore.

'She's going to have to walk back,' the co-pilot shouted. 'We can't land down there.'

Angie sensed a small outcropping of jagged rocks just before she would have crashed into them. She turned her body and floated the rest of the way to the rocks, placed the doll gingerly in a crevice between them, then pulled herself up on top.

The pilot swung the helicopter down by the rocks and spoke through a megaphone mounted above the light. 'Miss Gennaro, we cannot attempt evacuation. The walls are too close and there's no purchase.'

Angie nodded and waved tiredly, her body white in the harsh spotlight, strings of her long black hair clamped to her cheeks.

'Directly behind those rocks,' the pilot called over the megaphone, 'is a trail. Follow it down and keep turning left. You'll end up on Ricciuti Drive. There'll be someone there to meet you.'

Angie gave him a thumbs-up and sat down on the rocks, inhaled deeply, and placed the doll on her lap.

She shrank to nothing but a pale dot in a wall of black as the helicopter banked once again and shot up over the quarry walls, and the land raced far too quickly underneath as we dipped over the old railway route and then headed west for the ski slopes in the Blue Hills.

'The hell was she looking for down there?' The cop beside me lowered his rifle.

'The girl,' I said.

'Hell,' the cop said, 'we're going back in with divers.'

'At night?' I said.

The cop looked through his visor at me. 'Probably,' he said, with a bit of hesitation. 'Definitely in the morning.'

'I think she was hoping to find her before it got to that point,' I said.

The cop shrugged. 'Man, if Amanda McCready's in that quarry, only God decides whether we find her corpse or not.'

19

We landed on the bunny slope of the Blue Hills Reservation, dropped down neatly between the ski lift lines, and watched as the second helicopter did the same, settled gently about twenty yards away.

Several police cars and ambulances, two MDC ranger cars, and a few trooper units greeted us.

Broussard jumped out of the second helicopter and raced toward the first police car, pulled the uniformed cop from the driver's seat.

I jogged over as he started the engine. 'Where's Poole?'

'I don't know,' he said. 'He wasn't where we left him. He wasn't anywhere on the trail. I think he either tried to make it back down on his own or came up to the top when he heard the shots.'

Major Dempsey came rushing across the grass toward us. 'Broussard, what the hell happened up there?'

'Long story, Major.'

I climbed in beside Broussard.

'Where's the child?'

'There was no kid up there,' Broussard said. 'It was a setup.'

Dempsey leaned in the window. 'I heard the girl's doll was floating in the water.'

Broussard looked at me, eyes wild.

'Yeah,' I said. 'Didn't see her body, though.'

Broussard dropped the shift into DRIVE. 'Got to find Poole, sir.'

'Sergeant Raftopoulos called in two minutes ago. He's on Pritchett Street. Says we got some DOAs.'

'Who?'

'Don't know.'

Dempsey leaned back from the window. 'I have a ranger unit going over to Ricciuti Drive to get your partner, Mr Kenzie.'

'Thanks.'

'Who fired all the ordnance up there?'

'Don't know, sir. They pinned my ass down, though.'

The sudden whine of a turbine screeched into the field, and Dempsey had to shout to be heard.

'They can't get out!' Dempsey yelled. 'They're locked in! There's no way out!'

'Yes, sir.'

'No sign of the girl?' Dempsey seemed to think that if he asked the question enough, sooner or later he'd get the answer he was hoping for.

Broussard shook his head. 'Look, sir, with all due respect, Sergeant Raftopoulos had some sort of heart attack on the trail. I want to get to him.'

'Go.' Dempsey stepped aside and waved several cars into line behind us as Broussard punched the gas and drove down the slope, pinned the wheel at a line of trees and spun onto a dirt path, swung left a few seconds later, and sped down a crater-ravaged trail toward the expressway off-ramp that would lead around a rotary and onto Pritchett Street.

Two more dusty paths and we broke onto Quarry Street and raced down the southern side of the hills, with red and blue lights bouncing and swerving behind us in the rearview mirror.

Broussard didn't slow as he shot through a stop sign at the end of Quarry Street. He fishtailed over the shoulder and turned into the rotary, actually giving the gas pedal a deeper push. All four tires fought him for a second. The heavy car seemed to jerk in against itself and buckle, as if it would suddenly turn on its side, but then the wheels caught and the powerful engine moaned and we shot off the rotary. Broussard pinned the wheel again, and we tore over another shoulder, spewed grass and dirt up onto the hood, and burst past an abandoned mill on our right, saw Poole sitting against the rear quarter panel of the Lexus RX 300 on the left side of the road about fifty yards past the mill.

Poole's head lolled against the fender. His shirt was open to the navel, and he'd placed one hand against his heart.

Broussard slammed the car to a stop and jumped out, slid on the dirt, and dropped to his knees by Poole.

'Partner! Partner!'

Poole opened his eyes, smiled weakly. 'Got lost.'

Broussard felt his pulse, then put a hand to his heart, pushed up Poole's left eyelid with his thumb. 'Okay, buddy. Okay. You're gonna be . . . you're gonna be fine.'

Several police cars pulled past us. A young cop stepped out of the first one, a Quincy unit, and Broussard said, 'Open your back door!'

The cop fumbled with the flashlight in his hand, dropped it to the dirt. He reached down to pick it up.

'Open your fucking door!' Broussard screamed. 'Now!'

The young cop managed to kick the flashlight under the car before he reached back and opened the door.

'Kenzie, help me lift him.'

I got a grip on Poole's lower legs, and Broussard eased behind him and wrapped his arms around his chest, and we carried him to the back of the police car and slid him onto the seat.

'I'm fine,' Poole said, and his eyes rolled to the left.

'Sure you are.' Broussard smiled. He turned his head to look at the young cop, who appeared very nervous. 'You drive fast?'

'Uh, yes, sir.'

Behind us, several troopers and Quincy cops approached the front of the Lexus, guns drawn.

'Step out of the car now!' one trooper shouted, pointing his weapon at Gutierrez's windshield.

'Which hospital is closer?' Broussard asked. 'Quincy or Milton?'

'Uh, from here, sir, it's Milton.'

'How fast can you get there?' Broussard asked the cop.

'Three minutes.'

'Make it two.' Broussard slapped the cop's shoulder and shoved him toward the driver's door.

The cop hopped behind the wheel. Broussard squeezed Poole's hand and said, 'See you in a bit.'

Poole nodded sleepily.

We stepped back and Broussard shut the back door.

'Two minutes,' he repeated to the cop. The wheels of the unit spewed gravel and kicked up clouds of dust as the cop blew out onto the road, turned on his lights, and sped down the asphalt so fast he could have been shot from a rocket booster.

'Holy shit,' another cop said. He stood at the front of the Lexus. 'Holy shit,' he said again.

Broussard and I walked toward the Lexus and Broussard grabbed a pair of troopers, pointed at the abandoned mill building. 'Secure that building. Now.'

The troopers didn't even question. They placed hands to the guns on their hips and ran back up the road toward the mill.

We reached the Lexus, worked our way through the small crowd of cops blocking the front bumper, and looked through the windshield at Chris Mullen and Pharaoh Gutierrez. Gutierrez was in the driver's seat, Mullen riding shotgun. The headlights were still on. The engine was running. A single hole formed a small spiderweb in the windshield in front of Gutierrez. An identical hole was bored through the glass in front of Mullen.

The holes in their heads were pretty similar, too – both the size of a dime, both puckered and white around the edges, both spilling a thin stream of blood down the men's noses.

By the looks of it, Gutierrez had taken the first shot. His face registered nothing except a sense of impatience, and both his hands were empty and lying palms up on the seat. The keys were in the ignition, the shift in PARK. Chris Mullen's right hand gripped the gun in his waistband, and the look on his face was a sudden frozen seizure of fear and surprise. He'd had about half a second to know he was going to die, maybe less. But enough time for everything to turn slow-motion on him, a thousand terrified thoughts scrambling through his angry brain in the time it took for him to register the bullet that had killed Pharaoh, reach for his gun, and hear the spit of the next bullet punch through the windshield.

Bubba, I thought.

Fifty yards in front of the Lexus, the abandoned mill with its sagging widow's walk would have provided a perfect sniper's perch.

In the shafts of light cast by the car's headlamps, I could see the two Staties approaching it slowly, knees bent slightly, guns drawn and aimed up at the widow's walk. One of them pointed to the other, and they approached the side door. One threw it open, and the other stepped in front of it, gun pointed at chest level.

Bubba, I thought, I hope you didn't do this just for fun. Tell me you have Amanda McCready.

Broussard followed my gaze. 'How much you want to bet the angle of trajectory tells us the bullets were fired from that building?'

'No bet,' I said.

Two hours later, they were still sorting out the mess. The night had turned suddenly cold, and a light sleet fell and splattered windshields and stuck in our hair like lice.

The troopers who'd entered the mill had come back out with a Winchester Model 94 lever-action rifle they'd found, with LAD target scope attached. The rifle had been dumped in a barrel of ancient oil on the second floor, just to the right of the window that led to the widow's walk. The serial numbers had been filed off, and the first guy from Forensics who looked at it laughed when someone suggested the possibility of prints.

More troopers were sent into the mill to look for further evidence, but in two hours they hadn't found shell casings or anything else, and Forensics had been unable to get any prints off the railing of the widow's walk or the frame of the window leading out there.

The ranger who'd met Angie on the back side of the hill leading to Swingle's Quarry had given her a bright orange raincoat to cover herself and a pair of thick socks for her feet, but still she shivered in the night, kept rubbing her dark hair with a towel even though it had dried or frozen hours ago. Indian summer, it appeared, had gone the way of the Massachusetts Indian.

Two divers had attempted a search of the Granite Rail Quarry but reported visibility at absolute zero below thirty feet, and once the weather kicked in, the silt deposits loosened from the granite walls had turned even the shallow water into a sand-storm.

The divers quit at ten without finding anything but a pair of men's jeans hanging from a shelf about twenty feet below the water line.

When Broussard had reached the south side of the quarry, almost directly across from the cliff where Angie and I had seen the doll, a note had been waiting for him, placed neatly under a small boulder and illuminated by a pencil-thin flashlight hung from a branch above it.

Duck.

As Broussard reached for the note, the trees erupted with gunfire, and he dove out from the tree line onto the cliff plateau, grappling for his gun and walkie-talkie, leaving the money bag and his flashlight back at the tree line. A second barrage of bullets drove him to the edge of the cliff, where he lay in darkness, his only safety, and trained his gun on the tree line but didn't fire for fear the muzzle flashes would reveal his exact position.

A search of Broussard's last position found the note, the kidnapper's pencil light, Broussard's flashlight, and the bag, which was open and empty. Over a hundred spent shells had been found in the trees and ledges directly behind Broussard's cliff in the last hour and the trooper who radioed in said:

'We're gonna find a lot more. Looks like the shooters went house back here. Looks like Grenada, for Christ's sake.'

The troopers and rangers on our side of the quarry had called down to report finding evidence of at least fifty rounds fired into our cliff plateau or the trees behind us.

The consensus was pretty much summed up by a trooper we heard over the radio. 'Major Dempsey, sir, they weren't supposed to walk back out of here. No way in hell.'

All roads into and out of the area remained locked down, but based on the fact that the shots were fired from the southern side of Granite Rail Quarry, troopers, rangers, and local police with hounds were sent to concentrate their search for the suspects there, and even from the street on the northern side we could occasionally see the symphony of lights playing off the treetops.

Poole had suffered what doctors believed was a myocardial infarction, exacerbated by his walk downhill to Quarry Street. Once there, Poole, already disoriented and possibly delirious, had apparently seen Gutierrez and Mullen in the Lexus heading for Pritchett Street and had made his way over there in time to find their corpses and call in from the car phone in the Lexus.

Last we'd heard, Poole was in ICU at Milton Hospital, his condition critical.

'Anybody done the math yet?' Dempsey asked us. We were leaning against the hood of our Crown Victoria, Broussard smoking one of Angie's cigarettes, Angie shivering and slurping coffee from a cup with the seal of the MDC on it as I ran a hand up and down her back, trying to push some heat back into her blood.

'Which math?' I said.

'The math that puts Gutierrez and Mullen down on the road at about the same time you three were under fire.' He chewed a red plastic toothpick, touched it occasionally with his thumb and index, but never removed it from his mouth. ''Less they had a helicopter, too, and I don't think they did somehow . . . You?'

'I don't think they had a helicopter,' I said.

He smiled. 'Right. So, barring that, there's really no way they could have been on top of those hills and tooling around down here in their Lexus a minute or so later. Just seems – I dunno – impossible. You follow?'

Angie's teeth chattered as she said, 'So who else was up there?'

'That's the question, isn't it? Among others.' He looked back over his shoulder at the dark shape of the hills rising on the other side of the expressway. 'Not to mention, where's the girl? Where's the money? Where's the person or persons who unloaded a Schwarzenegger movie's worth of fire-power up there? Where's the person or persons who DOA'd Gutierrez and Mullen so smoothly?' He put his foot up on the fender, touched the toothpick again, and looked up at the cars racing past on the expressway just on the other side of the Lexus. 'Press is going to have a field day.'

Broussard took a long pull of his cigarette, and exhaled loudly. 'You're playing CYOA, aren't you, Dempsey.'

Dempsey shrugged, his owl eyes still on the expressway.

'CYOA?' Angie chattered.

'Cover Your Own Ass,' Broussard said. 'Major Dempsey does not want to be known as the cop who lost Amanda McCready, two hundred thousand dollars, and two lives in one night. Right?'

Dempsey turned his head until the toothpick pointed directly at Broussard. 'I would not want to be known as that cop, no, Detective Broussard.'

'So I will be.' Broussard nodded.

'You did lose the money,' Dempsey said. 'We let you play it your way, and this is how it turned out.' He raised his eyebrows at the Lexus as two coroner's assistants pulled Gutierrez's body from the driver's seat and laid it in the black bag they'd spread on the road. 'Your Lieutenant Doyle? He's been on the phone since eight-thirty with the Police Commissioner himself, trying to explain. Last time I saw him, he was trying to stick up for you and your partner. I told him it was a waste of time.'

'What exactly,' Angie said, 'was he supposed to do when they opened up on him like that? Have the presence of mind to grab the bag and dive off the cliff with it?'

Dempsey shrugged. 'That would have been one alternative, sure.'

'I don't fucking believe this,' Angie said. Her teeth stopped chattering. 'He risked his life for—'

'Miss Gennaro.' Broussard stopped her with a hand on her knee. 'Major Dempsey is not saying anything Lieutenant Doyle isn't going to say.'

'Listen to Detective Broussard, Miss Gennaro,' Dempsey said.

'Someone's got to take the fall for this cluster fuck,' Broussard said, 'and I'm elected.'

Dempsey chuckled. 'You're the only one running for the office.'

He left us there and walked over to a group of troopers, speaking into his walkie-talkie as he looked back up at the quarry hills.

'This isn't right,' Angie said.

'Yes,' Broussard said, 'it is.' He flicked his cigarette, smoked down to the filter, into the street. 'I fucked up.'

'*We* fucked up,' Angie said.

He shook his head. 'If we still had the money, they could live with Amanda being still missing or dead. But without the money? We look like clowns. And that's my fault.' He spit into the street, shook his head, and kicked the tire at his feet with the back of his heel.

Angie watched a Forensics tech slide Amanda's doll into a plastic bag, seal it, and write on the bag with black marker.

'She's in there, isn't she?' Angie looked up at the dark hills.

'She's in there,' Broussard said.

20

When dawn arrived, we were still there as the tow truck pulled the Lexus down Pritchett Street and turned into the rotary toward the expressway.

Troopers moved in and out of the hills, returning with bags filled with shell casings and several shards of bullets recovered from rock face and dug out from tree trunks. One of them had also recovered Angie's sweatshirt and shoes, but no one seemed to know who that trooper was or what he'd done with them. Over the course of our vigil, a Quincy cop had placed a blanket over Angie's shoulders, but still she shivered and her lips often looked blue in the combination of streetlights, headlamps, and lights set up to illuminate the crime scene.

Lieutenant Doyle came down from the hills around one and beckoned Broussard with a crooked finger. They walked up the road to the yellow crime scene tape strung around the mill building, and once they'd stopped and squared their shoulders toward each other, Doyle exploded. You couldn't hear the words, but you could hear volume, and you could see as he jabbed his index finger in Broussard's face that a 'Shucks, we tried' attitude wasn't informing his mood. Broussard kept his head down through most of it, but it went on a while, a good twenty minutes at least, and Doyle seemed only to get more agitated. When he was spent, Broussard looked up, and Doyle shook his head at him in such a way that even from a distance of fifty yards you could feel the cold finality in it. He left Broussard standing there and walked into the mill building.

'Bad news, I take it,' Angie said, as Broussard bummed another of her cigarettes from the pack sitting on the hood of the car.

'I'm to be suspended sometime tomorrow pending an IAD hearing.' Broussard lit the cigarette and shrugged. 'My last official duty will be to inform Helene McCready that we failed to recover her daughter.'

'And your lieutenant,' I said. 'The one who approved this operation. What's his culpability?'

'None.' Broussard leaned against the bumper, sucked back on the cigarette, exhaled a thin stream of blue smoke.

'None?' Angie said.

'None.' Broussard flicked ash into the street. 'I take the fall and all the responsibility, admit to covering up pertinent information so I could get all the glory for the collar, and I won't lose my badge.' He shrugged again. 'Welcome to department politics.'

Angie said, 'But—'

'Oh, yeah,' Broussard said, and turned to look at her. 'The lieutenant made it very clear that if you speak to anyone about this entire affair, he'll – let me see if I got this – "bury you up to your eyelids in the Marion Socia murder."'

I looked off at the mill building door where I'd last seen Doyle. 'He's got shit.'

Broussard shook his head. 'He never bluffs. If he says he can get you for it, he can.'

I thought about it. Four years ago, Angie and I had killed a pimp and crack dealer named Marion Socia in cold blood under the south-east expressway. We'd used unregistered guns and wiped them clean of prints.

But we'd left a witness, a gangbanger-to-be named Eugene. I never knew his last name, and I'd been pretty sure at the time that if I didn't kill Socia he'd kill Eugene. Not then, but soon. Eugene, I decided, must have taken a few pinches over the years – a career with Shearson Lehman hadn't seemed in the kid's future – and during one of those pinches he must have offered us up in return for a lighter sentence. Given the utter lack of evidence tying us to Socia's death in any other regard, I'm sure the DA had decided not to follow up, but someone had tucked the information away and passed it along to Doyle.

'He's got us by the balls, is what you're saying.'

Broussard glanced at me, then at Angie, and smiled. 'Euphemistically speaking, of course. But, yeah. He owns you.'

'Comforting thought,' Angie said.

'This week's been full of comforting thoughts.' Broussard tossed his cigarette. 'I'm going to go find a phone, call my wife, tell her the good news.'

He walked off in the direction of the cops and vans circled around Gutierrez's Lexus, his shoulders hunched, hands dug in his pockets, his steps just a bit uncertain, as if the ground felt different underfoot than it had half an hour ago.

Angie shuddered against the chill and I shuddered with her.

The divers went back to the quarry as morning rose in gradations of bruised purple and deep pink over the hills, and yellow tape and sawhorses were used to block off Pritchett and Quarry streets as the cops prepared for morning rush hour. A contingent of troopers formed a human barrier to the hills themselves. At 5 A.M., troopers were left stationed at the access points of all major roads, but traffic was allowed to flow through checkpoints, and the highway on and off ramps were opened. Pretty soon, as if they'd been waiting just around the bend, TV news vans and print reporters camped out on the expressway, clogged the breakdown lane, and shone their lights down on us and across at the hills. Several times a reporter called down to Angie to ask why she wasn't wearing shoes. Several times Angie answered with her head down and her middle finger rising up from where her hands lay on her lap.

At first the reporters had shown up because word had leaked that someone had unloaded a few hundred rounds from an automatic weapon in the Quincy quarries and two corpses had been found on Pritchett Street in what looked like a professional execution. Then, somehow, Amanda McCready's name slid down off the hills with the dawn breeze, and the circus began.

One of the reporters on the expressway recognized Broussard, and then the rest of them did, and pretty soon we felt like galley slaves as they shouted down to us.

'Detective, where is Amanda McCready?'

'Is she dead?'

'Is she in the quarry?'

'Where's your partner?'

'Is it true Amanda McCready's kidnappers were shot last night?'

'Is there any truth to the rumor that ransom money was lost?'

'Was Amanda's body retrieved from the quarry? Is that why you're not wearing shoes, ma'am?'

As if on cue, a trooper crossed Pritchett Street with a paper bag and handed it to Angie. 'Your stuff, ma'am. They sent it down with some pancake slugs.'

Angie kept her head down and thanked him, removed her Doc Martens from the bag, and put them on.

'The sweatshirt's going to be a harder act to pull off,' Broussard said, with a small smile.

'Yeah?' Angie slid off the hood and turned her back to the reporters as one of them tried to vault the guardrail and a trooper pushed him back with an extended nightstick.

Angie dropped the blanket and raincoat off her shoulders, and several cameras swung our way at the news of her bare flesh and black bra straps.

She looked at me. 'Should I do a slow strip, move my hips a bit?'

'It's your show,' I said. 'I think you have everybody's attention.'

'Got mine,' Broussard said, staring openly at the press of Angie's breasts against black lace.

'Oh, joy.' She grimaced and pulled the sweatshirt over her head, pulled it down her torso.

Someone on the expressway applauded, and someone else whistled. Angie kept her back to them as she pulled thick strands of her hair from the collar.

'My show?' she said to me, with a sad smile and

small shake of her head. 'It's their show, man. All theirs.'

Poole's status was changed from critical to guarded shortly after sunrise, and, with nothing to do but wait, we left Pritchett Street and followed Broussard's Taurus over to Milton Hospital.

At the hospital, we argued with the admitting nurse over how many of us could go into ICU when none of us were Poole's blood relatives. A doctor passed us and took one look at Angie and said, 'Are you aware your skin is blue?'

After another small argument, Angie followed the doctor behind a curtain to be checked for hypothermia, and the admitting nurse grudgingly allowed us into ICU to see Poole.

'Myocardial infarction,' he said, as he propped himself up on the pillows. 'Hell of a word, huh?'

'It's two words,' Broussard said, and reached out awkwardly and gave Poole's arm a small squeeze.

'Whatever. Friggin' heart attack was what it was.' He hissed against a sudden pain as he shifted again.

'Relax,' Broussard said. 'Christ's sake.'

'The fuck happened up there?' Poole said.

We told him the little we knew.

'Two shooters in the woods and one on the ground?' he said when we finished.

'That's the way it's looking,' Broussard said. 'Or one shooter with two rifles in the woods and one on the widow's walk.'

Poole made a face like he bought that theory about as much as he believed JFK was killed by a lone gunman. He moved his head on the pillow, looked at me. 'You definitely saw two rifles get dumped over the cliff?'

'I'm pretty sure,' I said. 'It was nuts out there.' I shrugged, then nodded. 'No, I'm sure. Two rifles.'

'And the shooter at the mill leaves his gun behind?'

'Yup.'

'But not the shell casings.'

'Right.'

'And the shooter or shooters in the woods get rid of the rifles but leave shell casings everywhere.'

'That is correct, sir,' Broussard said.

'Christ,' he said. 'I don't get this.'

Angie came into the ward then, dabbing at her arm with a cotton swab, flexing the forearm up against the biceps. She came over to Poole's bed and smiled down at him.

'What'd the doctor say?' Broussard asked.

'Low-grade hypothermia.' She shrugged. 'He shot me up with chicken soup or something, said I'd keep my fingers and toes.'

Color had returned to her flesh – not nearly as much as usual, but enough. She sat on the bed beside Poole and said, 'The two of us, Poole – we look like a couple of ghosts.'

His lips cracked when he smiled. 'I hear you emulated the famous cliff divers of the Galapagos Islands, my dear.'

'Acapulco,' Broussard said. 'There are no cliff divers in the Galapagos.'

'Fiji, then,' Poole said, 'and stop correcting me. Again, kids, what the hell is going on?'

Angie patted his cheek lightly. 'You tell us. What happened to you?'

He pursed his lips for a moment. 'I'm not real sure.

For whatever reason, I found myself walking down the hill. Problem was, I left my walkie-talkie and my flashlight behind.' He raised his eyebrows. 'Bright, wouldn't you say? And when I heard all the gunfire, I tried to head back up to where I'd come from, but no matter what I did, it seemed like I kept moving away from the noise, instead of toward it. Woods,' he said with a shake of his head. 'Next thing I know I'm at the corner of Quarry Street and the off-ramp from the expressway, and I see the Lexus shoot by. So I walk after it. Time I get there, our friends have received their head taps and I'm feeling kind of dizzy.'

'You remember calling it in?' Broussard asked.

'I did?'

Broussard nodded. 'On the car phone.'

'Wow,' Poole said. 'I'm pretty smart, huh?'

Angie smiled and took a handkerchief from the cart by Poole's bed, wiped his forehead with it.

'Christ,' Poole said, his tongue thick.

'What?'

His eyes rolled away from us for a moment, then snapped back. 'Huh? Nothing, just these drugs they got in me. Hard to concentrate.'

The admitting nurse parted the curtain by Broussard. 'You have to go. Please.'

'What happened up there?' Poole slurred.

'Now,' the nurse said, as Poole's eyes rolled to the left and he smacked his dry lips, batted his eyelashes. 'Mr Raftopoulos is not up to this.'

'No,' Poole said. 'Wait.'

Broussard patted his arm. 'We'll be back, buddy. Don't you worry.'

'What happened?' Poole asked again, his voice

fading into sleep as we stepped back from the bed.

Good question, I thought, as we walked out of ICU.

As soon as we got back to the apartment, Angie hopped in a warm shower and I called Bubba.

'What?' he answered.

'Tell me you have her.'

'What? Patrick?'

'Tell me you have Amanda McCready.'

'No. What? Why would I have her?'

'You took out Gutierrez and—'

'No, I didn't.'

'Bubba,' I said, 'you did. You had to.'

'Gutierrez and Mullen? No way, dude. I spent two hours with my face in the dirt at Cunningham Park.'

'You weren't even there?'

'I got hit. Someone was waiting, Patrick. I took a fucking sledgehammer or something in the back of my head, knocked me cold. I never even made it out of the park.'

'All right,' I said, and felt clouds of oil swimming through my head, 'tell me again. Slow. You got to Cunningham Park—'

'At about six-thirty. I take my gear, I cut through the park toward the trees. I'm just about to go into the trees and make my way to the hills when I hear something. I start to turn my head and fucking – *crack* – someone hits me in the back of the head. Which, you know, just annoys me at first, but fucks up my vision too, and I'm starting to duck and turn, and *crack* again. I go to one knee, and I take a third hit. I think there might have been a fourth, but next thing I know I'm waking up in a pile of blood and it's like eight-thirty. Time I get into the trees again, the woods are crawling with Staties. I go back, go to Giggle Doc's.'

Giggle Doc was the ether-snorting doctor Bubba and half the mob guys in the city used to repair injuries they couldn't report.

'You okay?' I said.

'Got some serious ringing in my head and things are still going black and then clearing, but I'll be all right. I want this motherfucker, Patrick. No one knocks me down, you know?'

I knew. Of all the things I'd heard in the last ten hours, this was by far the most depressing. Anyone fast enough and smart enough to take Bubba out of the equation was very, very good at his job.

Another thing: If you were to deal with Bubba in that way, why leave him alive? The kidnappers had killed Mullen and Gutierrez and tried to kill Broussard, Angie, and me. Why hadn't they just shot Bubba from a distance and been done with him?

'Giggle Doc said one more swing probably would have severed the tendons in back of my skull. Man,' he said, 'I am fucking pissed.'

'As soon as I know who it was,' I said, 'I'll pass it along.'

'I've been sending out my own questions, you know? I heard about the Pharaoh and Mullen from Giggle Doc, so I've got Nelson making some phone calls. Heard the cops lost the money, too.'

'Yup.'

'And no girl.'

'No girl.'

'You picked a fight with some serious mother-fuckers this time, dude.'

'I know.'

'Hey, Patrick?'

'Yeah.'

'Cheese would never be stupid enough to send someone to take a pipe to my head.'

'Not knowingly. Maybe he didn't expect you to be there.'

'Cheese knows how tight me and you are. He's got to half figure you'd bring me in for backup on something like this.'

He was right. Cheese was too smart at covering his bases not to expect Bubba might be involved. And Cheese also had to know that Bubba was capable of rolling a grenade into a group of Cheese's men just on the off chance he'd kill the guy who'd piped him. So, if Cheese had given the order . . . again, why hadn't he made it a termination contract? With Bubba dead, Cheese wouldn't have to sweat reprisal. But by leaving him alive, Cheese's only alternative, if he wanted to have any organization left by the time he got out of stir, was to hand over at least one of the players in the woods that night to Bubba. Unless he had other options I couldn't envision.

'Christ!' I said.

'Got another mind-fuck for you,' Bubba said.

I wasn't sure I could handle one more twist in my already knotted brain, but I said, 'Shoot.'

'There's a rumor going around about Pharaoh Gutierrez.'

'I know. He was teaming up with Mullen to take over Cheese's action.'

'No, not that one. Everyone knows that one. Thing I'm hearing is that Pharaoh wasn't one of us.'

'Then what was he?'

'A cop, Patrick,' Bubba said, and I felt everything in my brain slide to the left. 'Word is he was DEA.'

21

'DEA?' Angie said. 'You're kidding.'

I shrugged. 'Just what Bubba heard. You know street info: could be total bullshit, could be total truth. Too soon to tell.'

'So, what? Gutierrez was undercover for six years, working Cheese Olamon's operation, and then he gets involved in the kidnapping of a four-year-old and he doesn't pass that info on to his superiors?'

'Doesn't add up, does it?'

'No. But what else is new?'

I leaned back in the kitchen chair, resisted an urge to punch the wall. This was one of the most infuriating cases I'd ever worked. Absolutely nothing made sense. A four-year-old girl disappears. Investigation leads us to believe the child was kidnapped by drug dealers who'd been ripped off by the mother. A ransom demand for the stolen money arrives from a woman who seems to work for the drug dealers. The ransom drop is an ambush. The drug dealers are killed. One of the drug dealers may or may not be an undercover operative for the federal government. The missing girl remains missing or at the bottom of a quarry.

Angie reached across the table and put her warm

hand on my wrist. 'We have to at least try to get a few hours' sleep.'

I turned my wrist, took her hand in mine. 'Is there one single thing about this case that makes sense to you?'

'Now that Gutierrez and Mullen have been whacked? No. There's no one else in Cheese's organization who could pick up the slack. Hell, there's no one in his organization who's smart enough to have pulled this off.'

'Wait a minute . . .'

'What?'

'You just said it yourself. There's a power vacuum in Olamon's organization now. What if that was the point?'

'Huh?'

'What if Cheese knew Mullen and Gutierrez were planning a coup? Or maybe he knew Mullen was, at least, and he'd heard whispers that Gutierrez wasn't who he claimed to be?'

'So Cheese set all this up – the kidnapping, the ransom demands, et cetera – just so he could take out Mullen and Gutierrez?' She dropped my hand. 'You're serious?'

'It's a theory.'

'An idiotic one,' she said.

'Hey.'

'No, think about it. Why go to all this trouble when he could have hired a couple of jack boys to pop Mullen and Gutierrez while they slept?'

'But he's also pissed at Helene, wants his two hundred grand back.'

'So he tells Mullen to kidnap the kid, set up this elaborate child-for-money ruse, and then he has someone whack Mullen while it's going down?'

'Why not?'

'Because then where's Amanda? Where's the money? Who was firing from those trees last night? Who knocked Bubba out? How did Mullen not know he was being set up? Do you realize how many people in Cheese's organization would have had to be in on this huge, complicated conspiracy to pull it off? And Mullen wasn't stupid. He was the smartest guy in Cheese's crew. You don't think he would have sniffed out a plan from the inside to kill him?'

I rubbed my eyes. 'Christ. My head hurts.'

'Mine, too. And you're not helping.'

I scowled at her and she smiled.

'Okay,' she said, 'back to square one. Amanda is abducted. Why?'

'Two hundred grand her mother stole from Cheese.'

'Why didn't Cheese just send someone around to threaten her? I'm pretty sure she would have buckled. They'd know that, too.'

'It could have taken them three months just to figure out the money wasn't impounded by the police in the raid on the bikers.'

'Okay. But then they'd have moved fast. Ray Likanski had black eyes the day we met him.'

'You think he got them from Mullen?'

'Mullen would have given him a lot worse than black eyes if he thought he'd ripped him off. See, that's what I'm saying. If Mullen thought Likanski and Helene had ripped the organization off, he wouldn't kidnap Helene's kid. He'd just kill Helene.'

'So maybe it wasn't Cheese who had Amanda abducted?'

'Maybe not.'

'And the two hundred grand was a coincidence?' I tilted my head, cocked an eyebrow at her.

'You're saying that's a big coincidence.'

'I'm saying that's a coincidence the size of Vermont. Particularly when the note found in Kimmie's underwear said the two hundred grand equals a child's return.'

She nodded, pinched her coffee cup handle, and turned the cup back and forth on the table. 'Okay. So we're back to Cheese. And all those questions about why he'd go to all this trouble.'

'Which, I agree, makes no sense and doesn't sound like Cheese's MO.'

She looked up from her coffee cup. 'So where is she, Patrick?'

I touched her arm, slid my hand under the cuff of her bathrobe. 'She's in the quarry, Ange.'

'Why?'

'I don't know.'

'Someone abducts that girl, ransoms her, and kills her. Simple as that?'

'Yes.'

'Why?'

'Because she'd seen her kidnappers' faces? Because whoever was up in the quarries last night smelled police, knew we were trying to play both ends up the middle? I don't know. Because people kill kids.'

She stood up. 'Let's go see Cheese.'

'What about sleep?'

'We can sleep when we're dead.'

22

The sleet that had visited us briefly last night had returned this morning, and by the time we reached Concord Prison it sounded like nickels pelting the hood.

This time I wasn't with two members of law enforcement, so Cheese was brought out into the visitors' room and faced us through a pane of thick glass. Angie and I each picked up a phone in our cubicle and Cheese reached for his.

'Hey, Ange,' he said. 'Looking fine.'

'Hey, Cheese.'

'Maybe, I get out of here someday, we could have a chocolate malt or something?'

'A chocolate malt?'

'Sure.' He rolled his shoulders. 'A root beer float. Something like that.'

She narrowed her eyes. 'Sure, Cheese. Sure. Give me a call when you're released.'

'Goddamn!' Cheese slapped the glass with his thick palm. 'You *know* that.'

'Cheese,' I said.

He raised his eyebrows.

'Chris Mullen's dead.'

'I heard. Terrible shame.'

Angie said, 'You seem to be handling it well.'

Cheese leaned back in his seat, appraised us for a moment, scratched his chest idly. 'This business, you know? Motherfuckers die young.'

'Pharaoh Gutierrez, too.'

'Yeah.' Cheese nodded. 'Sad about the Pharaoh. Motherfucker could dress. Know what I'm saying?'

I said, 'Rumor I hear is Pharaoh wasn't just working for you.'

Cheese cocked an eyebrow and seemed momentarily bewildered. 'Come again, my brother?'

'I hear Pharaoh was a Fed.'

'Shit.' Cheese smiled broadly and shook his head, but his eyes remained wide and slightly unfocused. 'You believe everything you hear on the street, you should – I dunno – become a motherfucking cop or something.'

It was a weak-ass analogy and he knew it. So much of who Cheese was depended on everything coming out of his mouth smooth, fast, and funny, even the threats. And it was pretty obvious by his grasping speech that the possibility of Pharaoh being a cop had never occurred to him until now.

I smiled. 'A cop, Cheese. In your organization. Think what that'll do to your cred.'

Cheese's eyes regained their cast of bemused curiosity, and he leaned back in his chair, settled back into himself. 'Your boy Broussard, he come to see me about an hour ago, tells me Mullen and Gutierrez are no more out of the kindness of his heart. Said he thinks I aced my own boys. Said he gonna make me pay. Said I'm responsible for him getting suspended, his old-coot partner getting sick. Pissed off the Cheese, you want to know the truth.'

'Sorry to hear that, Cheese.' I leaned in toward the glass. 'Someone else is real pissed off, too.'

'Yeah? Who's that?'

'Brother Rogowski.'

Cheese's fingers stopped scratching his chest and the front legs of his chair came forward, touched the ground. 'Why's Brother Rogowski irate?'

'Someone from your team piped him in the back of the head several times.'

Cheese shook his head. 'Not *my* team, baby. Not *my* team.'

I looked at Angie.

'That's unfortunate,' she said.

'Yeah,' I said. 'Too bad.'

'What?' Cheese said. 'You know I'd never raise a hand to Brother Rogowski.'

''Member that guy?' Angie said.

'Which?' I said.

'The one a few years back, bigwig in the Irish mob, you know him—' She snapped her fingers.

'Jack Rouse,' I said.

'Yeah. He was, like, the Irish godfather or something, wasn't he?'

'Wait,' Cheese said. 'No one knows what happened to Jack Rouse. Just he pissed off the Patrisos or something.'

He looked at us through the glass as we both shook our heads slowly.

'Wait. You're saying Jack Rouse got clipped by—'

'Sssh,' I said, and held a finger up to my lips.

Cheese placed the phone on the table for a minute and looked up at the ceiling. When he looked back at us, he seemed to have shrunk by a foot, and the dampness in his bangs plastered the hair to his forehead and made him look ten years younger. He brought the phone back up to his lips.

'The bowling alley rumor?' he whispered.

A couple of years ago, Bubba, a hit man named Pine, myself, and Phil Dimassi had met Jack Rouse and his demented right hand, Kevin Hurlihy, in an abandoned bowling alley in the leather district. Six of us had gone in, four of us had walked out. Jack Rouse and Kevin Hurlihy, tied, gagged, and tortured by Bubba and a few bowling balls, never stood a chance. The hit was sanctioned by Fat Freddy Constantine, head of the Italian Mafia here, and those of us who walked back out knew that no one would find the corpses and no one would ever be dumb enough to go looking.

'It's true?' Cheese whispered.

I gave Cheese the answer in my dead gaze.

'Bubba's gotta know I had nothing to do with him getting piped.'

I looked at Angie. She sighed, looked at Cheese, and then down at the small shelf below the glass.

'Patrick,' Cheese said, and all the pseudo-Superfly intonations had left his voice, 'you have to let Bubba know.'

'Know what?' Angie said.

'That I had nothing to do with this.'

Angie smiled and shook her head. 'Yeah, sure, Cheese. Sure.'

He whacked the glass with the back of his hand. 'You listen to me! I had nothing to do with this.'

'Bubba doesn't see it that way, Cheese.'

'So, tell him.'

'Why?' I said.

'Because it's true.'

'I don't buy that, Cheese.'

Cheese pulled his chair forward, squeezed the phone so hard I expected it to crack in half. 'Fucking listen to me, you piece of shit. That psychotic thinks I piped him, I might as well shiv some guard, make sure I stay locked in solitary for life. That man is a walking fucking death sentence. Now you tell him—'

'Fuck you, Cheese.'

'What?'

I said it again, very slowly.

Then I said, 'I came to you two days ago and begged for the life of a four-year-old girl. Now she's dead. Because of you. And you want mercy? I'm going to tell Bubba you *apologized* for having him piped.'

'No.'

'Tell him you said you were sorry. You'll make it up to him somehow.'

'No.' Cheese shook his head. 'You can't do that.'

'Watch me, Cheese.'

I took the phone away from my ear and reached out to hang it up.

'She's not dead.'

'What?' Angie said.

I put the phone back to my ear.

'She's not dead,' Cheese said.

'Who?' I said.

Cheese rolled his eyes, tilted his head back in the direction of the guard standing watch by the door.

'You know who.'

'Where is she?' Angie said.

Cheese shook his head. 'Give me a few days.'

'No,' I said.

'You don't have a choice.' He looked back over his shoulder, then leaned in close to the window and whispered into the phone. 'Someone will contact you. Trust me. I got to clear some things first.'

'Bubba's very angry,' Angie said. 'And he has friends.' She glanced around the prison walls.

'No shit,' Cheese said. 'His pals, the fucking Twoomey brothers, just got dropped for a bank job in Everett. They'll be rotating in here next week for processing. So stop trying to scare me. I'm scared. Okay? But I need time. Call off the dog. I'll send a message to you, I promise.'

'How do you know for sure she's alive?'

'I know. Okay?' He gave us a rueful smile. 'You two don't have a clue what's really going on. Do you know that?'

'We know it now,' I said.

'You let Bubba know I'm clean when it comes what happened to him. You want me alive. Okay? Without me, that girl will be gone. Gone-gone. You understand? Gone, baby, gone,' he sang.

I leaned back in my chair, studied him for a minute. He looked sincere, but Cheese is good at that. He's made a career out of knowing exactly which things can hurt people most and then identifying the people who want those things. Need them. He knows how to dangle bags of heroin in front of addicted women, make them blow strangers for it, and then only give them half of what he promised. He knows how to dangle half-truths in front of cops and DAs and get them to sign on the dotted line, before he delivers a facsimile of what he originally promised.

'I need more,' I said.

The guard rapped the door and said, 'Sixty seconds, Inmate Olamon.'

'More? The fuck you need?'

'I want the girl,' I said. 'I want her now.'

'I can't tell—'

'Fuck you.' I banged on the glass. 'Where is she, Cheese? Where is she?'

'If I tell you, they'll know it came from me, and I'll be dead by the morning.' He backed up as he spoke, palms-up in front of him, terror filling his fat face.

'Give me something hard. Something I can follow up, then.'

'Independent corroboration,' Angie said.

'Independent what?'

'Thirty seconds,' the guard said.

'Give us something, Cheese.'

Cheese looked over his shoulder desperately, then at the walls holding him in, the thick glass between us.

'Come on,' he begged.

'Twenty seconds,' Angie said.

'Don't. Look—'

'Fifteen.'

'No, I—'

'Tick-tock,' I said. 'Tick-tock.'

'The bitch's boyfriend,' Cheese said. 'You know?'

'He blew town,' Angie said.

'Then find him,' Cheese hissed. 'It's all I got. Ask him what his part was the night the kid vanished.'

'Cheese—' Angie started.

The guard loomed up behind Cheese, put his hand on his shoulder.

'Whatever you think happened,' Cheese said, 'you're not even in the ballpark. You guys are so offtrack, you might as well be in motherfucking Greenland. Okay?'

The guard reached over him and pulled the phone from his hand.

Cheese stood up, allowed himself to be tugged toward the door. When the guard opened the door, Cheese looked back at us, mouthed one word:

'Greenland.'

He raised his eyebrows up and down several times, and then the guard pushed him through the door and out of our sight.

The next day, shortly after noon, divers in Granite Rail Quarry found a torn piece of fabric impaled on a sliver of granite that jutted out like an ice pick from a shelf along the southern wall, fifteen feet below the waterline.

At three o'clock, Helene identified the fabric as a scrap of the T-shirt her daughter wore the night she disappeared. The scrap had been torn from the rear of the T-shirt, up by the collar, and the initials A. McC. were written on the fabric with a felt-tip pen.

After Helene identified the shirt fabric in the living room of Beatrice and Lionel's house, she watched Broussard as he placed the pink scrap back in the evidence bag, and the glass of Pepsi she'd been holding shattered in her hand.

'Jesus,' Lionel said. 'Helene.'

'She's dead, isn't she?' Helene squeezed her hand into a fist and drove the shards of broken glass deeper into her flesh. Blood fell in fat parachutes to the hardwood floor.

'Miss McCready,' Broussard said, 'we don't know that. Please let me see your hand.'

'She's dead,' Helene repeated, louder this time. 'Isn't she?' She pulled her hand away from Broussard, and blood sprayed the coffee table.

'Helene, for God's sake.' Lionel put one hand on his sister's shoulder and reached for her damaged hand.

Helene spun away from him and lost her balance, fell to the floor, and sat there cradling her hand and looking up at us. Her eyes found mine, and I remembered telling her in Wee Dave's house that she was stupid.

She wasn't stupid, she was anesthetized – to the world at large, the real danger her child had been in, even the shards of glass digging into her flesh, her tendons and arteries.

The pain was coming, though. It was finally coming. As she held my gaze, her eyes paled and widened and the truth found them. It was a horrible awakening, a nuclear fusion of clarity that found her pupils, and with it came the awareness of what her neglect had cost her daughter, of how vile and acute the pain had probably been for her child, the nightmares shoved into her small skull with pistons.

And Helene opened her mouth and howled without making a sound.

She sat on the floor, blood pouring from her torn hand onto her jeans. Her body shook with abandonment and grief and horror, and her head dropped back to her shoulders as she looked up at the ceiling, and tears poured from her eyes and she rocked on her haunches and continued to howl without making a sound.

*   *   *

At six that night, before we'd had a chance to talk to him, Bubba and Nelson Ferrare walked into a bar Cheese owned in Lower Mills. They told the three skagheads and the bartender to take a lunch break, and ten minutes later most of the bar blew out into the parking lot. An entire booth cleared the front door and totaled a local alderman's Honda Accord, which had been illegally parked in a handicap spot. Firefighters who arrived on the scene had to don oxygen masks. The blast had been so powerful it had all but blown itself out, and hardly anything was aflame in the bar itself, but in the basement, fire-fighters met a blazing pyre of uncut heroin; after the first two through the basement door began vomiting, the firemen pulled back and let the heroin burn until they were properly protected.

I would have tried to get a message to Cheese to let him know Bubba had acted on his own, but at six-thirty Cheese slipped on a freshly mopped floor at Concord Prison. It was a hell of a slip. Cheese somehow managed to lose his balance so completely, he fell over the guardrail on the third tier and dropped forty feet to a stone floor, landed on his oversized, trash-talking yellow head, and died.

Part Two

Winter

Part Two

23

Five months passed, and Amanda McCready stayed gone. Her photograph – in which her hair fell limply around her face and her eyes seemed still and empty – stared out from construction sites and telephone poles, usually torn or decayed by weather, or on a newscast update every now and then. And the more we saw the photo, the more it blurred, the more Amanda seemed a fiction, her image just another in a steady barrage of images attached to billboards, sent out through picture tubes, until passersby noted her features with a detached wistfulness, unable to remember who she was anymore or why her picture was plastered to the light pole by the bus stop.

Those who did remember probably shrugged off the chill of her memory, turned their heads down to the sports page or up toward the approaching bus. The world is a terrible place, they thought. Bad things happen every day. My bus is late.

A month-long search of the quarries yielded nothing and ended when temperatures plummeted and November winds swept the hills. Come spring, divers promised they'd go back in, and once again proposals to drain and then cover the quarries with landfill were raised, and Quincy city officials who worried about the millions of dollars it would cost found strange bedfellows in preservationists who warned that filling the quarries would damage the environment and destroy a multitude of scenic vistas for hikers and walkers, deprive the people of Quincy of sites of great historical significance, and eradicate some of the best rock climbing in the state.

Poole returned to active duty in February, six months shy of his thirty, and was reassigned to narcotics and quietly demoted to detective first grade. Compared to Broussard, though, he was lucky. Broussard was busted down from detective first to patrolman, placed on nine months' probation, and assigned to the motor pool. We met him for drinks the day after his demotion, a little over a week after that night in the quarries, and he smiled bitterly at his plastic swizzle stick as he swirled it through the cubes of ice in his Tanqueray and tonic.

'So Cheese said she was alive, and someone else told you Gutierrez was DEA.'

I nodded. 'Far as being alive, Cheese said Ray Likanski can corroborate.'

Broussard's bitter smile lost its edge and turned forlorn. 'We had APBs out for Likanski both here and in Pennsylvania. I'll keep 'em active for you, if you want.' He gave me a small shrug. 'Won't hurt anything, I suppose.'

'You think Cheese was lying,' Angie said.

'About Amanda McCready being alive?' He removed the swizzle stick, sucked the gin off it, and placed it on the edge of the cocktail napkin. 'Yes,

Miss Gennaro, I think Cheese was lying.'

'Why?'

'Because he was a criminal and that's what they do. Because he knew you wanted her to be alive so bad you'd buy it.'

'So when you visited him that day, he didn't say anything like that to you?'

Broussard shook his head and removed a pack of Marlboros from his pocket. Smoking full-time now. 'He acted all surprised about Mullen and Gutierrez getting hit, and I told him I was going to fuck up his life if it was the last thing I ever did. He laughed. Next day he died.' He lit the cigarette, closed one eye against the flare of heat from the match. 'Swear to God, I wish I'd killed him. Shit, I wish I'd put a con up to it. Really. I just wish he died because someone who cared about that little girl iced him, and he knew that's why he was dying all the way down to Hell.'

'Who did kill him?' Angie asked.

'Word I get is they're looking at that psycho kid from Arlington, just got convicted of double homicide.'

'The kid who killed his two sisters last year?' Angie said.

Broussard nodded. 'Peter Popovich. He was there a month for processing, and supposedly Cheese and him had some words in the yard. Either that or Cheese really did slip on the floor.' He shrugged. 'Whichever, it works for me.'

'You don't find it suspicious that Cheese tells us he has information on Amanda McCready and the next day he gets killed?'

Broussard took a sip of his drink. 'No. Look, I'll

be honest. I don't know what happened to that girl, and it bugs me. Bugs me bad. But I don't think she's alive, and I don't think Cheese Olamon knew how to tell the truth even if it could help him.'

'What about Gutierrez as DEA?' Angie said.

He shook his head. 'No way. We'd have been told by now.'

'So,' Angie said quietly. 'What happened to Amanda McCready?'

Broussard looked down at the table for a bit, shaved off the white head of his cigarette against the rim of the ashtray, and when he looked up tears glistened in the red pockets under his eyes.

'I don't know,' he said. 'I wish to God I'd done everything differently. I wish I'd called in the Feds. I wish—' His voice cracked and he lowered his head and covered his right eye with the heel of his hand. 'I wish . . .'

His Adam's apple bobbed as he swallowed. Then he sucked a wet breath down into his lungs, but he didn't say anything more.

Angie and I took other cases throughout the winter, though none that had anything to do with missing children. Not that many distraught parents would have hired us in the first place. We'd failed to find Amanda McCready, after all, and the acrid odor of that failure seemed to follow us when we were out at night in the neighborhood or shopping in the supermarket on Saturday afternoons.

Ray Likanski stayed gone as well, something that bothered me more than anything else in the case. As far as he knew, the heat was off him; there was no reason for him to stay gone. For a few months, Angie and I would, on a whim, stake out his father's house for a day and a night and get nothing for our efforts but the taste of cold coffee, our bones and muscles drawn stiff by a car seat. In January, Angie bugged Lenny Likanski's phone, and for two weeks we listened to tapes of him calling 900 numbers and ordering Chia pets off the Home Shopping Network, but never once did he call or hear from his son.

One day we'd had enough and drove all night to Allegheny, Pennsylvania. We located the Likanski brood from the phone book and staked them out for a weekend. There was Yardack and Leslie and Stanley, three brothers and first cousins to Ray. All three worked at a paper plant that filled the air with fumes that smelled like toner in a Xerox machine, and all three drank every night at the same bar, flirted with the same women, and went back alone to the house they shared.

The fourth night, Angie and I followed Stanley into an alley, where he scored some coke from a woman who rode a dirt bike. As soon as the dirt bike left the alley, while Stanley spread a rough line on the back of his hand and snorted it, I stepped up behind him, tickled his earlobe with my .45, and asked him where Cousin Ray was.

Stanley urinated in place; steam rose off the frozen ground between his shoes. 'I don't know. I haven't seen Ray since two summers ago.'

I cocked the gun and dug it into his temple.

Stanley said, 'Oh, Jesus God, no.'

'You're lying, Stanley, so I'm going to shoot you now. Okay?'

'Don't! I don't know! I swear to God! Ray, Ray, I ain't seen Ray in almost two years. Please, Christ's sake, believe me!'

I looked over his shoulder at Angie, who stared up into his face. She met my eyes and nodded. Stanley was telling the truth.

'Coke makes your dick soft,' Angie told him, and we walked up the alley, got in our car, and left Pennsylvania.

Once a week, we visited Beatrice and Lionel. The four of us would hash over everything we knew and then everything we didn't, and the latter always seemed much larger and deeper than the former.

One night in late February as we left their home and they stood shivering on the porch to make sure, as they always did, that we reached our car without incident, Beatrice said, 'I wonder about headstones.'

We stopped as we reached the sidewalk and looked back at her.

Lionel said, 'What?'

'At night,' Beatrice said, 'when I can't sleep, I wonder what we'd put on her headstone. I wonder if we should get her one.'

'Honey, don't—'

She waved him away, tightened her cardigan around her. 'I know, I know. It seems like giving up, like saying she's dead when we want to believe she's alive. I know. But . . . see – you know? – nothing says she ever lived.' She pointed down at the porch. 'Nothing marks her as having been here. Our memories aren't good enough, you know? They'll fade.' She nodded to herself. 'They'll fade,' she said again, and turned back into the house.

                    *   *   *

I saw Helene once in late March when I was
shooting darts with Bubba down at Kelly's Tavern,
but she didn't see me – or pretended not to. She sat
at the corner of the bar, alone, and nursed a drink
for a full hour, staring into the glass as if Amanda
were waiting at the bottom.

Bubba and I had arrived late, and after we finished
with darts we moved on to pool as the last-call
crowd poured in and filled the place three-deep
within about ten minutes. Then last call had passed,
and Bubba and I finished our game, finished our
beers, and placed the empties on the bar as we
headed for the door.

'Thank you.'

I turned and looked down the bar, saw Helene
sitting in the corner, surrounded by stools the
bartender had already propped up on the mahogany
around her. I'd thought for some reason that she'd
left.

Or maybe I'd just hoped she had.

'Thank you,' she said again, very softly, 'for
trying.'

I stood there on the rubber tile and was aware that
I didn't know what to do with my hands. Or my
arms. Or any of my limbs, for that matter. My entire
body felt awkward and clumsy.

Helene kept her eyes on her drink, her unwashed
hair falling in her face, tiny among all those overturned stools, the dim lights that had fallen on the
bar at closing time.

I didn't know what to say. I wasn't even sure I
could speak. I wanted to go to her and hold her and
apologize for not saving her daughter, for not

                         317

finding Amanda, for failing, for everything. I wanted to weep.

Instead, I turned and headed for the door.

'Mr Kenzie.'

I stopped, my back to her.

'I'd do it all differently,' she said, 'if I could. I'd . . . I'd never let her out of my sight.'

I don't know if I nodded or not, gave any indication that I'd heard her. I know that I didn't look back. I got the hell out of there.

The next morning, I woke before Angie and brewed coffee in the kitchen, tried to shake Helene McCready from my head, those horrible words of hers:

'Thank you.'

I went downstairs for the paper, tucked it under my arm, and came back up. I made my cup of coffee and took it into the dining room with me as I opened the paper and discovered that another child had disappeared.

His name was Samuel Pietro, and he was eight.

He'd last been seen leaving his friends in a Weymouth playground and walking back toward home Saturday afternoon. It was now Monday morning. His mother hadn't reported him missing until yesterday.

He was a handsome kid with large dark eyes that reminded me of Angie's, and a friendly, crooked smile in the photo they'd cropped from his third-grade class picture. He looked hopeful. He looked young. He looked confident.

I considered hiding the paper from Angie. Ever since Allegheny, when we'd left that alley and all the steam had run out of us, all the determination, she'd become even more deeply obsessed with Amanda McCready. But it wasn't an obsession that found an outlet in action, since there was very little action to take. Instead, Angie pored over all our case notes, drew Time Line and Major Figures charts on poster board, and talked for hours with Broussard or Poole, always rehashing, always circling the same ground.

No new theories or sudden answers came from these long nights or burst from the poster board, but she kept at it anyway. And every time a kid went missing and it was reported on the national news, she watched, rapt, as the minuscule details unfolded.

She wept when they turned up dead.

Always quietly, always behind closed doors, always at times when she thought I was on the other side of the apartment and couldn't hear.

It was only recently that I'd realized how deeply her father's death had affected Angie. It wasn't the death itself, I don't think. It was the never knowing for sure how he died. Without a body to point to, to lower into the ground for one last look, maybe he'd never been completely dead to her.

I was with her once when she asked Poole about him, and I could see the fear of his own inadequacy in Poole's face as he explained that he'd barely known the man, just to see on the street occasionally, come across in a gambling raid, Jimmy Suave, always a perfect gentleman, a man who understood that the cops were doing a job just as he was doing his.

'Eats at you still, huh?' Poole had said.

'Sometimes,' Angie said. 'It's having to accept

someone's gone in your head, but your heart never gets completely . . . settled about the whole thing.'

And so it was with Amanda McCready. So it was with all those kids who went missing nationally and weren't found, dead or alive, over the long winter months. Maybe, I thought once, I'd become a private detective because I hated to know what happened next. Maybe Angie became one because she needed to know.

I looked down at Samuel Pietro's smiling, confident face, those eyes that seemed to drink you up just like Angie's did.

Hiding the paper, I knew, was stupid. There were always more papers, always TV and radio, always people talking in supermarkets and bars and while pumping gas at the self-serve.

Maybe forty years ago it was possible to escape the news, but not now. News was everywhere, informing us, bludgeoning us, maybe even enlightening us. But there. Always there. No room to duck from it, no place to hide.

I traced my finger around the outline of Samuel Pietro's face and, for the first time in fifteen years, said a silent prayer.

Part Three

The Cruelest Month

Part Three

24

By early April, Angie was spending most nights with her poster boards, Amanda McCready notes, and the small shrine she'd built to the case in the tiny second bedroom in my apartment, the one I'd previously used to store luggage and boxes I kept meaning to drop off at Goodwill, where small appliances gathered dust while they waited for me to take them to a repair shop.

She'd moved the small TV and a VCR in there and watched the newscasts from October over and over again. In the two weeks since Samuel Pietro had disappeared, she logged at least five hours a night in that room, photographs of Amanda staring out with that unexcitable gaze of hers from the wall above the TV.

I understand obsession in the same general sense most of us do, and I couldn't see that this was doing Angie too much harm – yet. Over the course of the long winter, I'd come to accept that Amanda McCready was dead, curled into a shelf 175 feet below the waterline of the quarry, flaxen hair floating with the soft swirls of the current. But I hadn't accepted it with the sort of conviction that allowed me to look derisively on anyone who believed she was still alive.

Angie held firmly to Cheese's assurance that Amanda lived, that proof of her whereabouts lay somewhere in our notes, somewhere in the minutiae of our investigation and that of the police. She'd convinced Broussard and Poole to loan her copies of their notes, as well as the daily reports and interviews of most of the other members of the CAC task force who'd been assigned to the case. And she was certain, she told me, that sooner or later all that paper and all that video would yield the truth.

The truth, I told her once, was that someone in Cheese's organization had pulled a double-cross on Mullen and Gutierrez after they'd dumped Amanda over a cliff. And this someone had taken them out and walked away with two hundred thousand dollars.

'Cheese didn't think so,' she said.

'Broussard was right about that. Cheese was a professional liar.'

She shrugged. 'I beg to differ.'

So at night she'd return to autumn and all that had gone wrong, and I would either read, watch an old movie on AMC, or shoot pool with Bubba – which is what I was doing when he said, 'I need you to ride shotgun on something down in Germantown with me.'

I'd only had half a beer by this point, so I was pretty sure I'd heard him right.

'You want me to go on a deal with you?'

I stared across the pool table at Bubba as some heathen chose a Smiths song on the jukebox. I

324

hate the Smiths. I'd rather be tied to a chair and forced to listen to a medley of Suzanne Vega and Natalie Merchant songs while performance artists hammered nails through their genitalia in front of me than listen to thirty seconds of Morrissey and the Smiths whine their art-school angst about how they are human and need to be loved. Maybe I'm a cynic, but if you want to be loved, stop whining about it and you just might get laid, which could be a promising first step.

Bubba turned his head back toward the bar and shouted, 'What pussy played this shit?'

'Bubba,' I said.

He held up a finger. 'One sec.' He turned back toward the bar. 'Who played this song. Huh?'

'Bubba,' the bartender said, 'now calm down.'

'I just want to know who played this song.'

Gigi Varon, a thirty-year-old alkie who looked a shriveled forty-five, raised her meek hand from the corner of the bar. 'I didn't know, Mr Rogowski. I'm sorry. I'll pull the plug.'

'Oh, Gigi!' Bubba gave her a big wave. 'Hi! No, never mind.'

'I will, really.'

'No, no, hon.' Bubba shook his head. 'Paulie, give Gigi two drinks on me.'

'Thank you, Mr Rogowski.'

'No problem. Morrissey sucks, though, Gigi. Really. Ask Patrick. Ask anyone.'

'Yeah, Morrissey sucks,' one of the old guys said, and then several other patrons followed suit.

'I put the Amazing Royal Crowns in next,' Gigi said.

I'd turned Bubba on to the Amazing Royal

Crowns a few months back, and now they were his favorite band.

Bubba spread his arms wide. 'Paulie, make it three drinks.'

We were in Live Bootleg, a tiny tavern on the Southie/Dorchester line that had no sign out front. The brick exterior was painted black, and the only indication the bar had a name at all was scrawled in red paint on the lower right corner of the wall fronting Dorchester Avenue. Ostensibly owned by Carla Dooley, aka 'The Lovely Carlotta,' and her husband, Shakes, Live Bootleg was really Bubba's bar, and I'd never been in the place when every stool wasn't filled and the booze wasn't flowing. It was a good crowd, too; in the three years since Bubba had opened it, there'd never been a fight or a line for the bathroom because some junkie was taking too long to shoot up in the stall. Of course, everyone who entered knew who the real owner was and how he'd feel if anyone ever gave the police reason to knock on his door, so for all its dark interior and shady rep, Live Bootleg was about as dangerous as the Wednesday night bingo game at Saint Bart's. Had better music, too, most times.

'I don't see why you're giving Gigi a small coronary,' I said. 'You own the jukebox. You loaded the Smiths CD.'

'I didn't load no friggin' Smiths CD,' Bubba said. 'It's one of those Best of the Eighties compilations. I had to live with a Smiths song 'cause it's got "Come on, Eileen" on it and a whole bunch of other good shit.'

'Katrina and the Waves?' I said. 'Bananarama? Real cool bands like that?'

'Hey,' he said, 'it's got Nena, so shut up.'

' "Ninety-nine Luftballoons," ' I said. 'Well, all right.' I leaned into the table, pocketed the seven. 'Now what's this about me accompanying you on a deal?'

'I need backup. Nelson's out of town and the Twoomeys are doing two-to-six.'

'Million other guys will help you for a C-note.' I dropped the six, but it kissed Bubba's ten on the way in, and I stepped back from the table.

'Well, I got two reasons.' He leaned over the table and banged the cue ball off the nine, watched it bounce around the table, and then shut his eyes tight as the cue dropped in the side pocket. For someone who plays so much pool, Bubba really sucks.

I put the cue back on the table, lined up for the four in the side. 'Reason number one?'

'I trust you and you owe me.'

'That's two reasons.'

'It's one. Shut up and shoot.'

I dropped the four, and the cue rolled slowly into a sweet lie across from the two ball.

'Reason number two is,' Bubba said, and chalked his stick with great squeaking turns, 'I want you to get a look at these people I'm selling to.'

I pocketed the two but buried the cue behind one of Bubba's balls. 'Why?'

'Trust me. You'll be interested.'

'Can't you just tell me?'

'I'm not sure if they are who I think they are, so you gotta join me, see for yourself.'

'When?'

'As soon as I win this game.'

'How dangerous?' I said.

'No more dangerous than normal.'

'Ah,' I said. 'Very dangerous then.'

'Don't be such a puss. Shoot the ball.'

Germantown is set hard against the harbor that separates Quincy from Weymouth. Given its name back in the mid-1700s when a glass manufacturer imported indentured laborers from Germany and laid out the town lots with ample streets and wide squares in the German tradition, the company failed and the Germans were left to fend for themselves when it became apparent that the cost of giving them their freedom would be less expensive than sending them someplace else.

A long line of failure followed, seemed to haunt the tiny seaport and the generations descended from the original indentured servants. Pottery, chocolate, stockings, whale-oil products, and medicinal salt and saltpeter industries all cropped up and fell by the wayside over the next two centuries. For a while the cod- and whale-fishing industries enjoyed some popularity, but they, too, picked up and moved north to Gloucester or farther south toward Cape Cod in search of better catches and better waters.

Germantown became a forgotten slip of land, its waters cut off from its inhabitants by chain-link fence and polluted by refuse from the Quincy Shipyards, a power plant, oil tanks, and the Procter & Gamble factory that formed the only silhouettes in its skyline. An early experiment with public housing for war veterans left its shoreline marred by cul-de-sac housing developments the color of pumice, each one a collection of four buildings housing sixteen units and curved in on each other in a horseshoe, skeletal metal clothesline structures rising out of pools of rust in the cracked tar.

The house Bubba parked his Hummer in front of was a block off the shore, and the homes on either side of it were condemned and cascading back into the earth. In the dark, the house seemed to sag as well, and while I couldn't make out much in the way of detail, there was an air of certain decay to the structure.

The old man who answered the door had a close-cropped beard that quilted his jawline in square tufts of silver and black but refused to grow in over the cleft of his long chin, leaving a pink puckered circle of exposed flesh that winked like an eye. He was somewhere between fifty and sixty, with a gnarled curve to his small frame that made him appear much older. He wore a weathered Red Sox baseball cap that looked too small even for his tiny head, a yellow half T-shirt that left a wrinkled, milky mid-riff exposed, and a pair of black nylon tights that ended above his bare ankles and feet and bunched up around his crotch so tightly his appendage resembled a fist.

The man pulled the brim of the baseball cap farther down his forehead and said to Bubba, 'You Jerome Miller?'

'Jerome Miller' was Bubba's favored alias. It was the name of Bo Hopkins's character in *The Killer Elite*, a movie Bubba had seen about eleven thousand times and could quote at will.

'What do you think?' Bubba's enormous body loomed over the slight man and obscured him from my view.

'I'm asking,' the man said.

'I'm the Easter Bunny standing on your doorstep with a gym bag filled with guns.' Bubba leaned in over the man. 'Let us the fuck in.'

The old man stepped aside, and we crossed the threshold into a dark living room acrid with cigarette smoke. The old man bent by the coffee table and lifted a burning cigarette from an overstuffed ashtray, sucked wetly on the butt, and stared through the smoke at us, his pale eyes all but glowing in the dark.

'So, show me,' he said.

'You want to turn on a light?' Bubba said.

'No light here,' the man said.

Bubba gave him a wide, cold smile, all teeth. 'Take me to a room that has one.'

The man shrugged his bony shoulders. 'Suit yourself.'

As we followed him down a narrow hallway, I noticed that the strap at the back of the baseball cap hung open, the ends too wide apart to clasp, and in general the back of the hat rode oddly on the man's head, too far up the skull. I tried to put my finger on who the guy reminded me of. Since I didn't know many old men who dressed in half T-shirts and tights, I would have figured the list of possibilities to be relatively small. But there was something familiar about the guy, and I had the feeling that either the beard or the baseball hat was throwing me off.

The hallway smelled like dirty bathwater left undrained for days, and the walls reeked of mildew. Four doorways opened off the hall, which led straight to the back door. Above us, on the second floor, something made a sudden soft thump. The ceiling throbbed with bass, the vibrations of speakers turned up loud, even though the music itself was so faint – a tinny whisper, really – that it could have been coming from half a block away. Soundproofing, I decided. Maybe they had a band up there, a group of old men in Spandex and half-shirts covering old Muddy Waters songs, gyrating to the beat.

We neared the first two doorways midway down the hall, and I glanced in the one on my left, saw only a dark room with shadows and shapes I guessed were a recliner and stacks of either books or magazines. The smell of old cigar smoke wafted from the room. The one on the right took us into a kitchen bathed so harshly in white light, I was pretty sure the fluorescent wattage was industrial, the kind normally found in truck depots, not private homes. Instead of illuminating the room, it washed it out, and I had to blink several times to regain my vision.

The man lifted a small object off the counter and tossed it sideways in my direction. I blinked in the brightness, saw the object coming in low and to my right, and reached out and snagged it. It was a small paper bag, and I'd caught it by the bottom. Sheaves of money threatened to spill to the floor before I righted the bag and pushed the bills back inside. I turned back to Bubba and handed it to him.

'Good hands,' the man said. He smiled a yellow tobacco-stained grin in Bubba's direction. 'Your gym bag, sir.'

Bubba swung the gym bag into the man's chest, and the force of it knocked him on his ass. He sprawled on the black-and-white tile, arms spread, and propped the heels of his hands on the tile for support.

'Bad hands,' Bubba said. 'How about I just put it on the table?'

The man looked up at him and nodded, blinked at the light above his face.

It was his nose that looked so familiar, I decided, the hawkish curve to it. It jutted out from the otherwise flat plane of the man's face like a precipice, hooked downward so dramatically the tip cast a shadow on the man's lips.

He got up off the floor and dusted the seat of his black tights, rubbed his hands together as he stood over the table and watched Bubba unzip the gym bag. Twin orange fires lit the man's eyes like the glints of taillights in the dark as he stared into the bag, and dots of perspiration speckled his upper lip.

'So these are my babies,' the man said, as Bubba pulled back the folds of the bag and revealed four Calico M-110 machine pistols, the black aluminum alloy glistening with oil. One of the strangest-looking weapons I've ever seen, the Calico M-110 is a handgun that fires a hundred rounds from the same helical-feed magazine used for its carbines. Roughly seventeen inches long, the grip and barrel take up the front eight inches, with the slide and the majority of the gun frame jutting back behind the grip. The gun reminded me of the fake ones we'd built as kids out of rubber bands, clothespins, and popsicle sticks to fire paper clips at one another.

But with rubber bands and popsicle sticks, we couldn't fire more than ten paper clips in a minute. The M-110, at full auto, was capable of unleashing one hundred bullets in roughly fifteen seconds.

The old man lifted one from the bag and laid it flat in the palm of his hand. He raised his arm up and down to feel the weight, his pale eyes glistening as if they'd been oiled like a gun. He smacked his lips as if he could taste the gunfire.

I said, 'Stocking up for a war?'

Bubba shot me a look and began counting the money from the paper bag.

The man smiled at the gun as if it were a kitten. 'Persecution exists on all fronts at all times, dear. One must be prepared.' He stroked the gun frame with the tips of his fingers. 'Oh, my my my,' he cooed.

And that's when I recognized him.

Leon Trett, the child molester Broussard had given me a picture of in the early days of Amanda McCready's disappearance. The man suspected in the rapes of over fifty children, the disappearance of two.

And we'd just armed him.

Oh, joy.

He looked up at me suddenly, as if he could sense what I was thinking, and I felt myself go cold and small in the wash of his pale eyes.

'Clips?' he said.

'When I leave,' Bubba said. 'Don't fuck up my counting.'

He took a step toward Bubba. 'No, no. Not when you leave,' Leon Trett said. 'Now.'

Bubba said, 'Shut up. I'm counting.' Under his breath, I could hear: '. . . four hundred fifty, sixty, sixty-five, seventy, seventy-five—'

Leon Trett shook his head several times, as if by

doing so he could make the clips appear, make Bubba turn reasonable.

'Now,' Trett said. 'Now. I want my clips now. I paid for them.'

He reached out for Bubba's arm and Bubba back-handed him in the chest, knocked him into the small table underneath the window.

'Motherfucker!' Bubba stopped counting, slammed the bills together in his hands. 'Now I gotta start all over.'

'You give me my clips,' Trett said. His eyes were wet and there was a spoiled eight-year-old's whine in his voice. 'You give them to me.'

'Fuck off.' Bubba started counting the bills again.

Trett's eyes filled and he slapped the gun between his hands.

'What's the matter, baby?'

I turned my head toward the sound of the voice and laid eyes on the largest woman I'd ever seen. She wasn't just an Amazon of a woman, she was a Sasquatch, bulky and covered in thick gray hair, at least five inches of it rising off the top of her head and then spilling down the sides of her face, obscuring her cheekbones and the corners of her eyes, billowing out on her wide shoulders like Spanish moss.

She was dressed in dark brown from head to toe, and the girth under those folds of loose clothing seemed to shake and rumble as she stood in the kitchen doorway with a .38 held loosely in one great paw of a hand.

Roberta Trett. Her photograph did not do her justice.

'They won't give me the clips,' Leon said. 'They're taking the money, but they won't give me the clips.'

Roberta took a step into the room, surveyed it with a slow roll of her head from right to left. The only one who hadn't acknowledged her presence was Bubba. He remained in the center of the kitchen, head down, trying to count his money.

Roberta pointed the gun quite casually in my direction. 'Give us the clips.'

I shrugged. 'I don't got 'em.'

'You.' She waved the gun at Bubba. 'Hey, you.'

'. . . eight hundred fifty,' Bubba said, 'eight hundred sixty, eight hundred seventy—'

'Hey!' Roberta said. 'You look at me when I'm talking.'

Bubba turned his head slightly toward her, but kept his eyes on the money. 'Nine hundred. Nine hundred ten, nine hundred twenty—'

'Mr Miller,' Leon said desperately, 'my wife is talking to you.'

'. . . nine hundred sixty-five, nine hundred seventy—'

'Mr Miller!' Leon's shriek was so high-pitched I felt it ring in my inner ears, buzz along the brain stem.

'One thousand.' Bubba stopped in the middle of the wad of money and placed the chunk he'd already counted in his jacket pocket.

Leon sighed audibly and relief sagged across his face.

Bubba looked at me as if unaware of what all the fuss was about.

Roberta lowered the gun. 'Now, Mr Miller, if we could just—'

Bubba licked the corner of his thumb and peeled off the top bill in the pile that remained in his hands.

'Twenty, forty, sixty, eighty, one hundred . . .'

Leon Trett looked like he'd suffered an embolism on the spot. His chalky face turned crimson and bloated and he squeezed the empty gun between his hands and hopped back and forth as if he needed a bathroom.

Roberta Trett raised the gun again, and this time there was nothing casual about it. She pointed it directly at Bubba's head and closed her left eye. She sighted down · the barrel and pulled back the hammer.

The harsh light of the kitchen seemed to etch her and Bubba's outlines as they stood in the center of the room, both of them the size of something you'd normally climb with rope and pitons, not give birth to.

I slid my .45 out of the holster at the small of my back, dropped it · down behind my right leg, and released the safety.

'Two hundred twenty,' Bubba said, as Roberta Trett took another step toward him, 'two hundred thirty, two hundred forty, dude, shoot this bitch, will ya, two hundred fifty, two hundred sixty . . .'

Roberta Trett stopped and cocked her head slightly to the left, as if unsure of what she'd heard. She looked unable to identify what her options were. She looked unfamiliar with that sensation.

I doubted she'd ever been ignored in her life.

'Mr Miller, you will stop counting now.' She extended her arm until it was T-bar straight and hard, and her knuckles whitened against the black steel.

'. . . three hundred, three hundred ten, three

hundred twenty, I said, shoot the big bitch, three hundred thirty . . .'

That time she was sure of what she'd heard. A tremor appeared in her wrist, and the pistol shook.

'Ma'am,' I said, 'put the gun down.'

Her eyes rolled right in their sockets, and she saw that I hadn't moved, that I wasn't pointing anything at her. And then she noticed that she couldn't see my right hand, and that's when I used my thumb to pull back the hammer on my .45, the sound cutting into the fluorescent hum of that bright kitchen as cleanly as a gunshot itself.

'. . . four fifty, four sixty, four seventy . . .'

Roberta Trett looked over Bubba's shoulder at Leon, and the .38 shook some more and Bubba kept counting.

Beyond the kitchen I heard the sound of a door open and close very quickly. It came from the back of the house, from the far end of the long hallway that split the building.

Roberta heard it too. Her eyes jerked to the left for a moment, then back to Leon.

'Make him stop,' Leon said. 'Make him stop counting. It hurts.'

'. . . six hundred,' Bubba said, and his voice grew an octave louder. 'Six ten, six twenty, six twenty-five – enough with the fives already – six thirty . . .'

A set of soft footsteps approached from the hall, and Roberta's back stiffened.

Leon said, 'Stop it. Stop that counting.'

A man even smaller than Leon went rigid as he stepped through the doorway, his dark eyes widening in confusion, and I removed the gun from behind my leg and pointed it at the center of his forehead.

He had a chest so sunken it seemed to have been produced in reverse, the sternum and the rib cage curling in while the small belly protruded like a pygmy's. His right eye was lazy and kept sliding away from us as if it were asea on a floundering boat. Small scratches over his right nipple reddened in the white light.

He wore only a small blue terry-cloth towel, and his skin was sheened with sweat.

'Corwin,' Roberta said, 'you go back to your room now.'

Corwin Earle. I guess he'd found his nuclear family after all.

'Corwin's going to stay right here,' I said, and extended my arm its full length, watched Corwin's good eye meet the hole in the barrel of the .45.

Corwin nodded and placed his hands by his sides.

All eyes but mine turned back to Bubba and gave him their full attention.

'Two thousand!' he crowed. He raised the wad of cash in his hand.

'We agree you've been compensated,' Roberta Trett said, and her voice shook like the gun in her hand. 'Now complete the transaction, Mr Miller. Give us the clips.'

'Give us the clips!' Leon shrieked.

Bubba looked over his shoulder at him.

Corwin Earle took a step back, and I said, 'That's a no-no.'

He swallowed and I waved the gun forward and he moved with it.

Bubba chuckled. It was a low, soft *heh-heh-heh*,

338

and it put a hard curve up the back of Roberta Trett's neck.

'The clips,' Bubba said, and turned back to Roberta, seemed to notice the gun pointed at him for the first time. 'Of course.'

He pursed his lips and blew a kiss to Roberta. She blinked and stepped back from it as if it were toxic.

Bubba reached toward the pocket of his trench coat, and then his arm shot back up.

'Hey!' Leon said.

Roberta jerked backward as Bubba slapped his wrist into hers and the .38 jumped from her hand, flew over the sink, and sped toward the counter.

Everyone but Bubba ducked.

The .38 hit the wall above the counter. Its hammer dropped on impact, and the gun fired.

The bullet tore a hole through the cheap Formica behind the sink and ricocheted into the wall beside the window where Leon crouched.

The .38 clattered loudly as it fell to the counter, and the barrel spun and ended up pointing at the dusty dish rack.

Bubba looked at the hole in the wall. 'Cool,' he said.

The rest of us straightened, except for Leon. He sat down on the floor and placed a palm over his heart, and those pale eyes of his hardened in such a way that I knew he was far less frail than his cringing act during Bubba's counting would lead us to believe. It was just a mask, a role he played, I assumed, to lull us into forgetting about him, and it dropped from his face as he sat on the floor and looked up at Bubba with naked hatred.

Bubba stuffed the second wad in his pocket. He

closed the distance between himself and Roberta, then tapped his foot on the floor in front of her until she raised her head and met his eyes.

'You had a gun pointed at me, Xena the Large.' He rubbed his jaw with his palm, filled the kitchen with the scratch of bristles against rough flesh.

Roberta placed her hands by her sides.

Bubba smiled gently at her.

Very softly, he said, 'So, should I kill you now?'

Roberta shook her head once from side to side.

'You sure?'

Roberta nodded, very deliberately.

'You pointed that gun at me, after all.'

Roberta nodded again. She tried to speak, but nothing came out but a gurgle.

'What was that?' Bubba said.

She swallowed. 'I'm sorry, Mr Miller.'

'Oh.' Bubba nodded.

He winked at me and there was that green and angry light dancing in his smiling eyes that I've seen before, the one that said anything could happen. Anything.

Leon used the kitchen table for support as he got to his feet behind Bubba.

'Little man,' Bubba said, his eyes on Roberta, 'you reach for that Charter twenty-two you got strapped under the table, and I'll unload it into your balls.'

Leon's hand fell from the edge of the table.

Sweat poured from Corwin's hair, and he blinked against it, placed his palm against the doorjamb to hold himself up.

Bubba walked over to me, kept his eyes on the room as he leaned in and whispered in my ear,

'They're armed to the fucking teeth. We're gonna be leaving in a rush. Got it?'

I nodded.

As he crossed back to Roberta, I watched Leon's eyes glance first at the table, then over at a cupboard, then at the dishwasher, which was rusty, caked with dirt along the door, and probably hadn't washed a dish since I was in high school.

I caught Corwin Earle doing the same; then he and Leon's eyes met for a moment, and the fear dissipated.

I had to agree with Bubba's assessment. We were, it seemed, standing in the middle of Tombstone. As soon as we dropped our guards, the Tretts and Corwin Earle would grab their weapons and show us their vivid reenactment of the OK Corral.

'Please,' Roberta Trett said to Bubba, 'go.'

'What about the clips?' Bubba said. 'You wanted the clips. Do you still want 'em?'

'I—'

Bubba touched her chin with the tips of his fingers. 'Yes or no?'

She closed her eyes. 'Yes.'

'Sorry.' Bubba beamed. 'Can't have 'em. Gotta go.'

He looked at me and cocked his head and headed for the doorway.

Corwin pinned himself against the wall and I trained my gun on the room as I backed out after Bubba, saw the fury in Leon Trett's eyes and knew they'd be coming out after us in a hurry.

I grabbed Corwin Earle behind the neck and shoved him into the center of the kitchen by Roberta. Then I met Leon's eyes.

'I'll kill you, Leon,' I said. 'Stay in the kitchen.'

The whiny, eight-year-old's voice was gone when he spoke. What replaced it was deep and slightly husky, cold as rock salt.

'You got to make the front door, boy. And it's a long walk.'

I backed into the hallway, kept the .45 trained on the kitchen. Bubba stood a few feet down the hall, whistling.

'Think we should run?' I whispered out of the side of my mouth.

He looked back over his shoulder. 'Probably.'

And he took off, charging toward the front door like a linebacker, his boots slamming the old floorboards, laughing maniacally, a booming *Ah-ha-ha*! tearing up through the house.

I dropped my arm and ran after him, saw the dark hall and the dark living room swing crazily from side to side as I charged behind Bubba and we ran full out for the front door.

I could hear them scrambling in the kitchen, the swing of the dishwasher door opening, then dropping on its hinges. I could feel target sights on my back.

Bubba didn't pause to open the screen door between us and freedom, he ran straight through it, the wood frame shattering on impact, the green webbing shrouding his head like a veil.

I risked a look back as I reached the threshold, saw Leon Trett step into the hallway, arm extended. I backed up and pointed down the dark hall at him, but I was outside now, and for a long moment Trett and I stared across the dark space at each other, guns pointed.

Then he lowered his arm and shook his head at me. 'Another time,' he called.

'Sure,' I said.

Behind me, on the lawn, Bubba made a great racket as he cast what remained of the door off his head and boomed that crazy laugh of his.

'Ah-ha-ha! I am Conan!' he shouted, and spread his arms wide. 'Grand slayer of evil gnomes! No man dare test my mettle or strength in battle! Ah-ha-ha!'

I came out on the lawn, and we jogged to his Hummer. I kept my back to the Hummer and my eyes on the house, gripping my gun in both hands as Bubba got in and unlocked my door. Nothing in the house moved.

I climbed in the fat, wide machine and Bubba peeled off from the curb before I'd even shut the door.

'Why'd you renege on the clips?' I asked, once we'd gotten a full block between us and the Tretts.

Bubba rolled through a stop sign. 'They annoyed me and fucked up my counting.'

'That's it? For that you held back the clips?'

He scowled. 'I hate when people interrupt my counting. Hate it. Really, really hate it.'

'By the way,' I said, as we turned a corner, 'what was with the evil gnomes thing?'

'What?'

'There were no evil gnomes in *Conan*.'

'You sure?'

'Pretty much.'

'Damn.'

'Sorry.'

'Why do you have to ruin everything?' he said. 'Man, you're no fun at all.'

343

25

'Ange!' I called, as Bubba and I came bounding into my apartment.

She stuck her head out of the tiny bedroom where she worked. 'What's up?'

'You've been following the Pietro case pretty closely, right?'

A needle of hurt pierced her eyes for a moment. 'Yeah.'

'Come into the living room,' I said, tugging her. 'Come on, come on.'

She looked at me, then at Bubba, who rocked back on his heels and blew a large pink balloon of Bazooka through his thick, rubbery lips.

'What have you two been drinking?'

'Nothing,' I said. 'Come on.'

We turned on lights in the living room and told her about our trip to the Tretts'.

'You two are friggin' chuckleheads,' she said, when we finished. 'Like little psycho boys going out to play with the psycho family.'

'Fine, fine,' I said. 'Ange, what was Samuel Pietro wearing when he disappeared?'

She leaned back in her chair. 'Jeans, a red sweatshirt over a white T-shirt, a blue and red parka, black mittens, and hi-top sneakers.' She narrowed her eyes at me. 'So what?'

'That's it?' Bubba said.

She shrugged. 'Yeah. That and a Red Sox baseball cap.'

I looked at Bubba and he nodded, then held up his hands.

'I can't go anywhere near this. Those are my guns in that house.'

'No problem,' I said. 'We'll call Poole and Broussard.'

'Call Poole and Broussard for what?' Angie said.

'You saw Trett wearing a Red Sox baseball hat?' Poole said, sitting across from us in a Wollaston coffee shop.

I nodded. 'Which was three or four sizes too small for him.'

'And this leads you to believe said hat belonged to Samuel Pietro.'

I nodded again.

Broussard looked at Angie. 'You going along with this?'

She lit a cigarette. 'Circumstantially, it fits. The Tretts are in Germantown, directly across from Weymouth, a couple of miles from the Nantasket Beach playground where Pietro was just before he disappeared. And the quarries, the quarries aren't too far from Germantown, and—'

'Oh, please!' Broussard crumpled an empty cigarette pack, tossed it to the table. 'Amanda McCready again? You think just because Trett lives within five miles of the quarries, then of course he must have killed her? You serious?'

He looked at Poole, and they both shook their heads.

'You showed us the pictures of the Tretts and Corwin Earle,' Angie said. 'You remember that? You told us Corwin Earle liked to pick up kids for the Tretts. You told us to keep our eyes peeled for him,' Angie said. 'That was you, Detective Broussard, wasn't it?'

'Patrol officer,' Broussard reminded her. 'I'm not a detective anymore.'

'Well, maybe,' Angie said, 'if we drop by the Tretts and poke around a bit, you will be again.'

Leon Trett's house was set off the road about ten yards in a field of overgrown grass. Behind the amber sheets of rain, the small white house looked grainy and smeared by large swirling fingers of grime. Near the foundation, however, someone had planted a small garden, and the flowers had begun to bud or bloom. It should have been beautiful, but it was unsettling to see such a tenderly cared for array of purple crocus, white snowdrops, bright red tulips, and soft yellow forsythia burgeoning in the shadows cast by such a greasy, decrepit house.

Roberta Trett, I remembered, had been a florist, a gifted one apparently, if she'd been able to coax color from the hard earth and long winter. I couldn't picture it – the same lumbering woman who'd held the gun to Bubba's head last night, thumbed back the hammer on her .38, had a gift for delicacy, for softness, for drawing growth from dirt and producing soft petals and fragile beauty.

The house was a small two-story, and the upper windows fronting the road were boarded up with black wood. Below those windows, the shingles were cracked or missing in several places, so that the upper third of the house resembled a triangular face with blackened eyes and a ragged smile of shattered teeth.

Just as I'd felt when I approached the house in the dark, decay permeated it like an odor, garden or no garden.

A tall fence with cyclone wire stretched on top divided the back of Trett's property line from his neighbor's. The sides of the house looked out on a half acre of weeds, those two condemned and abandoned homes, and nothing else.

'No way to approach but through that front door,' Angie said.

'Seems to be the case,' Poole said.

The screen door Bubba had destroyed last night lay in a tangle on the lawn, but the main door, a white wooden one with cracks in the center, had replaced it. This end of the street was still and had the empty feeling of a place few in the neighborhood ventured. In the time we'd been here, only one car had passed us.

The back door of the Crown Victoria opened and Broussard climbed in beside Poole, shaking rain from his hair, splattering drops on Poole's chin and temples.

Poole wiped at his face. 'You're a dog now?'

Broussard grinned. 'Wet out.'

'I noticed.' Poole pulled a handkerchief from his breast pocket. 'I repeat: You're a dog now?'

'*Ruff.*' Broussard gave his head another shake. 'The back door's where Kenzie said it was. Same approximate location as the front door. One upper

347

window on the east side, one on the west, one in back. All boarded up. Heavy curtains over all the lower windows. A locked bulkhead by the rear corner, about ten feet to the right of the back door.'

'Any signs of life in there?' Angie asked.

'Impossible to tell with the curtains.'

'So what do we do?' I said.

Broussard took the handkerchief from Poole and wiped his face, tossed it back on Poole's lap. Poole looked down at it with a mixture of amazement and disgust.

'Do?' Broussard said. 'You two?' He raised his eyebrows. 'Nothing. You're civilians. You go through that door or tip Trett's hand, I'll arrest you. My once and future partner and I are going to walk up to that house in a minute and knock on the door, see if Mr Trett or his wife wants to chat. When they tell us to fuck off, we'll walk back out and call Quincy P.D. for backup.'

'Why not just call for backup now?' Angie said.

Broussard looked at Poole. They both glanced at her and shook their heads.

'Excuse me for being retarded,' Angie said.

Broussard smiled. 'Can't call for backup without probable cause, Miss Gennaro.'

'But you'll have probable cause once you knock on the door?'

'If one of them's stupid enough to open it,' Poole said.

'Why?' I said. 'You think you're just going to look in through a crack and see Samuel Pietro standing there holding a HELP ME sign?'

Poole shrugged. 'It's amazing what you can hear through the crack of a partially opened door, Mr

Kenzie. Why, I've known cops have mistaken the whistling of a kettle for a child's screams. Now it's a shame when doors have to be kicked in and furniture destroyed and inhabitants manhandled over such a mistake, but it's still within the purview of probable cause.'

Broussard held out his hands. 'It's a flawed justice system, but we try to make do.'

Poole pulled a quarter from his pocket, perched it on his thumbnail, and nudged Broussard. 'Call it.'

'Which door?' Broussard said.

'Statistically,' Poole said, 'the front door draws more fire.'

Broussard glanced out through the rain. 'Statistically.'

Poole nodded. 'But we both know it's a long walk to that back door.'

'Through a lot of open ground.'

Poole nodded again.

'Loser gets to knock on the back door.'

'Why not just go together to the front door?' I asked.

Poole rolled his eyes. 'Because there's at least three of them, Mr Kenzie.'

'Divide and conquer,' Broussard said.

'What about all those guns?' Angie said.

Poole said, 'The ones your mystery friend said he saw in there?'

I nodded. 'Those, yeah. Callico M-110s, he seemed to think.'

'But no clips to go with them.'

'Not last night,' I said. 'Who knows if they had time to score some somewhere else in the last sixteen hours?'

Poole nodded. 'Heavy firepower, if they have the clips.'

'Fall off that bridge when we come to it.' Broussard turned to Poole. 'I always lose the coin toss.'

'Yet here's chance come knocking again.'

Broussard sighed. 'Heads.'

Poole flicked his thumb and the coin spun up through the half-dark of the backseat, caught some of the amber light woven on the rain, and shone, for just a millisecond, like Spanish gold. The quarter landed in Poole's palm and he slapped it over the back of his hand.

Broussard looked down at the coin and grimaced. 'Best two out of three?'

Poole shook his head, pocketed the coin. 'I have the front, you get the back.'

Broussard sat back against the seat, and for a full minute no one said anything. We stared through the slanted sheets of rain at the dirty little house. Just a box, really, with a prevalent sense of rot in the deep sag of the porch, the missing shingles and boarded windows.

Looking at the house, it was impossible to imagine love being made in its bedrooms, children playing in its yards, laughter curling up into its beams.

'Shotguns?' Broussard said eventually.

Poole nodded. 'Real western-style, pardner.'

Broussard reached for the door handle.

'Not to spoil this John Wayne moment,' Angie said, 'but won't shotguns seem suspicious to the occupants of the house if you're supposedly just there to ask questions?'

'Won't see the shotguns,' Broussard said, as he

opened his door to the rain. 'That's why God created trench coats.'

Broussard walked across and up the road to the back of the Taurus and popped the trunk. They'd parked the car by a tree as old as the town; large, misshapen, its roots having disgorged the sidewalk around it, the tree blocked the car and Broussard from view of the Tretts' house.

'So we're clear,' Poole said gently, from the back-seat.

Broussard pulled a trench coat from the trunk and shrugged it on. I looked back at Poole.

'If anything goes wrong, use your cellular phone and call Nine-one-one.' He leaned forward and placed an index finger up by our faces. 'Under no circumstances do you move from this vehicle. Are we understood?'

'Got it,' I said.

'Miss Gennaro?'

Angie nodded.

'Well, then, it's all fine.' Poole opened his door and stepped out into the rain.

He crossed the road and joined his partner at the back of the Taurus. Broussard nodded at something Poole said and looked over at us as he slipped a shotgun under the flap of his trench coat.

'Cowboys,' Angie said.

'This may be Broussard's chance to get back to detective rank. Of course he's excited.'

'Too excited?' Angie asked.

Broussard seemed to have read our lips. He smiled through the rivulets of water pouring down our windows and shrugged. Then he turned back to Poole, said something with his lips an inch from the older man's ear. Poole patted him on the back and Broussard walked away from the Taurus, strode up the road through the slanting rain, stepped into the east side of Trett's yard, ambled casually through the weeds, and made his way toward the back of the house.

Poole closed the trunk and pulled at his trench coat flaps until they covered his shotgun. The shotgun was nestled between his right arm and chest. He held his Glock behind his back in his left hand as he walked up the road, his head tilted up toward the boarded-up windows.

'You see that?' Angie said.

'What?'

'The window to the left of the front door. I think the curtain moved.'

'You sure?'

She shook her head. 'I said I "think."' She took her cellular phone from her purse, placed it on her lap.

Poole reached the steps. He raised his left foot toward the first step, and then he must have seen something there he didn't like, because he extended his leg over the first step, brought his foot down on the second, and climbed up onto the porch.

The porch sagged deeply in the middle, and Poole's body canted to the left as he stood there, the rain running off the porch between his feet in the gutter formed by the deep sag.

He looked over at the window to the left of the door, kept his head turned that way for a moment, then turned toward the right window, stared at it.

I reached into the glove box, pulled my .45 out.

Angie reached over me and removed her .38,

flicked her wrist and checked the cylinder, snapped it back into place.

Poole approached the door and raised the hand that held the Glock, rapped on the wood with his knuckles. He stepped back, waited. His head turned to the left, then to the right, then back to the door. He leaned forward and rapped the wood again.

The rain barely made noise as it fell. The drops were thin and the sheets fell at an angle, and except for the high-pitched moan of the wind, the road outside the car was silent.

Poole leaned forward and twisted the doorknob to the right and left. The door remained closed. He knocked a third time.

A car drove past, a beige Volvo station wagon with bicycles tied to the roof rack, a woman with a peach headband and a pinched nervous face hunched over the wheel. We watched her brake lights flare red at the stop sign a hundred yards down the road; then the car turned left and disappeared.

The blast of a shotgun from the back of the house ripped through the moaning wind, and glass shattered. Something shrieked in the whispering rain like the clack of damaged brakes.

Poole looked back at us for a moment. Then he raised his foot to kick in the door and disappeared in an eruption of splinters and fire and bursts of light, the chattering of an automatic weapon.

The blast blew him off his feet, and he hit the porch banister so hard it cracked and peeled back from the porch like an arm snapped free at the shoulder socket. Poole's Glock jumped out of his hand and landed in the flower bed below the porch and his shotgun clattered down the steps.

And the gunfire stopped as suddenly as it had started.

For a moment, we froze inside the car, inside the din left in the aftermath of the gunfire. Poole's shotgun slid off the last step and the stock disappeared in the grass as the barrel shone black and wet on the pavement. A strong gust blew the rain with renewed force, and the small house whined and creaked as the gust pushed hard against its roof, rattled its windows.

I opened the car door and stepped out on the road, kept myself low as I ran toward the house. In the soft hiss of the rain, I could hear the thump of my rubber soles on the wet tar and gravel.

Angie ran beside me, the cellular phone up by her right ear and the corner of her mouth. 'Officer down at 322 Admiral Farragut Road in Germantown. Say again: Officer down at 322 Admiral Farragut, Germantown.'

As we ran up the walkway leading to the steps, my eyes darted from the windows to the door and back again. The door had been eviscerated, as if large animals had attacked it with stiletto claws. The wood was gouged in ragged teardrops; in several places I could see through the holes into the house, catch quick glimpses of muted colors or light.

As we reached the steps, the holes were suddenly obscured by darkness. I swung out with my right arm, knocked Angie off her feet and onto the lawn as I dove left.

It was as if the world exploded. Nothing prepares you for the sound of a gun firing seven rounds a second. Through a wooden door, the rage of the bullets sounded almost human, a cacophony of biting, rabid homicide.

Poole flopped to his left as the bullets spit off the porch, and I reached down into the grass by my feet, curled my hand around the stock of his shotgun. I holstered my .45 and rose to one knee. I pointed through the rain and fired into the door, and the wood belched smoke. When the smoke cleared, I was looking at a hole in the center the size of my fist. I rose off my knee but slipped on the wet grass and heard glass tinkling to my left.

I spun and fired over the porch banister into the window, blew the glass and frame to pieces, ripped a hole in the dark curtain.

Inside the house, someone screamed.

The gunfire had stopped. Echoes of the shotgun blasts and the chatter of the automatic weapon stormed through my head.

Angie was on her knees by the bottom of the steps, a tight grimace on her face, .38 pointed at the hole in the door.

'You all right?' I said.

'My ankle's fucked up.'

'Shot?'

She shook her head, her eyes never leaving the door. 'I think it snapped when you pushed me to the ground.' She took a long breath through pursed lips.

'Snapped as in broken?'

She nodded, sucked in another breath.

Poole moaned, and blood slid from the corner of his mouth in a bright, swift current.

'I have to get him off the porch,' I said.

Angie nodded. 'I'll cover.'

I laid the shotgun on the wet grass and reached up, grabbed the top of the banister Poole had bent back when his body had slammed into it. I put my foot against the foundation of the porch and pulled down, felt the base of the banister wrench away from the rotted wood. I gave it another hard pull and the banister and half the railing ripped away from the porch. Poole tumbled back into me, knocked me to the wet grass.

He moaned again and writhed in my arms, and I slid out from under him, saw the curtain in the right window move.

I said, 'Angie,' but she'd already pivoted. She fired three rounds into the window and glass spit out of the frame, showered to the porch.

I crouched by the low bushes along the foundation, but no one returned fire and Poole's back arched off the lawn and a mist of blood burst from his lips.

Angie lowered her gun, took one last long look at the door and the windows, then scrambled across the walk toward us on her knees, her left ankle twisted and held aloft as she pulled herself forward. I drew my .45, pointed over her as she crawled past, and then slid over to the other side of Poole.

Another eruption of automatic weapon fire tore through the back of the house.

'Broussard.' Poole spit the word as he grabbed Angie's arm, his heels kicking at the grass.

Angie looked at me.

'Broussard,' Poole said again, a thick gurgle in his throat, his back arching off the grass.

Angie pulled her sweatshirt over her head, pressed it to the dark fountain of blood in the center of

Poole's chest. 'Sssh.' She placed a hand on his cheek. 'Sssh.'

Whoever was firing in the back of the house had a huge clip. For a full twenty seconds, I could hear the staccato screech of that gun. There was a brief pause, then it started again. I wasn't sure if it was the Calico or some other automatic weapon, but it didn't make much difference. A machine gun is a machine gun.

I closed my eyes for just a second, swallowed against a painfully dry throat, felt the adrenaline wash through my blood like toxic fuel.

'Patrick,' Angie said, 'don't even fucking think about it.'

I knew if I looked back at her, I'd never leave that lawn. Somewhere in the back of that house, Broussard was pinned down or worse. Samuel Pietro could be in there, bullets flying around his body like hornets.

'Patrick!' Angie screamed, but I'd already vaulted the three steps and landed on the crevice where the two sides of the ruined porch met.

The doorknob had been blown off in the ambush on Poole, and I kicked the door open and fired at chest level into the dark room. I spun right, then left, and emptied my clip, dropped it out of the butt and slammed a fresh one home as it hit the floor. The room was empty.

'Need immediate assistance,' Angie screamed into the cell phone behind me. 'Officer down! Officer down!'

The inside of the house was a dark gray that matched the sky outside. I noticed a swath of blood on the floor that had come from a body dragging

357

itself into the hallway. At the other end of the hall, light poured through bullet holes in the back door. The door itself dipped toward the ground, its lower hinge blown off the jamb.

Halfway down the hall, the swath of blood broke to the right and disappeared through the kitchen doorway. I turned in the living room, checked the shadows, saw the broken glass under the windows, the pieces of wood and curtain fabric that had come apart in the gun blasts, an old couch spilling stuffing and littered with beer cans.

The automatic gunfire had ceased as soon as I'd entered the house, and for the moment all I heard was the rain spitting against the porch behind me, the ticking of a clock somewhere in the back of the house, and the sound of my own breathing, shallow and ragged.

The floorboards creaked as I made my way across the living room, followed the blood into the hall. Sweat poured down my face and softened my hands as my eyes darted from the door at the end of the hall to the four separate doorways that lay ahead of me in the narrow corridor. The one ten feet up on my right was the kitchen. The one on the left spilled yellow light into the hall.

I flattened myself against the right wall and inched along until I had a partially obstructed view of the room to the left. It appeared to be a sitting room of some kind. Two chairs were positioned on either side of a wine cabinet built into the wall. One was the recliner I'd been able to make out in the dark last night. The other matched it. The wine cabinet hung in the center of the wall and the glass casing that usually ran over the shelves had been removed. The shelves were filled with stacks of newspaper and glossy magazines, and several more magazines were stacked on the floor beside the chairs. Two old-fashioned pewter ashtrays in three-foot stands stood by the arms of the leather chairs, and a half-smoked cigar still smoldered in one. I stood pressed against the wall, my gun pointed at the right side of that room, watching for moving shadows, listening for creaks on the floorboards.

Nothing.

I took two tight steps across the hall, pinned myself against the other wall, and pointed my gun into the kitchen.

The black-and-white tile floor glistened with streaks of blood and viscera. Wet hand prints, tinged a bright orange under the harsh fluorescent, stained the cupboards and refrigerator door. I saw a shadow spill out from the right side of the room, heard a ragged breathing that wasn't my own.

I took a long, deep breath, counted down from three, and then jumped across to the other side of the doorway, saw in a flash that the reading room to my right was empty, stared down the barrel of my gun at Leon Trett sitting up on the kitchen counter, his eyes fastened on me.

One of the Calico M-110s lay just inside the doorway. I kicked it under the table to my right as I entered.

Leon watched me come with a pained grin on his face. He'd shaved, and his soft, curdled skin had an unhealthy, raw sheen to it, as if the flesh had been scraped with a wire brush and then lathered in oil, as if it could be lifted from the bone with a spoon. Without the beard, his face was longer than it had appeared last night, the cheeks so sunken his mouth was a perpetual oval.

His left arm hung useless by his side, a hole pumping dark blood from the biceps. His right arm was crossed over his abdomen, trying to hold his intestines in. His tan trousers were saturated with his own blood.

'Come to give me my clips?' he said.

I shook my head.

'Got some of my own this morning.'

I shrugged.

'Who are you?' he said in a soft voice, his right eyebrow cocked.

'Down on the floor,' I said.

He grunted. 'Sweetie, you see me holding my guts in up here? How'm I supposed to move and keep them in?'

'Not my problem,' I said. 'Down on the floor.'

His long jaw clenched. 'No.'

'Get down on the fucking floor.'

'No,' he said again.

'Leon. Do it.'

'Fuck you. Shoot me.'

'Leon—'

His eyes flickered to his left for just a moment, and the tightness left his jaw. He said, 'Show some mercy, baby. Come on.'

I watched his eyes flicker again, saw the hint of a smile form on his lips, and I dropped to my knees as Roberta Trett fired at the place I'd been and blew her own husband's head off with a sustained burst from her M-110.

She screamed in shock and surprise as Leon's face disappeared like a balloon popped by a pin, and I rolled onto my back and squeezed off a round that hit her right hip and jerked her into the corner of the kitchen.

She spun back toward me, that great mass of gray hair swinging across her face, and unfortunately the M-110 came with her. One sweaty finger grasped for the trigger, kept sliding off the guard, and her free hand grasped at the wound on her hip as her eyes stayed locked on her husband's missing head. I watched the muzzle swing my way, and I knew that any second she'd come out of shock and find the trigger.

I dove out of the kitchen, back into the hall. I rolled to my right as Roberta Trett spun full circle and the Calico muzzle winked at me. I got to my feet and ran for the back door, saw the door getting closer and closer, and then I heard Roberta step out into the hall behind me.

'You killed my Leon, motherfucker. You killed my Leon!'

The hallway blew up like an earthquake as Roberta got her finger around the trigger and let loose.

I dove without looking into the room off to my left, discovered too late that it wasn't a room at all but a staircase.

My forehead rammed a stair about seven or eight steps up, and the impact of wood against bone rocked back through my teeth like electrical voltage. I heard Roberta's heavy footsteps as she stumbled down the hallway toward the staircase.

She wasn't firing her gun, and that terrified me more than if she were.

She knew she had me boxed in.

My shin screamed as it banged against the edge of a riser as I tore up the staircase, slipped once and kept going, saw a metal door at the top and prayed please God please God let it be open.

Roberta reached the opening below and I lunged for the door, hit it in the center with the heel of my hand, felt it give way like a burst of oxygen breaking from my lungs.

My chest bounced off the floor as Roberta unloaded her gun again. I rolled to my left and slammed the door behind me on a splatter of lead that banged off the metal like hail on a tin roof. The door was heavy and thick – the door to an industrial cooler or a vault – and bolt locks lined the inside: four of them from a height of about five and a half feet to a depth of about six inches. I threw them one by one as the bullets continued to ping and thunk off the other side. The door itself was bulletproof, the locks incapable of being shot out from the other side, sealed by sheets of layered steel on this side.

'You killed my Leon!'

The bullets had stopped and Roberta wailed from the other side of the door, a lunatic's wail so violated and sheared and steeped in sudden, awful aloneness that the sound of it wrenched something in my chest.

'You killed my Leon! You killed him! You will die! Fucking die!'

Something heavy slammed into the door, and I realized after a second thump that it was Roberta Trett herself, throwing that oversized body of hers against the door like a battering ram, over and over, howling and shrieking and calling her husband's name, and – *bam, bam, bam* – hurling herself at the only boundary between us.

Even if she lost her gun and I still had mine, I knew that if she got through that door she'd rip me to pieces with her bare hands, no matter how many rounds I fired into her.

'Leon! Leon!'

I listened for the sounds of sirens, the squawk of walkie-talkies, the bleat of a bullhorn. The police had to have reached the house by now. They had to.

That's when it hit me that I couldn't hear anything except Roberta, and only because she was directly on the other side of the door.

A bare forty-watt bulb hung over the room, and as I turned and took in my surroundings, I felt an express train of cold fear barrel through my veins.

I was in a large bedroom fronting the street. The windows were boarded up, thick black wood screwed into the molding, the dead silver eyes of forty or fifty flatheads apiece staring back at me from each window.

The floor was bare and strewn with the droppings of rodents. Bags of potato chips and Fritos and tortilla chips were scattered by the baseboards, their crumbs ground into the wood. Three bare mattresses, soiled with excrement and blood and God knew what else lay against the walls. The walls themselves were covered in thick gray sections of sponge and the Styrofoam soundproofing found in a recording studio. Except this wasn't a recording studio.

Metal posts had been hammered into the walls just above the bare mattresses, and handcuffs hung to small ringlets that had been welded to the ends of the posts. A small metal wastebasket in the western corner of the room held a variety of riding crops, whips, spiked dildos, and leather straps. The entire room smelled of flesh so soiled and tainted the taint had spilled into the heart and poisoned the brain.

Roberta had stopped banging into the door, but I could hear her muffled wailing in the stairwell.

I walked toward the east end of the bedroom, saw where a wall had been knocked down to open the room up, the ridge of plaster and dust still rising from the floor. A fat mouse with spiked fur ran past me, took a right at the east end of the room, and disappeared through an opening just past the end of the wall.

I kept my gun pointed ahead of me as I stepped through more bags of chips and NAMBLA newsletters, empty cans of beer with mold growing by their openings. Magazines, printed on the cheapest glossy paper, lay open and gaping: boys, girls, adults – even animals – engaged in something I knew wasn't sex, even though it appeared to be. Those photos seared their way into my brain in the half second before I could turn away, and what they'd captured and imprisoned on film had nothing to do with normal human interaction, only with cancer – cancerous minds and hearts and organs.

I reached the opening where the mouse had disappeared, a small space under the eaves of the house, where the roof slanted to the gutters. Beyond it was a small blue door.

Corwin Earle stood in front of the door, his back hunched under the eaves, a crossbow held up by his face, the stock resting against his shoulder, his left eye trying to squint down the sight and blink away sweat at the same time. His lazy right eye searched for focus, slid toward me again and again before it was pushed back to the right as if by a motor. He closed it eventually, resetting his shoulder against the crossbow stock. He was naked, and there was blood on his chest, a smattering of it on his protruding abdomen. A sense of defeat and weary victimization was imprinted in his sad crumble of a face.

'The Tretts don't trust you with the machine guns, Corwin?'

He shook his head slightly.

'Where's Samuel Pietro?' I said.

He shook his head again, this time more slowly, and flexed his shoulders against the weight of the crossbow.

I looked at the tip of the arrowhead, saw it wavering slightly, noticed the tremors running up and down the undersides of Corwin Earle's arms.

'Where's Samuel Pietro?' I repeated.

He shook his head again, and I shot him in the stomach.

He didn't make a sound. He folded over at the waist and dropped the crossbow on the floor in front of him. He fell to his knees and then tipped to his right in a fetal ball, lay there with his tongue lolling out of his mouth like a dog's.

I stepped over him and opened the blue door, entered a bathroom the size of a small closet. I saw the boarded-up black window, and a tattered shower curtain lying under the sink, and blood on the tile, the toilet, splashed against the walls as if hurled from a bucket.

A child's white cotton underwear lay soaked in blood in the sink.

I looked in the bathtub.

I'm not sure how long I stood there, head bent, mouth open. I felt a hot wetness on my cheeks, streams of it, and it was only after that double eternity of staring into the tub at the small, naked body curled up by the drain that I realized I was weeping.

I walked back out of the bathroom and saw Corwin Earle on his knees, his arms wrapped around his stomach, his back to me, as he tried to use his kneecaps to carry himself across the floor.

I stayed behind him and waited, my gun pointed down, his dark hair rising up from the other side of the black metal sight on the barrel.

He made a chugging sound as he crawled, a low *yuh-yuh-yuh-yuh-yuh* that reminded me of the chug of a portable generator.

When he reached the crossbow and got one hand on the stock, I said, 'Corwin.'

He looked back over his shoulder at me, saw the gun pointed at him, and scrunched his eyes closed. He turned his head, gripping the crossbow tight with a bloody hand.

I fired a round into the back of his neck and kept walking, heard the shell skitter on wood and Corwin's body thump against the floor as I turned left, back into the bedroom, and walked to the vault door. I unsnapped the locks one by one.

'Roberta,' I said, 'You still out there? You hear me? I'm going to kill you now, Roberta.'

I unsnapped the last of the locks, threw the door open, and came face-to-face with a shotgun barrel.

Remy Broussard lowered the barrel. Between his legs, Roberta Trett lay facedown on the stairs, a

366

dark red oval the size of a serving dish in the center of her back.

Broussard steadied himself against the railing as sweat poured like warm rain from his hairline.

'Had to blow the lock on the bulkhead and come up through the basement,' he said. 'Sorry it took so long.'

I nodded.

'Clear in there?' He took a deep breath, watched me steadily with dark eyes.

'Yes.' I cleared my throat. 'Corwin Earle is dead.'

'Samuel Pietro,' he said.

I nodded. 'I think it's Samuel Pietro.' I looked down at my gun, saw that it jumped from the tremors in my arm, the shakes wracking my body like a series of small strokes. I looked back at Broussard, felt the warm streams spring from my eyes again. 'It's hard to tell,' I said, and my voice cracked.

Broussard nodded. I noticed that he was weeping, too.

'In the basement,' he said.

'What?'

'Skeletons,' he said. 'Two of them. Kids.'

My voice didn't sound like my own as I said, 'I don't know how to respond to that.'

'I don't either,' he said.

He looked down at Roberta Trett's corpse. He lowered the shotgun and placed it against the back of her head, and his finger curled around the trigger.

I waited for him to blow her dead brains all over the staircase.

After a while, he removed the gun and sighed. He

took his foot and brought it down gently on the top of her head, and then he pushed her down.

That's what the Quincy police met as they reached the stairs: Roberta Trett's large corpse sliding down the dark staircase toward them and two men standing up top, weeping like children because they'd somehow never known the world could get this bad.

26

It took twenty hours to confirm that the body in the bathtub had, in fact, been that of Samuel Pietro. The work the Tretts and Corwin Earle had done on his face with a knife had made dental records the only sure means of identification. Gabrielle Pietro had gone into shock after a reporter from the *News*, acting on a tip, called before the police contacted her to ask for a statement regarding her son's death.

Samuel Pietro had been dead forty-five minutes by the time I found him. The medical examiner ascertained that in the two weeks since his disappearance he'd been sodomized repeatedly, flogged along his back, buttocks, and legs, and handcuffed so tightly that the flesh around his right wrist was worn down to the bone. He'd been fed nothing but potato chips, Fritos, and beer since he'd left his mother's house.

Less than an hour before we'd entered the Trett house, either Corwin Earle, one or both of the Tretts, or maybe all three of them – who the hell knew and ultimately what difference did it make? – had stabbed the boy in the heart and then drawn the knife blade across his throat and severed his carotid artery.

I'd spent the morning and most of the afternoon up in our cramped office, tucked in the belfry of St Bartholomew's Church, feeling the weight of the great building around me, the spires reaching for heaven. I stared out the window. I tried not to think. I drank cold coffee and sat, felt a soft ticking in my chest, in my head.

Angie's ankle had been set and plastered last night at the New England Med emergency room, and she'd left the apartment this morning as I was waking up, taken a taxi to her doctor's office so he could check the ER resident's work and tell her what to expect from time spent in a cast.

I left the belfry office, once I got the details regarding Samuel Pietro from Broussard, and descended the stairs into the chapel. I sat in the front pew in the still half-dark, smelled the remains of incense and the bloom of chrysanthemums, met the gem-shaped gaze of several stained-glass saints, and watched the lights of small votive candles flicker off the mahogany altar rail, wondered why an eight-year-old child had been allowed to live on this earth just long enough to experience everything horrific in it.

I looked up at the stained-glass Jesus, his arms held open above the gold tabernacle.

'Eight years old,' I whispered. 'Explain that.'

I can't.

Can't or won't?

No answer. God can clam up with the best of them.

You put a child on this earth, give him eight years of life. You allow him to be kidnapped, tortured, starved, and raped for fourteen days – over three hundred and thirty hours, nineteen thousand eight hundred long minutes – and then as a final image You provide him with the faces of monsters who shove steel into his heart, cleave the flesh from his face, and open his throat on a bathroom floor.

What's your point?

'What's Yours?' I said loudly, heard my voice echo off stone.

Silence.

'Why?' I whispered.

More silence.

'There's no goddamned answer. Is there?'

Don't blaspheme. You're in church.

Now I knew the voice in my head wasn't God's. My mother's probably, maybe a dead nun's, but I doubted God would get hung up on technicalities during such a time of dire need.

Then again, what did I know? Maybe God, if He did exist, was as petty and trivial as the rest of us.

If so, He wasn't a God I could follow.

Yet I stayed in the pew, unable to move.

I believe in God because of . . . what?

Talent – the kind Van Gogh or Michael Jordan, Stephen Hawking or Dylan Thomas were born with – always seemed proof of God to me. So did love.

So, okay, I believe in You. But I'm not sure I like You.

That's your problem.

'What good comes from a child's rape and murder?'

Don't ask questions your brain is too small to answer.

I watched the candles flicker for a while, sucked the quiet into my lungs, closed my eyes to it, and waited for transcendence or a state of grace or peace or whatever the hell it was the nuns had taught me you were supposed to wait for when the world is too much with you.

After about a minute, I opened my eyes. Probably the reason I'd never been a successful Catholic – I lacked patience.

The rear door of the building opened and I heard the clack of Angie's crutches against the door bar, heard her say, 'Shit,' and then the door closed and she appeared at the landing between the chapel and the stairs leading up to the belfry. She noticed me just before she turned toward the stairs. She swiveled around awkwardly, looked at me, and smiled.

She worked her way down the two carpeted steps to the chapel floor, swung her body past the confessionals and baptismal font. She paused by the altar rail in front of my pew, hoisted herself up onto it, and leaned her crutches against the rail.

'Hey.'

'Hey,' I said.

She looked up at the ceiling, the painting of the Last Supper, back down at me. 'You're inside the chapel and the church is still standing.'

'Imagine,' I said.

We sat there for a bit, neither of us saying anything. Angie's head tilted back as she scanned the ceiling, the detail carved into the molding atop the nearest pilaster.

'What's the verdict on the leg?'

'The doctor said it's a stress fracture of the lower left fibula.'

I smiled. 'You love saying that, don't you?'

'Lower left fibula?' She gave me a broad grin. 'Yeah. Makes me feel like I'm on *ER*. Next I'm going to ask for a Chem-Seven and BP count. Stat.'

'The doctor told you to stay off it, I suppose.'

She shrugged. 'Yeah, but that's what they always say.'

'How long you have to wear the cast?'

'Three weeks.'

'No aerobics.'

She shrugged again. 'No a lot of things.'

I looked down at my shoes for a bit, then back up at her.

'What?' she said.

'It hurts all over. Samuel Pietro. I can't get my head around it. When Bubba and I went to that house, he was still alive. He was upstairs and he was . . . we—'

'You were in a house with three heavily armed, very paranoid felons. You couldn't have—'

'His body,' I said, 'it . . .'

'They confirmed it was his body?'

I nodded. 'It was so small. It was so small,' I whispered. 'It was naked and cut into and . . . Jesus, Jesus, Jesus.' I wiped at acidic tears, leaned my head back.

'Who'd you talk to?' Angie said gently.

'Broussard.'

'How's he doing?'

''Bout the same as me.'

'Any word on Poole?' She leaned forward a bit.

'He's bad, Ange. They don't expect him to pull through.'

She nodded and kept her head down for a bit, her good leg swaying back and forth lightly off the rail.

'What did you see in that bathroom, Patrick? I mean, exactly?'

I shook my head.

'Come on,' she said softly. 'This is me. I can take it.'

'I can't,' I said. 'Not again. Not again. I think about it for a second – I see that room flash through my head – and I want to die. I don't want to carry it around with me. I want to die and make it go away.'

She slid gingerly off the rail and used the front of the pew to pull herself around to the seat. I moved over and she sat beside me. She took my face in her hands, but I couldn't meet her eyes, was sure that seeing the warmth and the love in them would make me feel more soiled, for some reason, more unhinged.

She kissed my forehead and then my eyelids, the tears drying on my face, brought my head down to her shoulder, and kissed the back of my neck.

'I don't know what to say,' she whispered.

'Nothing to say.' I cleared my throat, wrapped my arms around her abdomen and lower back. I could hear her heart beating. She felt so good, so beautiful, so everything that was right in the world. And I still felt like dying.

That night we tried to make love, and at first it was fine, fun actually, trying to work around the heavy cast, Angie giggling from the painkillers, but then once we were both naked in the light of the moon shining through my bedroom window, I'd see a flash of her flesh and it would meld with a snapshot image of Samuel Pietro's. I touched her breast and saw Corwin Earle's flabby stomach splattered with

374

blood, ran my tongue over her rib cage and saw blood splashed on the bathroom wall as if hurled from a bucket.

Standing over that bathtub, I'd gone into shock. I saw everything and it was enough to make me weep, but some part of my brain shut down as a protective impulse, so that the true horror of everything I was looking at didn't fully compute. It had been bad, bloody and unconscionable – I'd known that much – but the images had remained random, floating in a sea of white porcelain and black-and-white tile.

In the thirty hours since, my brain had collated everything, and I was alone and in that tub with Samuel Pietro's naked, ravaged, debased body. The door to the bathroom was locked, and I couldn't get out.

'What's wrong?' Angie said.

I rolled away from her, looked out the window at the moon.

Her warm hand stroked my back. 'Patrick?'

A scream died in my throat.

'Patrick, come on. Talk to me.'

The phone rang and I picked it up.

It was Broussard. 'How you doing?'

I felt a flush of relief at the sound of his voice, a sense that I wasn't alone.

'Pretty bad. You?'

'Pretty real fucking bad, if you know what I mean.'

'I do,' I said.

'Can't even talk to my wife about it, and I tell her everything.'

'I know what you mean.'

'Look . . . Patrick, I'm still in the city. With a

bottle. You want to drink some of it with me?'

'Yeah.'

'I'll be at the Ryan. That all right with you?'

'Sure.'

'See you when you get here.'

He hung up, and I turned to Angie.

She had pulled the sheet up over her body and was reaching across to her nightstand for her cigarettes. She placed the ashtray on her lap and lit the cigarette, stared through the smoke at me.

'That was Broussard,' I said.

She nodded, took another drag on the cigarette.

'He wants to meet.'

'Both of us?' She looked down at the ashtray.

'Just me.'

She nodded. 'Best get going, then.'

I leaned in toward her. 'Ange—'

She held up a hand. 'No apology necessary. Off you go.' She appraised my naked body and smiled. 'Put some clothes on first.'

I picked my clothes up off the floor and put them on as Angie watched from behind her cigarette smoke.

As I left the bedroom, she stubbed out her cigarette and said, 'Patrick.'

I stuck my head back in the door.

'When you're ready to talk, I'm all ears. Anything you need to say.'

I nodded.

'And if you don't talk, that's up to you. You understand?'

Again, I nodded.

She placed the ashtray back on the nightstand and the sheet fell away from her upper body.

For a long time, neither of us said anything.

'Just so we're clear,' Angie said eventually. 'I won't be like one of those cop wives in the movies.'

'How do you mean?'

'Nagging and begging you to talk.'

'I don't expect you to.'

'They never know when to leave, those women.'

I leaned back into the room, peered at her.

She shifted the pillows behind her head. 'Could you hit the light on your way out?'

I turned off the light, but I stood there for a few moments more, feeling Angie's eyes on me.

27

It was one very drunk cop I met in the Ryan playground. Only when I saw him wavering on a swing as I entered, no tie, wrinkled suit jacket scrunched under a topcoat stained by playground sand, one shoe untied, did I realize that it was the first time I'd ever seen him with so much as a hair out of place. Even after the quarries and a jump onto the leg of a helicopter, he'd looked impeccable.

'You're Bond,' I said.

'Huh?'

'James Bond,' I said. 'You're James Bond, Broussard. Mister Perfect.'

He smiled and drained what remained of a bottle of Mount Gay. He tossed the dead soldier into the sand, pulled a full one from his topcoat, and cracked the seal. He spun the cap off and into the sand with a flick of his thumb. 'It's a burden, being this good-looking. Heh-heh.'

'How's Poole?'

Broussard shook his head several times. 'Nothing's changed. He's alive, but barely. He hasn't regained consciousness.'

I sat on the swing beside his. 'And the prognosis?'

'Not good. Even if he lives, he's had several

strokes in the last thirty hours, lost a ton of oxygen to the brain. He'd be partially paralyzed, the doctors figure, mute most likely. He'll never get out of bed again.'

I thought of that first afternoon I'd met Poole, the first time I'd seen his odd ritual of sniffing a cigarette before snapping it in half, the way he'd looked up into my confused face with his elfin grin and said, 'I beg your pardon. I quit.' Then, when Angie'd asked if he'd mind if she smoked, he'd said, 'Oh, God, would you?'

Shit. I hadn't even realized until now how much I liked him.

No more Poole. No more arch remarks, delivered with a knowing, bemused glint in his eye.

'I'm sorry, Broussard.'

'Remy,' Broussard said, and handed me a plastic cocktail cup. 'You never know. He's the toughest bastard I ever met. Has a hell of a will to live. Maybe he'll pull through. How about you?'

'Huh?'

'How's your will to live?'

I waited while he filled half the cup with rum.

'It's been stronger,' I said.

'Mine, too. I don't get it.'

'What?'

He held the bottle aloft and we toasted silently, then drank.

'I don't get,' Broussard said, 'why what happened in that house has got me so turned around. I mean, I've seen a lot of horrible shit.' He leaned forward in his swing, looked back over his shoulder at me. 'Horrible shit, Patrick. Babies fed Drano in their bottles, kids suffocated and shaken to death, beat so

379

bad you can't tell what color their skin really is.' He shook his head slowly. 'Lotta shit. But something about that house . . .'

'Critical mass,' I said.

'Huh?'

'Critical mass,' I repeated. I took another swig of rum. It wasn't going down easy yet, but it was close. 'You see this horrible thing, that one, but they're spaced out. Yesterday, we saw all sorts of evil shit and it all reached critical mass at once.'

He nodded. 'I've never seen anything as bad as that basement,' he said. 'And then that kid in the tub?' He shook his head. 'A few months shy of my twenty, and I've never . . .' He took another swig and shuddered against the burn of alcohol. He gave me a slight smile. 'You know what Roberta was doing when I shot her?'

I shook my head.

'Pawing at the door like a dog. Swear to God. Pawing and mewing and crying about her Leon. I'd just climbed out of that cellar, found those two little kid skeletons sunk in limestone and gravel, the whole fucking place something out of a spook show, and I see Roberta at the top of the stairs? Man, I didn't even look for her gun. I just unloaded mine.' He spit into the sand. 'Fuck her. Hell's too good a place for that bitch.'

For a while we sat in silence, listening to the creak of the swings' chains, the cars passing along the avenue, the slap and scrape of some kids playing street hockey in the parking lot of the electronics plant across the street.

'The skeletons,' I said to Broussard after a bit.

'Unidentified. Closest the ME can tell me is that

one's male, one's female, and he thinks neither is older than nine or younger than four. A week before he knows shit.'

'Dentals?'

'The Tretts took care of that. Both skeletons showed traces of hydrochloric acid. The ME thinks the Tretts marinated them in the shit, pulled out the teeth while they were soft, dumped the bones in boxes of limestone in the cellar.'

'Why leave them in the cellar?'

'So they could look at them?' Broussard shrugged. 'Who the fuck knows?'

'So one could be Amanda McCready.'

'Most definitely. Either that or she's in the quarry.'

I thought about the cellar and Amanda for a bit. Amanda McCready and her flat eyes, her lowered expectations for all the things that kids should have the highest expectations for, her lifeless corpse being dropped in a bathtub filled with acid, her hair stripping away from her head like papier-mâché.

'Hell of a world,' Broussard whispered.

'It's a fucking awful world, Remy. You know?'

'Two days ago I would have argued with you. I'm a cop, okay, but I'm lucky, too. Got a great wife, nice house, invested well over the years. I'll leave all this shit soon as I hit my twenty and a wake-up call.' He shrugged. 'But then something like – Jesus – that carved-up kid in that fucking bathroom and you start thinking, "Well, fine, my life's okay, but the world's still a pile of shit for most people. Even if *my* world is okay, *the* world is still a pile of evil shit." You know?'

'Oh,' I said, 'I know. Exactly.'

'Nothing works.'

'What's that?'

'Nothing works,' he said. 'Don't you get it? The cars, the washing machines, the refrigerators and "starter" houses, the fucking shoes and clothes and . . . nothing works. Schools don't work.'

'Not public ones,' I said.

'Public? Look at the morons coming out of private schools these days. You ever talked to one of those disaffected prep-school fucks? You ask 'em what morality is, they say a concept. You ask 'em what decency is, they say a word. Look at these rich kids whacking winos in Central Park over drug deals or just because. Schools don't work because parents don't work because *their* parents didn't work because nothing works, so why invest energy or love or anything into it if it's just going to let you down? Jesus, Patrick, *we* don't work. That kid was out there for two weeks; no one could find him. He was in that house, we suspected it hours before he was killed, we're sitting in a doughnut shop *talking* about it. That kid got his throat cut when we should have been kicking in the door.'

'We're the richest, most advanced society in the history of civilization,' I said, 'and we can't keep a kid from getting carved up in a bathtub by three freaks? Why?'

'I don't know.' He shook his head and kicked at the sand by his feet. 'I just don't know. Every time you come up with a solution, there's a faction ready to tell you you're wrong. You believe in the death penalty?'

I held out my cup. 'No.'

He stopped pouring. 'Excuse me?'

I shrugged. 'I don't. Sorry. Keep pouring, will you?'

He filled my cup and sucked back on the bottle for a moment. 'You capped Corwin Earle in the back of the head, you're telling me you don't believe in capital punishment?'

'I don't think society has the right or the intelligence. Let society prove to me they can pave roads efficiently; then I'll let them decide life and death.'

'Yet, again: you executed someone yesterday.'

'Technically he had his hand on a weapon. And besides, I'm not society.'

'What the fuck's that mean?'

I shrugged. 'I trust myself. I can live with my actions. I don't trust society.'

'That why you're a PI, Patrick? The lone knight and all that?'

I shook my head. 'Piss on that.'

Another laugh.

'I'm a PI, because – I dunno, maybe I'm addicted to the great What Comes Next. Maybe I like tearing down facades. That doesn't make me a good guy. It just makes me a guy who hates people who hide, pretend to be what they're not.'

He raised the bottle, and I tapped my plastic glass into the side.

'What if someone pretends to be one thing because society deems he must, but in reality he's something else because *he* deems he must?'

I shook my head against the booze. 'Run that one by me again.' I stood up, and my feet felt unsteady in the sand. I crossed to the jungle gym opposite the swings and perched myself on a rung.

'If society doesn't work, how do we, as allegedly honorable men, live?'

'On the fringes,' I said.

He nodded. 'Exactly. Yet we must coexist within society or otherwise we're – what, we're fucking militia, guys who wear camouflage pants and bitch about taxes while they drive on roads paved by the government. Right?'

'I guess.'

He stood and wavered, grasped the swing chain, and tilted back into the pools of dark behind the swing-set arch. 'I planted evidence on a guy once.'

'You what?'

He tilted back into the light. 'True. Scumbag named Carlton Volk. He was raping hookers for months. Months. A couple pimps tried to stop him, he fucked them up. Carlton was a psycho, black-belt, prison-weight-room kind of guy. Couldn't be reasoned with. And our buddy Ray Likanski gives me a phone call, lets me in on all the details. Skinny Ray, I guess, had a soft spot for one of the hookers. Whatever. Anyway, I know Carlton Volk is raping hookers, but who's going to convict him? Even if the girls had wanted to testify – which they didn't – who would believe them? A hooker saying she was raped is a joke to most people. Like killing a corpse; supposedly it ain't possible. So I know Carlton's a two-time loser, out on probation; I plant an ounce of heroin and two unlicensed firearms in his trunk, way back under the spare where he'll never find 'em. Then I put an expired inspection sticker over the up-to-date one on his license plate. Who looks at their own plate until it's near renewal time?' He floated back into the dark again for a moment. 'Two weeks later, Carlton gets stopped on the inspection sticker, cops an attitude, et cetera, et cetera. Long story short, he gets dropped as a three-time felon for twenty years hard, no parole possibility.'

I waited until he'd swung back into the light again before I spoke.

'You think you did the right thing?'

He shrugged. 'For those hookers, yes.'

'But—'

'Always a "but" when you tell a story like that, ain't there?' He sighed. 'But a guy like Carlton, he thrives in prison. Probably goes through more young kids sent up for burglary and minor dope-dealing than he ever would have raped in hookers. So did I do right for the general population? Probably not. Did I do right for some hookers no one else gave a shit about? Maybe.'

'If you had to do it again?'

'Patrick, lemme ask you: What would you do with a guy like Carlton?'

'We're back to the death penalty again, aren't we?'

'The personal one,' he said, 'not the societal one. If I'd had the balls to whack Volk, no one gets raped by him anymore. That's not relative. That's black and white.'

'But those kids in prison, they'll still get raped by someone else.'

He nodded. 'For every solution, a problem.'

I took another swig of rum, noticed a lone star floating above the thin night clouds and city smog.

I said, 'I stood over that kid's body and something snapped. I didn't care what happened to me, to my life, to anything. I just wanted . . .' I held out my hands.

'Balance.'

I nodded.

'So you popped a cap in the back of a guy's head while he was on his knees.'

I nodded again.

'Hey, Patrick? I'm not judging you, man. I'm saying sometimes we do the right thing but it wouldn't hold up in court. It wouldn't survive the scrutiny of' – he made quotation marks with his fingers – 'society.'

I heard that *yuh-yuh-yuh* yammering Earle had made under his breath, saw the puff of blood that had spit from the back of his neck, heard the thump as he'd fallen to the floor and the spent shell skittered on the wood.

'In the same circumstances,' I said, 'I'd do it again.'

'Does that make you right?' Remy Broussard ambled over to the jungle gym, poured some more rum into my cup.

'No.'

'Doesn't make you wrong, though, does it?'

I looked up at him, smiled, and shook my head. 'No again.'

He leaned back into the jungle gym and yawned. 'Nice if we had all the answers, wouldn't it?'

I looked at the line of his face etched in the darkness beside me, and I felt something squirm and niggle in the back of my skull like a small fishing hook. What had he just said that bugged me?

I looked at Remy Broussard and I felt that fish hook dig deeper against the back of my skull. I watched him close his eyes and I wanted to hit him for some reason.

Instead I said, 'I'm glad.'

'About what?'

'Killing Corwin Earle.'

'Me too. I'm glad I killed Roberta.' He poured more rum into my cup. 'Hell with it, Patrick, I'm glad none of those sick pricks walked out of that house alive. Drink to that?'

I looked at the bottle, then at Broussard, searched his face for whatever it was about him that suddenly bothered me. Frightened me. I couldn't find it in the dark, in the booze, so I raised my cup and touched the plastic to the bottle.

'May their hell be a lifetime in the bodies of their victims,' Broussard said. He raised his eyebrows up and down. 'Can I get an amen, brother?'

'Amen, brother.'

28

I sat for a long time in the ashen, half-dark of my moonlit bedroom watching Angie sleep. I ran my conversation with Broussard over and over in my head, sipped from a large cup of Dunkin' Donuts coffee I'd picked up on my walk home, smiled when Angie mumbled the name of the dog she'd had as a child and reached out and stroked the pillow with the palm of her hand.

Maybe it was shell shock over the interior of the Tretts' house that had triggered it. Maybe it was the rum. Maybe it was just that the more determined I am to keep painful events at bay, the more likely I am to focus on the little things, minutiae, a casually dropped word or phrase that rings in my head and won't stop. Whatever the case, tonight in the playground, I'd found a truth and a lie. Both at the same time.

Broussard had been right: nothing worked.

And I had been right: facades, no matter how well built, usually come down.

Angie rolled onto her back and let out a soft moan, kicked at the sheet tangled up by her feet. It must have been that effort – trying to kick with a leg encased in plaster – that woke her. She blinked and raised her head, looked down at the cast, then turned her head and saw me.

'Hey. What're . . .' She sat up, smacked her lips, pushed hair out of her eyes. 'What're you doing?'

'Sitting here,' I said. 'Thinking.'

'You drunk?'

I held up my coffee cup. 'Not so's you'd notice.'

'Then come to bed.' She extended her hand.

'Broussard lied to us.'

She pulled the hand away, used it to push herself farther up the headboard. 'What?'

'Last year,' I said. 'When Ray Likanski bolted the bar and disappeared.'

'What about it?'

'Broussard said he barely knew the man. Said he was one of Poole's occasional snitches.'

'Yeah. So?'

'Tonight, with half a pint of rum in him, he told me Ray was his own snitch.'

She reached over to the nightstand, turned on the light. 'What?'

I nodded.

'So . . . so maybe he just made an oversight last year. Maybe we heard him wrong.'

I looked at her.

Eventually she held up a hand as she turned toward the nightstand for her cigarettes. 'You're right. We never hear things wrong.'

'Not at the same time.'

She lit a cigarette and pulled the sheet up her leg, scratched at her knee just above the cast. 'Why would he lie?'

I shrugged. 'I've been sitting here wondering the same thing.'

389

'Maybe he had a reason to protect Ray's identity as his snitch.'

I sipped some coffee. 'Possibly, but it seems awful convenient, doesn't it? Ray is potentially a key witness in the disappearance of Amanda McCready; Broussard lies about knowing him. Seems . . .'

'Shady.'

I nodded. 'A bit. Another thing?'

'What?'

'Broussard's retiring soon.'

'How soon?'

'Not sure. Sounded like very soon. He said he was closing in on his twenty, and as soon as he reached it he was turning in his shield.'

She took a drag off her cigarette, peered over the bright coal at me. 'So he's retiring. So what?'

'Last year, just before we climbed up to the quarry, you made a joke to him.'

She touched her chest. 'I did.'

'*Sí.* You said something like "Maybe it's time we retired."'

Her eyes brightened. 'I said, "Maybe it's time we hung 'em up."'

'And he said?'

She leaned forward, elbows on her knees, and thought about it. 'He said . . .' She jabbed the air with her cigarette several times. 'He said he couldn't afford to retire. He said something about medical bills.'

'His wife's, wasn't it?'

She nodded. 'She'd been in a car accident just before they were married. She wasn't insured. He owed the hospital big.'

'So what happened to those medical bills? You

think the hospital just said, "Ah, you're a nice guy. Forget about it"?'

'Doubtful.'

'In the extreme. So a cop who was poor lies about knowing a key player in the McCready case, and six months later the cop's got enough money to retire – not on the kind of money a cop gets after thirty years in, but somehow on the kind a cop gets after twenty.'

She chewed her lower lip for a minute. 'Toss me a T-shirt, will you?'

I opened my dresser, took a dark green Saw Doctors shirt from the drawer, and handed it to her. She pulled it over her head and kicked away the sheets, looked around the room for her crutches. She looked over at me, saw that I was chuckling under my breath.

'What?'

'You look pretty funny.'

Her face darkened. 'How's that?'

'Sitting there in my T-shirt with a big white cast on your leg.' I shrugged. 'Just looks funny is all.'

'Ha,' she said. 'Ha-ha. Where are my crutches?'

'Behind the door.'

'Would you be so kind?'

I brought them to her and she struggled onto them, and then I followed her down the dark hall into the kitchen. The digital display on the microwave read 4:04, and I could feel it in my joints and the back of my neck, but not in my mind. When Broussard had mentioned Ray Likanski on the playground, something had snapped to attention in my brain, started marching double time, and talking with Angie had only given it more energy.

While Angie made half a pot of decaf and pulled

cream from the fridge and sugar from the cupboard, I went back to that final night in the quarry, when it seemed we'd lost Amanda McCready for good. I knew a lot of the information I was trying to recall and sift through was in my case file, but I didn't want to rely on those notes just yet. Poring over them would just put me back in the same place I'd been six months ago, while trying to conjure it all back up from this kitchen could bring a fresh perspective.

The kidnapper had demanded four couriers to bring Cheese Olamon's money in return for Amanda. Why all four of us? Why not just one?

I asked Angie.

She leaned against the oven, crossed her arms, thought about it. 'I've never even considered that. Christ, could I be that stupid?'

'It's a judgment call.'

She frowned. 'You didn't question it.'

'I know I'm stupid,' I said. 'It's you we're trying to decide on.'

'A whole dragnet,' she said, 'swept those hills, locked down the roads around it, and they couldn't find anyone.'

'Maybe the kidnappers had been tipped off to an escape route. Maybe some of the cops had been paid off.'

'Maybe there was no one up there that night besides us.' Her eyes shimmered.

'Holy shit.'

She bit down on her lower lip, raised her eyebrows several times. 'You think?'

'Broussard fired those guns from his side.'

'Why not? We couldn't see anything over there. We saw muzzle flashes. We *heard* Broussard saying

392

he was under fire. But did we see him at all during that time?'

'Nope.'

'The reason, then, that we were brought up there was to corroborate his story.'

I leaned back in my chair, ran my hands through the hair along my temples. Could it be that simple? Or, maybe, could it be that devious?

'You think Poole was in on it?' Angie turned from the counter as steam rose from the coffeemaker behind her.

'Why do you say that?'

She tapped her coffee mug against her thigh. 'He was the one who claimed Ray Likanski was his snitch, not Broussard's. And, remember, he was Broussard's partner. You know how that works. I mean, look at Oscar and Devin – they're closer than husband and wife. A hell of a lot more blindly loyal to each other.'

I considered that. 'So how did Poole play into it?'

She poured her coffee from the pot even though the machine was still percolating and coffee dripped through the filter, sizzled off the heating pan. 'All these months,' she said as she poured cream into her cup, 'you know what's nagged me?'

'Give it to me.'

'The empty bag. I mean, you're the kidnappers. You're pinning a cop down to a cliff top and sneaking in to scoop up the money.'

'Right. So?'

'So you pause to open the bag and pull the money out? Why not just take the bag?'

'I don't know. Either way, what difference does it make?'

'Not much.' She turned from the counter, faced me. 'Unless the bag was empty to begin with.'

'I saw the bag when Doyle handed it to Broussard. It was bulging with money.'

'But what about by the time we reached the quarry?'

'He unloaded it during the walk up the hill? How?'

She pursed her lips, then shook her head. 'I don't know.'

I came out of my chair, got a cup from the cupboard, and it fell from my fingers, glanced the edge of the counter, and fell to the floor. I left it there.

'Poole,' I said. 'Son of a bitch. It was Poole. When he had his heart attack or whatever it was, he fell on the bag. When it was time to go, Broussard reached under him and pulled the bag out.'

'Then Poole goes down the side of the quarry,' she said in a rush, 'and hands off the bag to some third party.' She paused. 'Kills Mullen and Gutierrez?'

'You think they planted a second bag by the tree?' I said.

'I don't know.'

I didn't either. I could maybe buy that Poole had siphoned two hundred thousand in ransom money, but executing Mullen and Gutierrez? That was a stretch.

'We agree there had to be a third party involved.'

'Probably. They had to get the money out of there.'

'So who was it?'

She shrugged. 'The mystery woman who made the phone call to Lionel?'

'Possibly.' I picked up my coffee cup. It hadn't broken, and after checking for chips, I filled it with coffee.

'Christ,' Angie said and chuckled. 'This is a hell of a reach.'

'What?'

'This whole thing. I mean, have you been listening to us? Broussard and Poole orchestrated this whole thing? To what end?'

'The money.'

'You think two hundred thousand would be enough motive for guys like Poole and Broussard to kill a child?'

'No.'

'So, why?'

I fumbled for an answer, but didn't come up with one.

'Do you honestly think either of them is capable of killing Amanda McCready?'

'People are capable of anything.'

'Yeah, but certain people are also categorically incapable of certain things. Those two? Killing a child?'

I remembered Broussard's face and Poole's voice as Poole had talked about finding a child in watery cement. They could be great actors, but those were De Niro–caliber performances if they really did feel as indifferent to a child's life as they would to an ant's.

'Hmm,' I said.

'I know what that means.'

'What?'

'Your "hmm." It always means you're completely baffled.'

I nodded. 'I'm completely baffled.'

'Welcome to the club.'

I sipped some coffee. If just a tenth of what we were hypothesizing was true, a pretty large crime had been committed right in front of us. Not near us. Not in the same zip code. But as we'd knelt beside the perpetrators. Right under our noses.

Did I mention that we make our livings as detectives?

Bubba came to the apartment shortly after sunrise.

He sat on the living room floor with his legs crossed and signed Angie's cast with a black marker. In his large fourth-grader's scrawl, he wrote:

Angie
Brake a leg. Or too. Ha ha.
Ruprecht Rogowski

Angie touched his cheek. 'Aww. You signed it "Ruprecht." How sweet.'

Bubba blushed and swatted her hand, looked up at me. 'What?'

'Ruprecht.' I chuckled. 'I'd almost forgotten.'

Bubba stood up and his shadow fell across my entire body and most of the wall. He rubbed his chin and smiled tightly. ''Member the first time I ever hit you, Patrick?'

I swallowed. 'First grade.'

''Member why?'

I cleared my throat. 'Because I gave you shit about your name.'

Bubba leaned over me. 'Care to try again?'

'Ah, no,' I said, and as he turned away I added,

'Ruprecht.'

I danced away from his lunge and Angie said, 'Boys! Boys!'

Bubba froze and I used that time to put the coffee table between the two of us.

'Could we address the matter at hand?' She opened the notebook on her lap, uncapped a pen with her teeth. 'Bubba, you can beat up Patrick anytime.'

Bubba thought about it. 'This is true.'

'Okay.' Angie scribbled in her notebook, shot me a look.

'Hey.' Bubba pointed at her cast. 'How do you shower in that thing?'

Angie sighed. 'What did you find out?'

Bubba sat on the couch and propped his combat boots up on the coffee table, not an act I usually tolerate, but I was already on thin ice with the Ruprecht thing, so I let it slide.

'The word I get from what's left of Cheese's crew is that Mullen and Gutierrez didn't know nothing about a missing kid. As far as anyone knew, they went to Quincy that night to score.'

'Score what?' Angie said.

'What drug dealers usually score: drugs. Chat around the campfire,' Bubba said, 'was that after one hell of a dry spell the market was going to be flooded with China White.' He shrugged. 'It never happened.'

'You're sure about this?' I said.

'No,' he said slowly, as if talking to a slow child. 'I talked to some guys in Olamon's organization, and they all said Mullen and Gutierrez never mentioned going to the quarries with a kid. And no

397

one on Cheese's crew ever saw a kid hanging around. So, if Mullen and Gutierrez had her, it was strictly their deal. And if they were going to Quincy that night to dump a kid, that was strictly their deal, too.'

He looked at Angie, jerked a thumb at me. 'Didn't he used to be smarter?'

She smiled. 'Peaked in high school, I think.'

'Another thing,' Bubba said. 'I never could figure why someone didn't just kill me that night.'

'Me too,' I said.

'Everyone I talk to on Cheese's crew swears up and down they had nothing to do with piping me. I believe 'em. I'm a scary guy. Sooner or later, someone would have coughed it up.'

'So the person who piped you . . .'

'Probably isn't the type who kills on a regular basis.' He shrugged. 'Just an opinion.'

The phone rang from the kitchen.

'Who the hell calls here at seven in the morning?' I said.

'No one familiar with our sleeping patterns,' Angie said.

I walked into the kitchen, picked up the phone.

'Hey, brother.' Broussard.

'Hey,' I said. 'You know what time it is?'

'Yeah. Sorry about that. Look, I need a favor. Big one.'

'What is it?'

'One of my guys broke his arm chasing a perp last night and now we're one short for the game.'

'The game?' I said.

'Football,' he said. 'Robbery-Homicide versus Narcotics-Vice-CAC. I might be Motor Pool, but

I'm still Narco-Vice-CAC when it comes to ball.'

'And this,' I said, 'concerns me how?'

'I'm short a player.'

I laughed so loudly Bubba and Angie turned their heads in the living room, looked over their shoulders at me.

'That's hilarious?' Broussard said.

'Remy,' I said, 'I'm white and over thirty. I have permanent nerve damage to one hand, and I haven't picked up a football since I was fifteen.'

'Oscar Lee told me you ran track in college, played baseball, too.'

'To pay my tuition,' I said. 'I was second-string in both cases.' I shook my head and chuckled. 'Find another guy. Sorry.'

'I don't have time. Game's at three. Come on, man. Please. I'm begging you. I need a guy can tuck a ball under his arm and run short yards, play a little defensive end. Don't bullshit me. Oscar says you're one of the fastest white guys he knows.'

'I take it Oscar will be there.'

'Hell, yeah. Playing against us, of course.'

'Devin?'

'Amronklin?' Broussard said. 'He's their coach. Please, Patrick. You don't help me out, we're screwed.'

I looked back at the living room. Bubba and Angie were staring at me with perplexed faces.

'Where?'

'Harvard Stadium. Three o'clock.'

I didn't say anything for a bit.

'Look, man, if this helps, I play fullback. I'll be punching your holes for you, making sure you don't get a scratch.'

'Three o'clock,' I said.

'Harvard Stadium. See you there.'

He hung up.

I immediately dialed Oscar's number.

It was a full minute before he stopped laughing. 'He bought it?' he sputtered eventually.

'Bought what?'

'All that shit I sold him about your speed.' More laughter, loud and followed by a few coughs.

'Why's that so funny?'

'Whoo-ee,' Oscar said. 'Whoo-ee! He's got you playing running back?'

'That seems to be the plan.'

Oscar laughed some more.

'What's the punch line?' I said.

'The punch line,' Oscar said, 'is you better stay away from the left side.'

'Why?'

'Because I'm starting at left tackle.'

I closed my eyes, leaned my head against the fridge. Of all the appliances in the kitchen, the fridge was the most apt to touch my flesh to in the current situation. It was roughly the size, shape, and weight of Oscar.

'See you on the field.' Oscar hooted loudly several times and hung up.

I walked back through the living room on my way toward the bedroom.

'Where you going?' Angie said.

'To bed.'

'Why?'

'Got a big game this afternoon.'

'What sort of game?' Bubba said.

'Football.'

'What?' Angie said loudly.

'You heard me right,' I said. I went into the bedroom, closed the door behind me.

They were still laughing when I fell asleep.

29

It seemed like every other guy on the Narcotics, Vice, and Crimes Against Children squads was named John. There was John Ives, John Vreeman, and John Pasquale. The quarterback was John Lawn and one of the wide receivers was John Coltraine, but everyone called him The Jazz. A tall, thin, baby-faced narcotics cop named Johnny Davis played tight end on offense and free safety on D. John Corkery, night watch commander at the 16th precinct and the only guy with the team besides me who wasn't attached to Narco, Vice, or CAC, was the coach. A third of the Johns had brothers in the same squad, so John Pasquale played tight end and his brother Vic was a wide receiver. John Vreeman set up at left guard while his brother Mel crouched at right. John Lawn was supposedly a pretty good quarterback but took a lot of razzing for favoring passes to his brother Mike.

All in all, I gave up trying to put names to faces after ten minutes and decided to call everyone John until I was corrected.

The rest of the players on the DoRights, as they called themselves, had other names, but they all shared a similar look, no matter what their size or color. It was the cop look, the way they had of carrying themselves that was loose and wary at the same time, the hard caution in their eyes even when they were laughing, the sense you got from all of them that you could go from being their friend to their enemy in a split second. It didn't matter which way to them, it was your choice, but once the decision was made they would act accordingly and immediately.

I've known a lot of cops, hung out with them, drank with them, considered a few to be my friends. But even when one was your friend, it was a different kind of friendship than you had with civilians. I never felt completely at ease with a cop, completely sure I knew what one was thinking. Cops always hold something back, except occasionally, I assume, around other cops.

Broussard clapped his hand on my shoulder and introduced me around to the team. I got several handshakes, some smiles and curt nods, one 'Nice fucking job on Corwin Earle, Mr Kenzie,' and then we all huddled around John Corkery as he gave us the game plan.

It wasn't much of a plan. Basically it had to do with what a pack of prima-donna pussies the guys in Homicide and Robbery were, and how we had to play this game for Poole, whose only chance to make it out of ICU alive, apparently, was if we stomped the shit out of the other team. Lose, and Poole's death would be on our conscience.

While Corkery talked, I looked across the field at the other team. Oscar caught my eye and waved happily, a shit-eating grin on his face the size of the Merrimack Valley. Devin saw me looking and smiled, too, nudged a rabid-looking monster with the scrunched features of a Pekinese, and pointed across the field at me. The monster nodded. The rest of the Homicide and Robbery guys didn't look quite as big as our team, but they looked smarter, and quick, and had a leanness to them that spoke more of gristle than delicacy.

'Hundred bucks to the first guy knocks one of them out of the game,' Corkery said, and clapped his hands together. 'Kill the motherfuckers.'

That must have been it for the Rockne-like inspiration, because the team came off its haunches and banged fists and clapped hands.

'Where are the helmets?' I said to Broussard.

One of the Johns was passing as I said it, and he clapped Broussard's back and said, 'Fucking guy's hilarious, Broussard. Where'd you find him?'

'No helmets,' I said.

Broussard nodded. 'It's a touch game,' he said. 'No hard contact.'

'Uh-huh,' I said. 'Sure.'

Homicide-Robbery, or the HurtYous as they called themselves, won the coin toss and elected to receive. Our kicker drove them back to their eleven, and as we lined up, Broussard pointed to a slim black guy on the HurtYous and said, 'Jimmy Paxton. He's your guy. Stick to him like a tumor.'

The HurtYous' center snapped the ball and the quarterback dropped back three steps, fired the ball over my head, and hit Jimmy Paxton on the twenty-five. I had no idea how Paxton got past me, never mind to the twenty-five, but I made an awkward lunge that tapped his ankles at the twenty-nine, and the teams moved upfield to the line of scrimmage.

'I said like a tumor,' Broussard said. 'Did you get that part?'

I looked across at him and saw a hard fury in his eyes. Then he smiled, and I realized how far he'd probably gotten on that smile his whole life. It was that good, that boyish and American and pure.

'I'll see if I can adjust,' I said.

The HurtYous broke their huddle, and I saw Devin on the sideline exchange a nod with Jimmy Paxton.

'They're going to come right back at me again,' I said to Broussard.

John Pasquale, the cornerback, said, 'Might want to improve then, huh?'

The HurtYous snapped the ball and Jimmy Paxton streaked down the sideline and I streaked with him. His eyes flickered and he extended his back and said, ''Bye, white boy,' and I went up with him, spun my body around and extended my right arm, whacked at the air, hit pigskin instead, and swatted the ball out of bounds.

Jimmy Paxton and I came down together in a heap, banged off the ground, and I knew it was the first of many impacts that would probably keep me in bed all through tomorrow.

I got up first and reached down for Paxton. 'I thought you were going somewhere.'

He smiled and took the hand. 'Keep talking, white boy. You're getting winded already.'

We walked back down the sidelines toward the line of scrimmage and I said, 'Just so you don't have to keep calling me white boy, and I don't have to start calling you black boy, start a race riot at Harvard, I'm Patrick.'

He slapped my hand. 'Jimmy Paxton.'

'Nice to meet you, Jimmy.'

Devin ran the next play at me again, and once again I swatted the ball out of Jimmy Paxton's waiting hands.

'Fucking mean bunch you're with, Patrick,' Jimmy Paxton said, as we started the long walk back to scrimmage.

I nodded. 'They think you guys are pussies.'

Jimmy nodded. 'We might not be pussies, but we ain't cowboys like those crazy fuckers. Narco, Vice, and CAC.' He whistled. 'First ones through the door because they love the jizz.'

'The jizz?'

'The action, the orgasm. Forget the foreplay with those boys. They go right to the fucking. Know what I mean?'

The next play, Oscar lined up at fullback and leveled three guys at the snap, and the running back ran through a hole the size of my backyard. But one of the Johns – Pasquale or Vreeman, I had lost track – grabbed the ball carrier's arm on the thirty-six, and the HurtYous decided to punt.

The rain came five minutes later and the rest of the first half was a sloppy grind-it-out Marty Schottenheimer–Bill Parcells kind of game. Slogging and slipping and tripping through the mud, neither team made much progress. As running back, I gained about twelve yards on four carries, and as a safety I got burned twice by Jimmy Paxton, but I broke up another potential bomb and otherwise stuck to him so tight the quarterback chose other receivers.

Near the end of the half, the score was tied at zero but we were threatening. Down in the HurtYous' red zone, on a second and two with twenty seconds left, the DoRights ran an option and John Lawn tossed the ball to me and I saw a gaping hole and nothing but green beyond, did a little spin around a linebacker, stepped into the hole, tucked the ball under my arm, put my head down, and then Oscar loomed out of nowhere, his breath steaming through the cold rain, and hit me so hard I felt like I'd stepped into the path of a 747.

By the time I got off my back, the clock had run out and the hard rain splattered mud off the field into my cheek. Oscar reached down with one of those porterhouses he calls hands and lifted me to my feet, chuckling softly under his breath.

'You gonna puke?'

'Thinking about it,' I said.

He whacked me on the back in what I guess was a friendly show of camaraderie that almost sent me into a face plant in the mud.

'Nice bid,' he said, and walked off toward his bench.

'What happened to touch football?' I said to Remy on the sidelines, as the DoRights opened a cooler full of beer and soda.

'Soon as someone does what Sergeant Lee just did, the gloves come off.'

'So we get helmets for the second half?'

He shook his head, pulled a beer from the cooler. 'No helmets. We just get meaner.'

'Anyone ever died at one of these games?'

He smiled. 'Not yet. Could happen, though. Beer?'

I shook my head, waiting for the ringing to stop in there. 'Take a water.'

He passed me a bottle of Poland Springs, put a hand on my shoulder, and led me up the sideline a few yards, away from the rest. In the stands, a small group of people had gathered – runners, mostly, who'd stumbled on the game as they prepared to jog the steps, one tall guy sitting off to himself, long legs propped up on the rail, baseball hat pulled low over his eyes.

'Last night,' Broussard said, and let the two words hang in the rain.

I sipped some water.

'I said a thing or two I shouldn't have. Too much rum, my head gets a little fucked up.'

I looked out at the collection of wide Greek columns that rose beyond the stands. 'Such as?'

He stepped in front of me, his eyes dancing and bright. 'Don't try and play with me here, Kenzie.'

'Patrick,' I said, and took a step to my right.

He followed, his nose an inch from mine, that weird, dancing brightness filling his eyes. 'We both know I let slip something I shouldn't have. Let's leave it at that and forget about it.'

I gave him a friendly, confused smile. 'I don't know where this is coming from, Remy.'

He shook his head slowly. 'You don't want to play it this way, Kenzie. You understand?'

'No, I—'

I never saw his hand move, but I felt a sharp sting on my knuckles and suddenly my water bottle was lying at my feet, chugging its contents into the mud.

'Forget last night, and we'll be friends.' The lights in his eyes had stopped dancing but burned hard, as if embers were locked in the pupils.

I looked down at the water bottle, the mud

encasing the sides of the clear plastic. 'And if I don't?'

'That's not an "if" you want to bring into your life.' He tilted his head, peered into my eyes as if he saw something there that might require extraction, might not; he wasn't sure yet. 'Are we clear on this?'

'Yeah, Remy,' I said. 'We're clear. Sure.'

He held my eyes for a long minute, breathing steadily through his nostrils. Eventually, he raised his beer to his lips, took a long pull on the can, lowered it.

'That's Officer Broussard,' he said, and walked back upfield.

The second half of the game was war.

The rain and the mud and the smell of blood brought out something horrible in both teams, and in the carnage that ensued, three HurtYous and two DoRights left the game permanently. One of them – Mike Lawn – had to be carried off the field, after Oscar and a Robbery dick named Zeke Monfriez collided on either side of his body and damn near snapped him in half.

I sustained two heavily bruised ribs and one shot to the lower back that would probably have me pissing blood the next morning, but in view of all the bloody faces, noses flattened to pulps, and one guy spitting two teeth into the first-down hash mark, I felt comparatively fortunate.

Broussard switched to tailback and stayed away from me the rest of the game. He got a torn lower lip on one play, but two plays later clotheslined the guy who'd given it to him so viciously the guy lay on the field coughing and puking for a full minute before he could stand on legs so wobbly it looked like he was on the keel of a schooner in high seas. After he'd clotheslined the poor bastard, Broussard had kicked him while he was down for good measure, and the HurtYous went apeshit. Broussard stood behind a wall of his own men as Oscar and Zeke tried to get at him, called him a cheap-shot motherfucker, and he caught my eyes and smiled like a gleeful three-year-old.

He raised a finger caked with dark blood, and wagged it at me.

We won by a field goal.

As a guy who grew up as desperate to be a jock as any other guy in America, and one who still cancels most engagements on autumn Sunday afternoons, I suppose I should have been ecstatic at what would probably be my last taste of team sports, the thrill of conquest and the sexual intensity of battle. I should have felt like whooping, should have had tears in my eyes as I stood at midfield in the first football stadium ever built in this country, looked at the Greek columns and the rain boiling off the long planks of seating in the stands, smelled the last hint of winter dying in the April rain, the metallic odor of the rain itself, the lonely advance of evening in the cold purple sky.

But I didn't feel any of that.

I felt like we were a bunch of foolish, pathetic men unwilling to accept our own aging and willing to break bones and tear the flesh of other men just so we could move a brown ball a couple of yards or feet or inches down a field.

And, also, looking along the sidelines at Remy Broussard as he poured a beer over his bloody finger, doused his torn lip with it, and accepted high-fives from his pals, I felt afraid.

'Tell me about him,' I said to Devin and Oscar, as we leaned against the bar.

'Broussard?'

'Yeah.'

Both teams had chosen to convene the postgame party at a bar on Western Avenue in Allston, about a half mile from the stadium. The bar was called the Boyne, after a river in Ireland that had snaked through the village where my mother grew up, lost her fisherman father and two brothers to the lethal liquid combination of whiskey and the sea.

It was excessively well-lit for an Irish bar, and the brightness was heightened by blond wood tables and light beige booths, a shiny blond bar. Most Irish bars are dark, steeped in mahogany and oak and black floors; in the darkness, I've always thought, lies the sense of intimacy my race feels is necessary to drink as heavily as we often do.

In the brightness of the Boyne, it was clear to see how the battle we'd just fought on the field had spilled over into the bar. The Homicide and Robbery guys stuck to the bar and the small high tables across from it. The Narco-Vice-CAC cops took over the rear of the place, draped themselves over the backs of booths, and stood in packs near the tiny stage by the fire exit, talking so loudly that the three-piece Irish band quit playing after four songs.

I have no idea how the management felt about the fifty bloody men who'd piled into the sparsely popu-lated bar, if they had a team of extra bouncers waiting in the kitchen and a Def-Con alert called into the Brighton P.D., but they were definitely pulling down a profit, pouring beers and shots nonstop, trying to keep abreast of the calls for more coming from the rear of the bar, sending barbacks to wade through the men and sweep up the broken bottles and overturned ashtrays.

Broussard and John Corkery held court in the back, their voices rising loudly in toasts to the prowess of the DoRights, Broussard alternating a napkin and a cold beer bottle against his damaged lip.

'Thought you guys were buddies,' Oscar said. 'What, your moms won't let you play together anymore, or'd you have a spat?'

'The moms thing,' I said.

'Great cop,' Devin said. 'Bit of a showboat, but all those Narco-Vice guys are.'

'But Broussard's CAC. Hell, he's not even that anymore. He's Motor Pool.'

'CAC was recent,' Devin said. 'Last two years or so. Before that he did like a nickel in Vice, a nickel in Narco.'

'More than that.' Oscar belched. 'We came out of Housing together, did a year in uniform each, and he went into Vice, I went into Violent Crimes. That was 'eighty-three.'

Remy's head turned away from two of his men as they each chatted in his ear, and he looked across the bar at Oscar and Devin and me. He raised his beer bottle, tilted his head.

We raised ours.

He smiled, kept his eyes on us for a minute, then turned back to his men.

'Once Vice, always Vice,' Devin said. 'Those fucking guys.'

'We'll get 'em next year,' Oscar said.

'Won't be the same guys,' Devin said bitterly. 'Broussard's packing it in, so's Vreeman. Corkery hits his thirty in January, heard he's already bought the place in Arizona.'

I nudged his elbow. 'What about you? You gotta be close to thirty in.'

He snorted. 'I'm going to retire? To what?' He shook his head, threw back a shot of Wild Turkey.

'Only way we're leaving the job is on stretchers,' Oscar said, and he and Devin clinked their pint glasses.

'Why the interest in Broussard?' Devin said. 'Thought you two were bonded in blood after Trett's house.' He turned his head, slapped my shoulder with the back of his hand. 'Which, by the way, was a righteous piece of work.'

I ignored the compliment. 'Broussard just interests me.'

Oscar said, 'That why he slapped a water bottle out of your hand?'

I looked at Oscar. I'd been pretty sure Broussard had blocked the move with his body.

'You saw that?'

Oscar nodded his huge head. 'Saw the look he gave you after he clotheslined Rog Doleman, too.'

Devin said, 'And I can see how he keeps looking over here while we talk so friendly and casually.'

One of the Johns nudged his way between us, called out for two pitchers and three shots of Beam. He looked down at me, his elbow all but resting on my shoulder, then at Devin and Oscar.

'How's it going, boys?'

'Fuck you, Pasquale,' Devin said.

Pasquale laughed. 'I know you mean that in the most loving way.'

'But of course,' Devin said.

Pasquale chuckled to himself as the bartender brought the pitchers of beer. I leaned out of the way as Pasquale passed them back to John Lawn. He turned back to the bar, waited for his shots, drummed the bar with his fingers.

'You guys hear what our buddy Kenzie did in the Trett house?' He winked at me.

'Some of it,' Oscar said.

Pasquale said, 'Roberta Trett, I hear, had Kenzie dead to rights in the kitchen. But Kenzie ducked and Roberta shot her own husband in the face instead.'

'Nice ducking,' Devin said.

Pasquale received his shots, tossed some cash down on the bar. 'He's a good ducker,' he said, and his elbow grazed my ear as he pulled his shots off the bar. He caught my eye as he turned. 'That's more luck than talent, though. Ducking. Don't you think?' He turned so that his back was to Oscar and Devin, his eyes locked with mine as he threw back one of the shots. 'And the thing about luck, man, it always runs out.'

Devin and Oscar turned on their stools and watched him as he walked back through the crowd toward the back.

Oscar pulled a half-smoked cigar from his shirt pocket and lit it, his flat gaze staying on Pasquale. He sucked back on the cigar, and the black, torn tobacco crackled.

'Subtle,' he said, and tossed his match into the ashtray.

'What's going on, Patrick?' Devin's voice was a monotone, his eyes on the empty shot glass Pasquale had left behind.

'I'm not sure,' I said.

'You made an enemy of the cowboys,' Oscar said. 'Never a bright move.'

'Wasn't intentional,' I said.

'You got something on Broussard?' Devin said.

'Maybe,' I said. 'Yeah.'

Devin nodded and his right hand dropped off the bar, gripped my elbow tight. 'Whatever it is,' he said, and smiled tightly in Broussard's direction, 'let it go.'

'What if I can't?'

Oscar's head loomed around Devin's shoulder, and he looked at me with that dead gaze of his. 'Walk away, Patrick.'

'What if I can't?' I repeated.

Devin sighed. 'Then you might not be able to walk anywhere soon.'

30

In the blind hope that it might make a difference, we decided to drive over to see Poole.

The New England Medical Center sprawls across two city blocks, its various buildings and skywalks occupying a linchpin spot between Chinatown, the theater district, and what remains, gasping and gulping, of the old Combat Zone.

On an early Sunday morning, it's tough to find an open parking meter around New England Med: on a Thursday night, it's impossible. The Schubert was playing its umpteenth revival of *Miss Saigon* and the Wang was showing the latest bombastic Andrew Lloyd Webber or someone similar's piece of sold-out, overwrought, overdone, singing dung extravaganza, and lower Tremont Street was teeming with taxis, limos, black ties, and blond fur, angry cops blowing whistles and waving traffic in a wide arc around the triple-parked throng.

We didn't even bother circling the block, just turned into New England Med's parking garage, took our ticket, and drove up six levels before we found a spot. After I'd exited the car, I held Angie's door for her as she struggled onto her crutches, shut the door behind her as she worked her way out between the cars.

'Which way to the elevator?' she called back to me.

A young man with the tall, ropy build of a basketball player said, 'That way,' and pointed to his left. He leaned against the hatch of a black Chevy Suburban and smoked a slim cigar with the red Cohiba label still wrapped around it near the base.

'Thanks,' Angie said, and we proffered stock-friendly smiles as we passed him.

He smiled back, gave a small wave with the cigar. 'He's dead.'

We stopped, and I turned back and looked at the guy. He wore a navy-blue fleece jacket with a brown leather collar over a black V-neck and black jeans. His black cowboy boots were as weathered as a rodeo rider's. He tapped some ash from the cigar, put it back in his mouth, and looked at me.

'This is the part where you say, "Who's dead?"'

He looked down at his boots.

'Who's dead?' I said.

'Nick Raftopoulos,' he said.

Angie turned fully around on her crutches. 'Excuse me?'

'That's who you came to see, right?' He held out his hands, shrugged. 'Well, you can't, because he died an hour ago. Cardiac arrest due to massive trauma as a result of gunshot injuries incurred on Leon Trett's front porch. Perfectly natural, given the circumstances.'

Angie swung her crutches and I took a few steps until we were both standing in front of the man.

417

He smiled. 'Your next line is, "How do you know who we're here to see?"' he said. 'Take it, either one of you.'

'Who are you?' I said.

He slung his hand low in my direction. 'Neal Ryerson. Call me Neal. Wish I had a cool nickname, but some of us aren't so blessed. You're Patrick Kenzie, and you're Angela Gennaro. And I must say, ma'am, even with the cast and all, your picture doesn't do you justice. You're what my daddy'd call a looker.'

'Poole's dead?' Angie said.

'Yes, ma'am. 'Fraid so. Say, Patrick, could you shake my hand? It's a little tiring holding it out like this.'

I gave it a light squeeze, and he offered it to Angie. She leaned back on her crutches and ignored it, looked up into Neal Ryerson's face. She shook her head.

He glanced at me. 'Fear of cooties?'

He withdrew the hand and dug it into his inside coat pocket.

I reached behind my back.

'No fear, Mr Kenzie. No fear.' He withdrew a slim wallet and flipped it open, showed us a silver badge and ID. 'Special Agent Neal Ryerson,' he said, in a deep baritone. 'Justice Department. *Ta-da!*' He closed the wallet, slipped it back in his jacket. 'Organized Crime Division, if you need to know. Christ, you're a chatty couple.'

'Why are you bothering us?' I said.

'Because, Mr Kenzie, judging by what I saw at that football game this afternoon, you're kinda short of friends. And I'm in the friend business.'

'I'm not looking for one.'

'You might not have a choice. I may have to be your friend whether you like it or not. I'm pretty good at it, too. I'll listen to your war stories, watch baseball with you, generally pal around with you at all the hip watering holes.'

I looked at Angie, and we turned and started walking toward our car. I went to her side first, unlocked the door, and started to open it.

'Broussard will kill you,' Ryerson said.

We looked back at him. He took a puff of his Cohiba and came off the back of the Suburban, sauntered toward us with loose, long strides, as if he were walking off court at the end of a period.

'He's real good at that, killing people. Usually doesn't do it himself, but he plans it well. He's a first-rate planner.'

I took Angie's crutches from her and brushed Ryerson back with the rear door as I opened it to slide them in the backseat. 'We'll be fine, Special Agent Ryerson.'

'I'm sure that's what Chris Mullen and Pharaoh Gutierrez thought.'

Angie leaned against her open door. 'Was Pharaoh Gutierrez DEA?' She reached into her pocket, removed her cigarettes.

Ryerson shook his head. 'Nope. Informant for the OCD.' He stepped past me and lit Angie's cigarette with a black Zippo. 'My informant. I turned him. I'd worked him for six and a half years. He was going to help me bring down Cheese, and Cheese's organization was going to be next. After that, I was going after Cheese's supplier, guy named Ngyun Tang.' He pointed at the east wall of the garage. 'Chinatown bigwig.'

'But?'

'But' – he shrugged – 'Pharaoh got hisself iced.'

'And you think Broussard did it?'

'I think Broussard planned it. He didn't kill them himself because he was too busy pretending to get shot at up in the quarry.'

'So who killed Mullen and Gutierrez?'

Ryerson looked up at the garage ceiling. 'Who took the money out of the hills? Who was the first person found in the vicinity of the victims?'

'Wait a sec,' Angie said. 'Poole? You think Poole was the shooter?'

Ryerson leaned against the Audi parked beside our car, took a long puff of his cigar, and blew smoke rings up into the fluorescent lights.

'Nicholas Raftopoulos. Born in Swampscott, Massachusetts, 1948. Joined Boston Police Department in 1968, shortly after returning from Vietnam, where he was awarded the Silver Star and was, surprise, an expert-class marksman. His lieutenant in the field said Corporal Raftopoulos could, and I quote, "shoot the asshole ring out of a tse-tse fly from fifty yards."' He shook his head. 'Those military guys – they're so *vivid*.'

'And you think—'

'I think, Mr Kenzie, that the three of us need to talk.'

I took a step back from him. He was easily six-three, and his perfectly coiffed sandy hair, his easy bearing, and the cut of his clothes spoke of a man who'd come from money. I recognized him now: He'd been the spectator sitting alone at the far end of the stands in Harvard Stadium this afternoon, long legs hooked over the guardrail as he slouched low in his seat, baseball hat down over his eyes. I could see him at Yale trying to decide between law school and a job with the government. Either career held the promise of political office once the gray had blended in just right around his temples, but if he went with the government, he'd get to carry a gun. Outstanding. Yes, sir.

'Nice meeting you, Neal.' I walked around to the driver's door.

'I wasn't kidding when I said he'll kill you.'

Angie chuckled. 'And you'll save us, I suppose.'

'I'm Justice Department.' He placed a palm to his chest. 'Bulletproof.'

I looked over the roof of the Crown Victoria at him. 'That's because you're always behind the people you're supposed to be protecting, Neal.'

'Oooh.' His hand fluttered over his chest. 'Good one, Pat.'

Angie climbed in the car, and I followed. As I started the engine, Neal Ryerson rapped his knuckles on Angie's window. She frowned and looked at me. I shrugged. She rolled the pane down slowly, and Neal Ryerson dropped to his haunches, rested one arm on her windowsill.

'I got to tell you,' he said. 'I think you're making a big mistake by not hearing me out.'

'Made 'em before,' Angie said.

He leaned back from her door and took a puff of his cigar, blew the smoke out before he leaned back in.

'When I was a kid, my daddy'd take me hunting in the mountains not far from where I grew up, place called Boone, North Carolina. And Daddy, he always told me – every trip from the time I was eight till I was eighteen – that what you had to watch out for, *really* watch out for, wasn't the moose or the deer. It was the other hunters.'

'Deep,' Angie said.

He smiled. 'See, Pat, Angie—'

'Don't call him Pat,' Angie said. 'He hates that.'

He held up the hand with the cigar clenched between the fingers. 'All apologies, Patrick. How can I say this? The enemy is us. You understand? And "us" is going to come looking for you soon.' He pointed the thin cigar at me. ' "Us" already had words with you today, Patrick. How long before he ups the ante? He knows that even if you back off for a bit, sooner or later you'll come around again, asking the wrong questions. Hell, that's why you came to see Nick Raftopoulos tonight, am I right? Hoping he'd be coherent enough to answer some of your wrong questions. Now you can drive away. Can't stop y'all. But he'll come for you. And this'll just get worse.'

I looked at Angie. She looked at me. Ryerson's cigar smoke found the inside of the car and then the back of my lungs, clogged there like hair in a drain.

Angie turned back to him, waved him off the windowsill with a flick of her wrist. 'The Blue Diner,' she said. 'You know it?'

'Just a short six blocks away.'

'See you there,' she said, and we pulled out of our parking slot and headed for the exit ramp.

The exterior of the Blue Diner looks really cool at night. The only hint of neon fronting Kneeland Street at the base of the Leather District, a large white coffee cup hovers over its sign in a mostly commercial zone, so that the establishment appears, from the highway at least, like something straight out of Edward Hopper's night-washed daydreams.

I'm not sure Hopper would have paid six thousand dollars for a hamburger, though. Not that the Blue Diner charges quite that much, but it's in the ballpark. I've bought cars for less than I've paid for a cup of their coffee.

Neal Ryerson assured us the tab was on the Justice Department, so we splurged on coffee and a couple of Cokes. I would have ordered a hamburger, but then I remembered that the Justice Department budget was provided by my tax dollars, and Ryerson's generosity didn't seem like so much of a big deal.

'Let's start from the beginning,' he said.

'By all means,' Angie said.

He poured some cream into his coffee, passed it to me. 'Where did all this start?'

'With Amanda McCready's disappearance,' I said.

He shook his head. 'No. That's just where you two came into it.' He stirred his coffee, removed the spoon, and pointed it at us. 'Three years ago, Narcotics officer Remy Broussard busts Cheese Olamon, Chris Mullen, and Pharaoh Gutierrez doing a quality-control check of a processing plant in South Boston.'

'I thought all drug processing was done overseas,' Angie said.

'"Processing" is a euphemism. Basically, they were stomping the shit – cocaine, that time – cutting it with Similac. Broussard and his partner, Poole, couple of other Narcotics cowboys, bust Olamon, my boy Gutierrez, and a bunch of other fellas. Thing is, they don't arrest them.'

'Why not?'

Ryerson removed a fresh cigar from his pocket, then frowned when he noticed a sign that read NO CIGAR OR PIPE SMOKING PLEASE. THANK YOU. He groaned and put the cigar on the table, fingered the cellophane wrapping.

'They don't arrest them, because after they burned the evidence, there was nothing to arrest them for.'

'They burned the coke,' I said.

He nodded. 'According to Pharaoh, they did. There'd been rumors floating around for years that there was a rogue unit of the Narcotics Division that had been given a mandate to hit dealers where it hurt the most. Not with busts that would give the dealers street cred, news coverage, and a very dubious conviction rate. No. This rogue unit was alleged to destroy what they caught them with. And make them watch. It was, remember, a war on drugs, supposedly. And some enterprising Boston cops decided to fight it like a guerrilla war. These guys, rumor had it, were the true untouchables. They couldn't be bought. They couldn't be reasoned with. They were zealots. They ran a lot of smaller dealers out of business, ran a lot of newcomers straight back out of town. The bigger dealers – the Cheese Olamons, the Winter Hill gang types, the Italians, and the Chinese – pretty soon started factoring in these raids as the price of doing business, and ultimately, because the whole drug business went into a downswing, and because the raids never proved all that much more effective than anything else, the unit was rumored to have been disbanded.'

'And Broussard and Poole transferred to CAC.'

He nodded. 'Some other guys did, too, or stayed in Narcotics, or transferred to Vice or Warrants, what have you. But Cheese Olamon never forgot. And he never forgave. He swore that one day he'd get Broussard.'

'Why Broussard and not the other guys?'

'According to Pharaoh, Cheese felt personally insulted by Broussard. It wasn't just the burning of his product, it was that Broussard taunted him while they did it, embarrassed him in front of his men. Cheese took that to heart.'

Angie lit a cigarette, held out the pack to Ryerson.

He looked at his cigar, back at the sign that told him he couldn't smoke it, and said, 'Sure. Why not?'

He smoked the cigarette like a cigar, not really inhaling, just puffing, allowing the smoke to roll around on his tongue for a moment before exhaling it.

'Last autumn,' he said, 'Pharaoh makes contact with me. We meet, and he says Cheese has something on that cop from a few years back. Cheese, he promises me, is playing Payback's a Bitch, and Mullen has intimated to Pharaoh that everyone who was in that warehouse that night and had to sit by and be humiliated while Broussard and his boys burned the coke and laughed in their faces is going to enjoy this one. Now, besides everything else, I'm a little confused why Mullen and Pharaoh are suddenly so chummy that Mullen would intimate anything to him. Pharaoh gives me this bygones-be-bygones shit, but I don't buy it. I figure there's only one thing Pharaoh and Chris

Mullen would bond over, and that's greed.'

'So there was a palace coup in the works,' I said.

He nodded. 'Unfortunately for Pharaoh, Cheese got wind of it.'

'So what did Cheese have on Broussard?' Angie said.

'Pharaoh never told me. Claimed Mullen wouldn't say. Said it would ruin the surprise. The last word I ever got from Pharaoh was the afternoon of the night he died. He told me he and Mullen had been dragging cops all over the city the last few days, and that night they were going to collect two hundred grand, humiliate the cop, and go home. And as soon as that was done, and Pharaoh could figure what it was exactly that the cop had done, he was going to rat him and Mullen out to me, give me the biggest collar of my career, and then I'd be off his back for good. Or so he hoped.' Ryerson stubbed out his cigarette. 'We know the rest.'

Angie gave him a confused frown. 'We don't know anything. Shit. Agent Ryerson, have you come up with any sort of theory as to how Amanda McCready's disappearance plays into all this?'

He shrugged. 'Maybe Broussard kidnapped her himself.'

'Why?' I said. 'He just woke up one day, decided he wanted to kidnap a child?'

'I've heard of weirder things.' He leaned into the table. 'Look, Cheese had something on him. So, what was it? Everything keeps coming back to that little girl's vanishing. So let's look at it. Broussard kidnaps her, maybe as a way to force the mother's hand, come up with the two hundred grand Pharaoh told me she embezzled from Cheese.'

'Wait a second,' I said. 'This has bothered me forever: Why didn't Cheese send Mullen to beat the location of the stolen money out of Helene and Ray Likanski months before Amanda disappeared?'

'Because Cheese didn't find out about the scam until the day Amanda disappeared.'

'What?'

He nodded. 'The beauty of Likanski's scam – while shortsighted, I admit – was that he knew everyone would assume the money was impounded along with the bikers and the drugs. It took Cheese three months to find out the truth. The day he did was the same day Amanda McCready disappeared.'

'So,' Angie said, 'that points to Mullen being the kidnapper.'

He shook his head. 'I don't buy it. I think Mullen or someone working for Cheese went to Helene's that night to fuck her up bad and find out where the money was. But instead, they saw Broussard taking the kid. So now Cheese has something on Broussard. He blackmails him. But Broussard then plays both sides up against the middle. He tells the law enforcement side that Cheese kidnapped her and demands the ransom. He tells Cheese's side that he'll bring the money to the quarries that night and give it to Mullen, knowing he's going to drop them, dump the little girl, and scoot with the cash. He—'

'That's idiotic,' I said.

'Why?'

'Why would Cheese allow himself to be perceived as the kidnapper of Amanda McCready?'

'He didn't allow himself. Broussard set him up for it without telling him.'

I shook my head. 'Broussard *did* tell him. I was

there. We went to Concord Prison in October and quizzed Cheese about the disappearance. If he were complicitous with Broussard, they both would have had to agree that the blame would fall on Cheese's men. Now why would Cheese do that, if, as you say, he had Broussard by the balls? Why take the fall for the kidnapping and death of a four-year-old when he didn't have to?'

He pointed his unlit cigar at me. 'So *you* would believe it, Mr Kenzie. Haven't you two ever wondered why you were allowed so deeply into a police investigation? Why you were named to be at the quarry that night? You were witnesses. That was your role. Broussard and Cheese put on a show for you at Concord Prison: Poole and Broussard put on another one at the quarry. Your whole purpose was to see what they wanted you to see and accept it as truth.'

'By the way,' Angie said, 'how could Poole have *faked* a heart attack?'

'Cocaine,' Ryerson said. 'Seen it once before. It's risky as hell because the coke could easily trigger a real coronary. But if you *do* pull it off, a guy of Poole's age and occupation? Not many doctors would have thought to look for coke, just would have assumed a heart attack.'

I counted twelve cars pass by on Kneeland Street before any of us spoke again.

'Agent Ryerson, let's back up again.' Angie's cigarette had burned to a long curve of white ash in the ashtray, and she pushed the filter off the indented crevice that held it. 'We agree Cheese saw Mullen and Gutierrez as threats. What if he felt he had to take them out? And what if what he had on Broussard was so bad, he put him up to it?'

428

'Put Broussard up to it?'

She nodded.

Ryerson leaned back in the booth, looked out the window at the dark cast-iron buildings on the South Street corner. Over his shoulder, on Kneeland Street, I noticed the familiar urban sight of a boxy, nut-brown UPS truck idling with its hazards on, blocking a lane as the driver opened the back and took out a two-wheeler, pulled several boxes from the truck, and stacked them on the upright cart.

'So,' Ryerson said to Angie, 'your operating theory is that while Cheese thought he was putting one over on Mullen and Gutierrez, Broussard was putting one over on all three of them.'

'Maybe,' she said. 'Maybe. We have information that Mullen and Gutierrez thought they were picking up drugs at the quarry that night.'

The UPS guy jogged past the window, pushing the two-wheeler in front of him, and I wondered who got deliveries this late at night. Law firms burning the midnight oil on a big case, perhaps? Printers in a rush to make deadline, maybe. A high-tech computer firm doing whatever it was high-tech computer firms did while the rest of the world prepared for sleep.

'But, again,' Ryerson said, 'we keep coming back to motive. If what Cheese had on Broussard was that he kidnapped the girl? Fine. But why? What was Broussard thinking when he went to the house that night to grab a child he never met and take her away from her mother? It doesn't add up.'

The UPS guy was back in a flash, clipboard tucked under his arm, jogging faster now that the two-wheeler was empty.

'And another thing,' Ryerson said. 'If we accept that a decorated cop who works for a unit that *finds* kids would do something as loony and seemingly motiveless as snatching a kid from her home, how's he to do it? He watches the house on his own time until the woman leaves, knowing somehow that she'd leave her door unlocked? It's stupid.'

'But yet you think that's what happened,' Angie said.

'In my gut, yeah. I know Broussard took that girl. I just can't for the life of me figure out why.'

The UPS guy hopped in the truck and it slipped past the window, cut into the left lane, and disappeared from view.

'Patrick?'

'Huh?'

'You still with us?'

'Not with a criminal record, you can't.'

Angie touched my arm. 'What did you just say?'

I hadn't realized I'd said it aloud. 'You can't get a job driving for UPS if you have a criminal record.'

Ryerson blinked and gave me a look like he thought he should produce a thermometer, see if I had a fever. 'What the hell are you talking about?'

I glanced back at Kneeland Street, then looked at Ryerson, then Angie. 'That first day he was in our office, Lionel said he'd taken a bust – a hard bust – once, before he cleaned his act up.'

'So?' Angie said.

'So if there was a bust, there should be a record of it. And if there's a record of it, how'd he get a job working for UPS?'

Ryerson said, 'I don't see—'

'Ssshh.' Angie held up a hand, looked in my eyes. 'You think Lionel . . .'

I shifted in my seat, pushed my cold coffee away. 'Who had access to Helene's apartment? Who could open the door with a key? Who would Amanda readily leave with, no fuss, no noise?'

'But he came to us.'

'No,' I said. 'His wife did. He kept saying, "Thanks for listening to us, blah, blah, blah." Getting ready to brush us off. It was Beatrice who put the pressure on. What did she say when she was in our office? "No one wanted me to come here. Not Helene, not my husband." It was Beatrice who kept this thing alive. And Lionel – he loves his sister, okay. But is he blind? He's not stupid. So how does he not know about Helene's association with Cheese? How does he not know she has a drug problem? He acted surprised when he heard she did some coke, for Christ's sake. I talk to my own sister once a week, see her only once a year, but I'd know if *she* had a drug problem. She's my sister.'

'What you said about the criminal record,' Ryerson said. 'How's that play into it?'

'Let's say it was Broussard who busted him, had him on a hook. Lionel owed him. Who knows?'

'But why would Lionel kidnap his own niece?'

I thought about it, closed my eyes until I could see Lionel standing in front of me. That hound-dog face and sad eyes, those shoulders that seemed to have the weight of a metropolis pushing down on them, the pained decency in his voice – the voice of a man who truly didn't understand why people did all the shitty, neglectful things they did. I heard the volcanic

431

rage in his voice when he'd blown up at Helene in the kitchen that morning we'd confronted her about knowing Cheese, the hint of hatred in that volume. He'd told us he believed that his sister loved her child, was good for her. But what if he'd lied? What if he believed the opposite? What if he thought less of his sister's parenting skills than his own wife did? But he, the child of alcoholics and bad parents himself, had learned how to mask things, to cover his rage, would have had to in order to build himself into the kind of citizen, the kind of father, he'd become.

'What if,' I said aloud, 'Amanda McCready wasn't abducted by someone who wanted to exploit her or abuse her or ransom her?' I met Ryerson's slightly skeptical eyes, then Angie's curious, excited ones. 'What if Amanda McCready was abducted for her own good?'

Ryerson spoke slowly, carefully. 'You think the uncle stole the child . . .'

I nodded. 'To save the child.'

31

'Lionel's gone,' Beatrice said.

'Gone?' I said. 'Where?'

'North Carolina,' she said. She stepped back from the door. 'Please, come in.'

We followed her into the living room. Her son, Matt, looked up as we came in. He lay on his stomach in the middle of the floor, drawing on a pad of paper with a variety of pens, pencils, and crayons. He was a good-looking kid, with the smallest hint of his father's hound-dog sag in his jaw but none of the weight on his shoulders. He'd inherited his eyes from his mother, and the sapphire blazed under his pitch-black eyebrows and the wavy hair atop his head.

'Hi, Patrick. Hi, Angie.' He looked up with benign curiosity at Neal Ryerson.

'Hey.' Ryerson squatted by him. 'I'm Neal. What's your name?'

Matt shook Ryerson's hand without hesitation, looked in his eyes with the openness of a child who's been taught to respect adults but not fear them.

'Matt,' he said. 'Matt McCready.'

'Pleased to meet you, Matt. Whatcha drawing there?'

Matt turned the pad so we could all see it. Stick figures of various colors appeared to climb all over a car three times their height and as long as a commercial airliner.

'Pretty good.' Ryerson raised his eyebrows. 'What is it?'

'Guys trying to ride in a car,' Matt said.

'Why can't they get in?' I asked.

'It's locked,' Matt said, as if the answer explained everything.

'But they want that car,' Ryerson said. 'Huh?'

Matt nodded. ''Cause it—'

'*Be*cause, Matthew,' Beatrice said.

He looked up at her, confused at first, but then smiled. 'Right. Because it has TVs inside and Game Boys and Whopper Juniors and – uh, Cokes.'

Ryerson covered a smile with a wipe of his hand. 'All the good stuff.'

Matt smiled up at him. 'Yeah.'

'Well, you keep at it,' he said. 'It's coming along nice.'

Matt nodded and turned the pad back toward himself. 'I'm putting buildings in next. It needs buildings.'

And as if we'd been part of a dream, he picked up a pencil and turned back to the pad with such complete concentration, I'm sure we and everything else vanished from the room.

'Mr Ryerson,' Beatrice said. 'I'm afraid we haven't met.'

Her small hand disappeared in his long one. 'Neal Ryerson, ma'am. I'm with the Justice Department.'

Beatrice glanced at Matt, lowered her voice. 'So this is about Amanda?'

Ryerson shrugged. 'We wanted to check a few things with your husband.'

'What things?'

Ryerson had been clear before we left the diner that the last thing we wanted to do was spook Lionel or Beatrice. If Beatrice notified her husband that he was under suspicion, he could disappear for good, and Amanda's whereabouts might just go with him.

'Be honest with you, ma'am. The Justice Department has what's called the Office of Juvenile Justice and Delinquency Prevention. We do a lot of follow-up work with the National Center for Missing and Exploited Children, Nation's Missing Children Organization, and their databases. General stuff.'

'So this isn't a break in the case?' Beatrice kneaded her shirttail between her fingers and the heel of her palm, looked up into Ryerson's face.

'No, ma'am, I wish it were. As I said, it's just some basic follow-up questions for the database. And because your husband was first on the scene the night your niece disappeared, I wanted to go over it with him again, see if there was anything he might have noticed – a small thing here or there, say – which might produce a fresh way of looking at this.'

She nodded, and I almost winced to see how easily she bought Ryerson's lies.

'Lionel helps a friend of his who sells antiques. Ted Kenneally. He and Lionel have been friends since grade school. Ted owns Kenneally Antiques in Southie. Every month or so, they drive to North Carolina and drop some off in a town called Wilson.'

Ryerson nodded. 'The antiques center of North

America, yes, ma'am.' He smiled. 'I'm from those parts.'

'Oh. Is there anything I could help you with? Lionel will be back tomorrow afternoon.'

'Well, sure, you could help. Mind if I ask you a bunch of boring questions I'm sure you've been asked a thousand times already?'

She shook her head quickly. 'No. Not at all. If it can help, I'll answer questions all night. Why don't I make some tea?'

'That'd be great, Mrs McCready.'

While Matt continued to color, we drank tea and Ryerson asked Beatrice a string of questions that had long ago been answered: about the night Amanda disappeared, about Helene's mothering skills, about those early crazy days after Amanda had first disappeared, when Beatrice organized searches, established herself as media contact, plastered the streets with her niece's picture.

Every now and then Matt would show us his progress on the picture, the skyscrapers with rows of misaligned window squares, the clouds and dogs he'd added to the paper.

I began to regret coming here. I was a spy in their home, a traitor, hoping to gather evidence that would send Beatrice's husband and Matt's father to prison. Just before we left, Matt asked Angie if he could sign her cast. When she said of course, his eyes lit up and he took an extra thirty seconds finding just the right pen. As he knelt by the cast and signed his full name very carefully, I felt an ache creep behind my eyes, a boulder of melancholia settle in my chest at the thought of what this kid's life would be like if we were right about his father, and the law stepped in and blew this family apart.

But still, the overriding concern remained strong enough to stanch even my shame.

Where was she?

Goddammit. Where *was* she?

Once we'd left, we stopped at Ryerson's Suburban as he peeled the cellophane from another thin cigar, used a sterling silver cutter to snip the end. He looked back at the house as he lit it.

'She's a nice lady.'

'Yes, she is.'

'Great kid.'

'He's a great kid, yeah,' I agreed.

'This sucks,' he said, and puffed at the cigar as he held the flame to it.

'Yes, it does.'

'I'm going to go stake out Ted Kenneally's store. It's, what, like a mile from here?'

Angie said, 'More like three.'

'I didn't ask her the address. Shit.'

'There's only a few antique stores in Southie,' I said. 'Kenneally's is on Broadway, right across from a restaurant called Amrheins.'

He nodded. 'Care to join me? Could be the safest place for both of you right now with Broussard out there on the loose.'

Angie said, 'Sure.'

Ryerson looked at me. 'Mr Kenzie?'

I looked back at Beatrice's house, the yellow squares of light in the living room windows, thought of the occupants on the other side of those squares, the tornado they weren't even aware of circling their lives, gathering strength, blowing and blowing.

'I'll meet you guys.'

Angie gave me a look. 'What's up?'

'I'll meet you,' I said. 'I got to do something.'

'What?'

'Nothing big.' I put my hands on her shoulders. 'I'll meet you. Okay? Please. Give me some room here.'

After a long look in my eyes, she nodded. She didn't like it, but she understands my stubbornness as she understands her own. And she knows how useless it is to argue with me at certain times, the same way I recognize those moments in her.

'Don't do anything stupid,' Ryerson said.

'Oh, no,' I said. 'Not me.'

It was a long shot, but it paid off.

At two in the morning, Broussard, Pasquale, and a few other members of the DoRights football squad left the Boyne. By the way they hugged in the parking lot, I could tell they'd heard about Poole's death, and their pain was genuine. Cops, as a rule, don't hug, unless one of them has gone down in the line.

Pasquale and Broussard talked for a bit in the parking lot after the others drove off, and then Pasquale gave Broussard a last hard hug, rapped his fists on the big man's back, and they separated.

Pasquale drove off in a Bronco, and Broussard made his way with the careful, self-conscious steps of a drunk to a Volvo station wagon, backed out onto Western Avenue, and headed east. I stayed way back on the mostly empty avenue, and almost missed him when his taillights disappeared at the Charles River.

I speeded up because he could have turned onto Storrow Drive, cut over to North Beacon, or gone either east or west on the Mass Pike at that juncture.

From the avenue, as I craned my head, I picked up the Volvo as it slipped under a wash of light heading for the westbound tollbooths on the pike.

I forced myself to slow down and passed through the toll about a minute after he had. After about two miles, I picked up the Volvo again. It traveled in the left lane, doing about sixty, and I hung back a hundred yards and matched its speed.

Boston cops are required to live in the greater metro area, but several I know get around that by subletting their Boston apartments to friends or relatives while they live farther out.

Broussard, I discovered, lived way out. After over an hour and a departure from the turnpike onto a series of small dark country roads, we ended up in the town of Sutton, nestled in the shadows of the Purgatory Chasm Reservation and far closer to both the Rhode Island and Connecticut borders than it was to Boston.

When Broussard turned off into a steep, sloping driveway that led up to a small brown Cape, its windows obscured by shrubs and small trees, I kept going, drove until I'd reached a crossroad where the road ended at a towering forest of pine. I turned around, my lights arcing through the deep dark, so much blacker than the city dark, each beam of light seeming to promise sudden revelations of creatures foraging through the night, stopping my heart with glowing green eyes.

I turned back and found the house again, drove another eighty yards until my lights illuminated a

shuttered home. I pulled down a drive littered with
the mulch of last autumn's leaves, buried the Crown
Victoria behind a stand of trees, and sat in it for a
bit, as the crickets and the wind rustling the trees
made the only sounds in what seemed the heart of
the heart of pure stillness.

I woke the next morning to two gorgeous brown
eyes staring in at me. They were soft and sad and
deep as shafts in a copper mine. They didn't blink.

I jumped a bit in my seat as the long white-and-
brown nose tilted toward my window, and my
movement startled the curious animal. Before I was
even sure I'd seen it, the deer hopped over the lawn
and into the trees, and its white tail flashed once
between two trunks and was gone.

'Jesus,' I said aloud.

Another flash of color caught my eye, this one on
the other side of the trees directly in front of my
windshield. It was a rush of tan, and as I looked
through the opening to my right, Broussard's Volvo
sped past on the road. I had no idea if he was
heading down the road for milk or all the way back
to Boston, but in either case, I wasn't going to miss
the opportunity.

I took a set of lock picks from the glove compart-
ment, slung my camera over my shoulder, shook the
cobwebs from my head, and left the car. I walked up
the road, staying close to the soft shoulder, the first
warm day of the year beaming down on me from a
sky so blue with oxygen and free of smog I had a
hard time believing I was still in Massachusetts.

As I neared Broussard's driveway, a tall, slim
woman with long brown hair holding a child by the

hand stepped out at the bottom from around a corner of thick pine. She bent with the child as he picked up the newspaper at the base of the drive and handed it to her.

I was too close to stop, and she looked up and covered her eyes against the sun, smiled uncertainly at me. The child holding her hand was maybe three, and his bright blond hair and pale white skin didn't seem a match for either the woman or Broussard.

'Hi.' The woman rose and took the child with her, perched him on her hip as he sucked his thumb.

'Hi.'

She was a striking woman. Her wide mouth cut unevenly across her face, rose a bit on the left side, and there was something sensual in the skew, the hint of a grin that had discarded all illusions. A cursory glance at her mouth and cheekbones, the sunrise glow of her skin, and I could have easily mistook her for a former model, some financier's trophy wife. Then I looked in her eyes. The hard, naked intelligence there unsettled me. This was not a woman who'd allow herself to be put on a man's arm for show. In fact, I was certain this woman didn't allow herself to be *put* anywhere.

She noticed the camera. 'Birds?'

I looked at it, shook my head. 'Just nature in general. Don't see much of it where I'm from.'

'Boston?'

I shook my head. 'Providence.'

She nodded, glanced at the paper, shook off the dew. 'They used to wrap them in plastic to keep the moisture off,' she said. 'Now I have to hang it in the bathroom for an hour just to read the front page.'

441

The boy on her hip placed his face sleepily to her breast, stared at me with eyes as open and blue as the sky.

'What's the matter, sweetie?' She kissed his head. 'Tired?' She stroked his slightly chubby face, and the love in her eyes was a palpable, daunting thing.

When she looked back over at me, the love cleared, and for a moment I sensed either fear or suspicion. 'There's a forest.' She pointed down the road. 'Right down there. It's part of the Purgatory Chasm Reservation. Get some beautiful pictures there, I bet.'

I nodded. 'Sounds great. Thanks for the advice.'

Maybe the child sensed something. Maybe he was just tired. Maybe just because he was a little kid and that's what little kids do, he suddenly opened his mouth and howled.

'Oh-ho.' She smiled and kissed his head again, bounced him on her hip. 'It's okay, Nicky. It's okay. Come on. Mommy'll get you something to drink.'

She turned up the sloping driveway, bouncing the boy on her hip, caressing his face, her slim body moving like a dancer's in her red-and-black lumberjack shirt and blue jeans.

'Good luck with nature,' she called over her shoulder.

'Thanks.'

She turned a bend in the driveway and I lost sight of her and the child behind the same thicket that obscured most of the house from the road.

But I could still hear her.

'Don't cry, Nicky. Mommy loves you. Mommy's going to make everything all right.'

*   *   *

'So he has a son,' Ryerson said. 'So what?'

'First I heard of it,' I said.

'Me, too,' Angie said, 'and we spent a lot of time with him back in October.'

'I have a dog,' Ryerson said. 'First time you've heard about it. Right?'

'We've known you less than a day,' Angie said. 'And a dog isn't a child. You have a son and you spend a lot of time on stakeouts with people, you're going to mention him. He mentioned his wife a lot. Nothing big, just "Got to call my wife." "My wife is going to kill me for missing another dinner." Et cetera. But never, not once, did he mention a child.'

Ryerson looked in his rearview at me. 'What do you think?'

'I think it's odd. Can I use your phone?'

He handed it back to me and I dialed, looked out at Ted Kenneally's antiques store, the CLOSED sign hanging in the window.

'Detective Sergeant Lee.'

'Oscar,' I said.

'Hey, Walter Payton! How's the body?'

'Hurts,' I said. 'Like hell.'

His voice changed. 'How's that other thing?'

'Well, I got a question for you.'

'A rat-out-my-own-people sort of question?'

'Not necessarily.'

'Shoot. I'll decide if I like it.'

'Broussard's married, right?'

'To Rachel, yeah.'

'Tall brunette?' I said. 'Very pretty?'

'That's her.'

'And they have a kid?'

''Scuse me?'

443

'Does Broussard have a son?'

'No.'

I felt a lightness eddy in my skull, and the throbbing aches from yesterday's football game disappeared.

'You're sure?'

''Course I'm sure. He can't.'

'He can't or he decided not to?'

Oscar's voice became slightly muffled, and I realized he'd cupped the phone with his hand. His voice was a whisper. 'Rachel can't conceive. It was a big problem for them. They wanted kids.'

'Why not adopt?'

'Who's gonna let an ex-hooker adopt kids?'

'She was in the life?'

'Yeah, that's how he met her. He was on Homicide track until then, man, just like me. It killed his career, got him buried in Narco until Doyle bailed him out. But he loves her. She's a good woman, too. A great woman.'

'But no kid.'

His hand left the phone. 'How many times I got to tell you, Kenzie? No friggin' kid.'

I said thanks and goodbye, hung up, and handed the phone back to Ryerson.

'He doesn't have a son,' Ryerson said. 'Does he?'

'He has a son,' I said. 'He definitely has a son.'

'Then where'd he get him?'

It all fell into place then, as I sat in Ryerson's Suburban and looked out at Kenneally's Antiques.

'How much you want to bet,' I said, 'that whoever Nicholas Broussard's natural parents are, they probably weren't real good at the job?'

'Holy shit,' Angie said.

444

Ryerson leaned over the steering wheel, stared out through the windshield with a blank, stunned look on his lean face. 'Holy shit.'

I saw the blond boy riding Rachel Broussard's hip, the adoration she'd poured on his tiny face as she'd caressed it.

'Yeah,' I said. 'Holy shit.'

32

At the end of an April day, after the sun has descended but before night has fallen, the city turns a hushed, unsettled gray. Another day has died, always more quickly than expected. Muted yellow or orange lights appear in window squares and shaft from car grilles, and the coming dark promises a deepening chill. Children have disappeared from the streets to wash up for dinner, to turn on TVs. The supermarkets and liquor stores are half empty and listless. The florists and banks are closed. The honk of horns is sporadic; a storefront grate rattles as it drops. And if you look closely in the faces of pedestrians and drivers stopped at lights, you can see the weight of the morning's unfulfilled promise in the numb sag of their faces. Then they pass, trudging toward home, whatever its incarnation.

Lionel and Ted Kenneally had arrived back late, close to five, and something broke in Lionel's face as he saw us approach. When Ryerson flashed his badge and said, 'Like to ask you a couple of questions, Mr McCready,' that broken thing in Lionel's face broke even further.

He nodded several times, more to himself than to us, and said, 'There's a bar up the street. Why don't

446

we go there? I don't want to do this at my home.'

The Edmund Fitzgerald was about as small as a bar could get without becoming a shoeshine stand. When we first walked in, a small area opened up on our left with a counter running along the only window and enough space for maybe four tables. Unfortunately they'd stuck a jukebox in there, too, so only two tables fit, and both were empty when the four of us entered. The bar itself could sit seven people, eight tops, and six tables took up the wall across from it. The room opened up a bit again in back, where two darts players tossed their missiles over a pool table wedged so close to the walls that from three of four possible sides, the shooter would have to use a short stick. Or a pencil.

As we sat down at a table in the center of the place, Lionel said, 'Hurt your leg, Miss Gennaro?'

Angie said, 'It'll heal,' and fished in her bag for her cigarettes.

Lionel looked at me, and when I looked away, that constant sag in his shoulders deepened. The rocks that normally sat up there had been joined by cinder blocks.

Ryerson flipped a notepad open on the table, uncapped a pen. 'I'm Special Agent Neal Ryerson, Mr McCready. I'm with the Justice Department.'

Lionel said, 'Sir?'

Ryerson gave him a quick flick of the eyes. 'That's right, Mr McCready. Federal government. You have some explaining to do. Wouldn't you say?'

'About what?' Lionel looked over his shoulder, then around the bar.

'Your niece,' I said. 'Look, Lionel, bullshit time is over.'

He glanced to his right, toward the bar, as if someone there might be waiting to help him out.

'Mr McCready,' Ryerson said, 'we can spend half an hour playing No-I-Didn't/Yes-You-Did, but that would be a waste of everyone's time. We know you were involved in your niece's disappearance and that you were working with Remy Broussard. He's going to take a hard fall, by the way, hard as hard gets. You? I'm offering you a chance to clear the air, maybe get some leniency down the road.' He tapped the pen on the table to the cadence of a ticking clock. 'But if you bullshit me, I'll walk out of here and we'll do it the rough way. And you'll drop into prison for so long your grandkids will have driving licenses by the time you get out.'

The waitress approached and took our order of two Cokes, a mineral water for Ryerson, and a double scotch for Lionel.

While we waited for her return, no one spoke. Ryerson continued to use his pen like a metronome, tapping it steadily against the edge of the table, his level, dispassionate gaze locked on Lionel.

Lionel didn't seem to notice. He looked at the coaster in front of him, but I don't think he saw it; he was looking much deeper, much farther away than a table or this bar, his lips and chin picking up a sheen of sweat. I had the sense that what he saw at the end of his long inward gaze was the shoddy finale of his own unraveling, the waste of his life. He saw prison. He saw divorce papers delivered to his cell and letters to his son returned unopened. He saw decades stretching into decades in which he was alone with his shame, or his guilt, or merely the folly of a man who'd done a dumb thing society had stripped naked under klieg lights, exposed for public consumption. His picture would be in the paper, his name associated with kidnapping, his life the fodder for talk shows and tabloids and sneering jokes remembered long after the comics who'd told them were forgotten.

The waitress brought our drinks, and Lionel said, 'Eleven years ago, I was in a bar downtown with some friends. A bachelor party came in. They were all real drunk. One of them was looking for a fight. He picked me. I hit him. Once. But he cracked his skull on the floor. Thing is, I didn't hit him with my fist. I had a pool stick in my hand.'

'Assault with a deadly weapon,' Angie said.

He nodded. 'Actually, it was worse than that. The guy had been shoving me, and I'd said – I don't remember saying it, but I guess I did – I'd said, "Back off or I'll kill you."'

'Attempted murder,' I said.

Another nod. 'I go to trial. And it's my friends' words against this guy's friends' words. And I know I'm going to jail, because the guy I hit, he was a college student, and after I hit him, he claims he can't study anymore, can't concentrate. He's got doctors claiming brain damage. I can tell by the way the judge looks at me that I'm done. But a guy who was in the bar that night, a stranger to both parties, testifies that it was the guy I hit who said he was going to kill *me*, and that he'd thrown the first punch, et cetera. I walk, because the stranger was a cop.'

'Broussard.'

He gave me a bitter smile and sipped his scotch. 'Yeah. Broussard. And you know what? He lied up there on the stand. I might not be able to remember everything the guy I hit said, but I know for sure I hit him first. Don't know why, really. He was bugging me, in my face, and I got angry.' He shrugged. 'I was different then.'

'So Broussard lied and you walked, and you felt you owed him.'

He lifted his scotch glass, changed his mind, and set it back on the coaster. 'I guess. He never brought it up, and we became friends over the years. We'd run into each other, he'd give me a call every now and then. It was only looking back that I realized he was keeping tabs on me. He's like that. Don't get me wrong, he's a good guy, but he's always watching people, studying them, seeing if someday they'll be useful to him.'

'Lotta cops like that,' Ryerson said, and drank some mineral water.

'You?'

Ryerson gave it some thought. 'Yeah. I guess I am.'

Lionel took another sip of scotch, wiped his lips with the cocktail napkin. 'Last July, my sister and Dottie took Amanda to the beach. It was a really hot day, no clouds, and Helene and Dottie meet some guys who, I dunno, had a bag of pot or whatever.' He looked away from us, took a long pull on the scotch, and his face and voice were haunted when he spoke again. 'Amanda fell asleep on the beach, and they . . . they left her there, alone and unwatched, for hours. She roasted, Mr Kenzie, Miss Gennaro. She suffered deep burns to her back and legs, one stage less than third degree. One side of her face was so swollen it looked like she'd been attacked by bees. My fucking slut whore junkie

450

douche-bag piece-of-shit waste of a sister allowed her daughter's flesh to burn. They brought her home, and Helene calls me because Amanda, and I quote, "Is being a bitch." She wouldn't stop crying. She was keeping Helene up. I go over there and my niece, this tiny four-year-old *baby*, is burned. She's in pain. She's screaming, it's so bad. And you know what my sister had done for her?'

We waited while he gripped his scotch glass, lowered his head, took in a few shallow breaths.

He raised his head. 'She'd put beer on Amanda's burns. Beer. To cool her down. No aloe, no lidocaine, didn't even think about a trip to the hospital. No. She put beer on her, sent her to bed, and had the TV turned way up so she wouldn't have to listen to her.' He held a large fist up by his ear, as if prepared to strike the table, crack it in half. 'I could have killed my sister that night. Instead, I took Amanda to the emergency room. I covered for Helene. I said she'd been exhausted and both she and Amanda had fallen asleep on the beach. I pleaded with the doctor, and I convinced her, finally, not to call Child Welfare and report it as a neglect case. I don't know why, I just knew they'd take Amanda away. I just . . .' He swallowed. 'I covered for Helene. Like I been covering my whole life. And that night I took Amanda back to my house and she slept with me and Beatrice. The doctor had given her something to help her sleep, but I stayed awake. I kept holding my hand over her back and feeling the heat coming off it. It was – this is the only way I can put it – it was like holding your hand over meat you just pulled from the oven. And I watched her sleep and I thought,

This can't go on. This has to end.'

'But, Lionel,' Angie said, 'what if you had reported Helene to Child Welfare? If you'd done it enough times, I'm sure you could have petitioned the courts to allow you and Beatrice to adopt Amanda.'

Lionel laughed, and Ryerson shook his head slowly at Angie.

'What?' she said.

Ryerson snipped the end of a cigar. 'Miss Gennaro, unless the birth mother is a lesbian in states like Utah or Alabama, it is all but impossible to remove parental rights.' He lit the cigar and shook his head. 'Let me amend that: It *is* impossible.'

'How can that be,' Angie said, 'if the parent has proven herself consistently negligent?'

Another sad shake of the head from Ryerson. 'This year in Washington, D.C., a birth mother was given full custody of a child she's barely seen. The child has been living with foster parents since he was born. The birth mother is a convicted felon who gave birth to the child while she was on probation for murdering another of her children, who had reached the ripe old age of six weeks and was crying from hunger when the mother decided enough was enough and smothered her, tossed her in a trash bin, and went to a barbecue. Now this woman has two other kids, one of whom is being raised by the father's parents, the other of whom is in foster care. All four kids were fathered by different men, and the mother, who served only a couple of years for killing her daughter, is now – responsibly, I'm sure – raising the child she took back from the loving foster parents who'd petitioned the courts for custody. This,' Ryerson said, 'is a true story. Look it up.'

'That's bullshit,' Angie said.

'No, it's true,' Ryerson said.

'How can . . . ?' Angie dropped her hands from the table, stared off into space.

'This is America,' Ryerson said, 'where every adult shall have the full and inalienable right to eat her young.'

Angie had the look of someone who'd been punched in the stomach, then slapped in the face as she'd doubled over.

Lionel rattled the ice cubes in his glass. 'Agent Ryerson is right, Miss Gennaro. There's nothing you can do if an awful parent wants to hold on to her child.'

'That doesn't get you off the hook, Mr McCready.' Ryerson pointed his cigar at him. 'Where's your niece?'

Lionel stared into Ryerson's cigar ash, then eventually shook his head.

Ryerson nodded and jotted something in his notebook. Then he reached behind his back, produced a set of handcuffs, and tossed them on the table.

Lionel pushed his chair back.

'Stay seated, Mr McCready, or the next thing I put on the table is my gun.'

Lionel gripped the arms of the chair but didn't move.

I said, 'So you were angry at Helene about Amanda's burns. What happened next?'

I met Ryerson's eyes and he blinked softly, gave me a small nod. Going straight at the question of Amanda's whereabouts wasn't working. Lionel could just clam up, take the whole fall, and she'd stay gone. But if we could get him talking again . . .

'My UPS route,' he said eventually, 'covers Broussard's precinct. That's how we stayed in touch so easily over the years. Anyway . . .'

The week after Amanda's sunburn, Lionel and Broussard had gone out for a drink. Broussard had listened to Lionel pour out his concern for his niece, his hatred of his sister, his conviction that Amanda's chances to grow up to be anything but a mirror of her mother were slipping away day by day.

Broussard had bought all the drinks. He'd been generous with them, too, and near the end of the night, when Lionel was drunk, he'd put his arm around him and said, 'What if there were a solution?'

'There's no solution,' Lionel had said. 'The courts, the—'

'Fuck the courts,' Broussard had said. 'Fuck everything you've considered. What if there were a way to guarantee Amanda a loving home and loving parents?'

'What's the catch?'

'The catch is: No one can ever know what happened to her. Not her mother, not your wife, not your son. No one. She vanishes.'

And Broussard had snapped his fingers.

'*Poof*. Like she never existed.'

It took a few months for Lionel to go for it. In that time, he'd twice visited his sister's house to find the door unlocked and Helene gone over to Dottie's, her daughter sleeping alone in the apartment. In August, Helene dropped by a barbecue in Lionel and Beatrice's backyard. She'd been driving around with Amanda in a friend's car and she was fucked up on

454

schnapps, so fucked up that while pushing Amanda and Matt on the swings, she accidentally pushed her daughter off the seat and fell across it herself. She lay there, laughing, as her daughter got up off the ground, wiped the dirt from her knees, checked herself for cuts.

Over the course of the summer, Amanda's skin had blistered and scarred permanently in places because Helene occasionally forgot to apply the medicine prescribed by the emergency room doctor.

And then, in September, Helene talked about leaving the state.

'What?' I said. 'I never heard this.'

Lionel shrugged. 'Looking back, it was probably just another of her stupid ideas. She had a friend who'd moved to Myrtle Beach, South Carolina, got a job at a T-shirt shop, told Helene how it was sunny all the time, drinks were flowing, no more snow, no more cold. Just sit on the beach and occasionally sell T-shirts. For a week or so, it was all Helene talked about. Most times, I'd have brushed it off. She was always talking about living somewhere else, just like she was sure she'd hit for the lottery someday. But this time, I dunno, I panicked. All I could think was: She'll take Amanda. She'll leave her alone on beaches and in unlocked apartments and she won't have me or Beatrice around to pick up the slack. I just . . . I lost it. I called Broussard. I met the people who wanted to take care of Amanda.'

'And their names were?' Ryerson's pen hovered over the pad.

Lionel ignored him. 'They were great. Perfect. Beautiful home. Loved kids. Had already raised one perfectly, and now she'd moved out, they felt empty. They're great with her,' he said quietly.

'So you've seen her,' I said.

He nodded. 'She's happy. She really does smile now.' Something caught in his throat, and he swallowed against it. 'She doesn't know I see her. Broussard's first rule was that her whole past life had to be wiped out. She's four. She'll forget, given time. Actually,' he said slowly, 'she's five now. Isn't she?'

The realization that Amanda had celebrated a birthday he hadn't witnessed slid softly across his face. He shook his head quickly. 'Anyway, I've snuck up there, watched her with her new parents, and she looks great. She looks . . .' He cleared his throat, looked away from us. 'She looks loved.'

'What happened the night she disappeared?' Ryerson said.

'I came in from the back of the house. I took her out. I told her it was a game. She liked games. Maybe because Helene's idea was a trip down to the bar, play with the Pac-Man machine, honey.' He sucked ice from his glass and crushed it between his teeth. 'Broussard was parked on the street. I waited in the doorway to the porch, told Amanda to be real, real quiet. The only neighbor who could have seen us was Mrs Driscoll, across the street. She was sitting on her stoop, had a direct line on the house. She left the stoop for a second, went back in the house for another cup of tea or something, and Broussard gave me an all-clear signal. I carried Amanda to Broussard's car, and we drove away.'

'And no one saw a thing,' I said.

'None of the neighbors. We found out later,

though, that Chris Mullen did. He was parked on the street, staking out the house. He was waiting for Helene to come back so he could find out where she'd hid the money she stole. He recognized Broussard. Cheese Olamon used it to blackmail Broussard into retrieving the missing money. He was also supposed to steal some drugs from evidence lockup, give them to Mullen that night at the quarry.'

'Back to the night Amanda disappeared,' I said.

He took a second cube of ice from the glass with his thick fingers, chewed it. 'I told Amanda my friend was going to take her to see some nice people. Told her I'd see her in a few hours. She just nodded. She was used to being dropped off with strangers. I got out a few blocks away and walked home. It was ten-thirty. It took my sister almost twelve hours to notice her daughter was gone. That tell you anything?'

For a while we were so quiet, I could hear the thump of darts hitting cork near the back of the bar.

'When the time was right,' Lionel said, 'I figured I'd tell Beatrice, and she'd understand. Not right away. A few years down the road, maybe. I don't know. I hadn't thought that through. Beatrice hates Helene, and she loves Amanda, but something like this . . . See, she believes in the law, all the rules. She'd never have gone along with something like this. But I hoped, maybe, once enough time had passed . . .' He looked up at the ceiling, gave a small shake of his head. 'When she decided to call you two, I got in contact with Broussard and he said try and dissuade her, but not too hard. Let her do it if she has to. He told me the next day that if push came to shove, he had some things on you two. Something about a murdered pimp.'

Ryerson gave me a raised eyebrow and a cold, curious smile.

I shrugged and looked away, and that's when I saw the guy in the Popeye mask. He came in through the back fire exit, his right arm extended, a .45 automatic pointed at chest level.

His partner brandished a shotgun and also wore a plastic Halloween mask. Casper the Friendly Ghost's moony white face stared out as he came through the front door and shouted, 'Hands on the table! Everyone! Now!'

Popeye herded the two darts players in front of him, and I turned my head in time to see Casper throw the bolt lock on the front door.

'You!' Popeye screamed at me. 'You deaf? Hands on the fucking table.'

I put my hands on the table.

The bartender said, 'Oh, shit. Come *on*.'

Casper pulled a string by the window and a heavy black curtain fell across it.

Beside me, Lionel's breathing was very shallow. His hands, flat on the table, were completely still. One of Ryerson's hands dropped below the table, and one of Angie's did as well.

Popeye hit one of the darts throwers on the back of the spine with his fist. 'Down! On the floor. Hands behind your head. Do it. Do it. Do it now!'

Both men dropped to their knees and began locking their hands behind their necks. Popeye looked at them, his head cocked. It was an awful moment, filled with the worst sort of possibility. Whatever Popeye decided, he could do. Shoot them, shoot us, cut their throats. Whatever.

He kicked the older of the two in the base of the spine.

'Not on your knees. On your stomachs. Now.'

The men dropped to their stomachs by my feet.

Popeye turned his head very slowly, stopped on our table.

'Hands on the damn table,' he whispered. 'Or you fucking die.'

Ryerson withdrew his hand from under the table, held both empty palms to the air, then placed them flat on the wood. Angie did the same.

Casper came up to the bar across from us. He leveled the shotgun at the bartender.

Two middle-aged women, office workers or secretaries by the looks of their clothes, sat in the middle of the bar directly in front of Casper. When he extended the shotgun, it brushed the hair of one of the women. Her shoulders tensed and her head jerked to the left. Her companion moaned.

The first woman said, 'Oh, God. Oh, no.'

Casper said, 'Stay calm, ladies. This will all be over in a minute or two.' He pulled a green trash bag from the pocket of his leather bombardier's jacket and tossed it on the bar in front of the bartender. 'Fill it up. And don't forget the money from the safe.'

'There's not much,' the bartender said.

'Just get what there is,' Casper said.

Popeye, the crowd control, stood with his legs spread apart by roughly a foot and a half and bent slightly at the knees, his .45 steadily moving in an arc from left to right, right to left, and back again. He was about twelve feet from me, and I could hear his breathing from behind the mask, even and steady.

Casper stood in an identical stance, shotgun trained on the bartender, but his eyes scanned the mirror behind the bar.

These guys were pros. All the way.

Besides Casper and Popeye, there were twelve people in the bar: the bartender and waitress behind the bar, the two guys on the floor, Lionel, Angie, Ryerson, and me, the two secretaries, and two guys at the end of the bar closest to the entrance, teamsters by the look of them. One wore a green Celtics jacket, the other a canvas and denim thing, old and thickly lined. Both were mid-forties and beefy. A bottle of Old Thompson sat between two shot glasses on the bar in front of them.

'Take your time,' Casper said to the bartender, as the bartender knelt behind the bar and fiddled with what I assumed was the safe. 'Just go slow, like nothing's happening, and you won't spin past the numbers.'

'Please don't hurt us,' one of the men on the floor said. 'We got families.'

'Shut up,' Popeye said.

'No one's getting hurt,' Casper said. 'As long as you keep quiet. Just keep quiet. Very simple.'

'You know whose fucking bar this is?' the guy in the Celtics jacket said.

'What?' Popeye said.

'You fucking heard me. You know whose bar this is?'

'Please, please,' one of the secretaries said. 'Be quiet.'

Casper turned his head. 'A hero.'

'A hero,' Popeye said, and looked over at the idiot.

460

Without moving his mouth it seemed, Ryerson whispered, 'Where's your piece?'

'Spine,' I said. 'Yours?'

'My lap.' His right hand moved three inches to the edge of the table.

'Don't,' I whispered, as Popeye's head and gun turned back in our direction.

'You guys are fucking dead,' the teamster said.

'Why are you talking?' the secretary said, her eyes on the bar top.

'Good question,' Casper said.

'Dead. Got it? You fucking punks. You fucking humps. You fucking—'

Casper took four steps and punched the teamster in the center of the face.

The teamster dropped off the back of his stool and hit his head so hard on the floor that you could hear the crack when the back of his skull split.

'Any comment?' Casper asked the guy's friend.

'No,' the guy said, and looked down at the bar.

'Anyone else?' Casper said.

The bartender came up from behind the bar and placed the trash bag on top.

The bar was as silent as a church before a baptism.

'What?' Popeye said, and took three steps toward our table.

It took me a moment to realize he was talking to us, another moment to know with a complete certainty that this was all about to go terribly wrong terribly fast.

None of us moved.

'What did you just say?' Popeye pointed the gun at Lionel's head, and his eyes behind the mask skittered uncertainly over Ryerson's calm face, then came back to Lionel's.

'Another hero?' Casper took the bag off the bar, came over to our table with his shotgun pointed at my neck.

'He's a talker,' Popeye said. 'He's talking shit.'

'You got something to say?' Casper said, and turned his shotgun on Lionel. 'Huh? Speak up.' He turned to Popeye. 'Cover the other three.'

Popeye's .45 turned toward me and the black eye stared into my own.

Casper took another step closer to Lionel. 'Just yapping away. Huh?'

'Why do you keep antagonizing them? They have guns,' one of the secretaries said.

'Just be quiet,' her companion hissed.

Lionel looked up into the mask, his lips shut tight, his fingertips digging into the tabletop.

Casper said, 'Go for it, big man. Go for it. Just keep talking.'

'I don't have to listen to this shit,' Popeye said.

Casper rested the tip of the shotgun against the bridge of Lionel's nose. '*Shut up!*'

Lionel's fingers shook and he blinked against the sweat in his eyes.

'He just don't want to listen,' Popeye said. 'Just wants to keep talking trash.'

'Is that it?' Casper said.

'Everyone stay calm,' the bartender said, his hands held straight up in the air.

Lionel said nothing.

But every witness in the bar, deep in states of panic, sure they were going to die, would remember it the way the shooters wanted them to – that Lionel had been talking. That all of us at the table had. That we'd antagonized some dangerous men, and they'd killed us for it.

Casper racked the slide on the shotgun and the noise was like a cannon going off. 'Got to be a big man. Is that it?'

Lionel opened his mouth. He said, 'Please.'

I said, 'Wait.'

The shotgun swung my way, its dark, dark eyes the last thing I'd see. I was sure of it.

'Detective Remy Broussard!' I yelled, so the whole bar could hear me. 'Everyone got that name? Remy Broussard!' I looked through the mask at the deep blue eyes, saw the fear in there, the confusion.

'Don't do it, Broussard,' Angie said.

'Shut the fuck up!' It was Popeye this time, and his cool was slipping. The tendons in his forearm clenched as he tried to cover the table.

'It's over, Broussard. It's over. We know you took Amanda McCready.' I craned my neck out to the bar. 'You hear that name? Amanda McCready?'

When I turned my head back, the cold metal bores of the shotgun dug into my forehead, and my eyes met the curl of a red finger on the other side of the trigger guard. This close, the finger looked like an insect or a red and white worm. It looked like it had a mind of its own.

'Close your eyes,' Casper said. 'Close 'em tight.'

'Mr Broussard,' Lionel said. 'Please don't do this. Please.'

'Pull the fucking trigger!' Popeye turned toward his companion. 'Do it!'

Angie said, 'Broussard—'

'Stop saying that fucking name!' Popeye kicked a chair into the wall.

I kept my eyes open, felt the curve of metal against my flesh, smelled the cleaning oil and old gunpowder, watched the finger twitch against the trigger.

'It's over,' I said again, and it came out in a croak through my arid throat and mouth. 'It's over.'

For a long, long time, no one said anything. In that hard hush of silence, I could hear the whole world creak on its axis.

Casper's face tilted as Broussard cocked his head and I saw that look in his eyes that I'd seen yesterday at the football game, the one that was hard, that danced and burned.

Then a clear, resigned defeat replaced it and shuddered softly through his body, and his finger slipped from the trigger as he lowered the gun from my head.

'Yeah,' he said softly. 'Over.'

'Are you dicking me?' his partner said. 'We have to do this. We have to do this, man. We have orders. Do it! Now!'

Broussard shook his head, the moony face and child's smile of the Casper mask swaying with it. 'This is done. Let's go.'

'Fuck you, this is done! You can't cap these fuckers? Fuck you, you piece of shit. I can!'

Popeye raised his arm and pointed his gun in the center of Lionel's face as Ryerson's hand dropped into his lap and the first gunshot was muffled by the top of the table as it tore through the flesh of Popeye's left thigh.

His gun went off as he jerked backward, and

Lionel screamed, grabbed the side of his head, and toppled from his chair.

Ryerson's gun cleared the tabletop, and he shot Popeye twice in the chest.

When Broussard pulled the trigger of the shotgun, I distinctly heard the pause – a microsecond's worth of silence – between the trigger engaging the round and the blast that roared in my ears like an inferno.

Neal Ryerson's left shoulder disappeared in a flash of fire and blood and bone, just melted and exploded and evaporated all at the same time in a sonic boom of noise. A splatter of him hit the wall, and then his body toppled out of the chair as the shotgun rose through the smoke in Remy Broussard's hand and the table toppled to the left with Ryerson. His .9 mm fell from his hand and bounced off a chair on the way to the floor.

Angie had cleared her gun, but she dove to her left as Broussard pivoted.

I drove my head into his stomach, wrapped my arms around him, and ran straight back for the bar. I rammed his spine against the rail, heard him grunt, and then he drove the stock of the shotgun down onto the back of my neck.

My knees hit the floor, my arms fell back from his body, and Angie screamed, 'Broussard!' and fired her .38.

He threw the shotgun at her as I reached for my .45, and it hit her in the chest, knocked her to the floor.

He vaulted the two darts players and sprinted for the front door like a born athlete.

I closed my left eye and sighted down the barrel and fired twice as Broussard reached the front of the bar. I saw his right leg jerk and skitter away from him before he turned the corner, threw the bolt lock, and burst out into the night.

'Angie!'

I turned as she sat up amid a pile of overturned chairs. 'I'm fine.'

Ryerson shouted, 'Call an ambulance! Call an ambulance!'

I looked down at Lionel. He rolled on the floor, moaning, his head in his hands, blood pouring through the fingers.

I looked at the bartender. 'The ambulance!'

He picked up the phone and dialed.

Ryerson leaned back against the wall, most of his shoulder gone, and screamed up at the ceiling, his body convulsing wildly.

'He's going into shock,' I said to Angie.

'I got him.' She crawled toward Ryerson. 'I need all the towels from the bar, and I need 'em now!'

One of the secretaries hopped over the bar.

'Beatrice,' Lionel moaned. 'Beatrice.'

The rubber band holding Popeye's mask to his head had snapped when he dropped down the bar, Ryerson's bullets popping through his sternum. I looked down at the face of John Pasquale. He was dead, and he'd been right yesterday, after the football game: Luck always ran out.

I met Angie's eyes as she caught a towel the secretary tossed across the room to her. 'Get Broussard, Patrick. Get him.'

I nodded as the secretary rushed past me and dropped down by Lionel, placed a towel to the side of his head.

I checked my pocket for a second clip, found it, and left the bar.

33

I followed Broussard's trail across Broadway and up C Street, where it wound into the trucking and warehouse district along East Second. It wasn't a hard trail to follow. He'd discarded the Casper mask as soon as he left the bar, and it lay looking up at me as I stepped out, holes for eyes, a toothless smile. Drops of blood, so fresh they shone under street lamps, pointed out their owner's path in a jagged line. They grew thicker and wider in diameter the farther they led into the scantily lit, cracked-cobblestone blocks of dark depots, empty loading docks, and cubbyhole teamster bars with curtains drawn and small neon signs missing half the bulbs. Semis headed for Buffalo or Trenton rolled and heaved and bumped down the cracked streets, and their headlights flashed across the end of the trail, the place where Broussard had stopped long enough to jimmy a door. The blood dropping from a hole in his body had formed a puddle, splattered the door in thin streaks. I hadn't thought a leg could bleed like that, but maybe my bullet had blown apart the femur or savaged crucial arteries.

I looked up at the building. It was seven stories tall and built of the chocolate-brown brick they'd used at the turn of the century. Weeds rose to the windowsills on the first level, and the boards over the windows themselves were cracked and defaced by graffiti. It was wide enough to have served as storage for large objects or the manufacture and assembly of machines.

Assembly, I decided as I entered. The first thing I noticed was the silhouette of an assembly belt, pulleys and chains dropping from the rafters twenty feet above it. The belt itself and the rollers that had once been beneath it were gone, but the main frame remained, bolted to the floor, and hooks curled out from the ends of the chains like beckoning fingers. The rest of the floor was empty, everything of value either stolen by vagrants and kids or stripped by the final owners and sold.

To the right, a cast-iron staircase led to the next floor, and I climbed it slowly, unable to follow the trail of blood anymore in the darkness, peering through the black for holes rusted through the steps, gingerly reaching out for the rail before each step, hoping to press against metal and not the body of some angry, hungry rat.

My eyes adjusted somewhat to the dark as I reached the second floor, saw nothing but an empty loft space, the shapes of a few overturned pallets, the glow from dim streetlights pressing through lead windows shattered by rocks. The staircases were stacked one on top of each other at identical points on each floor, so that to reach the next, I had to turn left at the wall and follow it back about fifteen feet until I found the opening, looked up the stack of thick iron risers until I saw the rectangular hole up top.

As I stood there, I heard a heavy metallic groan from several levels up, the thump of a thick steel door as it fell back on its hinges and banged into cement.

I took the steps two at a time, stumbling a few times, turned the corner on the third floor, and jogged around to the next staircase. I went up a little faster, my feet beginning to pick up a rhythm, a sense where each riser rose through the dark.

The floors were all empty, and with each level the harbor and downtown skyline cast more light under the arches of the floor-to-ceiling windows. The staircases remained dark save for the rectangular openings at their tops, and as I reached the last one, bathed in moonlight and stretching to an open sky, Broussard called down to me from the roof.

'Hey, Patrick, I'd stay down there.'

I called back up. 'Why's that?'

He coughed. 'Because I got a gun pointed at the opening. Stick your head through, I'll take a chunk out of it.'

'Oh.' I leaned against the banister, smelled the harbor channel and the fresh cool night wafting through the opening. 'What're you planning to do up there, call for helicopter evac?'

He chuckled. 'Once in a lifetime's enough of that. No, I just thought I'd sit here for a bit, look at the stars. Fuck, man, you're a shitty shot,' he hissed.

I looked through the square of moonlight. From the sound of his voice, I was pretty sure he was to the left of the opening.

'Good enough to shoot you,' I said.

'It was a friggin' ricochet,' he said. 'I'm pulling tile out of my ankle.'

'You're saying I hit the floor and the floor hit you?'

'That's what I'm saying. Who was that guy?'

'Which?'

'The guy in the bar with you.'

'The one you shot?'

'That guy, yeah.'

'Justice Department.'

'No shit? I figured him for some sort of spook. He was way too fucking calm. Put three shots in Pasquale like it was target practice. Like it was nothing. I saw him sitting at that table, I knew the shit was going to turn bad.'

He coughed again, and I listened. I closed my eyes as he hacked uncontrollably for about twenty seconds, and I was certain by the time he finished that he was left of the opening by about ten yards.

'Remy?'

'Yo.'

'I'm coming up.'

'I'll put a bullet in your head.'

'No, you won't.'

'Yeah?'

'Yeah.'

His pistol snapped at the night air, and the bullet hit the steel staircase support clamped to the wall. The metal sparked like someone had struck a kitchen match off it, and I dropped flat against the stairs as the bullet clanged overhead, ricocheted off another piece of metal, and embedded itself with a soft hiss into the wall on my left.

I lay there for a bit, my heart squeezed into my esophagus and not too happy about the relocation, banging against the walls, scrambling to get back out.

'Patrick?'

'Yeah?'

'You hit?'

I pushed off the steps, straightened to my knees. 'No.'

'I told you I'd shoot.'

'Thanks for the warning. You're swell.'

Another round of hacking coughs, then a loud gurgle as he sucked it back into his lungs and spit.

'That didn't sound real healthy,' I said.

He gave a hoarse laugh. 'Didn't look too healthy, either. Your partner, man, she's the shooter in the family.'

'She tagged you?'

'Oh, yeah. Quick cure for smoking, what she did.'

I placed my back against the banister, pointed my gun up at the roof, and inched up the staircase.

'Personally,' Broussard said, 'I don't think I could have shot her. You, maybe. But her? I don't know. Shooting women, you know, it's just not something you want in your obit. "Twice decorated officer of the Boston Police Department, loving husband and father, carried a two-fifty-two bowling average, and could shoot the hell out of women." You know? Sounds . . . bad, really.'

I crouched on the fifth step from the top, kept my head below the opening, took a few breaths.

'I know what you're thinking: *But, Remy, you shot Roberta Trett in the back.* True. But Roberta wasn't no woman. You know? She was . . .' He sighed and then coughed. 'Well, I don't know what she was. But "woman" seems too limiting a term.'

I raised my body through the opening, gun extended, and stared down the barrel at Broussard.

He wasn't even looking my way. He sat with his back against an industrial cooling vent, his head tilted back, the downtown skyline spread out before us in a sweep of yellow and blue and white against a cobalt sky.

'Remy.'

He turned his head and stretched his arm out, pointed his Glock at me.

We stood there for quite a while that way, neither of us sure how this was going to go, if one wrong look, one involuntary twitch or tremor of adrenaline and fear would jerk a finger, punch a bullet through a flash of fire at the end of a muzzle. Broussard blinked several times, sucked at the pain, as what looked like the oversized bulb of a bright red rose gradually spread on his shirt, blooming, it seemed, opening its petals with steady, irrevocable grace.

Keeping his gun hand steady and his finger curled around the trigger, he said, 'Feel like you're suddenly in a John Woo movie?'

'I hate John Woo movies.'

'Me, too,' he said. 'I thought I was the only one.'

I shook my head slightly. 'Warmed-over Peckinpah with none of the emotional subtext.'

'What're you, a film critic?'

I smiled tightly.

'I like chick movies,' he said.

'What?'

'True.' On the other side of his gun, his eyes rolled. 'Sounds goofy, I know. And maybe it's 'cause I'm a cop, I watch those action movies, I keep saying, "Oh, bullshit." You know? But, yep, you toss *Out of Africa* or *All About Eve* in the VCR? I'm there, man.'

'You're a ton of surprises, Broussard.'

'That's me.'

It was tiring to hold a gun extended and pointed all this time. If we were going to shoot, we'd have probably done it by now. Of course, maybe that's what a lot of guys think just before they get shot. I noticed the advancing winter gray in Broussard's flesh, the sweat obscuring the silver along his temples. He couldn't last much longer. As tiring as it was for me, I didn't have a bullet in my chest and shards of floor in my ankle.

'I'm going to lower my gun,' I said.

'Your choice.'

I watched his eyes, and maybe because he knew I was watching them, he gave me nothing but an opaque, even gaze.

I raised my gun and slipped my finger off the trigger, held it up in my palm and climbed up the last few steps. I stood on the light gravel dusting the rooftop and looked down at him, cocked an eyebrow.

He smiled.

He lowered his gun to his lap and leaned his head against the vent.

'You paid Ray Likanski to draw Helene out of the house,' I said. 'Right?'

He shrugged. 'Didn't have to pay him. Promised to let him off the hook on some bust somewhere up the road. That was all it took.'

I crossed until I was in front of him. From there I could see the dark circle in his upper chest, the place where the rose petals grew. It was just right of center, and it still pumped brightly but slowly.

'Lung?' I said.

473

'Nicked it, I think.' He nodded. 'Fucking Mullen. Mullen wasn't there that night, it would have gone without a hitch. Dumb-ass Likanski doesn't tell me he ripped Olamon off. That would have changed things, I knew that. Believe me.' He shifted slightly and groaned from the effort. 'Forces me – me, for Christ's sake – to get into bed with a mutt like Cheese. Even though I was setting him up, man, that hurt the ego, I'll tell you.'

'Where is Likanski?' I said.

He tilted his head up toward me. 'Look over your shoulder and down to your right a bit.'

I tilted my head. The Fort Point Channel broke away from a white and dusty lip of land, rolled under bridges and Summer and Congress streets, stretched toward the skyline and the piers and the dark blue release of Boston Harbor.

'Ray sleeps with the fishes?' I said.

Broussard gave me a lazy smile. ''Fraid so.'

'How long?'

'I found him that night in October, right after you two came on to the case. He was packing. I interrogated him about the scam he ran on Cheese. Got to hand it to him, he never gave up the location of the money. Never thought he'd have that kind of spine, but two hundred grand gives some people balls, I guess. Anyway, he's planning to leave. I didn't want him to. Things got physical.'

He coughed violently, arching forward, and pressed a hand over the hole in his chest, gripped his gun tightly in his lap.

'We need to get you off this roof.'

He looked up at me, wiped at his mouth with the

back of his gun hand. 'I don't think I'll be going anywhere.'

'Come on. There's no point in dying.'

He gave me that wonderful, boyish grin of his. 'Funny, I'd argue the opposite about now. You got a cell phone to call for an ambulance?'

'No.'

He placed his gun on his lap and reached into his leather jacket, removed a slim Nokia. 'I do,' he said, and he turned and tossed it off the roof.

I heard it shatter distantly as it hit the pavement seven stories below.

'Don't worry.' He chuckled. 'Fucker comes with a hell of a warranty.'

I sighed and sat down on the small tar riser at the edge of the roof, faced him.

'Determined to die on this roof,' I said.

'Determined not to go to jail. A trial?' He shook his head. 'Not for me, pal.'

'Then tell me who has her, Remy. Go out right.'

His eyes widened. 'So you can go get her? Bring her back to that fucking *thing* society calls her mother? Kiss my ass, man. Amanda stays gone. You got that? She stays happy. She stays well-fed and clean and looked after. She has a few fucking laughs in her life and she grows up with a chance. You need brain surgery, you think I'm going to tell you where she is, Kenzie.'

'The people who have her are kidnappers.'

'Ah, no. Wrong answer. I'm a kidnapper. They're people who took a child in.' He blinked several times at the sweat bathing his face on a cool night, sucked in a long breath that rattled in his chest. 'You were at my house this morning. My wife called me.'

I nodded. 'She made the ransom call to Lionel, didn't she?'

He shrugged, looked off at the skyline. 'You at my house,' he said. 'Christ, that pissed me off.' He closed his eyes for a moment, then opened them. 'You see my son?'

'He's not yours.'

He blinked. 'You see my son?'

I looked up at the stars for a moment, a rarity in these parts, so clear on a cold night. 'I saw your son,' I said.

'Great kid. Know where I found him?'

I shook my head.

'I'm talking to this snitch in the Somerville projects. I'm alone, and I hear this baby screaming. I mean screaming like he's being bitten by dogs. And the snitch, the people walking down the corridor, they don't hear it. They just don't hear it. 'Cause they hear it every day. So I tell the snitch to beat it, I follow the sound, kick in the door of this shit-smelling apartment, and I find him in the back. The place is empty. My son – and he is my son, Kenzie, fuck you if you don't think so – he's starving. He's lying in a crib, six months old, and he's starving. You can see his ribs. He's fucking hand-cuffed, Kenzie, and his diaper is so filled it's leaking through the seams, and he's stuck – *he's fucking stuck to the mattress, Kenzie!*'

Broussard's eyes bulged, and his whole body seemed to lunge against itself. He coughed blood onto his shirt, wiped it with his hand, and smeared it on his chin.

'A baby,' he said eventually, his voice almost a

whisper now, 'stuck to a mattress by his own bedsores and fecal matter. Left in a room for three days, crying his head off. And nobody cares.' He held out his bloody left hand, let it drop to the gravel. 'Nobody cares,' he repeated softly.

I placed my gun on my lap, glanced over at the city skyline. Maybe Broussard was right. A whole city of Nobody Cares. A whole state. A whole country, maybe.

'So I took him home with me. I knew enough guys who'd forged fake identities in their time, and I paid one off. My son has a birth certificate with my surname on it. The records of my wife's tubal ligation were destroyed and a new one was created, showing she consented to the procedure after the birth of our son, Nicholas. And all I had to do was get through these last few months and retire, and we'd move out of state and I'd get some lame security consultant job and raise my child. And I'd have been very, very happy.'

I hung my head for a moment, looked at my shoes on the gravel.

'She never even filed a missing person's report,' Broussard said.

'Who?'

'The skaghead who gave birth to my son. She never even looked for him. I know who she is, and for a long time I thought of just blowing her head off for the fuck of it. But I didn't. And she never looked for her child.'

I raised my head, looked into his face. It was proud and angry and profoundly saddened by the depths of the worlds he'd seen.

'I just want Amanda,' I said.

'Why?'

'Because it's my job, Remy. It's what I was hired to do.'

'And I was hired to protect and serve, you dumb-ass. You know what that means? That's an oath. To protect and serve. I've done that. I've protected several children. I've served them. I've given them good homes.'

'How many?' I asked. 'How many have there been?'

He wagged a bloody finger at me. 'No, no, no.'

His head shot back suddenly, and his whole body stiffened against the vent. His left heel kicked off the gravel and his mouth opened wide into a soundless scream.

I dropped to my knees by him, but all I could do was watch.

After a few moments, his body relaxed and his eyes drooped, and I could hear oxygen entering and leaving his body.

'Remy.'

He opened one weary eye. 'Still here,' he slurred. He raised that finger to me. 'You know you're lucky, Kenzie. One lucky bastard.'

'Why's that?'

He smiled. 'You didn't hear?'

'What?'

'Eugene Torrel died last week.'

'Who's . . . ?' I leaned back from him and his smile broadened as I realized: Eugene, the kid who'd seen us kill Marion Socia.

'Got himself stabbed in Brockton over a woman.' Broussard closed his eyes again and his grin soft-ened, slid to the side of his face. 'You're very lucky.

Got nothing on you now but a worthless deposition from a dead loser.'

'Remy.'

His eyes flickered open and the gun fell from his hand into the gravel. He tilted his head toward it, but left his hand on his lap.

'Come on, man. Do something right before you die. You got a lot of blood on your hands.'

'I know,' he slurred. 'Kimmie and David. You didn't even figure me for that one.'

'It was gnawing at the back of my brain the last twenty-four hours,' I said. 'You and Poole?'

He gave his head a half shake against the vent. 'Not Poole. Pasquale. Poole was never a shooter. That's where he drew the line. Don't debase his mem'ry.'

'But Pasquale wasn't at the quarries that night.'

'He was nearby. Who do you think cranked Rogowski in Cunningham Park?'

'But that still wouldn't have given Pasquale the time to reach the other side of the quarries and kill Mullen and Gutierrez.'

Broussard shrugged.

'Why didn't Pasquale just kill Bubba by the way?'

Broussard frowned. 'Man, we never killed anyone wasn't a direct threat to us. Rogowski didn't know shit, so we let him live. You, too. You think I couldn't have hit you from the other side of the quarry that night? No, Mullen and Gutierrez were direct threats. So was Wee David, Likanski, and, unfortunately, Kimmie.'

'Let's not forget Lionel.'

The frown deepened. 'I never wanted to hit Lionel. I thought it was a bad play. Someone got scared.'

'Who?'

He gave me a short harsh laugh that left a fine spray of blood on his lips and closed his eyes tight against the pain. 'Just remember – Poole wasn't a shooter. Let the man's death have dignity.'

He could have been bullshitting me, but I didn't see the point, really. If Poole hadn't killed Pharaoh Gutierrez and Chris Mullen, I'd have to refigure some things.

'The doll.' I tapped his hand and he opened one eye. 'Amanda's shirt fragment stuck to the quarry wall?'

'Me.' He smacked his lips, closed his eye. 'Me, me, me. All me.'

'You're not that good. Hell, you're not that smart.'

He shook his head. 'Really?'

'Really,' I said.

He snapped his eyes open, and there was a bright, hard awareness in them. 'Move to your left, Kenzie. Let me see the city.'

I moved and he stared out at the skyline, smiled at the lights flickering in the squares, the red pulse of the weather beacons and radio transmitters.

''S pretty,' he said. 'You know something?'

'What?'

'I love children.' He said it so simply, so softly.

His right hand slid into mine and squeezed, and we looked off over the water to the heart of the city and its shimmer, the dark velvet promise that lived in those lights, the hint of glamorous lives, of sleek, well-fed, well-tended existences cushioned behind glass and privilege, behind redbrick and iron and steel, curving staircases, and moonlit views of water, always water, flowing gently around the islands and peninsulas that made up our metropolis, buffeted it against ugliness and pain.

'Wow,' Remy Broussard whispered, and then his hand fell from mine.

34

'. . . at which point the man later identified as Detective Pasquale responded, "We have to do this. We have orders. Do it now."' Assistant District Attorney Lyn Campbell removed her glasses and pinched the flesh between her eyes. 'Is that accurate, Mr Kenzie?'

'Yes, ma'am.'

'"Ms Campbell" will do fine.'

'Yes, Ms Campbell.'

She slid her glasses back up on her nose, looked through the thin ovals at me. 'And you took that to mean what exactly?'

'I took that to mean that someone besides Detective Pasquale and Officer Broussard had given the order to assassinate Lionel McCready and possibly the rest of us in the Edmund Fitzgerald.'

She flipped through her notes, which – in the six hours I'd been in Interrogation Room 6A of the BPO's District 6 station – had grown to take up half the notepad. The sound of her turning sheets of paper made brittle and curled inward by her furious scribbling with a sharp ballpoint reminded me of the late-autumn rustle of dead leaves against curbstone.

Besides myself and ADA Campbell, the room was

occupied by two homicide detectives, Janet Harris and Joseph Centauro, neither of whom seemed to like me even a little bit, and my attorney, Cheswick Hartman.

Cheswick watched ADA Campbell turn the pages of her notes for a while, and then, he said, 'Ms Campbell.'

She looked up. 'Hmm?'

'I understand this is a high-pressure case with what I'm sure will be extensive press coverage. To that end, my client and I have been cooperative. But it's been a long night, wouldn't you say?'

She turned another crisp page. 'The Commonwealth is not interested in your client's lack of sleep, Mr Hartman.'

'Well, that's the Commonwealth's problem, because I am.'

She dropped a hand to her notes, looked up at him. 'What do you expect me to do here, Mr Hartman?'

'I expect you to go outside that door and speak to District Attorney Prescott. I expect you to tell him that it's patently obvious what occurred in the Edmund Fitzgerald, that my client acted as any reasonable person would, is not a suspect in either the death of Detective Pasquale or of Officer Broussard, and that it is time for him to be released. Note, too, Ms Campbell, that our cooperation has been total up to this point and will continue to be so as long as you show us some common courtesy.'

'Fucking guy shot a cop,' Detective Centauro said. 'We're going to let him walk, counselor? I don't think so.'

Cheswick crossed his hands on the table, ignored

Centauro, and smiled at ADA Campbell. 'We're waiting, Ms Campbell.'

She turned a few more pages of her notes, hoping to find something, anything, on which to hold me.

Cheswick was inside another five minutes checking on Angie as I waited on the front steps, getting enough glares from the cops coming in and out of the building to know I'd better not get pulled over for speeding for a while. Maybe for the rest of my life.

When Cheswick joined me, I said, 'What's the deal?'

He shrugged. 'She's not going anywhere for a while.'

'Why not?'

He looked at me like I needed a shot of Ritalin. 'She killed a cop, Patrick. Self-defense or not, she killed a cop.'

'Well, shouldn't you be—'

He cut me off with a wave of his hand. 'You know who the best criminal lawyer in this city is?'

'You.'

He shook his head. 'My junior partner, Floris Mansfield. And that's who's in there with Angie. Okay? So chill out. Floris rocks, Patrick. Understand? Angie's going to be fine. But she's still got a lot of hours ahead of her. And if we press too hard, the DA will say, "Fuck it," and push it to a grand jury just to show the cops he's on their side. If we all play ball and make nice, everyone will begin to cool down and get tired and realize that the sooner this goes away the better.'

We walked up West Broadway at four in the

morning, the icy fingers of dark April winds finding our collars.

'Where's your car?' Cheswick said.

'G Street.'

He nodded. 'Don't go home. Half the press corps is there. And I don't want you talking to them.'

'Why aren't they here?' I looked back at the precinct house.

'Misinformation. The duty-desk sergeant purposefully let it leak that you were all being held at headquarters. The ruse'll hold until sunup; then they'll come back.'

'So where do I go?'

'That's a really good question. You and Angie, intentionally or unintentionally, just gave the Boston Police Department its blackest eye since Charles Stuart and Willie Bennett. Personally, I'd move out of state.'

'I meant now, Cheswick.'

He shrugged and pressed the slim remote attached to his car keys, and his Lexus beeped once and the door locks slid open.

'The hell with it,' I said. 'I'll go to Devin's.'

His head whipped around in my direction. 'Amronklin? Are you crazy? You want to go to a cop's house?'

'Into the belly of the beast.' I nodded.

At four in the morning, most people are asleep, but not Devin. He rarely sleeps more than three or four hours a day, and then it's usually in the late hours of the morning. The rest of the time, he's either working or drinking.

He opened the door to his apartment in Lower

Mills, and the stench of bourbon that preceded him told me he hadn't been working.

'Mr Popularity,' he said, and turned his back to me.

I followed him into his living room, where a book of crossword puzzles sat open on the coffee table in between a bottle of Jack Daniel's, a half-full tumbler, and an ashtray. The TV was on, but muted, and Bobby Darin sang 'The Good Life' from speakers set to whisper volume.

Devin wore a flannel robe over sweatpants and a Police Academy sweatshirt. He pulled the robe closed as he sat on the couch and lifted his glass, took a sip, and stared up at me with eyes that, while glassy, were as hard as the rest of him.

'Grab a glass from the kitchen.'

'I don't feel much like drinking,' I said.

'I only drink alone *when* I'm alone, Patrick. Got it?'

I got the glass, brought it back, and he poured an overly generous drink into it. He raised his.

'To killing cops,' he said, and drank.

'I didn't kill a cop.'

'Your partner did.'

'Devin,' I said, 'you're going to treat me like shit, I'll leave.'

He raised his glass toward the hallway. 'Door's open.'

I tossed the glass on the coffee table, and some bourbon spilled out of it as I got out of the chair and headed for the door.

'Patrick.'

I turned back, my hand on the doorknob.

Neither of us said anything, and Bobby Darin's silk vocal slid through the room. I stood in the doorway with all that had gone unspoken and unconfronted in my friendship with Devin hanging between us as Darin sang with a detached mourning for the unattainable, the gulf between what we wish for and what we get.

'Come on back in,' Devin said.

'Why?'

He looked down at the coffee table. He removed the pen from the crossword book, closed it. He placed his drink on top of it. He looked at the window, the dark cast of early morning.

He shrugged. 'Outside of cops and my sisters, you and Ange are the only friends I got.'

I came back to the chair, wiped the spill of bourbon with my sleeve. 'This isn't over yet, Devin.'

He nodded.

'Someone ordered Broussard and Pasquale to do that hit.'

He poured himself some more Jack. 'You think you know who, don't you?'

I leaned back in the chair and took a very light sip from my glass, hard liquor never having been my drug of choice. 'Broussard said Poole wasn't a shooter. Ever. I'd always had Poole pegged for the guy who took the money out of the quarries, capped Mullen and Pharaoh, handed the money off to someone else. But I could never figure who that someone else was.'

'What money? What the hell are you talking about?'

I spent the next half hour running it down for him.

When I finished, he lit a cigarette and said, 'Broussard kidnapped the kid; Mullen saw him. Olamon blackmails him into finding and returning the two hundred grand. Broussard runs a double-cross, has someone take out Mullen and Gutierrez, has Cheese whacked in prison. Yes?'

'Killing Mullen and Gutierrez was part of the deal with Cheese,' I said. 'But otherwise, yes.'

'And you thought Poole was the shooter.'

'Until the roof with Broussard.'

'So who was it?'

'Well, it's not just the shooting. Someone had to take the money from Poole and make it disappear in front of a hundred and fifty cops. No flatfoot could pull that off. Had to be high command. Someone above reproach.'

He held up a hand. 'Ho, wait a minute. If you're thinking—'

'Who allowed Poole and Broussard to breach protocol and proceed with the ransom drop without federal intervention? Who's dedicated his life to helping kids, finding kids, saving kids? Who was in the hills that night,' I said, 'roving, his whereabouts accountable only to himself?'

'Aw, fuck,' he said. He took a gulp from his glass, grimaced as he swallowed. 'Jack Doyle? You think Jack Doyle's in on this?'

'Yeah, Devin. I think Jack Doyle's the guy.'

Devin said, 'Aw, fuck,' again. Several times actually. And then there was nothing but silence and the sound of ice melting in our glasses for a long time.

35

'Before forming CAC,' Oscar said, 'Doyle was Vice. He was Broussard and Pasquale's sergeant. He approved their transfers to Narcotics, brought them on board with CAC a few years later when he made lieutenant. It was Doyle who kept Broussard from getting transferred to academy instructor after he married Rachel and the brass went nuts. They wanted Broussard busted down to nothing. They wanted him gone. Marrying a hooker is like saying you're gay in this department.'

I stole one of Devin's cigarettes and lit it, immediately got a head rush that sucked all the blood out of my legs.

Oscar puffed from his ratty old cigar, dropped it back in the ashtray, flipped another page in his steno pad. 'All transfers, recommendations, decorations Broussard ever received were signed off by Doyle. He was Broussard's rabbi. Pasquale's, too.'

It was light outside by now, but you wouldn't know it from Devin's living room. The shades were drawn tight, and the room still bore that vaguely metallic air of deep night.

Devin got up from the couch, removed a Sinatra

CD from the tray, and replaced it with *Dean Martin's Greatest Hits*.

'Worse part of all this,' Oscar said, 'is not that I might be helping bring down a cop. It's that I might be helping bring down a cop while listening to this shit.' He looked over his shoulder at Devin as Devin slid the Sinatra CD back into the rack. 'Man, play some Luther Allison, the Taj Mahal I gave you last Christmas, anything but this. Shit, I'd rather hear that crap Kenzie listens to, all those skinny suicidal white boys. Least they got some heart.'

'Where's Doyle live?' Devin came over to the coffee table and lifted his mug of tea, having passed on the Jack Daniel's shortly after he'd called Oscar.

Oscar frowned as Dino warbled 'You're Nobody Till Somebody Loves You.'

'Doyle?' Oscar said. 'Has a house in Neponset. 'Bout half a mile from here. Though once I went to a surprise sixtieth birthday party for him at a second house in a little town called West Beckett.' He looked at me. 'Kenzie, you really think he has that girl?'

I shook my head. 'Not sure. But if he's in on this, I bet he has someone's kid up there.'

Angie was released at two in the afternoon, and I met her at the rear door and we skirted the mob of press out front, drove up onto Broadway, and pulled behind Devin and Oscar as they turned off their hazards and rolled across the bridge toward the Mass Pike.

'Ryerson's going to pull through,' I said. 'They're still not sure if they can save his arm.'

She lit a cigarette, nodded. 'Lionel?'

'Lost his right eye,' I said. 'Still under sedation. And that teamster Broussard hit suffered a severe concussion, but he'll recover.'

She cracked her window. 'I liked him,' she said softly.

'Who?'

'Broussard,' she said. 'I really liked him. I know he came to that bar to kill Lionel, and maybe us, too, and he had that shotgun swung my way when I fired . . .' She raised her hands but then dropped them back in her lap.

'You did the right thing.'

She nodded. 'I know. I know I did.' She stared down at the cigarette shaking in her hand. 'But I just . . . I wish it hadn't gone down that way. I liked him. That's all.'

I turned onto the Mass Pike. 'I liked him, too.'

West Beckett was a Rockwell painting in the heart of the Berkshire Mountains. White steeples formed bookends to the town itself, and Main Street was bordered by red pine boardwalks and delicate antiques and quilt shops. The town lay in a small valley like a piece of china in a cupped hand, the dark green hills rising up around it, pocked with remnants of snow that hovered in all that green like clouds.

Jack Doyle's house was, like Broussard's, set back off the road and up on a slope, obscured by trees. His, however, was far deeper in the woods, at the end of a drive a quarter mile long, the nearest house a good five acres to the west and shuttered tight, its chimney cold.

We buried the cars twenty yards off the main

road, about halfway up, and walked the rest of the way through the woods, slow and cautious, not only because we were neophytes in nature but because Angie's crutches didn't find purchase as easily as they would on level ground. We stopped about ten yards short of the clearing that circled Doyle's lodge-style one-story and peered at the wraparound porch, the logs stacked under the kitchen window.

The driveway was empty, and the house appeared to be as well. We watched for fifteen minutes, and nothing moved past the windows. No smoke flowed from the chimney.

'I'll go,' I said eventually.

'He's in there,' Oscar said, 'he'll have the legal right to shoot you as soon as you step on his porch.'

I reached for my gun and remembered that it was in the custody of the police at the same moment my fingers touched an empty holster.

I turned to Devin and Oscar.

'No way,' Devin said. 'Nobody's shooting any more cops. Even in self-defense.'

'And if he draws on me?'

'Find the power of prayer,' Oscar said.

I shook my head, parted the small saplings in front of me, raised my knee to step forward, and Angie said, 'Wait.'

I stopped and we listened, heard the engine as it purred toward us. We looked to our right in time to see an ancient Mercedes-Benz jeep with a small snowplow blade still attached to the front grille as it bumped up the road and pulled into the clearing. It parked by the steps, the driver's side facing us, and the door opened and a round woman with a kind, open face stepped out. She took a sniff of the air and stared through the trees, seemed to be looking right at us. She had marvelous eyes – the clearest blue I've ever seen – and her face was strong and bright from mountain living.

'The wife,' Oscar whispered. 'Tricia.'

She turned from the trees and reached back into the car, and at first I thought she'd come back with a bag of groceries, but then something leapt and died at the same time in my chest.

Amanda McCready's chin fell to the woman's shoulder, and she stared through the trees at me with sleepy eyes, one thumb in her mouth, a red and black hat with ear flaps covering her head.

'Somebody fell asleep on the ride home,' Tricia Doyle said. 'Didn't she?'

Amanda turned her head and nestled it into Mrs Doyle's neck. The woman removed Amanda's hat and smoothed her hair, so bright – almost gold – under the green trees and bright sky.

'Want to help make lunch?'

I saw Amanda's lips move but didn't hear what she said. She tilted her chin again, and the shy smile on her lips was so content, so lovely, it opened my chest like an ax.

We watched them for another two hours.

They made grilled-cheese sandwiches in the kitchen, Mrs Doyle over the frying pan and Amanda sitting up on the counter handing her cheese and bread. They ate at the table, and I climbed up a tree, feet on one branch, hands on another, and watched them.

They talked around their sandwiches and soup,

leaned into one another, and gestured with their hands, laughed with food in their mouths.

After lunch, they did the dishes together, and then Tricia Doyle sat Amanda McCready up on the counter and dressed her again in coat and hat, watched with generous approval as Amanda placed her sneakers up on the counter and tied them.

Tricia disappeared into the rear of the house for her own coat and shoes, I assumed, and Amanda remained on the counter. She looked out the window and a sense of agonized abandonment gradually filled her face, pulled at it. She stared out the window at something beyond those woods, beyond the mountains, and I was unsure whether it was the marrow-sapping neglect of her past or the crushing uncertainty of her future – one I'm sure she had yet to believe was truly real – that tore her features. In that moment, I recognized her as her mother's daughter – Helene's daughter – and I realized where I'd seen that look on her face before. It had been on Helene's face the night she'd seen me in the bar and promised, if she ever had a second chance, that she'd never let Amanda out of her sight.

Tricia Doyle came back into the kitchen, and a cloud of confusion – of old and new hurts – drifted across Amanda's face before being replaced by a hesitant, warily hopeful smile.

They came out on the porch as I climbed down from the tree and there was a squat English bulldog with them, its coat a patchwork of brindle and white that matched a swath of hillside behind them where the ground was open and bare save for a ridge of frozen snow anchored between two rocks.

Amanda rolled with the dog, shrieked as he got on top of her and a gob of drool dripped toward her cheek. She escaped him, and he followed her and jumped at her legs.

Tricia Doyle held him down and showed Amanda how to brush his coat, and she did so on her knees, gently, as if brushing her own hair.

'He doesn't like it,' I heard her say.

It was the first time I'd heard her voice. It was curious, intelligent, clear.

'He likes when you do it better than me,' Tricia Doyle said. 'You're gentler than I am.'

'I am?' She looked up into Tricia Doyle's face and continued brushing the dog's coat with slow, even strokes.

'Oh, yes. Much gentler. My old woman's hands, Amanda? I have to grip the brush so hard, I sometimes take it out on old Larry here.'

'How come you call him Larry?' Amanda's voice turned musical on the name, riding up on the second syllable.

'I told you that story,' Tricia said.

'Again,' Amanda said. 'Please?'

Tricia Doyle chuckled. 'Mr Doyle had an uncle when we were first married who looked like a bulldog. He had big, droopy jowls.'

Tricia Doyle used her free hand to grip her own cheeks and pull the skin down toward her chin.

Amanda laughed. 'He looked like a dog?'

'He did, young lady. He even barked sometimes.'

Amanda laughed again. 'No suh.'

'Oh, yes. *Ruff!*'

'*Ruff!*' Amanda said.

Then the dog got into it as Amanda placed the

brush aside and Mrs Doyle let Larry go and the three of them faced one another on their haunches and barked at each other.

In the trees, none of us moved or spoke for the rest of the afternoon. We watched them play with the dog and play with each other, build a mini-version of the house out of old numbered building blocks. We watched them sit on the bench set against the porch rails with an afghan pulled over them against the gathering cold and the dog at their feet, as Mrs Doyle spoke with her chin on Amanda's head and Amanda lay on her chest and spoke back.

I think we all felt dirty in those woods, petty and sterile. Childless. Proven, as of yet, inept and unable and unwilling to rise to the sacrifice of parenting. Bureaucrats in the wilderness.

They had gone back in the house, hand in hand, dog squirming between their legs, when Jack Doyle pulled into the clearing. He climbed out of his Ford Explorer with a box under his arm, and whatever was in it made both Tricia Doyle and Amanda shriek when he opened it in the house a few minutes later.

The three came back into the kitchen and Amanda perched on the counter again and talked nonstop, her hands pantomiming her brushing of Larry, her fingers gripping her cheeks as she aped Tricia's description of distant Uncle Larry's jowls. Jack Doyle threw back his head and laughed, smothered the small girl against his chest. When he raised himself up from the counter, she clung to him and rubbed her cheeks against his five o'clock shadow.

Devin reached into his pocket and removed a cell phone, dialed 411. When the operator answered, he said. 'West Beckett Sheriff's office, please.' He repeated the number under his breath as she gave it to him, then punched the numbers into his cell phone keypad.

Before he could press SEND, Angie put a hand on his wrist. 'What are you doing, Devin?'

'What are you doing, Ange?' He looked at her hand.

'You're going to arrest them?'

He looked up at the house, then back at her and scowled. 'Yes, Angie, I'm going to arrest them.'

'You can't.'

He pulled his hand away from her. 'Oh, yes, I can.'

'No. She's—' Angie pointed through the trees. 'Haven't you been watching? They're good for her. They're . . . Christ, Devin, they *love* her.'

'They kidnapped her,' he said. 'Were you awake for that part?'

'Devin, no. She's . . .' Angie lowered her head for a moment. 'If we arrest them, they'll give Amanda back to Helene. She'll suck the life out of her.'

He stared down at her, peered into her face, a stunned disbelief in his eyes. 'Angie, listen to me. That's a cop in there. I don't like busting cops. But in case you've forgotten, that cop engineered the deaths of Chris Mullen, Pharaoh Gutierrez, and Cheese Olamon, if not implicitly, then tacitly. He ordered Lionel McCready and the two of you probably to be murdered. He's got Broussard's blood on his hands. He's got Pasquale's blood on his hands. He's a killer.'

'But . . .' She looked desperately toward the house.

'But what?' Devin's features were screwed up into a mask of anger and confusion.

'They love that girl,' Angie said.

Devin followed her gaze to the house, to Jack and Tricia Doyle, each holding one of Amanda's hands as they swung her back and forth in the kitchen.

Devin's face softened as he watched, and I could feel an ache invade him as a cloud crossed his face and his eyes grew wide as if opened by a breeze.

'Helene McCready,' Angie said, 'will destroy that life in there. She will. You know it. Patrick, you know it.'

I looked away.

Devin took a deep breath, and his head snapped to the side as if he'd taken a punch. Then he shook his head and his eyes grew small and he turned back from the house and pressed SEND on his phone.

'No,' Angie said. 'No.'

We watched as Devin held the phone to his ear and the phone on the other end rang and rang. Eventually he lowered it from his ear and pressed END.

'No one there. Sheriff's probably out delivering the mail, a town this size.'

Angie closed her eyes, sucked in a breath.

A hawk flew over the treetops, cut the cold air with its sharp call, a piercing sound that always makes me think of sudden outrage, reaction to a fresh wound.

Devin shoved the phone in his pocket and removed his badge. 'Fuck it. Let's do it.'

I turned toward the house and Angie grabbed my arm, turned me back. Her face was feral, torn, her hair falling in her eyes.

'Patrick, Patrick, no, no, no. Please, for God's

sake. No. Talk to him. We can't do this. We can't.'

'It's the law, Ange.'

'It's bullshit! It's . . . it's wrong. They love that child. Doyle's no danger to anyone anymore.'

'Bullshit,' Oscar said.

'Who?' Angie said. 'Who's he a danger to? With Broussard dead, no one knows he was involved. He has nothing to protect. No one's a threat to him.'

'We're a threat!' Devin said. 'You on fucking drugs?'

'Only if we do something about it,' Angie said. 'If we leave this place now, never tell anyone what we know, it's over.'

'He's got someone else's kid in there,' Devin said, his face an inch from hers.

She spun toward me. 'Patrick, listen. Just listen. He . . .' She pushed at my chest. 'Don't do this. Please. Please!'

There was nothing resembling logic in her face, nothing reasonable. Just desperation and fear and wild longing. And pain. Rivers of it.

'Angie,' I said quietly, 'that child does not belong to them. She belongs to Helene.'

'Helene is arsenic, Patrick. I told you that a long time ago. She'll suck everything bright out of that girl. She'll imprison her. She . . .' Tears poured down her cheeks and bubbled in the corners of her mouth, and she didn't notice. 'She's death. You take that child out of that home, that's what you're sentencing her to. A long death.'

Devin looked at Oscar, then at me. 'I can't listen to any more of this.'

'*Please!*' The word came out of Angie at the

pitch of a kettle's whistle, and her whole face sank around it.

I put my hands on her arms. 'Angie,' I said softly, 'maybe you're wrong about Helene. She's learned. She knows she was a lousy parent. If you could have seen her the night I—'

'Fuck you,' she said, with a steel chill in her voice. She pulled her arms out of my hands and wiped the tears violently off her face. 'Don't give me that you-saw-her-and-she-looked-sad shit. Where'd you see her, Patrick? In a bar, wasn't it? Fuck you and this "people learn" bullshit. People don't learn. People don't change.'

She turned away from us, to fish in her bag for her cigarettes.

'It isn't our right to judge,' I said. 'It's not—'

'Then whose right is it?' Angie said.

'Not theirs.' I pointed through the trees at the house. 'Those people have chosen to judge certain people on whether they're fit to raise children. Who gives Doyle the right to make that decision? What if he meets a kid and doesn't like the religion he's being raised in? What if he doesn't like parents who are gay or black or have tattoos? Huh?'

A squall of icy anger darkened her face. 'We're not talking about that, and you know it. We're talking about this particular case and this particular child. Don't give me all that pampered classroom philos-ophizing the Jesuits taught you. You don't have the balls to do what's right, Patrick. None of you do. It's that simple. You don't have the balls.'

Oscar looked up into the trees. 'Maybe we don't.'

'Go,' she said. 'Go arrest them. But I won't watch you.' She lit the cigarette, and her back stiffened against her crutches. She placed the cigarette between her fingers and curled her hands around the grips of her crutches.

'I'll hate all three of you for this.'

She swung the crutches forward, and we watched her back as she carried herself through the woods toward the car.

In all the time I've been a private detective, nothing has ever been quite so ugly or exhausting as the time I spent watching Oscar and Devin arrest Jack and Tricia Doyle in the kitchen of their home.

Jack didn't even put up a fight. He sat in the chair by the kitchen table, shaking. He wept, and Tricia scratched at Oscar as he pulled Amanda from her arms, and Amanda screamed and batted Oscar with her fists and cried, 'No, Grandma! No! Don't let him take me! Don't let him!'

The sheriff answered Devin's second call and pulled up the drive a few minutes later. He walked into the kitchen with a confused look on his face as Amanda lay limp in Oscar's arms and Tricia held Jack's head to her abdomen, rocked him as he wept.

'Oh, my God,' Tricia Doyle whispered, her eyes open to the end of their life with Amanda, the end of freedom, the end of everything.

'Oh, my God,' she whispered again, and I found myself wondering if He heard her, if He heard Amanda whimper against Oscar's chest, Devin reading Jack his rights; if He heard anything at all.

Epilogue

The Mother and Child Reunion

The Mother and Child Reunion, as the headline of the *News* called it the next morning, was transmitted live at 8:05 P.M. EST, on all local channels on the evening of April 7.

Bathed in hot white light, Helene bounded off her front porch, through a stream of reporters, and took Amanda from the arms of the social worker. She let out a yelp and, with tears streaming down her face, she kissed Amanda's cheeks and forehead, eyes and nose.

Amanda wrapped her arms around her mother's neck and buried her face in her shoulder, and several neighbors broke out in raucous applause. Helene looked up at the sound, confused. Then she smiled with a demure shyness, blinked into the lights, rubbed her daughter's back, and the smile grew broader.

Bubba stood in the living room in front of my TV and looked over at me.

'Everything's all right, then,' he said. 'Right?'

I nodded at the TV. 'Sure seems like it.'

He turned his head as Angie hopped down the

hallway with another box, placed it on the stack just outside the front door, and hopped back into the bedroom.

'So why's she leaving?'

I shrugged. 'Ask her.'

'I did. She won't tell me.'

I gave him another shrug. I didn't trust myself to speak.

'Hey, man,' he said, 'I don't feel good helping the woman move. You know? But she asked me.'

'It's okay, Bubba. It's okay.'

On TV, Helene told a reporter she considered herself the luckiest woman in the world.

Bubba shook his head and left the room, picked up the stack of boxes in the doorway, and trudged down the stairs with them.

I leaned in the bedroom doorway, watched Angie pull shirts from the closet, toss them on the bed.

'You going to be okay?' I said.

She reached up, grabbed a stack of hangers by the necks. 'Be fine.'

'I think we should talk about this.'

She smoothed wrinkles from the top shirt in the stack. 'We did talk about it. In the woods. I'm talked out.'

'I'm not.'

She unzipped a garment bag, lifted the pile of shirts and slid them inside, zipped the bag.

'I'm not,' I repeated.

She said, 'Some of these hangers are yours. I'll get them back to you.'

She reached for her crutches and swung toward me.

I stayed where I was, blocking the doorway.

She lowered her head, looked at the floor. 'You going to stand there forever?'

'I don't know. You tell me.'

'I'm just wondering whether I should put the crutches down or not. After a while, my arms get numb if I'm not moving.'

I stepped aside and she moved through the doorway, met Bubba as he came back up the stairs.

'There's a bag on the bed,' she said. 'That's the last of it.'

She swung out to the stairs and I heard her clack the crutches together, hold them in one hand, while she held the banister in the other and hopped down the stairs.

Bubba picked the garment bag up off the bed.

'Man,' he said, 'what did you do to her?'

I thought of Amanda lying on the porch bench in Tricia Doyle's arms, the Afghan pulled around them against the chill, the two of them talking quietly, intimately.

'Broke her heart,' I said.

Over the weeks that followed, Jack Doyle, his wife, Tricia, and Lionel McCready were all indicted by a federal grand jury on charges of kidnapping, forced incarceration of a minor, child endangerment, and gross child negligence. Jack Doyle was also indicted in the murders of Christopher Mullen and Pharaoh Gutierrez and in the attempted murders of Lionel McCready and Federal Agent Neal Ryerson.

Ryerson was released from the hospital. Doctors had saved his arm, but it was withered and useless, at least temporarily and maybe forever. He returned to Washington, where he was assigned desk duty in the Witness Protection Program.

I was summoned before the grand jury and asked to testify to my knowledge of all aspects of what the press had dubbed the Copnapping Scandal. No one seemed to grasp that the term itself suggested cops being abducted as opposed to doing the abducting, and the label was soon as synonymous with the case as Watergate had been to Nixon's multitude of treasons and petty corruptions.

Before the grand jury, my comments regarding Remy Broussard's last few minutes with me were disallowed because they could not be corroborated. I was restricted to testifying as to exactly what I'd observed on the case and what I'd noted in my case file.

No one was ever indicted for the murders of Wee David Martin, Kimmie Niehaus, Sven 'Cheese' Olamon, or Raymond Likanski, whose body was never found.

The federal prosecutor told me he doubted Jack Doyle would be convicted in the deaths of Mullen and Gutierrez, but because it was patently obvious he'd been involved, he'd take a hard fall on the kidnapping charges, never see the outside of a prison again.

Rachel and Nicholas Broussard disappeared the night Remy died, taking off for parts unknown with, most on the prosecution side assumed, two hundred thousand dollars of Cheese's money.

The skeletons found in Leon and Roberta Trett's basement were determined to be those of a five-year-old boy who'd disappeared from western Vermont two years ago and a seven-year-old girl who has yet to be identified or claimed.

*   *   *

In June, I dropped by Helene's.

She gave me a tight hug with bony wrists that bruised muscles in my neck. She smelled of perfume and wore bright red lipstick.

Amanda sat on the couch in the living room, watching a sitcom about a single father of two precocious six-year-old twins. The father was a governor or senator or something similar and he always seemed to be at the office yet, as far as I could tell, had no babysitter. A Hispanic handyman dropped in all the time and complained a lot about his wife, Rosa, who always had a headache. His jokes were nonstop sexual entendres, and the twins laughed knowingly while the governor tried to look stern and hide a smile at the same time. The audience loved it. They went wild for every joke.

Amanda just sat there. She wore a pink nightdress that needed a wash or at least some Woolite, and she didn't recognize me.

'Sweetie, this is Patrick, my friend.'

Amanda looked at me and raised a hand.

I returned the wave, but she was already looking back at the TV.

'She loves this show. Don't you, honey?'

Amanda said nothing.

Helene walked through the living room, her head tilted as she fastened an earring to her lobe. 'Man, Bea really hates you for what you did to Lionel, Patrick.'

I followed her into the dining room as she scooped things off the table into her purse.

'Probably why she hasn't paid my bill.'

'You could sue her,' Helene said. 'Right? You could. Couldn't you?'

I let it go. 'How about you? You hate me?'

She shook her head, patted the hair on the sides of her head. 'You kidding? Lionel took my kid. Brother or not, fuck him. She could have been hurt. You know?'

Something small twitched in Amanda's face when her mother said 'fuck.'

Helene ran her hand through three bright pastel plastic bracelets, shook her arm so they'd drop to her wrist.

'Going out?' I said.

She smiled. 'You know it. This guy? He saw me on TV, thinks I'm – like, a big star.' She laughed. 'Ain't that a riot? Anyway, he asked me out. He's cute.'

I looked at the child on the couch.

'What about Amanda?'

Helene gave me a big smile. 'Dottie's gonna watch her.'

'Dottie know that?' I asked.

Helene giggled. 'She will in about five minutes.'

I looked at Amanda as the image of an electric can opener was reflected from the TV and played across her face. I could see the can opening like a mouth on her forehead, her square chin bathed in blue and white, her eyes open and watching without interest as the jingle played. An Irish setter replaced the can opener, leapt across Amanda's forehead, rolled in a field of green.

'The caviar of dog food,' the announcer said. 'Because doesn't your dog deserve to be treated like a member of the family?'

Depends on the dog, I thought. Depends on the family.

A savage pang of weariness stabbed me just under

my rib cage, sucked the breath out of me, and left as quickly as it had come, trailed by a throbbing ache that settled into my joints.

I mustered up the strength to cross the living room. 'Goodbye, Helene.'

'Oh, you leaving? Bye!'

I stopped at the door. ''Bye, Amanda.'

Amanda's eyes remained on the TV, her face bathed in its pewter glow. ''Bye,' she said, and for all I knew she was talking to the Hispanic handyman as he went home to Rosa.

Outside, I walked for a while, finally came to a stop in the Ryan playground, sat on the swing where I'd sat with Broussard, looked out at the basin of the unfinished frog pond where Oscar and I had saved a child's life from the madness of Gerry Glynn.

And now? Now what had we done? What crime had we committed in the woods of West Beckett, in the kitchen where we'd taken a child from parents who had no legal right to her?

We'd returned Amanda McCready to her home. That's all we'd done, I told myself. No crime. We'd returned her to her rightful owner. Nothing more. Nothing less.

That's what we'd done.

We'd taken her home.

Port Mesa, Texas

October 1998

In Crockett's Last Stand one night, Rachel Smith joins in a drunken conversation about what's worth dying for.

Country, a guy fresh from the service says. And the others toast.

Love, another guy says, and catches a round of jeers.

The Dallas Mavericks, someone yells. We been dying for them ever since they entered the NBA.

Laughter.

A lot of things are worth dying for, Rachel Smith says, as she comes over to the table, her shift over, scotch glass in her hand. People die every day, she says. Over five dollars. Over locking eyes with the wrong person at the wrong time. Over shrimp.

Dying is no measure of a person, Rachel says.

What is? someone calls out.

Killing, Rachel says.

There's a moment's silence as the men in the bar consider Rachel, and that hard, calm thing in her voice matches the thing that's in her eyes sometimes, the thing that can make you nervous if you look too close.

Elgin Bern, captain of Blue's Eden, *the best shrimper in Port Mesa, eventually says, What would you kill for, Rachel?*

Rachel smiles. She raises her scotch glass so that the fluorescent light over the pool table is reflected and trapped in the ice cubes.

My family, Rachel says. And only my family.

A couple of guys laugh nervously.

Without a second thought, Rachel says. Without a look back.

Without a moment's pity.

THE END

CORONADO
By Dennis Lehane

Stories from the award-winning author of
Mystic River and *Shutter Island*.

A small southern town gives birth to a dangerous
man with a broken heart and a high-powered rifle . . .
A young girl, caught up in an inner-city gang war, crosses
the line from victim to avenger . . . An innocent man is
hunted by government agents for an unspecified
crime . . . A boy and a girl fall in love while ransacking
a rich man's house during the waning days of the
Vietnam War . . . A compromised psychiatrist confronts
the unstable patient he slept with . . . A father and son
wage a lethal battle of wits over the whereabouts of a
stolen diamond and a missing woman.

In turn suspenseful, surreal, romantic and tragically
comic, these tales journey headlong into the heart of our
myths – about class, gender, freedom and regeneration
through violence – and reveal that the truth waiting for
us there is not what we'd expect.

This collection includes the acclaimed play *Coronado*.

'BOY, DOES HE KNOW HOW TO WRITE'
Elmore Leonard

'ONE OF THE GREATS OF CRIME WRITING'
Guardian

059305752X
9780593057520

BANTAM PRESS